Daughter of Immigrants

Pearl Kastran Ahnen

PublishAmerica

Baltimore

First printing

ISBN: 1-59286-832-0
PUBLISHED BY PUBLISHAMERICA, LLLP
www.publishamerica.com
Baltimore

Printed in the United States of America

Dedicated to the memory of my dear YiaYia Eleni and my sweet Mother,
who taught me that the "impossible dream" just takes a little longer.

For Presvytera Catherine
& Father James.
My very best wishes.
Enjoy!

Fondly—
Pearl Kastrun Abner
9-28-03

Acknowledgments

I am grateful to Ron Hansen who saw "Tula's" potential from the very beginning, and to my other creative writing instructors, friends, librarians and family members for their generous advice. Thank you to Rebecca S. Embree, who was the first one to welcome me to PublishAmerica and to Ed Mixon who led the way. I was fortunate to have the computer expertise of Lori Morren, Sue Poolman and Penny Kramer. And finally thank you to my children, Steve and Deneen, their spouses, Chelle and Curt, and my grandchildren, Jessica and Drew for their love and support. My dear husband, Bill, who died before this novel was published, was with me from the very beginning with encouragement, love, advice and wisdom. Thank you God, for with your guidance, all things are possible.

Part I

When she was young, she held
the earth like a huge sphere.
The Odyssey

THE PALESTES FAMILY

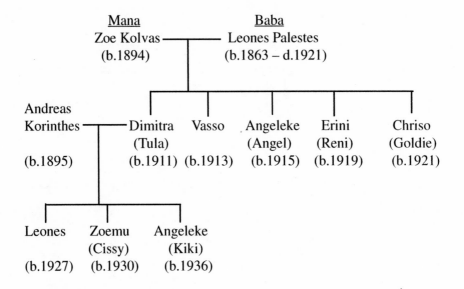

Mana
Zoe Kolvas
(b.1894)

Baba
Leones Palestes
(b.1863 – d.1921)

Andreas
Korinthes

(b.1895)

Dimitra
(Tula)
(b.1911)

Vasso

(b.1913)

Angeleke
(Angel)
(b.1915)

Erini
(Reni)
(b.1919)

Chriso
(Goldie)
(b.1921)

Leones

(b.1927)

Zoemu
(Cissy)
(b.1930)

Angeleke
(Kiki)
(b.1936)

Zoe's brother, Ondoni (b.1896)
Tula's friend, Photi   (b.1908)

Book of Secrets

Chicago, November, 1986

I saw the worn blue clothbound book for the first time the day she died. Earlier that day she called to remind me that we were having dinner that evening at her house.

"Don't forget, seven o'clock. I'm making your favorite, spinach pie," she said. "And I'm going to give you something special. I've had it a long time."

"What is it?"

"Can't tell you. It's a surprise, full of memories. See you at seven, honey. Goodbye."

That evening shortly after eight, I struggled with the lock on her front door, a sudden downpour drenching me. The small overhang over the door did not shelter me from the pouring rain and to complicate matters I was very late and the key would not turn in the lock. I was beginning to wonder if I had the right key. And why was the house so dark, except for a lamp burning in the hallway? Didn't she call and say she was making my favorite dinner? Yet, I was late. Perhaps she had grown weary of waiting for me and gone to bed.

The front door finally opened and the first thing I saw was a worn blue clothbound book. It lay at the foot of the stairs beside her. I stood for a moment looking at her – I couldn't breathe. Then I knelt beside her, touched my mouth to hers. I was too late, I couldn't save her. She was dead. I went crazy.

* * *

After the ambulance left, I sat alone in her living room, second-guessing her last moves. It was my fault! I was late. She had rushed down the stairs, tripping over the loose runner. It was my fault I hadn't had the runner replaced. It was my fault she lived alone. It was my fault. My fault! I could not accept the fact that she was dead.

Slowly I walked to the stairs, picked up the open book. Was this the surprise? On the first page in the handwriting of a ten-year-old, she had written, "I was born July 17, 1911, in Chicago. It is now November 10, 1921, and my father died a month ago. My Uncle Ondoni gave me this book. He's also my godfather, and my friend. When he gave me the book he told me I should never show it to anyone, especially my mother. She hates Uncle Ondoni, calls him an evil man. He is her brother, but she says I should "cross the street" when I see him. Uncle Ondoni made me promise to finish school, earn the education that was denied him, and become a teacher. He also wants me to get out of the slums, that's what he calls the west side of Chicago. I promised him I would."

In the middle of the book pressed between two pages was a flower, a Black-eyed Susan. Fragile from age the tissue-thin petals were a burnished amber, the center a powdery ebony. Beneath the pressed flower, scrawled in her teen-age handwriting were these words:

That man, Andreas, gave me this flower on my thirteenth birthday.
He calls me his "Black-eyed Susan." He says my dark eyes remind
him of the flower. I hate that name. My name is Tula.

This is Tula's story. And I am Tula's daughter.

Chapter 1

1921—

Wind rushed down Halsted Street on Chicago's west side and swept a smoky trail from the old Greek Orthodox priest's censer into the funeral procession. The poignant fragrance of the incense mingled with the strong street odors: ripe vegetables in a peddler's cart, unbearable smells from the sewers, and sweat from the four white horses pulling the hearse. The priest swung his censer in a wide arc, enveloping the black carriage and the horses. One of the horses neighed, causing the old priest to stop momentarily and reach into the folds of his cloak for a silver cross hanging from a velvet cord. His black cloak served to mute the sound of his censer's chains, while his monk-like cowl hid all but the barest traces of his gray beard.

Behind this grim figure walked a child. Her frightened eyes fixed on his stooped shoulders. She pressed a black-bordered handkerchief against her mouth.

Another blast of wind penetrated the cortege slowly making its way down the street, and the child's black straw bonnet was thrown back and dangled limply from its ribbons around her neck. Waves of chestnut brown hair cascaded out.

Above a drum's slow rumbling, the priest chanted, "Lord God, blessed art thou. May the soul of Leones Palestes be everlasting."

The child, Tula, walked behind the hearse. She reached up to touch the shiny black carriage. Through the windows she saw the casket. With back erect and shoulders squarely set, she was determined not to cry. She was ten, too big to cry. There was no time to dwell on herself this October day – a windy day, the kind of day that her father, who had loved Chicago, said occurred only here and only in October, when the autumn wind tore across Lake Michigan and white clouds crowned the city.

Tula moved closer to her mother and managed to tuck herself into the shadow cast by the hearse. Her mother's sobs joined the fussing of the baby in her arms. Tula's tightly coiled fingers gripped a bouquet of violets. Violets were what her father had always brought to her mother.

Now she had the feeling that something was reaching for her. The eeriness echoed nightmares that had begun three days ago when her father died. *Leave them behind*, she told herself. In a few hours, she could pour everything out to her godfather, her *Nouno* Ondoni, as she never could with her mother, Zoe. That was only one of the differences between Zoe and her brother, Ondoni. While Zoe was short and plump, with black eyes and glossy dark hair combed back from a widow's peak into a bun, Ondoni had a tall, lean frame, cobalt blue eyes and blond hair.

Tula wished *Nouno* Ondoni wasn't so far back in the procession. She wanted to walk beside him the way she often did. But she didn't want to hear him talk about money. Ondoni was obsessed with money. He had always known he was cleverer than most of the other young Greek men his age, which was twenty-five, and he had considered it his destiny to be a wealthy man. "I'm not going to wash dishes, shine shoes, and end up with a fat wife and a bunch of kids like those other Greeks. That's not for me," he'd say.

When a gust of wind parted Tula's worn black sweater, sending a shiver through her, she quickly buttoned it. Tula was a thin child with long legs and dark brooding eyes like her mother. Now her heart pounded in time with the drum, its melancholy sound carried by the wind drowned in the mourners' laments. She glanced back over her shoulder at the endless stream of people coming off of Polk Street. As she searched for signs of Ondoni, she also looked for Photi Kokkenos, her best friend. There he was among the other children, taller than, many of them, his dark curly hair ruffled by the wind, a black armband on his old tan jacket. His lean body tilted forward when she caught his eye. He gave her a sad smile, revealing a chipped front tooth, a reminder of one of the blows his father had given him.

Tula nodded to him and then concentrated on the hearse, trying to penetrate it with her eyes, to see inside the coffin, to see her father, still and cold. She tugged at Zoe's shawl, demanding, "Why did Baba die?"

In a whisper, Zoe said, "*Ola kala.*"

"No! All is *not* well."

Tula glared at her mother. Why couldn't she speak American English like Ondoni? He would say to her, "Sister, you're still Zoe from Greece, a greenhorn. Learn to speak American! You're in America now."

"I learn American and steal, like you? You no brother, you thief!" Zoe would say.

Tula put her hands to her mouth as if to silence her disrespectful thoughts. For all their closeness, her mother seemed very much a stranger just then.

"I'm scared," Tula said, holding on to her mother's shawl.

The procession moved slowly. Halsted Street, like many main streets on the west side of Chicago, was lined with stores, a grocery, a coffeehouse, a fish market, a Chinese laundry, and a dry goods store. On a street where nothing much ever happened, shop owners and customers spilled onto the sidewalk and gave the procession their full attention. Women clutching grocery sacks wept, men smoked cigars and talked among themselves, a child sat cross-legged on the curb. Tula supported her mother's elbow and guided her behind the hearse. She tightened her grip to steer Zoe away from the puddles of early morning rain.

The procession stopped at her father's bakery. Etched in gold letters on the window was "Dimitra's Fancy Bakery." Dimitra was Tula's baptismal name. Her father had named the bakery after her—"Dimitra, the goddess of wheat." Only he called her Dimitra. To everyone else she was Tula, the pet name her godfather Ondoni had given her.

Across the street from the bakery, a social worker in her starched white middy blouse leaned out of a window of Hull House and looked down at the procession. A dark-haired boy climbed up a tree, snapping branches under his weight, while another scaled Hull House's iron fence to gape at the mourners.

The priest censed the black wreath on the bakery door. Down the block, high in the dome of Holy Trinity Greek Orthodox Church, the bells tolled. Suddenly, Zoe passed the sleeping baby to Tula and walked to the door, sobbing "Leones, Leones!" Then she beat her fists on the door. "Leones!"

Tula gasped, the infant in her arms awoke and wailed. Ondoni raced from the back of the procession, "Zoe, please."

Out of control, Zoe leaned forward and shouted hoarsely, "Ex-oh! Out! Get away!" Her face cold with contempt, she pushed her brother away.

"What?" He touched her arms.

"Take hands off me." This time she spoke in English. She shouted her words so all could hear. "You no my brother. You put last nail in Leones' coffin." Her hands shook when she reached for baby Reni and straightened the black bonnet that covered the infant's head. The rage in Zoe's eyes sent shivers down Tula's spine. Tula looked up at her godfather towering over her, dressed in a custom-made navy blue serge suit and polished black leather shoes. His blue eyes blazed in anger. The solid line of his jaw was rigid.

Zoe glared at her brother and hissed, "*Poostee*, whore's man."

Red-faced, Ondoni rushed back to the end of the procession. Tula did not understand. She knew from quarrels overheard between her parents that the bakery had begun losing money as soon as Ondoni started working there. And that her father had to borrow from Gus Lambredes to save it. Tula cringed when she thought of Gus Lambredes, with his huge black walrus mustache, his beady brown eyes, his shiny black hair, his short, fat body. As for *Nouno* Ondoni, Tula realized as well that Zoe had lost all respect for her brother.

Now the old priest made the sign of the cross and the mourners moved forward. Tula's younger sisters, Vasso and Angeleke, kept pace. Vasso's dry brown eyes stared ahead, while Angeleke's gray eyes filled with tears. Tula, walking slowly beside her mother, felt a tug on her sweater.

"I'm cold." It was six-year-old Angeleke, her long blond hair whipping across her face. "How far to church?"

"See, there it is," Vasso said, pointing to the onion-shaped dome. The church dominated the block, its red brick wet from the morning rain, its imposing marble stairs rising to the entrance, two huge brass doors.

Vasso and Angeleke, were dressed in somber black cotton dresses, black sweaters, black stockings, black bonnets. Only Angeleke's bonnet hung loose from its ties, her hair flowing free. Tula brushed Angeleke's hair back, adjusted the bonnet, and tied the ribbons under her chin. Then she gave her attention to Vasso. *Poor Vasso.* She had cold brown eyes and a hot temper. She was only eight years old, but the family had learned a long time ago to watch her mouth. Whenever she bit her lower lip, it was a warning signal of a storm brewing. She clamped her teeth on her lip now, as she saw Ondoni standing once again next to Zoe.

The huge brass doors swung outward. The black-clad pallbearers struggled with the casket. The priest, following the casket, raised his censer to brush the sign of the cross on it. Mourners spilled into the church, standing shoulder to shoulder, men on the left, women on the right. There were no pews. The priest nodded to the black-robed cantor, who walked to the altar and lifted the lid of the coffin. Mists of incense hovered over it.

"Leones!" Zoe cried. A faint cry echoed from the baby in her arms.

"Please, Zoe," Ondoni said. He put his arms around his sister. She numbly followed him to the altar. Vasso and Angeleke, flushed from the long walk stood with Tula. "Is Baba in heaven now, Tula?" Angeleke asked.

"Yes." Tula looked up at the high-domed ceiling, a kaleidoscope of icons, saints, holy men, and angels against a starry sky. And in the center, Jesus, with his compassionate eyes, looking down.

The funeral chants seemed endless as mourners moved past the casket, making the sign of the cross on their chests.

After the last mourners had paid their respects, the priest nodded to Zoe. It was time to say good-bye. She walked to the casket, choking back the tears, and kissed her husband. She made the sign of the cross, lifted baby Reni to the casket, and said, "Say good-bye to Baba." Sobbing, she walked back to her girls, clutching Reni to her breast. Tula pressed against her, trying to absorb her pain.

Vasso, dry-eyed and somber, approached the casket. A weak "Bye-bye, Baba" was all she managed to murmur before she raced back to her mother's side.

Angeleke's mouth gaped, her gray eyes opened wide. She walked slowly to the casket. Standing on tiptoes, she touched her father's cheek, smoothed his hair. "Please, Baba don't die. I'm truly sorry if I was bad. I'll be good." Then she crammed the corner of her black-bordered handkerchief into her mouth and ran to Zoe.

"I can't say good-bye," Tula cried. "Why did you leave me, Baba?"

The pain inside her was like an explosion, a scorching invasion of her body, the ache spreading all the way to her heart. Ondoni came to her side and drew her close. He whispered, "You must say good-bye to your Baba."

She did not want to see him like this. This was the most terrible moment of her life. Clutching the wilted violets, Tula walked a few paces behind Ondoni. Drawing a deep gulp of air, she emptied her mind of all thoughts, of her mother, of her sisters, of all anger. When she reached the casket and saw his face, she wanted to erase the frown lines. He was sleeping. She wanted to wake him up, ruffle his hair, hug him. Instead she simply bowed her head and placed the violets on his chest.

Chapter 2

Vultures circle above Tula, waiting. The lake is in the distance. Baba runs through a field and stops at the water's edge. He points. Ondoni's body is floating in the water, his eyes two horrible black hollows, his mouth open in a silent scream. The birds circle closer. Tula plunges in. She thrashes in the water. Ondoni drifts farther and farther away. On shore, Baba shouts. "He is dead!" Tula cannot see where she is going. She cannot see where she has been. Baba's laughter rings in her ears. "Ondoni is dead!"

Tula sat up in bed and screamed.

Then she saw her mother at the door. "Same nightmare? Forty days since Baba die. Still you troubled by nightmare?"

Tula nodded and drew the quilt up to her chin. Vasso and Angeleke squeezed over to make room for their mother on the bed. The family was all there, except for baby Reni.

"Tula scared me." Angeleke rubbed her eyes.

"She woke me up. Again!" Vasso turned and stretched her long legs out from under the covers.

"*Zhoo-pah*, hush," Zoe said.

Tula wished she could ask her mother to hold her, protect her the way she had done when she was little. But she was ten now, a big girl. Somehow Angeleke had managed to snuggle up to her mother in the bed the sisters shared.

In the bedroom, Tula was surrounded by treasures Leones had showered on his bride the first year of their marriage: an ornately carved chair with a red velvet cushion, a brass double bed, and a walnut table. A faded, hand-woven, multicolored carpet from Greece covered the hardwood floor. In one corner was an old trunk, the only possession Zoe brought to the marriage, filled with her *preka*, her dowry. There were no mirrors in the bedroom. The two windows in the room were hung with lace curtains.

"Don't be frightened," Zoe said. Since her husband's death, Zoe had begun to speak English, the language of her daughters. Now she kissed Tula's cheeks.

"I – I'm all right now, honest," Tula said.

14

Zoe nodded. "Get some sleep, my daughters. Tomorrow we make the *kolyeva*." She gave each girl a kiss and walked out of the room, closing the door after her.

In the morning, Tula helped her mother boil the wheat. Using a wooden spoon, she leaned over the gas stove, mixing in honey, raisins, and almonds to make the *kolyeva* that when blessed by the priest would ensure peace for Leones' soul. At the sink, Zoe waved a hand, "Mix, good!" Soapsuds ran down her heavy arms while she rinsed a crystal bowl. Then she poured the *kolyeva* into it, spoonful by spoonful. Finally, she sprinkled powdered sugar over the top and covered it with her best linen napkin.

At church Tula carried the bowl of wheat to the altar. During the service, she stared at the crystal bowl. Would the nightmares stop now? She took a deep breath and let it out slowly.

Back at the flat, when she opened the door to the parlor, she frowned at the sight, hating how the room looked, gloomy like in a scary Lon Chaney movie. A dim light came through the narrow parlor windows. She felt her way through the semi-dark room, where mirrors, photographs and painting all were shrouded in black.

"We uncover pictures," Zoe stood at the door, Reni in her arms, her voice flat as she smoothed Reni's hair.

"Yes, Mana." Tula knelt on the brown leather sofa and tugged at the black cloth covering the oval mirror, all the while muttering to herself, *"ola kala."* She flipped the black cloth from the picture over the mantel, the one of Zoe as a child in the village riding her horse. Vasso raised the cloth from the family portrait, taken only a month before Leones died.

At the other end of the room, Angeleke had climbed onto a chair and forcefully pulled a black cloth from another photo, one of the sisters in their sailor outfits.

For generations, the legend had come down in Greek families, passed from mother to daughter, that the souls of the dead stalked the house for forty days. To release the soul, mirrors and pictures had to be draped in black.

Maybe it was superstition—Tula had just learned that word—but she sensed her father in the room. Tula shook her head. She had to get rid of this feeling.

Zoe placed Reni in a basket. "My back," she said, and stretched with both hands against the small of her back. She walked out of the room.

Vasso said, "Hurry, let's get this over with. I want to see the puppet show at Hull House." She looked at Angeleke. "You're a slowpoke."

"No, I'm not."

"Yes, you are. And you're so short you can't even reach up."

"No, I'm not. No, I'm not. You're just mad because I can spell better than you. Go ahead. Ask me to spell *dictionary*," Angeleke said.

"Cut that out, you two," Tula said.

"See, you're taking her side," Vasso said.

"Ask me to spell a hard word, *mythology*, *geography*, ask me."

"Shut up." Vasso bit her lower lip.

"All you do is get mad," Angeleke said.

"Hey, will you two quit it? We're sisters," Tula said.

"Sisters," Angeleke said.

Then, without knowing exactly how it happened or who started it, Tula found herself caught up in a big hug with Angeleke.

Vasso, sullen had turned to walk away but Tula opened the circle to take her in. Tula felt her sisters' bodies and their love—and they laughed and cried.

"Come on we're almost done," Tula said.

Vasso continued removing the cloths and folding them haphazardly. She was tall and thin, and she towered over Angeleke, or Angel, as she was called by the family. Tula knew that Vasso was jealous of Angel, jealous of her beauty, her knack for spelling, her gentle nature. Angel stood out among her sisters because of her blond hair and gray eyes. Tula, Angel, and even baby Erini, who was called Reni, had pet names. Only Vasso didn't.

Now Reni slept in a basket by the pot-bellied stove, her chubby cheeks pink from the heat, her tiny thumb in her mouth. Tula thought of how the baby would grow up without her father. *She'll never hear his voice, listen to his dreams.* He had big dreams for Tula. He always said, "Dimitra is our scholar. She'll make a fine teacher."

With trembling fingers, Tula removed Reni's thumb from her mouth. Her heart pounded and yet she felt a strange relief. She would be a teacher. At that thought, the weight of her grief for her father lifted a little. Tula left the sleeping baby and went to her parents' bedroom, at the rear of the flat. She looked about the room as though seeing it for the first time, a worn braided rug, its colors muted against the stark white walls, a brass bed in one corner, an oak chest in the other, and the wedding picture in a large oval frame hanging over the chest. Thank God, Vasso hadn't uncovered it yet. Tula thought it was too soon for her mother to face that picture.

She lifted the cloth and saw her mother; young, shy, and frightened, dressed in a white lace gown, standing beside a high backed velvet chair. In the chair sat her father, wearing a black suit, a white shirt with a high collar, and a black silk scarf loosely tied into an artist's bow. His hand clasped the small hand of his bride. In her other hand, she held violets.

When Tula heard Zoe's footsteps, she quickly covered the wedding photo. On a shelf next to the photo was an icon of *Panayea*, the Virgin Mary. This was the only image not cloaked in black. Suspended from the ceiling by a brass chain was the holy lamp. She stared at the red glass lamp, the *kanteelee*. The flaming wick in the oil appeared wavy and sparkling, as though she was looking at it through water.

"Tula?" Zoe asked. She was at the bedroom door, her face white.

"Yes?"

"You touch picture?"

"No." Tula stared at the rug. She could hear her sisters in the kitchen. She could hear her mother's deep sigh as she sank into the bed. How pale the light was at the window, how pale Zoe looked as she lay in bed.

"Leones, *te than ka-no meh tora*," Zoe said, appealing to her late husband for help.

Tula bent over, clasped her mother's hand, and kissed it.

Zoe took Tula's cheek between her thumb and forefinger and squeezed gently. "*Ella, Tula, katse.*" She patted the side of the bed. "*Katse.* Sit. We need to talk."

"Yes." Tula sat on the edge of the bed.

"Your Baba was good man." Zoe spoke in English now, so Tula knew she was trying to say something important.

"Your Baba force me to marry. Use *pistola*," Zoe began.

"Pistol?" Tula repeated, shocked.

Wringing her hands, Zoe said. "Way back, I young, fifteen years, and come to America with my Baba to marry man, not know he old. What madness was it make me leave village?" Zoe made a queer sound in the back of her throat and pressed her hands against her mouth. Finally, she continued. And Tula listened while her mother told the story.

The year was 1909, and Leones was thinking of marriage. He was forty-six years old. His landlord, George Kukkones, told him about Zoe, a fifteen-year-old girl from his village in Greece. She would make a fine wife. So Leones began writing to Zoe's father, and soon photos were exchanged. Six months later, Leones proposed and sent passage money for Zoe and her father to come to America.

Zoe stopped talking for a while. Then she blurted out, "He lie to us. He not thirty years, but forty-six, too old for me, my Baba said. We pack to leave for Greece. But–" Tears welled in Zoe's eyes.

"Don't cry, *Mana*."

Zoe sobbed, rocked back and forth on the edge of the bed. "Your Baba lock us in, stand at door with *pistola*. Big *pistola*. He tell me I must marry him or else! I scared, run hide under table. My Baba curse, scream at Leones. But I stay in America and marry him. In years I have you, Vasso, Angel, Reni, all my girls. Baba good man, but sad. I have no sons. This one–Zoe caressed her belly and smiled. "This one will be son for Leones."

Tula sat at the edge of the bed. A son! Oh, God, please let it be a son. But wait, what were they going to do now? Their savings were almost gone, and another baby was coming. Tula was the one who went to the bank with her mother. She was the one who signed her mother's name under her X mark. And Zoe didn't want her brother Ondoni to help.

Since Baba's death, *Nouno* Ondoni had tried to see his sister, but she always shut the door in his face. Then he stopped coming. Only yesterday Tula had learned he was sick. She must go to him, against her mother's wishes.

Tula left Zoe and walked to the kitchen. She looked out the window, the white curtains against her, touching her. Glancing around the room, she thought. She had lived there all her life. It was second floor of a building owned by George Kukkones. It was here her father courted Zoe. It was here Baba died.

She had to see *Nouno* Ondoni. He was someone she could always count on, who would always care. She remembered the books he had given her. Not schoolbooks but novels, history books, geography books. Her father had built bookshelves to hold them.

Should she change into a dress for the visit? She was tired of her old black skirt and middy blouse. Inside her blouse hung the gold cross *Nouno* Ondoni had placed around her neck at her baptism. On second thought, the middy blouse and black skirt would do fine. She turned to see a flash of lightning through the kitchen window, followed by a loud crack of thunder. Another November storm from the lake. Did she dare wear her mother's black leather high-button shoes? The soles of her own shoes were worn through and would soak up the rain.

Now Tula caught Vasso grabbing a heel of bread off the table and stuffing it in her pocket. Vasso spent a lot of time hiding food because she was always famished. Tula suspected that even her mother, who was a magician at stretching the *soupa* with chicken wings and necks, was getting weary of the sameness of their meals—*soupa*, potato sandwiches, and *dolmathes*, stuffed grape leaves filled with rice.

Not aware that she had been seen, Vasso said, "If Angel doesn't hurry, we'll be late. And it looks like it's going to rain."

Then Angel came into the room, twisting her hand in her blond locks, breathless. "Everything's done. Went through all the rooms."

"Good," Vasso said. "Let's go to the puppet show."

"Wait a minute," Tula said. "Be back by four."

"Why? Where're you going?" Vasso asked.

"To see my *Nouno* Ondoni."

"Does Mana know?"

There was a long pause. "No, and don't you tell her!"

When Vasso and Angel returned, the sky was cloudy and gray. Later, when Tula reassured herself that baby Reni was napping in her basket and Zoe asleep in her bedroom, she left for Ondoni's. She had to tell him about her mother, how she had changed, what had happened to the woman who used to speak up and talk about the future. But she wouldn't tell him about her nightmare of him drowning. Somehow she couldn't tell him that.

From the hall tree, Tula took her turquoise shawl, the one *Nouno* Ondoni had given her so long ago. Handmade of fine wool, it was crocheted by an old village woman. Her reputation for making fine shawls had traveled as far as Athens, Ondoni had said. Tula wrapped the shawl around her shoulders and grabbed her father's black umbrella from the hall tree as she raced out into the downpour. At the door of Ondoni's boarding house, cringing as lightning pierced the sky, Tula ducked under the canopied doorway.

She had been there only once, the day her Baba had died. Now she wrinkled her nose at the musty smell of the old building. Down the dimly lit hallway, she saw a woman and a man arguing. "Don't hold out on me," he said.

"I'm not."

"You bitch!" The man slapped her face.

This sobered the woman. She pointed a finger at him. "I'm telling Ondoni."

Tula was so stunned by this that she turned and ran. Unseen by the couple and trying to compose herself, she walked to the door of Ondoni's room. It was partway open. She pushed it. Inside she set her wet umbrella in a corner. Ondoni was lying on a metal bed huddled under a thin quilt. His pale face was drained of color, his hair not blond but ashen, and under his eyes was the smudge of sickness. The groaning door roused him. He reached for the quilt.

Slowly, his eyes opened, and he managed a smile. "Tula, my godchild, come in. Light the lamp."

"*Nouno* Ondoni," she said. Striking a match, she lit the gas lamp on the bedside table.

Ondoni fell back, releasing a painful sigh. "Damn, I can't even sit up."

"Can I help?"

"Dr. Voles will be here soon. Sit down, little doll."

She sat on a straight-back wooden chair and glanced around the sparsely furnished room. Its yellow floral wallpaper was peeling. In one corner, spread out on a table, were street maps, file folders, and newspapers. A maple dresser with a framed beveled mirror dominated another corner of the room. Books were piled on a humpback trunk. Some silver coins and a book lay on a small table near the bed.

"Did you tell your Mana you were coming here?"

She stammered. "No, I didn't. She said that whenever I see you, I should cross the street."

"Tula, you are brave to disobey her. Brave or foolish."

Her cheeks grew hot. In her mind, she could hear Zoe saying in her firm voice. "*Kakos anthropos*! evil man!"

No, he wasn't an evil man! He was the only one who was honest with her, the only one with whom she could share her feelings, the only one who could help her family.

Now dots of cold sweat peppered Ondoni's upper lip, signs of the recurring fever he had contracted on his trip to America ten years ago. He had left his village in Greece to be Tula's godfather, making the trip on an overcrowded ship, packed into steerage awash with vomit and urine. There, amid the wretched living conditions, he made his vow never to be poor again. Although he admired money, it was only a means to an end—power, he'd tell his sister. Zoe had told Tula about Ondoni's long convalescence and how during it he had taught himself to read, devouring books from the library. But the fever kept coming back. There was something different about Ondoni since the fever, Zoe often said.

Now Tula spoke. "Mana needs you. I mean, all of us need you. You must get well quickly. Our money is almost gon—"

A sharp rap on the door startled her. Dr. Voles hurried into the room, shaking a wet umbrella. He was short and heavy, with a paunch only partly concealed by his gray suit. He looked at Tula in surprise. "What are you doing here?"

"I had to see *Nouno*."

"Your mother would not approve, young lady."

Tula gazed at the worn hardwood floor.

Ondoni glared at the doctor. "Voles, shut up."

"Your illness hasn't done much for your temper." Dr. Voles said. He searched in his medicine bag and pulled out a thermometer, shook it, and popped it into Ondoni's mouth.

"That will keep you quiet!" The doctor busied himself taking Ondoni's pulse and listening to his chest.

Ondoni coughed, and the thermometer fell from his mouth. "Here, let me check that thing," Dr. Voles said. "You sure do have a fever. Better stay in bed."

"For how long?"

"A week at least. Don't forget that brain fever did some damage. How much is anyone's guess. Stay put. Your business can take care of itself for a while. And the girls, too." He winked.

What did he mean by that? Tula thought.

Ondoni struggled to get up. "I can't stay in bed!"

"That's an order. Don't do anything foolish." Dr. Voles turned and looked at Tula, who had been standing by the bed. "And you, young lady, belong home. Especially now, so soon after your Baba's death. Your Mana needs you. He was a good man. God rest his soul." He made the sign of the cross. "So sad. He didn't have to die. But he didn't take care of himself. I warned him. How is your Mana?"

Tula shrugged. "She cries. Once I saw her punching her belly."

"What?" Dr. Voles asked. "She has to think of the baby. It might be a boy. That's what your Baba prayed for."

Tula nodded. She pulled a handkerchief from her pocket and rubbed it over her face, the tears welling up.

Ondoni looked at her. "Tula, please. I will help."

Off in a corner, Dr. Voles scribbled a prescription on his pad. "You need this medicine, right away," he told Ondoni.

"I'll get it," Tula said.

"No, I don't want her running to the drug store. She has to go home," Ondoni said.

"Please let me go," she said.

Dr. Voles said, "Maybe you're right, Ondoni. We'll send someone else." He took off his steel-framed spectacles and rubbed his eyes. "Tula, go home."

Ondoni leaned forward, raising his head.

"Stay put. Can't you understand?" The doctor snapped his case shut. He turned to Tula. "Run along, young lady. God, the older you get, the more you look like your Mana, with those black eyes and long hair. Only you're taller. Take care of your Mana."

Tula nodded. "Yes, I will. Will *Nouno* be all right?"

"If he obeys orders. If not—I don't know."

"Don't scare the kid, Voles," Ondoni said.

"Scare her? Hell, I'm trying to scare *you*."

Ondoni grinned and reached for two silver dollars and the book on the bedside table. "Well, you haven't." He smiled at Tula and pressed the silver dollars into her hand. "For you, my godchild, for your nameday. I'm a little late, I know. I bought you this journal. See it says Friendship Book on the cover. It's fitting because we are more than godfather and godchild, we are friends, yes?"

"Yes."

"I want you to fill it with your dreams, your thoughts."

Tula flipped through the blank pages of the blue cloth-bound book. "Thank you, *Nouno*. Yes, I will."

"Good." And then Ondoni winced.

"See, what did I tell you?" Dr. Voles said. He bent over his patient and whispered. "You shouldn't encourage her. You're a bad influence."

Bad influence? Puzzled, Tula reached the door and waved good-bye, her hand on the doorknob.

Suddenly, the door flew open, and Tula moved aside when a young woman rushed past her, dropped her coat on the floor, and headed for the bed. In the dim lamplight, her face appeared familiar. She was the woman in the hallway. But she wasn't a woman, only a girl, with her smooth face marred by an ugly red mark. She wore a shiny blue satin dress which made her look far older than her true years. Her red hair was piled high on her head. From the way her small breasts bounced and the way the dress caressed her hips, it looked as if she wore nothing underneath.

She brushed past Tula as if she weren't there. "Hi, honey, how are you?" she asked Ondoni.

Ondoni grinned. "Maggie, my dear Maggie O'Grady. How's my girl?" Then he frowned. "What happened to your face?"

Her hands flew to her face. "I'll tell you about it later."

The tension relaxed when Dr. Voles said, "Ah, Maggie, just the person we're looking for. We have an errand for you to go on."

Tula, sensing that she was an intruder in the room, had to make her escape. All she could think about was her urgent errand to ask *Nouno* Ondoni to help them. And she had failed.

She fled the room and raced down the hallway. The sound of the heavy outer door as she forced it open and banged it against the wall echoed in the darkness. Tula stormed out into the rain.

Later, when she was alone in her bedroom in the flat, she slipped the Friendship Book out from within the folds of her shawl, ran her hand along the smooth cloth cover, and traced her fingers over the gold lettering: *Friendship Book.* In her Palmer script, she wrote her name on the inside cover and, on the second page, scribbled her first entry: "This book was given to me by my *Nouno* Ondoni, because we are more than godfather and godchild, we are *friends*. He said I should write my thoughts and my dreams in it." Then for a moment she chewed on her pencil. "After seeing *Nouno* Ondoni, I am certain he wants to help us, if Mana will let him. I'm also certain that I don't like that Maggie O'Grady."

Chapter 3

More than a month had passed since Tula's visit to Ondoni, and she had never said a word to her mother about seeing him nor about the two silver dollars and the Friendship Book he had given her. She kept the silver coins in her drawer, tucked into the pages of the Friendship Book.

Now she slipped the coins into her camisole pocket and once again flipped through the pages of her Friendship Book to take out the autographed photos of Mary Pickford and Theda Bara. Yesterday she received five-by-seven black-and-white glossies of the silent film stars in the mail. That made twenty photos she had in her collection. The more photos she received, the closer she felt to her "friends" the silent film stars and the movies they appeared in.

Tula started walking when she heard Zoe calling her. "I'm coming." She reached for her satchel on the dresser and slipped the photos into it. She was anxious to show the pictures to her best friend, Photi.

They had been friends almost forever, and they shared many things. Although Photi was two years older, they were in the same grade in school. Photi's father had kept his son home for two years to help with the horses in the barn. Photi, with his curly brown hair and bright hazel eyes, was much taller than the other boys in her class. Stronger, too from working with the horses. She began to feel a warm glow thinking of him.

She strolled into the kitchen and sat down at the table, where a steaming cup of coffee laced with milk and butter, waited for her.

"You late," Zoe said.

"No, I've got time." She worked at tracing a circle with her fingers on her chest to feel the coins. It was not on a whim that she had taken the coins. It was for luck because she was going to play the Virgin Mary in the Christmas pageant at school. Photi was going to be Joseph. He could have cared less. In fact, he had tried for the part only to please her. As for Tula, she desperately wanted to be perfect in her role. Acting that's what she loved. Would she be an actress, a teacher? One day it was one thing, the next day it was the other.

Today she wanted to be an actress on the silent screen, like Theda Bara or Mary Pickford, because of the photos she had received in the mail. And also because of the dream she'd had last night. Not the old nightmare, thank God, but a dream about the Nativity pageant. In the dream, she played the Virgin Mary to perfection. The dream ended with shouts of "Bravo" from the audience and thunderous applause. Now the dream eluded her and faded, and Tula's thoughts returned to the present. Theda Bara was her favorite. She had three other photos of her in her Friendship Book, one of her dressed as the Arabian princess Sheba, another in beads and spangles, and one in a long satin gown, reclining on a sofa, a vamp.

The fresh scent of pine tar soap filled the kitchen. Zoe had just washed her long brown hair and was sitting at the pot-bellied stove brushing it. Flickers of red and yellow flames danced behind the isinglass windows. Angel had put a miniature wooden Santa Claus and a sleigh on the floor near the stove. It was a toy her father had given her last year. Last year, they'd had a merry time at Christmas. But Christmas would soon be here again and they didn't have a tree, not so much as a Christmas wreath. Tula thought that everyone in Chicago would have a Merry Christmas except them. Zoe was sad. She seemed to live in a world all her own since Leones died. Would she ever come back to them? They still could have a Merry Christmas, if only Zoe would allow Ondoni to help them.

Zoe put her brush down.

"You look beautiful, Mana." Tula put her hands on her mother's face as if she were the child. Zoe was silent as tears filled her eyes. Not knowing how to comfort her, Tula finished her coffee and leaned over to fasten her old high-button shoes. She tried to imagine what it would be like to have new shoes, and to have her father back, alive, here in the kitchen. What it would be like to hear his voice, to hear her mother laugh.

Tula watched her mother smooth her apron over her swollen belly. She wore the same black dress that she had worn at the funeral, only now the dress had been let out and patched at the waist.

"*Ola kala*," Tula said.

"No! Not all right," Zoe cried. "He no care. He drank too much. And Ondoni *kakos*, bad. Two years Baba working to bring Ondoni here. Ondoni, a boy of fifteen. Bring him to be your *Nouno* to baptize you." Zoe held her breath, and her face began to redden. "The baby kick." She caressed her belly. "Baba prayed for son, to carry name. Please, God, give me son. I love my daughters, but four enough." Zoe wept as she made the sign of the cross on her chest. "Please, God."

Tula sat there rooted, her heart pounding. "Don't cry. The baby will be a boy."

Zoe took her daughter's face between her hands. "Go, you be late. And today big day, the Christmas play." She patted Tula's cheek. "Tula, grow up fast, be woman. Hurry, Tula. You save family."

"Yes, Mana." She was trembling. She looked into her mother's eyes. "I'll hurry."

"Good. Now go to school. Take lunch. My back hurt, much." She rubbed the small of her back.

Tula grabbed the brown lunch bag and her leather satchel. After pulling a knit hat over her ears, she struggled into her wool coat, closed the door behind her, and walked into the dark, damp hallway. She skipped over the last two steps and stumbled over someone at the bottom.

"Damn it, kid! Watch it!" the old woman screamed, huddled in the corner. A battered hat covered her gray hair. Her eyes, crusted with sleep, blinked. She pulled a threadbare coat close to her. She smelled of wine and fish gone bad. Tula had stumbled over Old Nell.

Old Nell had found shelter in the hallways of the flats on the west side of Chicago and begged for food from the tenants. Zoe often gave her bread and soup. At night, Nell roamed the streets and for pennies flashed her toothless grin and danced, lifting her dirty dress, exposing skinny legs. She wandered up and down the streets at all hours of the night and slept in hallways during the day.

Zoe had told her that Old Nell wasn't crazy, only poor and homeless. Once she had been in vaudeville. Tula thought that if she became an actress, she wouldn't go into vaudeville, not if vaudeville led to sleeping in hallways.

"Sorry," Tula said. She pulled on the heavy door. Sunlight and a cold blast hit both of them.

"Shut that damn door, and get the hell out of here!" The old woman shielded herself from the cold and inched deeper into the corner, trying to recapture the sleep she'd lost. Tula slammed the door, sealing the darkness, and raced down the street, the icy air filling her lungs.

She'd never catch up with Vasso and Angel, but she didn't care. She liked walking to school alone. Swinging into Halsted Street, she caught an aroma of fresh bread from the bakery up ahead and saw that her name had been painted out of the sign. How dare they! She knew that the family wasn't welcome in the bakery now that Baba was dead, but she didn't know why. No more "Dimitra's Fancy Bakery," just "Fancy Bakery" now. She reached into her school bag for a piece of chalk and scribbled on the sidewalk in front of the bakery door: DIMITRA'S FANCY BAKERY. There! Baba would be proud. She ran fast, not looking back, her cold breath coming out in cloud like puffs.

At the school's door, she pulled out her lunch bag and threw it into the barrel. She hated fried potato sandwiches, and that's all her mother ever gave her for lunch.

The marching beat of the piano urged her into the hall, where she saw the others lining up. The final bell rang. Photi made room for her.

"You just made it."

"Just almost." Tula knew that Photi would save a place for her in line. "Thanks for letting me take cuts."

"Silence!" said rosy-cheeked Miss MacMann. Although she had been in the States since she was a child, she still spoke with an Irish brogue. She was Tula's teacher, and this year she also was director of the Christmas play. She wielded a yardstick, flicking it occasionally at a misbehaving child in line.

The morning passed in a haze of excitement and anticipation for Tula. She was seated in the rear at a double desk with a freckled-faced blond, Esther DeAngelo, and the two hurried to finish their work. Esther no longer had braids. Her blond hair was bobbed in the new Buster Brown fashion. She wished *she* could have short blond hair, instead of ugly long brown hair.

At lunchtime, Tula huddled in a corner of the cafeteria, talking with Photi and Esther. Since she had thrown away her potato sandwich, she ate half of Photi's grape jelly sandwich and all of his lemon cream pie. She also ate two of Esther's Italian sugar cookies.

"I'm so nervous, I can't stop eating," Tula said, munching on a cookie. "I want to be an actress for the rest of my life."

"I thought you wanted to teach," Photi said. He grinned. "Isn't that why you help me with my homework, for practice?"

"Well, today I'm going to be an actress. See my pictures of Theda Bara and Mary Pickford?" Tula pulled the photos from her notebook. "Doesn't Mary Pickford look like the Virgin Mary with her long blond hair wrapped in a scarf and those big eyes?"

"Douglas Fairbanks, the pirate, is my favorite," Photi said. "Say we still have time to go on the swings. Want me to push you high into the clouds?"

Tula looked at Photi, her brave knight in shining armor.

One summer when Tula was almost five and Photi seven, they mixed droplets of blood from their little fingers. Tula had her eyes shut during the "operation." When Photi said the pin had done the trick and they were "blood brothers," only then did she open her eyes.

After that, there wasn't anything Tula couldn't tell Photi. As for Photi, for the longest time he wouldn't tell her that his father beat him. When he'd come to school with a black eye or bandages on his arms, he'd say it was an accident or he had fallen. One day, he ran up to Tula's flat with tears streaming down his face, his nose bloodied and his eyes bruised. "Hide me!" he cried.

And Zoe had hidden him in the closet. Later, his father came storming up the stairs, his bald head glistening with sweat, demanding his son.

Now Photi raced Tula and Esther to the swings. He pushed them, high, higher. Tula felt as if she were flying free.

When the bell rang, the children marched into the auditorium and rushed backstage, Esther to work the curtains and Photi to get into his costume. For a moment, Tula stood in the dark auditorium remembering how Baba had enjoyed it when she acted out a story for him.

He would gather her in his arms, and Tula would know that he had been drinking, for she smelled the wine on his breath. She didn't care. She loved him even though he drank.

"Dimitra," he'd say, "Which will you be? An actress or a teacher? I think a teacher, you have that air about you."

"I like to pretend I'm Miss MacMann, helping everyone. But today I want to be an actress. I don't know."

"Ah, but your Mana knows. Our Dimitra will be a teacher, right, Zoe?"

Now she walked to the front row. Framed by the auditorium lights, the stage rose above her. Tula hugged herself, feeling the two silver coins against her.

"Better hurry, Tula, it's almost time," Miss MacMann said, herding three shepherds across the stage.

"Yes, ma'am."

In the dressing room Tula fastened a veil over her hair and tied a rope tassel around her muslin gown. She looked at her younger sister, Angeleke. "Need help with those wings? You sure look like an angel with your long blond hair."

Angeleke smiled. "Thanks, I'm scared, though."

When Tula turned, she saw Vasso, her teeth clamped firmly on her lower lip. "What's the matter?"

"I don't want to be a dumb wise man. What if Mana comes and sees me in this stupid beard?"

"She's not coming."

"How do you know?"

"She's sick. Her back hurts her."

Later, when the heavy curtains parted to show the lit stage, the crowd applauded and some children yelled. It was then that Miss MacMann marched on stage, dressed in a navy wool high-waisted dress with a white collar, and raised her hands to quiet the audience.

Tula was calm enough through the first act. But when the second act began, her thoughts went again to her father. She could not concentrate. Her mind wasn't on the big scene. Two palm trees made of papier-mache took up a corner of the stage, which was dark except for a star light over the manger. Tula, cradling the baby doll, knelt beside Photi. She looked at him. His brown, curly hair was covered by a gray muslin scarf held in place with a black cord. Now more than ever he looked like her favorite movie star, Rudolph Valentino. He put his hand on her shoulder, and it felt warm through her thin gown. He smiled, revealing his chipped front tooth.

Tula stifled a giggle when Angel walked on stage with only one wing. Angel appeared when Photi said, "Mary, in my dream an angel told me to take you and the child and flee to Egypt. Come, we must go."

He slipped his hand in hers, and the two ran across the stage. "Hurry," he said, letting go of her hand. As she ran behind him, all she could see was his flowing robe. Suddenly, she tripped and crashed into the palm trees, knocking them off their stands. The baby doll flew from her arms into the front row. Tula lay sprawled on the stage, sobbing.

"Holy smoke!" Photi cried, and he knelt beside her. Angel leaped off the stage, crawled under a front-row seat, and came up clutching the baby doll. Vasso laughed so hard her beard fell off. Someone in the crowd shouted, "Bravo, Tula!" Esther pulled the curtain, and it came down with a thud. There was pandemonium on stage, backstage, and in the auditorium. Children were standing on their seat. The lights came on just as Esther peeped around the curtain and saw Miss MacMann trying to push through the crowd on the stage to get to Tula, who was stumbling along crying, her hands over her face as if someone had hit her. A stunned Photi trailed behind her.

"Tula, are you all right?" Miss MacMann asked.

"No! I wish I were dead!" She was shaking all over. She ran into the dressing room, slamming the door after her. It was then she decided that she could never be an actress. She frowned at her reflection in the mirror. Yes, she had failed. But someone else's face had come into view—it was Angel. "Are you all right?" she asked.

"I'm okay." She glanced at Vasso, who was behind Angel.

"Reni's here, but not with Mana," Vasso said.

"What? She can't be here without her," Tula said.

"Old Nell has her," Vasso said. "They're in the back row."

"Let's see what she's doing with our Reni," Tula said.

Vasso and Angel followed their sister at a run.

"What are you doing with Reni?" Tula demanded.

The old woman, with the sleeping Reni on her lap, sniffed and wiped her nose with the back of her hand. "Your ma told me to bring the baby here. It's her time. She called Dr. Voles, and he's at the flat now. She couldn't get anyone else to stay with Reni."

"What'll we do?" Vasso asked.

"Oh, Lordy, I don't know," moaned the old woman, rocking Reni in her arms.

For a moment, Tula stood very still. "What do you mean? We're going home." And then she remembered the two silver dollars. She pulled up her costume and searched for the coins in her camisole. "We've got to get home fast. I've got some money for a taxi." She raced out of the auditorium, grabbed her coat from the cloakroom, and flung open the door. "Come on!"

Vasso blocked the door. "We can't go in our costumes."

"Vasso's right, we've got to change," Angel said.

"There's no time. Mana needs us."

Vasso's face twisted. "She's got Dr. Voles."

Tula shrugged and smiled with a trace of pity. "A lot you know. We *have* to be there—now. It's important to Mana, or she wouldn't have sent Old Nell after us." Then she turned to Nell. "I'm sorry, I didn't mean to call you old—"

"I've been called worse, darlin'. Don't fret about it. But maybe you should change."

Tula fastened the buttons on her coat as she talked. "I'm going, and I don't care if no one comes. Mana needs us!" She pushed Vasso aside and ran outdoors.

"Wait for me!" Angel said, slipping her coat over her costume. Vasso, too, scrambled to button her coat.

Dr. Voles greeted them at the door of the flat.

"We want to see our *Mana*," Tula said. "Is she going to have her baby now?"

"Soon." Dr. Voles smiled. "She's resting now. I don't think it's a good idea for you girls to see her. Not just yet."

He addressed Tula. "Why don't you take the girls into the kitchen, make some cocoa for them? Perhaps some bread and feta. They look hungry. I've got to tend to your mother."

"Are you sure she's all right?" Angel asked.

"Yes. Now run along with Tula."

Tula took the sleeping Reni from Nell's arms, plumped up a sofa pillow, and placed Reni on it. The new baby would take Reni's place, Tula thought. And it would be a boy. That's what Baba wanted, prayed for, a boy. Did he die because he didn't have a son to carry on his name? Tula turned her gaze toward Vasso as she moved around the room. Vasso asked Tula, "What're we going to do?"

"First I'm going to make some cocoa, and you're going to help. Then we'll help Mana have her baby," Tula said.

"Ah, I don't think you can help much," began Nell. "But a wee prayer won't do any harm."

Vasso said, "I'm scared."

Tula had felt brave and full of hope when they walked into the flat, but now she was tired and hungry. Angel settled on the sofa next to Reni. Vasso stared out the window.

Nell said, "Angel, get up. Come on, girls, into the kitchen. Let's make that cocoa."

"Wait a minute, Nell," Dr. Voles said as he emerged from Zoe's room, wiping his hands. "I'll need you. Wash up. And we'll need some hot water. Put the kettle on, girls."

"Need m-me?" Nell stammered. "I don't know a thing about birthing. I ain't ever had a kid of my own."

"No problem. Just do as I say. Simple enough." A moan from the bedroom sent Dr. Voles running. "I've got to go. Zoe needs me."

"I can help," Tula said. She stumbled over her words and blushed crimson.

"No, Tula. You see to the girls," Dr. Voles said. "Come along, Nell. Don't forget the kettle."

"Yes, Doc, but for all the good I'll do, you might as well get Angel to help."

Angel giggled. "Me help Mana? I can't help, but I can spell. Want me to spell *baby*? B-A-B-"

"That's enough. Be quiet, Angel," Tula said.

"*Zhoo-pha*," Voles scolded.

And the girls were silent as Dr. Voles had asked.

Nell grabbed the kettle. "I'll help all I can, but I don't know nothin'." She followed Dr. Voles to the bedroom.

In the corner, the girls whispered as they sipped their cocoa.

"How is Mana going to have her baby?" Angel asked.

"I'm not sure," Tula said. "I think Dr. Voles is going to open her belly—with a knife. It won't hurt. And the baby will pop out. Then he'll sew her up."

"Tula, you're really stupid. Pop out of her belly, that's dumb," Vasso said. "I know how. Some girl told me at recess."

"Well, smarty, if you know, tell us," Angel said.

"You know where you do your pee-pee, down there?" Vasso began. She blushed. "Well, it comes out from down there."

"You're a liar!" Tula cried. "You don't know what you're talking about. Where we pee—you're crazy. It could never happen."

"That's what this girl told me. Her ma has seven kids, and she should know," Vasso said.

"Really?" Angel asked.

Hours later, when Zoe's labor began in earnest, Reni, Angel, and Vasso were asleep in their bed. Tula slept fitfully on the sofa, waking only when she heard her mother moaning. Finally, when she gathered enough nerve to peek into the back bedroom, she was alarmed to see that her mother's eyes were squeezed shut and her legs were shaking uncontrollably. Zoe screamed.

Dr. Voles said, "Now, now, don't worry. I'm here, even Nell is here to help you, and everything will be all right." As soon as Tula's wide-eyed stare met Dr. Voles' eyes, he said, "Tula, go back to your bed, immediately!"

Tula did as she was told, or pretended to. She closed the door and pressed her ear against it. Mana was suffering. Mana was hurting. She heard her mother scream.

She heard her gasp. "Something is wrong!"

Tula was getting anxious. Why wasn't Dr. Voles doing his job! Why didn't he open up Mana's belly and pull the baby out? Why was her mother in so much pain?

Then Zoe cried out again. Not a scream this time, but a series of sounds: huffing, choking, coughing, even cursing.

Please don't let Mana die, Tula prayed silently.

Zoe screamed from deep down in her chest. Tula couldn't stand it. *Hurry, Dr. Voles, open up Mana's belly, please. Get that baby out!* Tula squeezed her eyes shut.

Finally, Tula heard a sound, a cry. No, it wasn't Mana. It was a baby's cry.

Minutes later, Dr. Voles came into the parlor. "Still up, are you? Everyone else seems to be in bed."

"Mana?" Tula asked. She rubbed the sleep out of her eyes. In the doorway, she saw Nell, with Zoe's white apron on. Nell was smiling.

"Well, I never thought I'd help with a birthing, but I did."

"Yes, you were a big help," Dr. Voles said.

"How is Mana? I heard her crying."

"She's fine now," Dr. Voles said. "She's sleeping, and the baby is fine, too."

"The baby is here, born?"

"Yes. Come here, sit down," he said. He patted the sofa seat. "Your mother has named the new baby Chreso. How's that for a baby born at Christmas time?"

"It's a boy, isn't it?" Tula asked. "A boy for Baba! I'm so happy, so happy. A boy, a boy, a boy!"

"No," Dr. Voles said. "You have a new baby sister."

"Another girl?" Tula turned away from Nell and the doctor. She retched, opened her mouth, and vomited all over the front of her muslin costume. She gasped, and then she stood sobbing and retching, her body shaking.

Dr. Voles raced to the kitchen. "Nell, help me get some water, a cloth to clean up Tula."

Nell pulled out a handkerchief, gritted her teeth, took a deep breath, and cleaned Tula's face, all the while repeating, "Lord, the poor child's sick! The poor child's sick!"

Tula cried, "No! It *can't* be another girl! Baba prayed for a son!"

Chapter 4

Tula was nearly resigned to the fate that had abruptly changed her life when her father died two years ago. Now it was sealed on this October morning 1923, when Gus Lambredes slowed the horses to a stop in front of the flat. It was strange to look down at him from the flat, to see him sitting in her father's bakery wagon. She fought with all her strength not to think evil of this fat, short man who was going to help them move.

Alongside Gus Lambredes sat Photi, in his old overalls and heavy work boots. Photi jumped out of the front seat and looked up at Tula. "Well, here we are." His voice wasn't that cheerful, in fact it was sad. He was going to help them move two miles down Halsted Street, but he didn't want them to move. Photi's father, George Kokkenos, was nowhere in sight. He had evicted Tula's family. Something about Leones keeping secrets from him—something about Leones owning property and not telling him. Zoe also had been ignorant about the building on Blue Island Avenue, and when she found the deed among her husband's papers, she showed it to Tula, who suggested that Mr. Kokkenos look at it, since he was a knowledgeable man. That's when he blew up. Tula could still see his angry face, his baldhead glistening.

"What? Leones had a flat and said nothing to me?" The words exploded from his mouth. "Me, his best friend."

Zoe, in tears, tried to explain. "Leones never told me."

Now Tula sighed and shook her head. In the kitchen, she glanced at the old newspaper before wrapping a dish in it. A front-page article told of a royal wedding in England—"in the splendor of Westminester Abbey, the Duke of York and Lady Elizabeth Bowes-Lyon became man and wife." Tula sighed. She finished wrapping the dish and placed it in the barrel. Vasso swept the linoleum floor for the last time. Reni and Angel raced through the empty rooms. The table and ladder-back chairs were already in the wagon, as well as the beds, dressers, mirrors, trunk, everything except Tula's Friendship Book and her collection of movie star photos. She would not trust them to a box or barrel. She carried them in her arms.

Tula paused a minute from packing to gaze out the kitchen window for one last time. When she turned, she saw her mother. She was such a small, gentle-looking woman, Tula thought.

"You angry with me, that we move?" Zoe asked.

"No—"

"George bad for not letting us stay. His terrible temper."

Tula just shrugged.

"We will fix up Baba's flat. Clean the rooms, put paint on the walls, set traps for mice, yes?" Zoe said. "Girls we go. We must not keep Mr. Lambredes waiting." Once on the sidewalk, Zoe, with the baby in her arms, got into the front of the wagon. Reni sat between her mother and Gus Lambredes. Photi heaved the last box filled with clothing onto the wagon and jumped in after it. Tula, Vasso, and Angel climbed in, squeezing in among the barrels, boxes, and furniture.

As the horses ambled down the street, Tula thought about Mr. Lambredes, suspecting that he did not have their best interests at heart.

It all began a month ago when Gus Lambredes came to visit wearing the same shining, tight suit that he had worn at her father's funeral. While he sat drinking coffee, Gus Lambredes, his walrus mustache newly waxed, talked in a soothing voice and produced some papers from his suitcase. "Only a formality," he said. "Make your mark, and Tula will sign your name, Zoe. It's called power of attorney. I've been running the bakery since Leones passed away. Haven't I been giving you an allowance? Just a formality, that's all. Poor Leones, may his soul rest in peace." He made the sign of the cross.

Zoe wept.

Tula remembered everything. Her mother might as well have signed her life away, because after that they were not allowed in the bakery. Also the allowance that Gus Lambredes gave Zoe was growing smaller. And Baba's saving account at the Atlas Bank was another worry. The sums were dwindling away.

Tula stared at the street they passed in silence, but once their old flat was behind them, Vasso burst out with the question the rest of them had been too afraid to ask. "We're going to a bad part of town, aren't we, Tula?"

"No, it's not that bad," Tula said, but her words could not erase the decaying tenements they passed.

Angel began to weep, saying over and over again with childish despair, "We're going to a bad house."

Tula smiled and patted Angel's blond hair. "Don't say that, Angel. Baba's house isn't bad, honest." Tula's smile faded when the wagon stopped in front of a boarded-up storefront with two flats above it. Tula looked up at the soot-stained windows. Her black eyes flashed angrily.

"It's a dump," Vasso said.

"Shut up," Tula said.

"It ain't that bad," Photi said, standing up in the wagon. "Just needs cleaning and some paint. Let's get you moved."

After the last piece of furniture was carried up crumbling steps to the second floor, Gus Lambredes and Photi left.

"Must go to the bakery," Gus Lambredes said.

"Gotta help my *Baba* with the horses," Photi said.

Zoe thanked them and turned to her girls. "Be careful."

Just walking the floors in the flat was treacherous, littered as they were with broken plaster and remains of vermin. Tula followed her mother through the ghostly rooms and doorless doorways.

Zoe cautioned her daughters not to unpack at least until the kitchen had been scrubbed—windows, floors mopboards, everything. The first order of business was to boil water on the old gas stove.

"Clean first," Zoe said.

"This is a dirty place. We'll never get it cleaned. I bet not one has lived here in a hundred years," Angel said.

"Don't be silly," Vasso said.

"Get a rag, and start cleaning," Tula said.

They attacked the kitchen. A barn like room, it was the largest in the flat, with dirty gray walls, soot-stained window panes, and a worn, gray linoleum covering the floor.

"Holy cow, was that a mouse?" Angel cried as a furry creature scampered across the floor and disappeared through a small hole near the sink.

"We must set traps, close holes," Zoe said.

A week later, Tula walked through Dorr School early in the morning, past the principal's office, the gymnasium, the music room. It occurred to her that when the teachers and children were gone the school slept. The heels of her high-button shoes clicked as she climbed the stairs to Miss MacMann's classroom. She was glad for the early hour. Nervously, she tugged at the hem of her blue cotton dress. All her dresses were too short for her. Since her father's death two years ago, she had grown four inches. She was the tallest girl in her sixth-grade class.

Tula carried a sack containing a bottle of Baba's homemade wine. It was a farewell gift for Miss MacMann. The gift eased the small guilt she felt— although why she should feel guilt was an interesting thought. She refused to probe for what else was on her mind. *Only the wine for Miss MacMann, nothing else*, she told herself as she reached Miss MacMann's room.

She stood outside the door, holding the paper sack and wondering what would happen next. She had never imagined anything other than going to Dorr School, and if she could not do that, what was left?

She opened the sack, took out the bottle of wine and looked at the red liquid, the wine Baba had made. She could still hear his voice, "*Ella*, Tula, help me make the good wine." And she was there with him back in the cellar. She could feel his strong arms lifting her up and into the trough lined with oil cloth and filled with red grapes. While he clapped his hands, Tula stomped, squishing the juice through her toes, the strong, pungent smell of grapes pricking her nose and penetrating the damp cellar walls. She had shared this bond with him. Now she felt a surge of anger that she would never have that experience again.

Reluctantly, she opened the classroom door and faced Miss MacMann, for what she thought was the last time.

"Good morning, Tula. You're early." Miss MacMann's easy cheerfulness wasn't what Tula needed this morning. "What have you got there?" Miss MacMann eyed the paper sack.

"Some wine from my mother."

"Oh, thank you. You did tell her I enjoyed the last bottle? How thoughtful of your mother. And how is she?" She scooped up the bag and hid it in the closet.

"She's….there is something that I…."

"What's the matter? You look so sad. Here, sit down. Tell me about it." She picked up a chair that was near her desk and set it down beside her. "Sit," she said, patting the chair.

Tula sat. The chair faced the bright clean windows. Only last week, she had stayed after school to wash them. Now the panes sparkled.

"Miss MacMann, I'm leaving Door School," she blurted out.

"What? Why?"

"My mother wants us to go to Greek school. She wants us to learn Greek, to be Greek. She's afraid for us. We moved to an old place down Halsted. Too many things have happened since my father died. We just can't stay at Dorr School."

"There must be something I can do," Miss MacMann said. "You can't leave. I'll talk to your mother, work something out."

"I want to stay at Dorr School, but tomorrow we have to go to Socrates

Greek School." Tula stared at her teacher for a moment, and then her face collapsed.

Miss MacMann embraced her. "It will be all right," the teacher said. "I don't want you to cry." There were tears in Miss MacMann's eyes when she released Tula.

Tula thought it didn't matter what you wanted, it didn't matter. Miss MacMann, Esther, and Photi were her friends, but she would never see them again. Miss MacMann talked, outlining what she would do to keep Tula at Dorr School. Tula nodded but no longer heard; she was in her own thoughts, unraveling the feelings stirred up by this visit and the memory of Baba's wine.

The rest of Tula's day seemed to played in slow motion, as if in a movie. Esther came in, smiled at her, then the others filled the room. Finally, Photi ran in, almost late, as the final bell rang. There wasn't time to talk. Tula stood up straight at her desk, too tall, bone-skinny, long legs, and hopelessly confused. She couldn't bring herself to talk to Esther and Photi about leaving Dorr School.

When the closing bell rang, dismissing the children for the day, Tula did not seek out her friends. Instead, she went to Vasso and Angel, who gathered around her, as if guarding her, and the three walked home together.

That night in the cluttered flat, with the sounds of the scampering mice within the wall, Tula, a blanket around her shoulders looked out of the window at the full moon. Her Friendship Book lay open in her lap. She was tempted to climb out onto the fire escape to be alone, but the neighborhood was too new, and she was frightened. It had turned cold, and below her the street that had been filled with people a few hours ago was dark and threatening.

She flipped through the pages of her Friendship Book and located one of Baba's sayings: "Don't fear what has already happened." She had written that after she found out that her *Nouno* had gotten better. By chance she saw him at the corner grocery, but he did not see her.

Now thoughts of Photi took over. Was he her knight in shining armor? She smiled. Yes, he was brave. Last week, he had fought two boys who chased her into an alley. If it wasn't for Photi, who knows what they would have done to her? Tall, lanky fourteen-year-old Photi was in the sixth grade with Tula, all because of his father, a father who beat him. She was angry that she couldn't help Photi. Angry that she had to leave Dorr School. And angry that they had to move to this dirty flat, with the paint peeling off the walls, and the mice. It really would take them years to clean it up. Oh, how she missed the old flat, the clean smell of it, the lace curtains on the windows.

Boxes of books and barrels of dishes still unpacked crowded the small, dingy bedroom. The wedding picture, wrapped in a towel, leaned against the bedroom wall. Tula glanced at the bed where Vasso, Angel and Reni all slept. Tula would sleep on a cot in a corner of the room. But she was not sleepy now. She wrote in her Friendship Book by the light of the moon: "Dear God, grant me the wisdom and knowledge to escape from this place. Grant me the strength to accept this life until I can change it. Please, God—"

Voices coming from the kitchen interrupted her writing. Zoe was talking to baby Chreso. The sisters called her Goldie because Chreso means gold in Greek, and the name was more American.

Zoe's voice was comforting, soothing. *I want to keep her happy*, Tula thought. *How? I must hurry and grow up—to be a teacher like Miss MacMann. She will be happy then.*

Tula glanced at the Big Ben clock on the dresser. It was nine-thirty. She heard Zoe's soft voice talking to Goldie. Tula crept to the door and opened it a crack. By the soft light of the gas lamp, she saw her mother sitting in a rocking chair with the baby in her arms. She smiled as she watched. Maybe they *could* make this small flat into a home. A tap on the kitchen door surprised her, but she remained quiet in the dark room.

"Yes, who is it?" Zoe asked in her halting English. She moved toward the door with Goldie in her arms.

"It's me, Miss MacMann, Tula's teacher. I'm sorry to be calling so late."

"Miss MacMann?" Zoe asked in surprise. She unlatched the door.

From her place in the dark bedroom, Tula smiled. She had come after all! Zoe put Goldie back in the basket and offered Miss MacMann some coffee.

"Yes, coffee sounds good. Oh, the baby is so sweet!"

Miss MacMann unbuttoned her brown wool coat and put the plaid scarf, which had been wrapped around her neck, in her pocket. Then she made herself comfortable in the chair. "It's awfully cold," she said, trying to make conversation. "Can't wait for spring, but in Chicago it takes its sweet time."

"Yes, no grass, no trees here."

Tula squirmed. She couldn't hear everything they said. She missed words, even sentences, occasionally when she yawned. But she heard most of it. "Tell her. Tell Mana I mustn't go to Socrates. Tell her!" Tula whispered to herself.

Zoe took the pot from the stove and searched in a barrel for some cups.

Miss MacMann said, "I see you're getting settled in your flat. I imagine Tula's been a big help. It's Tula I've come to talk about. Tula and her schooling."

"Yes, Tula much help. Good girl. Smart girl."

"She's very smart, and an excellent student. She wants to become a teacher, and I want to help her. That's why I'm here. I want her to stay at Dorr School, where I can see she has the best."

"No, sorry, she go to Socrates. She needs Greek," Zoe said. "How can I say? She need own country language. She need own people. I widow. Nobody help. Must have Tula become good Greek. Go to Greek school, learn of old country."

"But she still can be a good Greek and go to Dorr School. And we can offer her so much more. We mustn't lose her," Miss MacMann said.

"No! Tula must go to Socrates. Me alone, no husband. Tula has no father, no brothers."

"Surely you'll remarry—in time, I mean. You must think of Tula's future.'

Zoe exploded, "Marry! Me? Never! Leones my only husband!"

Miss MacMann paused. "What I'm saying is—you have a good future, you're still young. I didn't mean to upset you. I didn't think."

"Leones my husband forever! Tula my oldest, my firstborn, she must hurry—grow up fast. Hurry!"

In the dark bedroom, Tula cringed. She hated being the oldest, she hated being a girl. Oh, dear God, she thought, *Miss MacMann has failed.* She would have to go to Socrates, which she hated. *No!* She wouldn't go.

As if through a fog, she heard Miss MacMann and her mother talking about her. Tula kneeled at the door, tasting the salty tears streaming down her cheeks. She heard her mother speak in halting English.

"My Tula will learn about my country at Socrates. She will read to me. I read bad, know little. She teach me. She safe at Socrates." Zoe sighed.

"She's safe at Dorr, and she is learning a great deal about this country America. Greek is well and good, but this is America, this is her country. Give her a chance."

Zoe shook her head. "Tula must learn Greek, be good Greek."

Miss MacMann didn't answer that. "I see I can't change your mind. I'm sorry." She finished her coffee and got up to leave. She slid her coat on, picked up her scarf, and went to the door. Zoe followed.

Miss MacMann said, "We could have done great things with Tula at Dorr School."

"She will do good at Socrates."

The two women said their good-byes, and Zoe latched the door.

Tula wrote in her Friendship Book: "Never, never trust grown-ups. They tell you they'll make it better, and everything will be *ola kala* and then it isn't. They lie, and they don't even know it."

Then Goldie woke up crying.

"*Ella, kukla,*" Zoe said. It was a while before Goldie went back to sleep and Zoe finished her coffee.

Tula, sobbing now, wondered how her mother could be so cruel. She got up, walked to the dresser, and gazed into the mirror at her tear-stained face. She vowed that nothing would stop her. She *would* be a teacher, without Miss MacMann's help. She could not control the anger coming up in her, and her rage took on an Old World form. She knelt on the floor and rocked back and forth, moaning, weeping.

After a while, there was a sharp rap on the kitchen door. It grew louder, more urgent. Tula went back to her post at the bedroom door, to look and listen.

"Open up, Zoe. It's me, Ondoni."

Zoe opened the door. "Why you here?" she demanded.

"Since I did not hear from you, even when I was sick, I went to the other flat, and George told me you had moved. Why?"

Her face grew red. "Why? He kick us out."

"That bald-headed bastard."

"I was fool, show George papers. Not know about this building. Leones keep secret from me. Didn't know what deed building mean, and Tula no understand. This *kata-stro-fe-a*, this catastrophe, my Leones' secret. He no tell me. Why?" Her voice was shaking so Tula couldn't hear all the words.

Ondoni didn't hear either, "What did you say?"

"Leones keep secret from me."

"Maybe he had plans to clean it up and surprise you. I can help, now that I've gotten over that damn fever. Or better still, I can get someone who knows what he's doing to help you."

"No!"

"I worry about you," Ondoni said. "That thief Gus Lambredes, is going to swindle you. Is he giving you any money? Maybe you can rent the lower flat. You will need money. I'll help you. I've got money."

"No!" She spoke scornfully, and the look on her face showed she would never allow him to help her.

"God damn it, why not?"

"Because I no want your money." She walked over to the baby and touched her tiny hand.

He followed her with his eyes and smiled. "Maybe I should find you a good husband. You're young."

"What? I had best husband. No more husbands for me, no more babies for me." She spit out the words.

Tula sat very still in the dark bedroom. *Why do I get the feeling that Mana is saying something more?*

Ondoni said, "No more husbands, no more babies? Oh, I see. And what's this I hear about you sending the girls to Socrates? Want to make greenhorns of them, too?"

Zoe said, "I want good Greek girls. Go."

He rose and fumbled in his pocket for some bills and put them on the table. "Here, take this. It will help some."

"No want whore's money." She tore the bills and threw them in his face. "*Na!*" She cursed him. "*Bad—putana's* money."

"Please don't. I want to help you."

"*Ex-oh!*" She pointed to the door.

He walked to the door and closed it after him.

Tula watched as Zoe sat at the kitchen table, put her head in her hands, and wept. Finally, she wiped her tears with the back of her hand, covered the baby in the basket with a blanket, and walked into the bedroom, where she found Tula sitting on the floor. "Tula, what you doing up?"

"I couldn't sleep."

"It's late. You catch cold on the floor. Sleep."

"*Ola kala*," Tula said. "All is well, don't worry."

"*Ola kala*." She touched Tula's hair in a caress.

Chapter 5

The kitchen was flooded with yellow sunlight the second Saturday in May. It shone through the sheer white curtains on the sparking windows. The flat was clean. It had taken Zoe and her daughters weeks of scouring with lye soap before the stench of rodents had finally vanished from the flat.

Tula stood in the kitchen gazing down into the alley, a canyon formed by two walls of tenements with a sea of decaying garbage at the foot of each wall.

She felt tired. It was the moving, the cleaning, the long hours. There was an ache in her chest and in her eyes. A constant refrain ran through her mind: What was going to happen to them? How could they get some money? Real money, not just pennies they earned crocheting lace collars, selling them to their teachers. Never enough money, never.

Looking down at the desolate landscape, she saw a boy searching through the garbage and thought of Photi, growing up to be a stupid peddler, like his father, living in poverty. A wild surge of anger rose in her, followed by fear, fear for Photi. She had to see him. Now!

After searching in her drawer for some pennies and finding six for carfare, three cents for each way, Tula left the flat and took the streetcar to the old neighborhood. On a Saturday morning, the streetcar was crowded with women, some with leather shopping bags folded on their laps, others with wicker baskets. All ready for a day at the Halsted Street Department Store, where the finest cotton and linens were sold and the richest silk embroidery threads from France, or at Maxwell Street, where in a carnival atmosphere peddlers sold everything from their pushcarts—pots, pans, dresses, shoes, furniture, live ducks and chickens, carpets, linens, sheets, towels and bedspreads.

Tula rarely found a window seat, especially on a Saturday. She did find an aisle seat and sat down. Her thoughts turned to Photi. She knew he'd be in the barn grooming his father's bay. He was always there on Saturdays. But she was worried about him, and she was afraid of his father, although he always treated her with cold politeness.

Photi wasn't her only worry. She was also concerned about her mother and the dwindling bank account. She was afraid that one day, she would wake up as old as her mother, with children living in squalor. All these thoughts were going through her mind, and before she knew it she was standing in front of the old stable. As soon as she pushed open the doors, she realized that something was wrong. There was no sound, just an eerie stillness broken by the racing of her heart. "Photi!" she called. No answer.

She turned the corner and saw the bay in one of the stalls with his nose in his feed bag. She reached over and patted his long, sleek neck. "Where's Photi?" she asked. The bay neighed. She smiled.

Then she heard a rustling sound, and her relief vanished as all her premonitions of disaster returned. She turned a corner and nearly stumbled over Photi lying in the darkest, out-of-the way place in the barn. He was tied to a post, his hands behind his back, his legs fastened together with a leather belt. His cries were muffled by a kerchief covering his mouth. She screamed. "Photi, what happened?" When she pulled off the kerchief and saw his swollen face, she knew. Frantically, she fumbled with the ropes. She loosened the leather belt. He leaned against the post, rubbing his wrists.

"Tula," he began. The fear in his voice scared her. Photi had always been tough.

"What happened?"

He said, "I thought I was tough, could stand up to him. Here I am crying like a baby. He said I was spying on him."

She faced him, drying his eyes with her hands. "You *are* tough. Come on, let's get out of here." They hurried past the stalls and opened the barn doors. Now the radiant sun warmed her. Why was she so cold? Gently she touched his cheek. "Come home with me."

He shook his head, "No, I can't. He'll find me."

On the way out the door, Tula turned and saw George staggering down the street. "He's coming back."

Photi said, "Go. There'll be more trouble if he finds you here."

She didn't move. "If there's trouble, I can help. There'd be two of us."

Now George was at the barn door, drunk and carrying a bottle. When he staggered into the barn, she was surprised to hear herself say, "If you hurt Photi again, I'm calling the police."

He roared at her. "God damn it, go—call them!"

Photi said, "I'm leaving."

"Like hell you are." He turned on his son and swung his fist, catching him on the cheekbone. Photi's mouth filled with blood. "Didn't get enough eh?

I'll teach you."

George dragged him into a stall, took off his belt and doubled it in his hand. He struck Photi with the belt, cursing him in a thick, drunken voice. Photi fell to his knees, stunned from the blow, crying.

Helpless, Tula watched. She didn't know what to do. She knew she was no match for George, even in his drunken condition. Finally, his chest heaving, George looked down at this son and said, "You think you're leaving? I'll kill you first with my bare hands." He threw his belt down and moved in closer. Photi ran and hid behind the bay. "Go ahead and hide, you son of a bitch. And you, Tula, get the hell out of here."

Tula's lips were trembling. She backed into a corner, not daring to move. She could not hide the hatred she felt for George at this moment. "You devil," she said.

"Get the hell out of here, or do you want the same?" He leaned against the stall post, rubbed his baldhead, and drank from the bottle. He seemed very drunk, his brown eyes had a crazy glint in them, and now Tula wasn't frightened anymore. She was mad. George looked down at this son. "I'll cut your heart out next time I catch you spying on me." He faced Tula. "I said, get out."

She flew out of the barn door and ran all the way home, breathless, confused, and angry. She was so frightened of what George had done to Photi that when she got home, she cried hysterically. Between sobs, she tried to tell Zoe what had happened. It was only after Tula's tears subsided that Zoe understood.

Finally, Zoe said, "That George is devil—not father." She cursed him. "*Na!*" she said, spitting out the curse. "May his soul rot in hell. Why must boy suffer. A poor motherless child."

"Can't we do anything?"

"Only God help him," Zoe said.

Mother and daughter sat talking for the next hour until it was time for supper. As Tula was setting the table, a knock came at the door. "I'll get it," Tula said, hoping it was Photi. She opened the door and saw a man looking down at her, a tall man with smiling hazel eyes. He wore a broad-brimmed brown hat. "Yes?" she asked, blocking the door with her small body.

"Hello," he said. He took off his hat and wiped his forehead with his forearm. "I'm Andreas Korinthes. And you have to be Zoe's daughter. With those black eyes, you look just like your mother when she left Greece." He spoke with a thick Greek accent, weighing each word. When he smiled, he revealed two dimples and white even teeth. He held out his hand. She stared at it, and he put it back in his pocket.

"What do you want?" She guarded the door.

"Doesn't' Zoe Palestes live here? And her brother, Ondoni?"

"Yes. No. I mean, yes my mother is Zoe Palestes, and she lives here, but my Uncle Ondoni doesn't."

Suddenly, Tula realized she was not alone with this tall stranger. Turning her head, she saw her mother observing, and behind her were her sisters, craning their necks in the background.

"Andreas, no see you in many years," Zoe said. "You no change, only grow taller. You man now. What twenty-three, twenty-four years old? Why you here in Chicago? You live in Nebraska with your brother, yes? Come in."

"Thank you. I'm twenty-seven, same age as Ondoni. Glad I found you," Andreas Korinthes said. "I got tired of the wide-open spaces of Nebraska. Wanted to taste city life." He walked into the room. Inside the kitchen, Andreas turned and looked down into Tula's eyes. "And this must of course be Black-eyed Susan. What beautiful eyes, just like the Black-eyed Susans that grow in Nebraska." He said it as if it was the most natural remark for a stranger to make even before being introduced. Tula stared at him, her mouth open in wonder.

There was a twinkle in Zoe's eyes. "No Black-eyed Susan. She Dimitra. We call her Tula. No Black-eyed Susans grow in Chicago, no flowers here."

Angel, close behind Tula, spelled softly, "B-l-a-c-k-e-y-e-d S-u-s-a-n."

"Shut up!" Tula said. No one had ever called her Black-eyed Susan. Her name was Tula. For a minute, she didn't know what to do with her hands.

Zoe said, "Please sit, Andreas, join us at humble meal. *Katse*, sit." Zoe brought in a small platter of chicken wings and necks and made room at the table for him. She placed herself between Andreas and Tula, but Tula was conscious of his nearness.

"Thank you. It's been a long time since I've tasted *avgo-lemono soupa*. I'm looking forward to this. So, Zoe, these are your daughters?"

Angel giggled.

Vasso turned to Angel and whispered, "Don't giggle, Shorty."

Zoe said, "Yes, my daughters." Pointing to each, Zoe introduced them. "You know my Tula, and this Vasso, my second, Angeleke, my fair-haired, we call Angel. Reni, with curls and last my baby, Chreso, we call Goldie. They help me when Leones die."

"I heard. I'm sorry." He made the sign of the cross. "God rest his soul. I'd heard he was a good man."

Zoe's eyes misted as she sipped her soup.

Andreas drew a breath. "Is Ondoni here?"

The girls ate their soup in silence, their eyes fastened on their bowls. Tula avoided a head-on look at the man who had traveled such a great distance to see her mother and uncle. She found it hard to cope with his easy manner, his cheerfulness. *He is too friendly*, she thought. But she was curious about him.

Zoe fed the baby some soup from her bowl. "No, Ondoni no here," she said. "He lives in a boarding house. No see him." Then she paused and looked at Tula, and Tula knew she wanted to steer the conversation away from Ondoni. "But tell about Nebraska?"

Sensing her mother's discomfort, Tula said, "Yes, tell us."

For a while, Andreas talked about Nebraska. He told them it was much bigger and greener than Chicago, or for that matter the state of Illinois. It had fields and fields of corn. It was flat land, not like the mountains of Greece. And there were many animals there—horses, cows, pigs, sheep, chickens, birds, geese.

"Yes, plenty of animals. Zoe, you're used to the goats and sheep of Greece, but in Nebraska I can't count the number of animals there. Too many." He laughed. "My brother, Tasso, is too busy chasing the Chautauqua."

"What's that?" Tula asked, and then, embarrassed at her boldness, blushed.

"It's a huge tent show, speeches, music, book learning, theater, all mixed together. We'd make sandwiches, my brother's wife would bake pies and cakes, and Tasso would take them to the Chautauqua, to the crowds." Andreas finished his soup first. He placed a palm over his bowl when Zoe offered to fill it again, then settled back. "It was a good business, and Tasso's daughters helped, but they are much older than yours. How old is Black-eyed Susan?"

"Tula twelve in two month, July."

Angel and Vasso giggled.

"*Zhoo-pha*. Quiet," Zoe said, and the girls remained silent. Andreas continued with his story. He told about going to high school, playing on the football team. After graduation, he worked for Tasso. But he was tired of the country. He wanted to see the big city of Chicago.

"So here I am," he said. "I also want to see Ondoni. We were such good friends in Greece. How can I reach him?"

Zoe looked at her daughters. "Girls, take Goldie downstairs for air. Tula, no do dishes. You go too. But first pour coffee."

Tula watched as Andreas stretched out in the chair near the stove and stared at the fire through the isinglass windows, his eyes half closed against the glare of the coals in the stove. Zoe pulled up a chair and sat beside him.

Tula poured him another cup of coffee. Who was this man, so full of laughter, so quick to make a joke? Who was this man from Nebraska, who claimed to be friends with Ondoni?

"You have a pleasant flat here, Zoe. All is well?"

"Well—" she began, and then turned to Tula. "Thank you. Now go with the girls."

As Tula closed the door, she heard her mother say, "Ondoni not same Ondoni you know in village. He change—was very sick, do strange things."

Changed? Doing strange things? Tula wondered.

*   *   *

It was the second week in June and Tula was almost hating her mother for her unhappiness. Not only did she hate Greek school, she hated the distance she had to walk. It was a mile, less if she cut through a deserted park, which she often did. She finally became resigned to it, running most of the way alone, not waiting for her sisters.

The long walk, the teachers, the school, the religious classes, the Greek classes, everything about Socrates irritated her. Thank God this was the last week of the semester.

When she dressed that morning, she thought about Andreas, how he had teased her with the name, Black-eye Susan. She didn't like him, and she didn't like that name. Andreas had become a frequent visitor, and he often brought chocolates to her mother and toys for Goldie. Tula thought he was becoming too much a part of their lives. Everyone except Tula looked forward to his visits. He had found work in a candy store near the Loop. With every visit, he brought a new confection from the store, much to the sisters' delight.

Tula was unhappy. She had no one to talk to and poured all her thoughts in her Friendship Book. "I worry about Mana," she wrote, "And that Andreas is trying to push himself into our family. I don't like him. I don't like his candy he bribes us with. I want to go back to the old neighborhood, be with my friends, Esther and Photi."

Now in the kitchen, she closed her Friendship Book and filled her cup with hot milk and coffee. She would come to grips with her problems, she told herself. By the time she finished her coffee, she would have solved her problems, once and for all! But her coffee grew cold, and she continued to sit at the table.

Her thoughts always came back to the bakery, Gus, and the power of attorney that Zoe had signed to receive the meager allowance. Tula knew that her mother worried about money. Money for food, money for clothes, money for school, books, money for church, money for the gas bill. And yet, Tula thought, with all this, her mother was sometime careless with money. She bought the best French embroidery thread, the best virgin olive oil, the best feta cheese. And many times she would call Dr. Voles for an ailing child, where other mothers would give home remedies and wait for the fever to pass.

"You be late, Tula," Zoe said.

"I've got time. And maybe I won't go to that school, ever."

Zoe was removing slices of toast from the oven. She slapped the plate of toast on the table, the bread scattering, and said, "You go to school!" The look she gave Tula made her face hot.

Tula's mouth quivered. She put her cup down and tucked her Friendship Book into her satchel. "Yes," she said. "I'm going. I don't know why, but I am." She grabbed her straw hat and rushed out, slamming the door.

She held her breath, putting off the moment she'd have to breathe in the musty smell of mice, stale fish, and cheap wine that still clung to the hallway. While she raced down the stairs, she thought there wasn't even Old Nell to scold her. She'd welcome a scolding from Old Nell.

Tula reached Socrates Greek School, the only frame building on Taylor Street. It was next door to Holy Trinity Greek Church, which stood like a jewel among the tenements, with its ornate gold dome.

She shook her hair free from the ribbons of the straw hat. She wore a somber navy blue uniform. Her face still burned with anger at her mother. She prayed she wouldn't have to speak to anyone. A procession of students walked past her. No one stopped, and no one talked to her. On her way to class, she passed the cafeteria, where the tantalizing smell of bacon came from within. In her haste to get out of the house, she hadn't eaten. Now she was hungry. Miss Kaloda saw her.

"Tula, come have breakfast with us. We've fifteen minutes before the final bell." She spoke in Greek. Right behind her was the principal, Mr. Gracas.

He said, "Please do. As a new student, you'll have to give me your opinion of Miss Kaloda's cooking."

Miss Kaloda's brown eyes suddenly grew coy and sparkling. She almost simpered. "I haven't heard any complaints yet."

Tula followed them into the small kitchen next to the cafeteria. The bacon sizzled in a pan. On the other burner, a pot of coffee simmered. There were a table and four chairs in the room, painted a stark white. Thick slices of bread were on a plate. Mr. Gracas stroked his mustache with this thumb and forefinger. "How do you like it here?" he asked as Tula put a fork into her scrambled eggs.

Tula said, "It's all right, I guess." She, too, spoke in Greek. Greek was the only language spoken at Socrates, except in the English classes.

Miss Kaloda poured Tula a glass of milk.

Mr. Gracas sat beside her, drinking his coffee. Miss Kaloda settled down in the other chair. "I'm glad you joined us for our quiet time and breakfast," she said.

"Quiet time before the storm, she means," Mr. Gracas said.

Tula stared at them. "This food's delicious. I haven't had eggs in such a long time, I mean—" She spoke in English, then blushed when she realized what she had done.

"You speak excellent English," Miss Kaloda said. "Do you converse in English at home?"

"No, not really. Maybe with my sisters. But my Mana doesn't know much English. She's trying, though. Getting better."

"And you speak Greek like a native, like one from the village," Mr. Gracas said.

Tula grinned. "Mana said I have the right accent. Is that what you call it?"

"The proper term is *fraces*. Now, let's hear you say it."

"*Fraces*."

"Good." He nodded. "Are you happy here at Socrates?"

Tula looked suspiciously at him. Did he know that she was miserable there? Did he know she longed to be back at Dorr School with her friends?

"Don't you like it here?" Miss Kaloda asked.

Tula decided to be honest. "I didn't want to come here. Mana made me. I wanted to stay at Dorr School."

"Dorr School, eh? That public school with all kinds of roughnecks," the principal said.

"No! They're not rough. Even if they are, I don't care. I liked it there." Tula had not meant to say that, and she would not say any more.

Used to the discipline of Miss MacMann at Dorr School, Tula found it hard to cope with the easy cheerful manner of Miss Kaloda and the friendly concern of the principal.

After finishing her breakfast in silence while Miss Kaloda and the principal chatted, Tula escaped to the hallway, her thanks drowned in the clang of the school bell. The hall filled with children scrambling to get into line. When Tula spotted Vasso and Angel in line, she squeezed in between them.

"Guess where I've been?" she whispered.

"In the principal's office, because you're bad," Vasso said.

"Showing your pictures of movie stars to the kids," Angel said.

"No, silly. Both of you are wrong. I just had breakfast with Miss Kaloda and Mr. Gracas."

"Really?" Angel asked, her gray eyes wide with wonder. "What did you eat? They really asked you?"

"I had bacon and eggs. And yes, they asked me."

"Bacon and eggs!"

Vasso's eyes narrowed, and she bit her lower lip. "You're lying! Teachers don't ask kids to breakfast, especially new kids. You're lying!"

"It's the truth, and I don't care if you don't believe it."

"I believe you," Angel said.

* * *

After school, Tula walked home alone, the rain and wind penetrating to her very bones. Although it was June, there was a chill in the air. She dreaded going home. She didn't want to face her mother after that morning's quarrel. Her gloom matched that day. There was no sun in the overcast sky. She walked through the park. Across the street from the park was Lady of Pompeii Catholic School.

Two boys stood in front of the school, leaning against the building watching her. "Hey, greasy Greek from Socrates. Want to get jazzed?" one of them hollered.

"Geez, don't ask her, let's do it. Jazz her!"

The boys broke into a trot and crossed the street.

Tula began to run. She glanced back over her shoulders, terrified. "Keep going!" she commanded her legs. The boys gained on her.

"Get that damn Greek!" the tall one shouted.

She looked around wildly. They were almost upon her. She felt pain in her side from running. She made a wild dash and turned the corner. She could hear their threats and taunts close behind. Glancing back, she saw the boys turn the corner and slam into a portly man, knocking him down.

"What the hell's going on?" he demanded, his eyes blazing mad. "Where's the fire?"

Sheepishly, the boys apologized while helping him up. A short distance away, she heard them shout. "We'll get you yet, you Greek! We'll jazz you good next time."

Gasping for breath, she stopped and leaned against the wall of a building. Tears rained down her face. She drew in her breath in suffocating sobs.

A shining black car drove slowly down the street. It stopped where she was huddled.

"Tula," she heard someone call from inside the car. She stood dazed, sobbing, looking into the car. The door opened. "Get in," the driver commanded. Suddenly, strong arms grabbed her and helped her in. It was Ondoni. "Want a ride home?" He held her until she stopped crying. Then he put the car into gear and started off. "It's all right, Tula. You're okay."

"Th-they wanted to j-jazz me. I was s-scared."

"*Jazz* you! Why, those bastards!"

Tula was ignorant of that meaning of *jazz*. She knew it was a sex act, but she didn't know anything about sex. And it didn't interest her. Tula was an avid reader but she never sought out the books that would give her any information about it.

Her mother had babies. How and why it happened never concerned her. Even when her father was alive, sex was not discussed. The word certainly was never mentioned. The act was performed only behind closed doors in the dark of night. She had never seen her parents unless they were fully clothes. The only time she had seen her father in bed was when he was dying.

Last summer, when she'd turned eleven, she had noticed red stains on her bloomers. She thought she had cut herself. She searched her body for a cut. The bleeding stopped within in a few days, and she soon forgot about it. Two months later, it started again, and this time it was more intense. Was she bleeding to death? She started writing about it in her Friendship Book. If she was going to die, she wanted a record of her last days: "I don't want to die. But I don't know how to tell Mana." She lay in bed at night next to Vasso in confused terror, frantically writing. "I'm afraid to close my eyes because I know that's when death will come."

One day, alone in her room, she cried. Zoe heard her. "What is the matter?"

Tula looked at her, terrified, then squeezed her eyes shut. "It's too terrible."

"Baba die. That too terrible."

"That's it. Baba dying. And now I'm dying." She blurted out the words burying her head in her hands.

Zoe gently lifted Tula's head. "Now tell me. Why you cry?"

"I'm bleeding to death. It's getting worse now because it hurts, too. I'm dying!"

Zoe closed her eyes for a moment, and then she opened them wide. She smiled. "Tula, it happens to all women, every month. Tell me when flow comes. I give you clean rags to catch it. If you have pain, small glass of cognac help. You woman now."

A woman! Tula felt her face get hot.

Now, nestled beside her uncle in the black car as he drove through the rain, Tula felt a sharp pain in her side. Was it because of the running? Or was it because the flow had started? She wasn't afraid anymore. "I'm a woman," she whispered to herself.

"What did you say?" Ondoni said, his eyes on the traffic.

"Oh, nothing." She looked up at him. Did he see the change in her? Did he see her as a woman? She knew she wasn't a little girl. Did he know that, too? "I'm glad you're here."

"So am I,' he said.

Chapter 6

Tula reached for her Friendship Book and jotted: "It's July 17, 1924 my thirteenth birthday. Happy day! It looks like it's going to be a hot one. I've pinned my hair up in braids, just like Mana's."

From the open kitchen window, she heard a peddler cry, "rags o lay." Leaning out, she saw the old man encouraging his gray mare with a light tap of his whip to walk the hot brick street, leaving ripples of dust behind him. Vasso sneaked up behind her and held her while Angel gave her fourteen licks, one for each year and one to grow on.

"Stop it, stop it!" Tula yelled.

"What's happening?" Zoe asked. "Don't hit sister. Shame. Especially on Sunday and birthday." Tula noticed that her mother's English was improving. *Someday she'll be just like us*, Tula thought. Then again, maybe it was because of Andreas.

"Mana, it's just for fun," Vasso said. Changing the subject, she said, "Can't we eat?" Her thin lips were pressed together.

"You know better, Vasso. We take communion today. We fast."

"Not even water?" Angel asked. "I'm thirsty."

"Try to think of something else," Zoe said. "Tula your hair? You look older—" Her voice trailed off. "*Na ta katosteethes.* May you live to be a hundred," she said, smiling and draping her arm around Tula's shoulders. "My firstborn. Now a woman."

Tula stood there basking in the warm glow. "But I don't want to live to be a hundred. I know it's an old Greek saying, but I'll settle for ninety-nine."

"You'll be all wrinkled and old," Vasso said.

Tula just grinned. Nothing could spoil this day for her, not even Vasso. "So what? I've seen old, wrinkled *yiayias*, grandmothers in church, and they look sweet."

Reni chanted, "Tula is a *yiayia*."

"Enough, enough," Zoe said.

"And Tula isn't getting any presents. Wrinkled old Tula isn't getting N-O-T-H-I-N-G," Angel said.

"Shut up. And quit spelling." Tula didn't want to think about her birthday anymore. Because that's when she remembered how angry her mother got when Ondoni gave her birthday presents. He went against another Greek tradition, to give gifts only on name days. Tula knew that her mother thought it had been a mistake for Ondoni to be her godfather, because he didn't go to church and because she called him an evil man. Tula never had understood why he was evil in her mother's eyes.

Tula still cherished the turquoise wool shawl he had given her. Zoe had said when she first laid eyes on Ondoni at Ellis Island, he'd been tagged and addressed like a parcel, yet he clung to a large brown paper sack containing the shawl. Wrapped in folds of the shawl had been a gold cross and a fine gold chain, purchased in Athens, a hand-crocheted white baby bonnet and sweater, tiny slippers of butter-soft white leather, and a white linen christening gown embroidered with violets.

Zoe's voice snapped Tula out of her reverie. She reach for the gold cross hanging around her neck.

"Enough about birthdays, enough about presents," Zoe said. "Girls, come."

In a few minutes they were on their way, passing other families headed down the street. Leones had been dead for more than three years. Now the women and men greeted Zoe with special attention and Tula knew why. The news had traveled among the Greeks in the neighborhood that a man was visiting Leones' widow.

When they reached the church, Tula saw Miss Kaloda on the steps. She ran to greet her teacher.

"And how are you, Tula? My, you look so grown-up today."

"It's my birthday. I'm thirteen."

"*Na ta katosteethes.*"

"Thank you."

They had become friends. Tula had discovered during the years at Socrates School that Miss Kaloda was an avid movie fan and enjoyed going to the theater almost as much as she did.

One day, Tula showed Miss Kaloda her collection of movie star pictures. Miss Kaloda wanted some photos of her own. She asked Tula to write for her. When photos of John Gilbert and Rudolph Valentino came to Miss Kaloda, personally autographed, she was in Tula's debt.

Dorr School was a faint, pleasant memory now. Tula had changed her allegiance to Socrates Greek School. In the fall, she would be in the eighth grade. How excited she was at the prospect. She was going to become a teacher, she knew it! Her only regret was her father would not be there to see

55

his prediction come true.

Half of her still hated to think about him. It made her sad. It made her angry. He was gone. But half of her was proud that she had had him, even for a little while.

In church, she saw Andreas. She must not look at him. She made her way down the aisle through the crowd, and when she looked up, he was beside her. His hand touched her shoulder.

"How's my Black-eyed Susan?" he whispered. She turned away from him. Her hands felt damp. What was he doing on the women's side? Why didn't he move—go on the men's side? She wanted to run out of the church.

Zoe glanced over and frowned. In the past year, Andreas and Zoe had become close. *Are they more than friends?* Tula wondered. He had helped her mother in many ways, such as going to the court hearings about the bakery. He had even had an electrician install electricity in the flat after Reni had burned her hand on the gas jet flame. He would come to the flat, unannounced, his arms full of groceries and candy. *There are too many questions*, thought Tula. Her head was reeling. She felt tears welling up.

Andreas' eyes showed concern when he looked at her. An usher came to where Andreas was standing beside Tula. He whispered something.

"No!" said Andreas. "I will not move."

The usher said, "The blues with the blues, the pinks with the pinks."

Andreas took a deep breath. "No!" He remained by Tula's side. Goldie and Reni stared at him. Vasso and Angel, eyes wide and mouths open, gaped. Zoe frowned.

Why doesn't he move? thought Tula. Finally, she said, "You shouldn't be here."

This time, Andreas' face reddened. He half smiled, revealing his dimples, and sharply turned and walked to the men's side.

After the service, she moved quickly through the crowd. A woman stopped to chat with Zoe. Andreas, leaning on the church's iron fence, grinned when he saw Tula.

He walked up to her and pressed a small box into her hands. "This is for you, Black-eyed Susan. Happy birthday."

"But—but," she stammered.

"Open it, please."

She opened the box. Inside was a miniature porcelain box with a flower etched on the lid. The stem was in gold leaf, the black disc surrounded by fourteen golden petals.

"Happy birthday, Black-eyed Susan."

It was beautiful. She stared at him, puzzled. Why did he give her such a precious gift? "It's lovely. I don't know if I should keep it."

He laughed. "But of course you should keep it. It's a Black-eyed Susan. Now you know what the flower looks like. See the black center? Just like your eyes. It's a ring box. It has a brass clasp, to lock it, so you won't lose your rings. I'll show you how to work the clasp." He took the box and unfastened the clasp. "See? I bought it in Nebraska, just before I left. I wanted a reminder of home. I want you to have it."

Angel came in closer to see. "What is it?" Tula opened the box for her. "My, it's pretty."

Vasso and Reni stared at the box. Reni whistled. Zoe joined Andreas and her daughters. She held Goldie in her arms. She nodded to Andreas, "So you made scene and stood on women's side?" she said in Greek.

"Yes, I did make a scene. Just wanted to see if the ushers were paying attention. I have to do that every now and then, to keep them in line."

"Andreas, no matter how long I know you, I will never know you," Zoe said.

"True," Andreas said.

Tula held the gift in her hand. Should she interrupt their conversation? Should she keep the gift? Finally, she said, "Mana, look what Andreas gave me."

Zoe examined the box. "Isn't that nice?"

"I don't think I should keep it."

"It's a thoughtful gift. Yes, keep it. But it's not your name day."

"I couldn't wait for her name day," Andreas said. "May I walk you home?"

"Yes, please," Zoe said. "You can carry Goldie."

Andreas lifted Goldie.

It was getting hotter as the day wore on. They crossed the street where some cars had stopped for a red light. They passed a large thermometer nailed to the front of a drug store. It registered an incredible 98 degrees. Tula was glad she had put her hair up. Her white dress felt pasted to her body.

"Boy, it's hot," Angel gasped.

"It's not heat but humidity," Zoe said. "It get cooler tonight, and we can sit outside."

Tula knew that after the sun set, after the supper dishes were done, her mother enjoyed sitting with the other women in the neighborhood, gossiping. They laughed and cried about their youth and their homeland, while their children played nearby. Families and children were the main topics. Zoe had made several friends in the neighborhood. Her best friend was Sophie, who was called *Thea* Sophie by the girls, to show respect. Sophie became Goldie's godmother. Also a widow, she was Zoe's confidante now. Sophie, who was more American than Zoe, introduced her to fortune-tellers. Often they would visit an old gypsy in a neighborhood store.

At the flat, when Andreas reached the foot of the stairs, he put Goldie down.

"Come up," Zoe offered.

"Not today. I'll come back sometime this week. Good-bye, girls. Good-bye, Zoe. And once again, happy birthday, Black-eyed Susan. May you live to be a hundred." And then he walked down the street.

"Black-eyed Susan!" Angel taunted.

"Black-eyed Susan!" Vasso repeated.

"Shut up!" Tula said, her face growing hot. She ran up the stairs.

"Girls, don't tease Tula. That not nice."

I have to get away, Tula thought. She reached the dark hallway and the door to the flat. Andreas shouldn't have given her that box. She held it in her hand. In frustration, she kicked the locked door. What was taking her mother so long?

The hallway was dark. Her foot caught on something. She kneeled down and picked it up. It was wrapped in the thinnest tissue paper, layers of it. It smelled like springtime. She remembered that fragrance from somewhere. She tore through the tissue and found a delicate bunch of violets tied with a purple velvet ribbon. Attached to the ribbon was a birthday card. It was from Ondoni.

"May you live to be a hundred, my dear goddaughter." He signed it, "*Agape*, love, your *Nouno* Ondoni." Tula buried her face in the violets and cried.

Chapter 7

As Zoe sipped her coffee, she was unusually quiet. It was a Saturday morning in August. Tula stood at the kitchen counter and sliced some bread. She loved Saturdays, because she could have some time with her mother alone. Her sisters were out playing stickball in the street. Even Goldie tagged along. She was at the age, two and a half, where she was into everything. But she was such a cheerful child that no one was ever angry with her for long.

Zoe poured more coffee into the cups. Tula watched her, her eyes bright, a smile on her lips. Suddenly, she was sure that she loved her mother more than her mother loved her. She turned and looked out the open window. She heard the "rags o lay" man. Yesterday, Tula had gathered the odds and ends of flour sacks after Zoe had used them to make slips and underwear for her daughters and sold the rags to the "rags o lay" man for twenty-five cents.

Tula stared at her shoes. She had put them on this morning on a whim, saying to herself she must break them in. These were the shoes Andreas had bought for her a week ago.

"They look fine," he had said while the shoe clerk fitted Tula.

"They cost too much," Tula had said.

"No, not at all. We'll take them," he had said.

Angel chose a pair of black T-straps. She wore them out of the store. Vasso picked a pair of Buster Browns, and Reni and Goldie settled for high-button shoes. While the clerk fitted her sisters, Tula watched Zoe and Andreas.

Would Andreas become Tula's stepfather? He had become a family friend, and Zoe sought his advice. He made good money at the candy store and had a promising future. He often brought them gifts, food, toys for Goldie, candy for the others. At first, Zoe would not accept the gifts. That's when Andreas became angry and said, "I want to help you. We are friends, aren't we? Don't you want me as a friend?"

In the shoe store, Andreas had insisted that the girls also needed dresses to go with their new shoes. Since he'd insisted, Zoe said, "Let's go to Maxwell Street, more bargains there."

Why was he buying them clothing? Tula was confused. She pushed her way through the loaded carts of Maxwell Street. Zoe also rushed ahead. She knew Maxwell Street, it was her territory. She paused at a stall where dresses were piled high in the cart. Others hung on a rope over the cart. The peddler began, "Dresses, nice dresses for the girls? Bargains. Bargains, lady." He looked at Andreas. "Bargains, Mister."

Andreas grinned. "Bargains, eh? Well, we'll see."

Tula's eyes were caught by a lavender crepe that fell in soft folds from its wooden hanger. The neck was round, and it was sleeveless, the bodice lavishly stitched with tiny gray and purple beads. She touched it, felt the soft fabric, the beads.

The peddler took it down and patted it with his huge hand. "A masterpiece, fit for a princess." He turned it inside out. "Stitched by hand."

Tula heard Zoe whisper to Andreas in Greek. "It's too fancy. Perhaps the cotton ones on the cart. Bargain with him. See if you can get them at a good price."

Now the cotton dresses hung in the bedroom closet, Tula thought and she sipped her coffee.

Zoe put her cup down and sighed. "How I wish I could read the coffee grounds better, like Sophie. She does it so well. Then I can tell fortunes." She spoke in Greek.

Zoe turned her cup upside down into the saucer, waited a minute, and then turned it back up again and studied the inside of the cup, where the fine coffee grounds had settled into a pattern. "I see something. Yes, it's a man."

Tula felt her face grow hot. Her thoughts had turned to Andreas. Was her mother thinking of him, too? She remembered the time Andreas had to tell Zoe that Gus had won and taken over Baba's bakery. She remembered how her mother found comfort in Andreas' arms. She had watched them, dry-eyed.

Now Zoe lightly tapped the spoon in her coffee cup, touching the depressions the fine grounds made. "Yes, see the high valley, the high ridge? That means change, a big change, for the better."

"I hope so," Tula said. "Even though it's bunk. Bunk like the old gypsy tells you and Thea Sophie. Maybe the change is that old Gus will take Baba's flats, just like he took the bakery."

"Hush. Be still."

Reading coffee grounds, going to the gypsy—everything was a fake, Tula thought. Why did she believe? "It's stupid."

"Listen Tula, I have something important to say." Zoe smiled.

It must be good news. She is smiling, Tula thought.

"We have to think of our future," Zoe began. "And you, being the oldest, have the most responsibility."

"I know. Haven't I helped, with the cooking, with the baking, with the cleaning? Haven't I taken care of Goldie?"

"Yes, you've done more than your share. I'm very proud of you. I can't do without you. It's just that there is another matter that I must talk to you about. It's about Andreas."

So that's why Andreas hadn't been over lately. Mana had said he was too busy at the candy store, but she had lied. She was planning something with Andreas. Tula wanted to blurt out that Andreas did not belong in their family. They could make it without him. Tula looked at her mother, at her eyes, so black, so much like her own, so bright.

"What about Andreas?" Tula asked.

"You remember when Thea Sophie was here, about two weeks ago? Andreas was here, too, remember?"

"Yes, when Vasso and I went to the show to see Edmund Lowe in *Don Juan*."

Zoe stared at her hands, folded in her lap. Tula had never seen her mother this way. Zoe was her mother, not some girl from school who wanted to share her secrets. Tula expected Zoe was going to tell her something she didn't want to hear.

There were tears in Zoe's eyes. "Tula, I want you to think about something."

Tula didn't speak.

"Are you listening?"

"Yes."

Zoe's voice quivered. "You're the oldest. Almost like myself when I was your age. At fifteen I married. In time you will do the same. Marry, have babies to love, to cry over. All the same, all the same."

"No! You're wrong. I'm going to school. I'm going to be a teacher. Maybe someday I'll marry, but not for a long, long time."

"A long, long time?"

"Yes."

"Child, will you promise me something?"

"Yes."

"Hold on to your dreams, whatever happens."

"Yes."

Zoe blurted out, "Tula, Andreas wants to marry you. I have given my approval."

"What?" Tula asked, shocked. "I can't marry Andreas. I can't marry anyone. I want to go to school. He doesn't want to marry me. He wants *you!* Mana, he wants *you!*"

"My poor Tula, my poor child, you must save us." Zoe cried. "We lost the bakery, we might lose the flats, we need Andreas, you *must* marry him!"

"*You* marry him! I don't want to get married, understand? *You* marry him!" Tula trembled with anger. She wiped the tears from her face, made a fist, and banged the table. "So that is what you and Thea Sophie have been cooking up. Planning *my* life. I'll never marry him, never!"

Zoe said, "You must marry Andreas. We will wait a year, maybe longer, until you are almost fifteen. That was the age I married." She wiped the tears from her eyes. "I will announce the engagement in October, on your name day. You have two months to get used to the idea. I will give Andreas the diamond ring your Baba gave me. It will be your engagement ring. I'm not asking you, Tula. I'm telling you. It's settled."

"I won't marry him! I'll run away first!" Tula ran into her bedroom and slammed the door shut after her. She remained in the gloom of the tiny room most of the day. She sat cross-legged on the bed and poured her heart out into her Friendship Book.

In the book she kept pictures of Esther and Photi, of baby Goldie, of Baba in front of the bakery, of her favorite teachers. Miss MacMann on stage at the Christmas play and Miss Kaloda holding autographed pictures of Rudolph Valentino and Theda Bara.

Pasted on some of the book's pages were newspaper and magazine clippings. In a special section in the back of the book, she had printed in black letters, "SOCIETY." In the caption of a newspaper picture of Queen Sophia of Greece, it said: "Queen Sophia of Greece, sister of Wilhelm the former Kaiser and widow of the dethroned King Constantine. At the right is the queen's daughter, Helene, crown princess of Rumania." Next to Helene's face, Tula had scribbled, "Tula, crown princess of Chicago."

Listlessly, Tula flipped through the pages. The book held her most private thoughts, her treasured photos.

Then she wrote: "Why do girls leave home? Is it the call of great cities? Is it the freedom of adventure? Or is it disagreement with parents, dissatisfaction with home life? Is it a deadly sickness that comes from germs? I think that mothers are the most important reason for girls leaving home."

Tula put her pencil down. She wished she could erase what had just happened from her mind. She flung her book on the bed and put her hands over her face and cried. It isn't true! It's a lie. Mana doesn't want me to get married.

Later she wrote: "Commandments for mothers who want to keep their daughters at home. (1) Thou shalt not take all thy daughter's dreams away from her. (2) Remember to keep the birthdays and holidays. (3) Give thy daughter praise for her achievements. (4) Thou shalt help thy daughter to obtain a good education. (5) Thou shalt not deceive thy daughter by not being frank with her. Tell her the truths of life. Do not allow her to believe in Santa Clause too long. (6) Thou shalt not sell thy daughter to marriage."

Tula put her pencil down. It was quiet in the room and she could hear voices in the kitchen. Exhausted from her feverish writing, she stretched out on the bed.

Part II

Chapter 8

I'm going to have to tell Photi sooner or later, Tula thought. She hurried into the stable and instantly smelled the musty odor of manure and horses. One consolation, Tula thought, it was cooler inside the barn on this hot August day.

She spotted Photi near the door before he saw her, and she watched as he shaded his eyes against the strong sun with one hand. With the other hand, he swept a brush down the big bay's flank.

"So here you are," Tula said. "Are you hiding?"

"You think I'm hiding from my father?" His voice was flat as he continued brushing the bay. "What are you doing here? You're a long way from home."

Tula sat on a three-legged stool. "I—I was worried about you. And I have to tell you something." Now Photi had changed. He was taller and, at fifteen, almost a man. "Are you sure you're all right?"

"I'm okay," he said. "I'm just—well, look at my horse. Groomed to perfection. Grooming a horse is like cleaning the barn. You clean it, it gets dirty, you clean it again." Photi patted the flanks of the bay.

"Well, I guess you're in this barn because you like it, even if it does stink." Tula wrinkled her nose.

"I like it fine here. You didn't answer my question, or maybe you did. Why are you here? You're worried about me?" Photi asked.

Tula watched as he moved the brush in swift strokes, one way and then another, his hand and the brush moving as one. Tiny beads of sweat covered his forehead. He reached for a rag hanging from the stall and wiped his forehead. "If I'd known you were coming, I'd have dressed up." He brushed hay from his worn blue pants.

"I wanted to see you. It doesn't matter if you're not dressed up. You look fine to me, quite handsome." She smiled, tried to coax a smile out of him.

"What?" He frowned.

"I said you look handsome." Yes, there was something appealing about his thick brown hair curling low at the nape of his neck, his broad shoulders, his clear brown eyes. If Photi had changed so much in a few months, had she? She no longer wore her long hair loose. It was braided and twisted in a coronet on top of her head. The white middy blouse and blue pleated skirt had been replaced by a simple cotton dress. Did Photi notice that she was no longer a child.

They looked at each other for a moment. It was impossible for her to tell him about Andreas. And just as impossible for her not too. She rose and went to the barn door. He followed her.

"Tula," he said and when she turned and looked up at him, he kissed her check and she accepted the kiss. Tula touched his cheek. "Photi."

He turned away. His face grew red. To change the subject, he said, "It's cool in here. You wouldn't think it was August."

"Cool and stinking," Tula said.

"Not that bad. Last night, I slept here. Made a bed of straw. Used an old saddle for a pillow. It was peaceful. Even the horses didn't bother me. I had a dream—about us—"

Tula nodded.

"I had a job in the Indiana steel mills and made lots of money. We were walking down Michigan Avenue, or Lake Shore Drive or some fancy street, can't remember. And everyone was looking at us. Some whispering, 'Look at that big shot from the steel mills and his wife, the teacher.' I can see it, Tula. Can you?"

She walked over and patted the horse.

"Something's wrong, Tula." It was a statement.

"No, nothing's wrong."

"Then why do you look like you're going to cry?"

She turned away, grasping for words to explain to him. Her stomach felt weak. "My Mana has promised me—"

"Your Mana promised what?"

"She's promised me in marriage to this man Andreas."

"Marriage?"

"Yes," Tula said. "Mana says I must marry this man."

Photi steadied the bay's snapping head with his hand and stared at her. "Marriage? Are you crazy?" He dropped the brush, startling the bay. Then he calmed him using soothing words. "Easy, boy, easy, easy." His hands were knotted into tight fists. "It's a joke. You're kidding, of course."

"No, it's not a joke."

He kicked the post in the stall and shook his head.

"You don't mean that—"

"I don't want to marry Andreas," Tula began. "Mana has given her word to him. When I'm fifteen, I have to marry him. I don't like him. I hate him! Why did my Baba die? Why? I loved him, Photi." She began to weep.

"I know. Don't cry. Please don't cry."

"He didn't take care of himself, and he died. He left us alone…" She sobbed.

"Tula, please, don't."

With her hands, she wiped her eyes. She took a deep breath. "I'm okay now. I shouldn't cry. Babies cry. I'm a woman now. Mana says I'm a woman. And I have to—"

"You have to finish school, Tula."

"I know. That's why I want to run away. Let's run away, Photi. Like in your dreams. Let's go to Indiana."

"Run away?"

Tula looked at him. With surprise she realized that Photi could not run away with her. She was embarrassed for him. It was only a dream he'd had. She felt foolish.

"Sure, we can run away," he said nervously.

"Photi, I…" And then she stopped, not able to go on. "Forget what I said. I've got to go. Goldie and Reni are waiting for me at Hull House."

"Don't go. I want you to stay. Let's talk. We can do it. Run away I mean."

"I must go."

"Stay awhile. We'll figure something out. I don't want you to marry Andreas. It's time I did something my Baba—it's time I—"

"I have to go. It's late," she said.

"When will I see you again?" he asked.

"I don't know. Maybe in a few weeks. I'll see."

"I have to see you again. We can walk to the Loop," Photi said.

"Okay. I'll meet you at the Hull House courtyard one day in two weeks, before school starts."

"Okay."

There was so much pain in his eyes, Tula had to get away. When she stepped out of the barn, she lifted her head to the warm August sunlight. Then she started running down Halsted Street. She stopped only when she reached the huge brick building, Hull House. With her hand, she wiped the sweat running down her face and felt the wetness under her armpits beneath her cotton dress. She stared at the building and recalled the story of Jane Addams, who had made Hull House a place where foreigners like Mana could learn American ways. Tula swung into the courtyard and saw a small crowd of children watching Reni climb the monkey tree.

There was no grass in the cement courtyard, only playground equipment—a sand box, a slide, swings and an elaborate eight-foot-high steel structure, which the children nicknamed the *monkey tree.*

It was a maze of steel squares, resembling the skeleton structure of a building, a challenge to the older children, a frustration for the younger ones. Reni seemed to be up to the challenge, thought Tula as she smiled up at her sister. As agile as a monkey, Reni climbed from one rung to the other.

How Tula loved this courtyard. It was a special place. She remembered the many times she had climbed to the top of the steel structure, savoring the freedom of swinging high above everyone. She was no older than Reni when she had made her first climb to the top, the wind blowing in her face—a happy time.

Now the sun hung over the courtyard, casting rays down onto the laughing children. Billowy clouds indented the blue sky. There was no breeze to cut the heat. Flies buzzed around the children. A settlement worker watched the children, her hands plunged into the pockets of her brown smock.

"Isn't this fun, Tula?" Goldie said.

Reni, hanging upside down on the bars, her bloomers showing with the "Flour" emblem plainly visible, shouted, "Can we stay, please?"

"Yes, we can."

"Tula, come up here. Climb with me," Reni coaxed.

"I don't think I should," Tula said.

"Why not?" Reni asked, still upside down.

Tula felt the blood rush to her checks. Would it ever be magic time again?

Hull House had been her refuge. She looked across the courtyard and saw the library, where she had spent many happy hours. She had become the librarian's helper at nine. At ten, she was president of the Young Readers Club. And as a prize for reading ten books one summer, she was given the novel *Little Women*, which she had read many times over.

Hull House had been her universe. Tula knew little of the world outside the west side of Chicago. What was country? What was a forest, or a river, or a stream? What did a cow sound like? They were pictures in books. The real world was Hull House and Chicago. The real world was living in a flat and enjoying the pleasures of Hull House.

Now Tula looked up at the monkey tree and Reni almost at the top. "Wait for me, Reni." Her legs flew as she climbed from one bar to another with ease. Her cotton dress fluttered in the breeze.

"Go, go!" Goldie said.

When Tula reached the top, a breeze brushed her hair and beads of perspiration dotted her forehead. She shouted, "Hey, look at me! I'm king of the hill!"

Reni, a few rungs down, said, "Look at Tula, king of the hill!"

The children took up the chant: "Tula is a king of the hill!"

Tula, standing high up on the bars, laughing, enjoying the cheers, did not see him. He stood at the edge of the crowd and looked up at her, smiling. And then their eyes met, and Tula stopped laughing. She felt her face grow hot.

He said, "Black-eyed Susan is *queen* of the hill!"

Goldie turned and looked up. "Andreas, carry me." He picked her up and put her on his shoulders. "Now I can almost touch Tula," she said.

Tula came down the bars quickly and silently. When she got down, Andreas walked up to her. "That was quite a climb," he said.

She kicked a stone. When she looked at Andreas, she felt the door into her life slowly close. She couldn't speak. No, he was not going to go away.

Andreas dug in his pocket, pulled out three candy bars, and offered one to Goldie. "Oh, goody," she said.

Reni who trailed behind Tula, smiled at Andreas. "One for me, too?" she asked. "It's my favorite."

"I know," Andreas said, and he watched her peel off the silver foil. Then he offered one to Tula. "Your favorite, too?"

"No, thanks," she said.

He returned the candy to his pocket and put Goldie down.

"I thought we might talk," he said to Tula.

Tula did not look at him. "Yes," she said. "Let's talk."

Andreas led the girls through the courtyard. Goldie held his hand, and Reni skipped on ahead, avoiding the cracks in the sidewalk.

Andreas glanced at Tula. "You should be in Greece. There are lots of mountains to climb there."

"The *monkey tree* isn't hard. I do it all the time," Tula said. She was angry.

He grasped her hand. It was the first time he had touched her. Quickly, she freed herself.

"Black-eyed Susan," he began, "There is only one person I care about, and that's you. You'll be happy, I promise."

Finally, she looked up at him. She caught her breath before she spoke. "You don't understand. I don't want to get married. Not to you, not to anyone.

I want to finish school."

"You can go to school while we are engaged. You have a whole year. After we get married, you'll have other things to do, and you'll forget about school."

"I won't. I'll never forget school. I want to be a teacher. Don't you understand?"

"Yes, I do. That's your dream. I had dreams, too, but I had obligations. And you have obligations to your *Mana*. There were ten children in my family, six of them girls. Do you know what that means? I had to help with their dowries—before I even thought of marriage. I had to save my money, send it to my *Mana* in Greece."

"But this is America, it's different," Tula said.

"No, my Black-eyed Susan, it's not different. Your Mana has no sons. You are the oldest, you must help her, help the family." His accent still held trace of the old country. "Marriage was out of the question for me," Andreas said, "Until all my sisters were promised and their dowries paid. Then I was free to plan my own future. That is when I came to Chicago. Then everything changed for me when I saw you."

At the flat now, Reni and Goldie raced upstairs. Tula paused and sullenly asked, "Are you coming up?"

"No, not today."

"Good-bye, then," she said.

"Good-bye."

She watched as Andreas strolled down the street, his arms swinging. With every bone in her body, she wished that he had never entered her life.

On the second floor, Tula heard her mother screaming in Greek at someone. Worried, she slowed down. When she came into the flat, she saw her mother and *Nouno* Ondoni nose to nose both red-faced, eyes flashing.

Tula started to turn into the hallway toward her bedroom, but the angry look in Ondoni's eyes stopped her.

"Ah," he said. "The lamb is off to the slaughter. Tula's just a child, Zoe. You're insane to promise her to Andreas. You don't make sense."

Zoe gave her brother one burning look and said, "Tula, go into the parlor. Take Goldie."

Ondoni glared at his sister. "No, Zoe, don't chase her away. She has to hear this." He looked at Tula with pity and love. "Don't do this to her."

"I don't understand," Tula said.

Zoe face went white. "Tula and I have discussed it. She knows what she has to do. She agrees. It's all settled."

"Settled?" asked Ondoni. "You give the orders, she obeys, is that it?"

Zoe ignored him and turned to Tula. "Didn't I tell you to go in the parlor?"

Tula stood facing her mother, her cheeks burning in anger. Inside, she felt the familiar despair and hopelessness. She choked on the closeness of the air in the kitchen. Tula was about to speak, answer him, but in the end she just shook her head. Then Ondoni swung sideways, cupped her face in his hands, and started down at her. "Tula, I realized something a while ago. I wasn't being truthful with you, wasn't in fact being truthful about myself."

"What?" Tula asked.

Zoe flared up. "Don't! I want you out of my house."

"I'll go in time, sister. I have to talk to Dimitra."

As Tula watched *Nouno* Ondoni, her heart leaped into her throat. He had called her Dimitra, exactly like Baba used to. In one more second, he would grab her and spin her around, laughing, calling her his Dimitra, his actress, his teacher. In another instant Baba would start that slow smile, and he would say—

"Tula, my godchild..."

Tula's eyes squeezed shut against Ondoni's voice. She took a deep breath. She stood there, numb.

All this time, Zoe was silent. She waited for her brother to speak his piece. She rested, gathering up her strength for the quarreling that lay ahead.

Tula's mother had changed with Andreas's visits. She appeared courageous now, without fear of life and its dangers. She was strong, wary, and alert. Her only weakness was a lack of that natural cunning and shrewdness, which her brother had. It was a gift that Vasso shared with him.

Ondoni said, "What can you do, Tula? You can finish school. That's what *I* want you to do. Get an education. Get out of this hell you live in. I'll help you. Come live with me, my godchild."

"Out!" Zoe shouted. She smacked him in the chest. "Tula live with you? I'd rather have her dance naked down Halsted Street." Zoe's voice was heavy with sarcasm.

"You're ruining her life." Ondoni turned to Tula. "Do you want to marry Andreas?" He reached over and pushed her hair off her forehead. "Do you, Tula?"

Tula looked across at her mother in her black dress. Her mother sighed. "You don't have to answer him," Zoe said.

Ondoni shook his head. "She has a mouth, she can speak. Answer me,

Tula."

"I *don't* want to marry Andreas!" Tula said hotly.

"Calm down, Tula," Zoe said. "You should be happy. Andreas is a good man. He will make you a fine husband."

"*You* marry him, Mana!"

"That's enough!" Zoe reached over and slapped Tula on the side of the face. "Respect!"

"No!" Ondoni said. "Don't touch her again, Zoe." He went to Tula, touched her stung cheek. "Are you all right?"

Tula nodded.

"She has to marry, save the family, since my Leones—" Zoe began to cry.

"Always crying," Tula said. "You act like you're the only one who misses him. You walk around this flat, crying. You didn't love Baba half as much as—" Tula wiped her eyes with the back of her hand. "You got mad at him when he drank too much. That's what killed him, you said. But it wasn't that—it was the bakery. And now you're trying to ruin my life!" Without looking at her mother or Ondoni, she ran to her bedroom.

She sat on the edge of the bed and listened to the noises from the kitchen. Tula heard Ondoni storm out of the flat.

"I hate you, Andreas," Tula said. She went to the mirror and looked at her red-rimmed eyes, her tangled hair. From the top drawer in the dresser, she pulled out her Friendship Book and wrote: "Ondoni wants me to live with him and go to school. Photi said he wants to run away with me. I don't know what to do. But I do know I don't want to marry Andreas."

Chapter 9

In her bedroom, hours after the argument between Ondoni and her mother, Tula thought about the strange moment of intimacy that had existed between Photi and her in the barn when he kissed her. She wrote in her Friendship Book: "Photi kissed me. Not on the lips, but on my cheek. It felt—I can't explain how it felt. Not like when we became blood brothers. But more like holding your breath, like having a feather touch your heart, like listening to music. It was something—"

Two weeks later, she was waiting for Photi at Hull House. She needed to talk to him before they went back to school. She needed to walk with him to the Loop. She needed to have him by her side as they looked at the boats crossing the Canal Street Bridge. She needed this time with him, before—

She saw him running toward her. She ran to meet him, grinning, laughing.

"Sorry I'm late," he said. And then she noticed his face, his black eye, his swollen lip.

"What happened?"

"He got drunk again and beat me up."

She touched his lips. "I'm sorry."

"It doesn't hurt much, now. Let's go. I'm running away, and soon. I hate him. He's always telling me I'll never amount anything to please him. Sometimes I feel so bad, I want to die. I want to kill myself."

She stared at him, speechless. Then she said slowly, "No, please don't say that. That's crazy."

"I'm not crazy. Sometimes I feel I can't fight him anymore. I can't win."

Tula threw her arms around him, her hair falling across his face. "You'll win."

She stepped back, looking at him. "Remember all the fun we had at Dorr School? Remember the play and the swings? Miss MacMann? Remember the lunches I talked you out of because I hated my potato sandwiches? Remember?"

"Yes, I remember," he said. "Are you really going back to school, Tula?"

"Yes, why shouldn't I go back? Mana said I could."

"It's time you woke up. If you go to school, the kids will laugh at you.

They'll want to know why you're getting married."

"Mana says I must get married. But *she's* the one who should get married. I know why she doesn't want to. Once I heard her whispering to some women after church. She said she's had enough babies. *I* don't want babies, not now. I want to go to school."

He bit his lower lip and avoided her gaze but did not answer her.

"Don't do that," she said.

"What am I doing?"

"Not talking. Remember when we were little, and you wouldn't answer me, and I'd hit you, hit you hard?"

"We were just kids, kids fighting."

"I feel guilty about it now, hitting you as hard as I could," Tula said. "And you never hit back. I'd keep punching you until I got tired."

"Tula, you were only six years old. You couldn't punch hard enough to hurt a fly."

"You're not saying that just to make me feel better?"

"You were just a snotty kid, just six."

She began to laugh through her tears.

"You all right?" he asked.

"*Oka kala,*" she said.

"No more tears?"

"No more. I promise."

They walked in silence. In the distance, the tall buildings of the Loop cast huge shadows. When they crossed over the bridge, the wooden planks echoed with the sound of their footsteps. They didn't talk, just walked shoulder to shoulder, hand in hand.

A small chug boat tooted its horn as it came to the bridge. A sailboat glided on the smooth, glass like water. A carriage pulled by a large bay ambled across the bridge, the horse snorting, its nostrils flaring.

Tula was caught up in the spell of the calm water, the clippity-clop of the horse's hooves on the bridge, the crack of the whip. Although Photi was here beside her, holding her hand, she already felt the pain of parting.

"Look at the boats," Photi said. "I know we've seen them a lot, but somehow now it's all new. Look, there's one near our favorite rock. See?"

"Yes."

"I love the water. I love to swim. I want to take you on one of those boats and sail around the world. Just the two of us," he said.

While he looked out into the water, she gazed at him, tried to memorize his face, so she could keep him in her thoughts forever. She knew that even those you love are hard to remember with the passing of the years. The image of her father had faded. She didn't want it to happen, but it did. Now she concentrated on Photi, his face, his clear brown eyes, his unruly hair, his strong body. Then, out of the blue, she asked, "Come to my engagement party."

"What?"

"Please. Take Esther, and come to my house—"

"You're going through with it?" he asked.

She nodded. She could not speak. It was too painful.

Photi, seeing the pain in her eyes, changed the subject. "We can go to the museum and sit on those stone lions in front. Remember when we went there for the first time with Miss MacMann, and I climbed on the lion's head?"

"And you didn't want to get down." She smiled. *He knows just what to say to make me smile*, she thought.

They walked to Marshall Fields Department Store and stared into the windows.

"Do you want that fur coat, Tula? I'll buy it for you."

"Yes, yes, and the blue silk dress, and the shoes to match. Everything!"

"Someday, when I'm a big shot, I'll buy them all for you."

They walked through the theater district, hand and hand. The Oriental Theater had a poster of Milton Berle with the banner "Next Attraction" across his chest. The State and Lake Theater announced a new Greta Garbo film. They walked passed the Rialto Burlesque. A girl with full breasts loose under a cotton blouse was at the ticket window. She winked at Photi.

"Let's go. We're not going in there. That's a bad place. My godfather Ondoni told me that wasn't a place for kids."

"Anything you say, Tula. Besides, we don't have any money. Did you think I was interested in that girl? She's probably a gangster's moll."

"Sure looks like one, like the ones in the movies."

"Maybe she's *his* moll." Photi pointed to a short man across the street. His gray hat was at an angle over his right eye. His suite was a black pinstripe, and he wore a red tie.

"Do you think he'll rob a bank?"

The high, shrill scream of a siren ripped the air, as two squad cars raced down Michigan Avenue.

The man in the gray hat ran into the Rialto.

"Let's get out of here," Photi said. Tula found herself thrust into a doorway with him, and she was content to stay there watching the people, the cars, rushing around them. Another siren sounded, making her jump.

Photi grabbed her, held her tight, his arms around her, his face close to hers. She felt her heart pounding in her chest, her palms moist in his hands. She wished she hadn't looked up into his eyes. Her next impulse was to leave, to race out of the doorway and run down the street, after the sirens, after the police cars.

He held her close, cupped her face with his hands, looked into her eyes, and with great care kissed her—first one cheek, then the other. Then a soft, gentle kiss on the lips.

"What'd you do that for, Photi?"

"Tula, let's run away!"

Chapter 10

Tula chewed on her pencil. Her Friendship Book lay open beside her on the bed. "Baba, you've been dead three years," she wrote. "I miss you more now. Where are you Baba? Do you know that today is October 26, 1924, my name day and my engagement day? If you were here, things would be different. 'Help me make the wine, Tula,' you would say, lifting me up. 'Stomp on the grapes.' And after, I would sit in your lap, listening while you read to me from Homer. 'Tula, you are my Scholar.' But now Mana wants me to marry Andreas. I don't think I will ever forgive her."

Tula dropped the book on her bed and began pacing, back and forth, back and forth. In one corner, high up, the red flame of the holy lamp glowed and in contrast to her mood gave off a calm golden light that enveloped everything in the bedroom. The sound of voices came from the kitchen, yet Tula heard nothing-nothing except her mother's voice in her mind: "You have to marry Andreas!"

She wanted to take Andreas by the throat and choke him until he understood. She wanted to say, "I don't want to get married, to you or anyone else. I want to go to school. I want to have a chance to grow up. I don't want a husband. I want to be a teacher."

She took a few steps toward the cedar chest, where she had put her turquoise shawl, the one her godfather had given her long ago. Her mother didn't want her to wear it anymore. She opened the chest and pulled out the shawl, felt its softness, smelled the aroma of cedar.

At that moment, Angel ran into the bedroom and put her arms around her. "It's your engagement day." Her face, framed in blond curls, was glowing, and as she caught Tula's eyes, she smiled. "Your name day, too. How do you feel on this big day?"

"Awful! I don't want to be engaged."

"You can't back out now. It's too late." It was Vasso's voice. Tula turned and saw her at the door.

"Leave her alone," Angel said. "Can't you see she's upset?"

"Too bad," Vasso yelled hotly over her shoulder as she walked back into the hallway.

"You're stupid!" Angel yelled back.

Tula put her hands over her eyes. She didn't want to cry. Babies cry. She didn't want to ruin the dress, the one Andreas had bought for her, the lavender crepe she had admired that day in Maxwell Street. She smoothed the billowy skirt, forcing herself to be calm.

"You okay?" Angel asked.

Tula nodded.

"I'd better finish dressing, then."

The sister parted, Tula headed for the kitchen and Angel the bathroom. In the kitchen, her self-doubt prevailed. *No, no*, she thought. Her hands trembled. *Stop it! This is real. Where is* Nouno *Ondoni?* Had he deserted her? She drank some water to calm herself. Poised now, she turned and faced her mother.

"You look very nice," Zoe said, her hands kneading the meat and rice for the stuffed grape leaves. Zoe and Thea Sophie sat at the kitchen table, sleeves rolled up, white aprons on covering their good black dresses. Tula frowned.

"Smile. This is your day, a happy day!" Thea Sophie said.

And she did smile, her lips slightly parted, showing her teeth, but her eyes revealed the sadness in her heart.

"Ah, now, that's better, child."

"She's not a child," Zoe said. "This is her day, and she is a young lady. She is all grown up, a lady, not a child. Andreas will be here soon, and all our friends, and the priest, to bless the engagement. Yes, a happy day. No more frowning today, Tula."

Tula saw her mother's face take on a light of triumph.

A sharp rap on the door started them.

"Answer it, please. It's probably Andreas," Zoe said.

Tula opened the door. He stood in the hallway, a small bouquet of violets in one hand.

"Am I early?"

"No, come in."

"Come in," Zoe said. "You're not early. We're just finishing the dolmates."

"How do you find time to do all this?" His hand waved over the trays of dolmates and the platters filled with pastries on the counter.

"Thanks to you, Andreas, for the money."

Tula felt her face grow hot.

Thea Sophie said, "Are those violets for me?"

He laughed. "Sorry, they're for Tula."

He bowed and offered them to her. "For you."

"Thank you."

"Tula, take Andreas into the parlor. The kitchen is no place for you young people."

In the parlor, he said, "The violets match your dress. You look beautiful."

Tula frowned. She had lain awake most of the night, and when she finally did sleep, she'd had the old nightmares of Baba and *Nouno* Ondoni. Now she looked beautiful?

With a slightly uncomfortable look on his face, Andreas walked across the floral carpet and sat on the sofa. "Sid down," he said, patting the place next to him. He unbuttoned his suit jacket.

Tula sat beside him, and her eyes swept the length of the room. She shifted positions on the sofa and inched away from him.

"I couldn't remember the exact color of your dress," he began. "I only knew it reminded me of violets. Violets and Black-eyed Susans. They're your flowers. I tried to find some Black-eyed Susans, but not a one in the whole city of Chicago."

"I don't want any flowers. I don't want to marry you. I want to finish school." Her voice trembled. There were beads of perspiration on her upper lip. "I don't—" She breathed deeply, to calm herself, long slow breaths until the quivering in her heart died and impulse to fling angry words at him subsided.

She put her hands to her face and held herself very still, shielding her eyes. She didn't want him to see her crying.

Andreas reached for her hands, drew them away from her face, saw the tears. "I'm sorry," he said. "Our marriage will be a good one. Don't cry. You'll soon forget about school."

"No! No!" she said.

In a quiet voice, he went on. "I'll work hard. We will never go hungry. I will take care of your mother and sisters, and we will find fine husbands for your sisters when they are old enough, when the time comes. Almost as good as me." He smiled. He waited for her to smile, but she did not.

She looked at the violets on her lap. *Help your Mana and your sisters.* She heard the words in her mind. *No! I can't sit here discussing the future with him. I can't. It's not my future.*

She knew that Andreas had spared no expense for the engagement party. "You only get engaged once," he had said. Zoe had objected to the expense, but finally they reached an agreement. He would buy the food and she would cook. Andreas had bought a whole spring lamb. Zoe had made dolmates, baklava, butter cookies and holiday egg bread. Feta cheese, black olives and Ouzo were on the buffet. Baba's wine cooled in the dark hallway.

When the guests started to arrive, Andreas and Tula arranged folding chairs borrowed from the undertaker, in the parlor and dining rooms. Vasso and Angel sliced bread and feta cheese, making themselves useful in the kitchen. Reni and Goldie spent their time running down the stairs, watching for guests, and announcing their arrival by racing up the stairs before them.

The bearded priest was the last to arrive. Everyone rushed forward when he came to the door. Zoe quickly tossed her apron aside and led him into the parlor, where the women sat in chairs gossiping and the men gathered in groups drinking wine.

Zoe slipped the three silver dollars Andreas had given her into the priest's hand. With dignity, he placed them in a pocket of his vestments. Zoe smiled and accepted the priest's thanks and blessings.

All eyes were on Tula and Andreas as the priest led them to the center of the parlor. Tula stared at the floral wallpaper. She was in another world.

Andreas smiled down at her and held her hand. They faced the priest. She did not look at him, only nodded and gave the proper responses when called upon. The priest blessed the ring and Andreas put it on the ring finger of her right hand. It was the diamond ring Baba had given Mana when they were married. Andreas had had it reset in a platinum band with twin sapphires on the sides.

Tula wanted to cry; she was terrified. *Run, run!* she thought.

And then Andreas leaned over, took her face in his hands, and kissed her gently on the lips. She felt nothing. It wasn't the same as Photi's kiss, when she had felt a feather touch her heart. Instinctively, she pushed him away.

Zoe gasped.

The look in Andreas' eyes was sad. He blushed when Thea Sophie said, "To the engaged couple, a long and happy life." A glass of wine that Thea Sophie had drank earlier seemed to have mellowed her. She giggled.

"More wine," Thea Sophie said.

Tula left Andreas and went to the open window. She pulled back the lace curtains to get a better view of the street. And then she saw the big bay pulling a wagon. It stopped in front of the flat. Photi's father, George, staggered from the wagon dragging a tearful Esther. What was he doing to Esther? Where was Photi? They told her they were coming to the party together.

She heard George cursing on the stairs. He burst into the room holding

Esther's wrist. Zoe, hearing the commotion, ran to the door. "What's the matter? What are you doing here, George? What in God's name are you doing with Esther?" She fired the questions at him in Greek. "Let go of the girl."

After George released her, Esther said, "I was coming to your house for the party, and then I saw him, and he pulled me into the wagon. I talked to Photi yesterday, and he said he just couldn't come. He thinks I know where Photi is, and I don't. Honest."

"She's lying," George said. He staggered and pointed a finger at Zoe. "Or are you hiding my son, Zoe?" He grabbed her arm.

"Take your hands off me, you drunk."

"Drunk am I? So, you don't want the likes of me at your fancy party. How much did Andreas pay for Tula? Did you get a good price for your girl?" He laughed.

Small as she was, Zoe raised her hand to strike him. George quickly grabbed both her hands and held them in his huge fists. Andreas fought his way through crowd of people that had gathered at the door. "Take your hands off Zoe."

They were face to face. George's eyes shifted from side to side under Andreas' gaze. His baldhead glistened. He turned his eyes red, his thin lips set. "Damn you, Andreas, the quarrel is between Zoe and me. Get the hell out of here. She's hiding my son."

George swung at Andreas and missed.

Andreas grabbed him, pulled him away from the door, away from the crowd, but George gripped the doorjamb and hung on. Andreas struck him hard across the face and he fell. Andreas lifted him up and his shirt ripped in Andreas' hand.

"No, your quarrel is with me!" Andreas said. He punched him in the face. Andreas continued to swing his fists in George's face, his chest, his stomach, until George came crashing down in the hallway with Andreas on top of him.

"Stop it, stop it!" Tula cried.

In the heat of the battle, Andreas shouted, "You son of a bitch! You ever step foot in this flat again and I'll kill you!"

George refused to look at him. He lay on the floor, his hands over his face, moaning.

"Get up, and get the hell out of here!"

George inched himself up painfully and then slowly walked down the stairs.

Chapter 11

The next morning, Tula slipped off her engagement ring and put it in the small porcelain box Andreas had given her. When she closed the box, her fingers traced the etching of the Black-eyed Susan on the lid. She fastened the clasp and held the box for a moment, then tucked it in the top drawer of her dresser underneath her black stocking. She examined her finger to see if there were any ring marks.

What would she do if Miss Kaloda or one of the kids at school asked her about the engagement? She mustn't think about it. She had made her sister promise not to say anything about it at school, not even to Miss Kaloda.

Tula fastened her braids into buns and pinned them close to her ears. She looked in the mirror and saw a scared girl in a school uniform, not a woman at all. She walked into the kitchen.

"Tula, hurry. You'll be late for school," Zoe said. She poured coffee, milk, and a spoonful of butter into a cup and placed some toast beside it. Goldie and Reni, sitting at the table, watched Tula.

"I'm not hungry," Tula said. She didn't sit down.

"Can I have her toast?" Reni asked.

"Not hungry?" Zoe asked.

"I'm going to school. Don't feel like eating," Tula said. For a moment, there was an uncomfortable silence. Even Goldie and Reni were still. Both shared Tula's toast.

Zoe's eyes searched Tula's face. "Are you going to tell them you're engaged?"

"No!"

"You can't hide it for long. You're going to get hurt," Zoe said. "Someone will say something."

"I don't care. I'm not going to tell anyone. They can't tell I'm engaged. See? I took the ring off."

A hint of harshness crept into Zoe's voice. "You should be proud to wear that ring. Your *Baba* gave it to me. Now it is yours. Beside, Andreas is a fine man."

"If he is so fine, *you* marry him!"

"Tula, stop that talk!"

At that instant, Tula hated her mother. How dare she sell her to Andreas? She raced out the door, flying down the stairs like an animal in flight.

Outside, she rubbed her ring finger. Was there a mark? She looked at her finger, examined it, studied it. When she had convinced herself that there was no mark, she walked down Blue Island Avenue.

Later, in the classroom, she felt that all eyes were on her. Did they know? She raced to her seat.

Miss Kaloda stood up from behind her desk and said. "Tula, I'd like to see you in the hall." With a sweep of her hand, Miss Kaloda motioned for Tula to follow her. Out in the hallway, they sat on a bench. Miss Kaloda smoothed her dark brown skirt around her. A wide belt encircled her slim waist. Her black oxfords were newly polished. Tula's high-button shoes were scuffed.

Miss Kaloda said, "First, I want to thank you. I received a photo of Douglas Fairbanks in the mail, and it was personally autographed. I think he is a fine actor. I can't thank you enough."

"It's okay. I like Douglas Fairbanks, too. I have a couple of pictures of him. He's my friend Photi's favorite."

"Yes. Many people like Douglas Fairbanks." Then she said. "Did you have a nice weekend? It was your name day, wasn't it?"

Tula nodded.

She leaned over and took Tula's hand. Her gold watch, suspended on a chain from her neck, swung out.

"You know how gossip travels," Miss Kaloda said. "Well, there is something that I heard, and I wanted to ask you about it."

Tula clenched a fist.

"Of course," the teacher said, adjusting a large hairpin in her bun, "Some rumors are false."

Tula closed her eyes for a moment and then opened them. She smoothed her uniform skirt with her hands. "We had a party at my house," she said.

Miss Kaloda sighed and looked into Tula's eyes. "Want to tell me about it?"

Tula felt her face get hot. "It….it…was an engagement party. My engagement to Andreas."

"An engagement party? Then the rumors are true."

Gathering strength from within, Tula began to talk. She hadn't planned what she was going to say. It just came out. She talked about her mother. She talked about Baba. She talked about their money problems, Gus and the bakery, the building Baba owned in secret. She must have made sense because Miss Kaloda responded. She smiled and took Tula's hand. "You're too young to get married. You must finish school. You're my best student. I'll talk to your mother."

"No, you can't do anything. I *have* to get married."

"You *have* to get married?"

"Yes."

"Child, what have you done?"

"Mana says I have to save the family." Tula looked down at her high-button shoes. "I don't want to get married, but when I turn fifteen, I have to."

"Listen, Tula, we have more than a year. I'll think of something."

Tula looked at Miss Kaloda's sad eyes. She knew the teacher could do nothing to change her mother's mind. Tula wanted to scream. Instead, she followed Miss Kaloda back into the classroom.

Later, in the lunchroom, Tula bit off a corner of her fried potato sandwich, catching a bit of potato with her fingers before it fell to the table. It was the same old sandwich. She hated it. Vasso and Angel sat beside her. The three sisters were a silent oasis in the midst of the noise and shouts of the other children.

Angel put her sandwich down and said, "Did you tell Miss Kaloda?"

"Yes. She's going to talk to Mana."

"What good will that do?" Vasso asked. "You know she won't change her mind."

"I know," Tula said. She got up. She squeezed the sandwich in her hands, mashing the bread and potatoes, then tossed it into the brown bag and walked to the wastebasket.

A boy, shorter than Tula, with a large nose that supported thick eyeglasses, stood in front of her, blocking her way. His stringy brown hair fell over his forehead. He said, "Y're getting married, ain't you? Do ya have ta? Do ya?" He snickered.

Tula faced him. "None of your business."

"Married lady! Married lady!" he chanted.

"Shut up, you runt!" Tula said. Then she hit him in the chest with her fists, beating, pounding, knocking him against the wastebasket.

A crowd gathered around them. "That's it, Tula! Give it to him," a child shouted.

It was some time before a teacher made her way through the crowd of children and separated them. The boy, glasses broken, face bruised, cried, "She's nuts! She tried to kill me!"

Tula raced down the hall, pulled open the main door, and stormed out. She ran to the playground and sat on a swing, gasping, crying, gulping for air. She saw Vasso and Angel running toward her. When they reached the swing, they stood a moment in embarrassed silence.

"That teacher's mad at you," Vasso said.

"Are you all right?" Angel asked. "Let's go back inside."

"No." Tula shook her head. She sat on the swing and looked up at the sky. The gray clouds hung low, and she felt the rain on her face. "No. I'm not going back. Not today, not ever."

Tula knew it would never be the same.

"Don't say that," Angel said.

"If you're not going in, I am. I'm getting soaked out here." Vasso began walking back to the school building.

"Please come," Angel took Tula's arm.

"Don't beg her." Vasso was at the door.

"Go with her, Angel." Tula shrugged her shoulders. "I'm okay, honest." Then she began the difficult task of pushing her troubles back into some corner of her mind where they could rest and where she could forget about them. She gave herself a push on the swing and sailed high into the rain, pumping, pumping, higher and higher. The rain fell in a steady stream, wetting her face, her school uniform, her hair. It cleansed her. She pumped the swing, flying skyward toward the gray, stormy clouds.

Chapter 12

Tula sat alone by the window in the kitchen, drinking her coffee and writing in her Friendship Book. "How many mothers really know their daughters? A daughter will have a certain look on her face of unhappiness, and the mother just sits there talking and sipping her coffee."

Tula's book fell neglected into her lap as she absently watched a peddler hoist a bundle of rags onto his pushcart. On this cold October morning, another empty day stretched before Tula. What should she do today? Walk to Hull House and get some books? Or wait until her mother got back from Maxwell Street and ask her for a dime to go to the show?

Sometimes she wished she hadn't said that she would never go back to Socrates. Although she missed school, she wouldn't go back. No one could change her mind. Not even Miss Kaloda, who had come many times to talk to her. Miss Kaloda wanted to help, but there was nothing she could do. Tula knew that if she went back to school, the kids would stare at her, whisper about her being engaged. What was she, anyway, a vaudeville act? Being engaged wasn't something she wanted to talk about with the other kids. It was something she had to do until—until?

The knock on the door cut through her thoughts. Maybe it would be Ondoni, with a plan to stop the wedding. Or maybe it would be Photi? She opened the door. Was that Photi? The tall, dark-haired man in the hallway? There he was with a suitcase in his hand.

"Tula, we're running away. *Ola kala.*"

Tula's mouth flew open. "What?"

"*Ola kala,*" Photi said quietly, and he reached out and put his hands on her shoulders. "Pack some things. We're leaving."

Stunned, she nodded. All the anxiety, all the worry, all the stress came out in full force when she saw him, and she couldn't keep from crying.

"You've got to pull yourself together. Stop crying."

"I'll try." Then she saw the bruise on his face, touched it gently.

"I can't take it anymore," he said.

She rushed to the hall closet, bought back her Baba's carpetbag, and set it on the floor in the kitchen. Another dash to her bedroom for some clothing.

While she packed, they talked about going to Indiana. Just what they were going to do after they got there, they weren't sure, but they knew they would be together.

"Let's go before your Mana gets back," Photi said.

"Wait a minute." She ran into her bedroom again, searched the top drawer for her ring box with the Black-eyed Susan on the cover. Carefully, she removed her diamond ring and placed it in the box, fastened it with its lock, and tucked it into the carpetbag.

She grabbed her Friendship Book from the kitchen table. She couldn't run away without that. She thought about writing a note to her mother but what would she say? A note might give too many clues to where they were going.

From the hall tree, she gathered her turquoise shawl. The miracle had happened, she thought, wrapping the shawl around her shoulders. It didn't matter to Tula that its wool strands were unraveling. She would wear the shawl until she was an old lady. It was like having *Nouno* Ondoni's arms around her.

Photi was going to save her. She wasn't going to marry Andreas.

"Let's go."

It took them twenty minutes on the streetcar to get to the Canal Street Bridge. After they jumped off the streetcar, they raced to their rock, a huge boulder, actually the largest of several boulders sunk into the deep water with the only access at one end where a portion of the boulders rested on the beach. Cautiously, they scaled the ten-foot high boulder, the biggest of the slippery group. At the top, they stood on the rock's flat surface and drank in the spectacular view of the lake, its waves high, frothy at the tips.

"What a sight," Photi said. "I came here on your engagement day. I wanted to be here on our rock. I knew my *Baba* was looking for me. I didn't care. And now we're here to say good-bye to this special place."

Tula nodded, remembering in summers past, how she had cheered as Photi soared from the boulder, a lone eagle in flight, then breaking the blue surface, splashing into the deep water. It was a feat Photi prided himself on, sometimes identifying himself with the great divers of Mexico whom he had seen in newsreels. Photi would say that those divers were like giant condors flying off cliffs of great height into a narrow cove to reach the water below.

For a few minutes, they were content to sit in silence on the boulder overlooking Lake Michigan.

Photi smiled and reached for her hands. He told her of his plans. "I have some money. I've been saving for years from what little my *Baba* would give me or when I helped the other peddlers load their wagons or brush down their horses. Every penny I saved." He took some bills from his pocket.

Tula opened her Baba's carpetbag, removed the ring box, unfastened the clasp, and examined her diamond. "I can sell my ring. I can get a lot of money for it. It's a real diamond."

"Don't worry. I have enough for us until I get a job. Remember my dream? I'm going to be a big shot in Indiana. You don't have to sell the ring. It was the one your Baba gave your Mana, right?"

She leaned forward, her long hair falling across her face. She glanced at the ring in the box, turned the box this way, that way, the light from the sun catching the diamond, making it sparkle. She closed the lid and secured the clasp.

She moved to sit higher on the boulder while Photi entertained her with talk of their future. She failed to realize how engrossed she had become when a change in the wind caught her attention. Just like the lake in October, angry waters, she thought and looked down from the boulder and watched a woman and a small red-headed boy walk around the far side of the boulders. She waved. The woman nodded a greeting. The youngster grinned. He lifted a toy sailboat in the air. "See my boat?" the boy said. "I'm going to sail it."

Photi smiled. "Good. A little rough for sailing, though." He looked up at the blue sky with silver-white clouds moving forcefully. Sun warmed his upturned face.

"Better weather for running away," Tula said. She smiled a bright smile and kissed his cheek. Photi blushed. Oh, he was so shy. He put his hands in the pockets of his gray jacket. He wore his Sunday best blue pants and a clean white shirt.

Thank God for Photi!

Tula watched him. She noticed everything about him, his strong body, his kind face, his gentle hands. He was definitely handsome.

Photi said, "Amazing what the water holds. Sometime it's calm. Now it's raging like it's fighting with something. And it's got a mean undercurrent. I know. I've felt it, once or twice. I'm a strong swimmer, so it doesn't bother me."

She nodded and looked at this broad face and fine straight nose. Thick brown brows, following the curve of this eyes, long black lashes, and brown eyes, mostly hooded to hide his thoughts. And the chipped front tooth, a reminder of his father's anger. By far his best feature was his mouth, large but very well shaped. There was a particular firmness to the way he held it, as if perhaps if he were to relax, it might give away secrets about what he was really like.

He was watching her watch him. For a moment, his eyes held hers, wide open and alert.

Suddenly, he kissed her firmly on the mouth. Not a lingering kiss, a fleeting one. Once again, she felt the feather in her heart. She blushed.

Photi sighed and looked into Tula's eyes. "Are we blood brothers?"

Tula nodded and held his hand. *This is our day*, she thought. *And nothing matters except our escape to a new life. We can do it. In spite of our fears*, she thought. Once again she held the ring box, and with her finger traced the etching of the Black-eyed Susan on its cover. She turned her head to see the small red-headed boy running, holding a taut string in his fist, waving at his boat in the water.

As she rose to wave to him, the ring box slid from her lap and tumbled down the boulder, into the deep water.

"Oh, my ring box! My God, my diamond's in it!"

A distance away on the beach, two men strolled by smoking cigars. When they heard Tula's cry, they stopped and looked up at the huge boulder.

"What?" said the taller one.

"Seems she dropped something, a tiny box, I think. See, it's floating in the water," the other said.

"Yes. The current's got it. She'll never get it," the tall one said.

"I'll get it!" Photi kicked off his shoes and shed his jacket.

Tula cried. "What are you doing?"

"Don't worry. The water's not that bad. I can see the ring box. I'll get it." Head down, he dove from the boulder into the deep water and slid smoothly through it until he spotted the box floating in the distance. Cupping his hands around his mouth, he called, "I see the box."

On the beach, the mother and boy had spotted Photi.

Laughing, they waved to him. Tula watched as he put his head down again and swam a little farther, almost, but not quite, touching the ring box. The boy shouted, encouraging him. "You almost got it!"

"Please, God." The words were barely more than a whisper as they escaped Tula's lips. She turned and looked up at the sky, which had somehow changed. "Something's wrong," she said. The wind had fallen off.

The two men on the beach watched Photi. They looked worriedly at the sky, too.

With measured strokes, Photi swam through the high waves. In a victory swing, he grabbed the ring box and raised it above his head.

Tula smiled and cheered. *He's a good swimmer*, she thought. *He'll make it to shore soon.* Facing into the wind, standing on the high boulder, Tula watched as the black clouds devoured the sun. Despite the fact that it was daylight, there was an eerie twilight glow. The blue water suddenly turned dark gray and frothy with white caps. The waves beat forcefully against the boulder. A sudden gust caught Tula, knocking her down. Her lips moved in a silent prayer. She knew that Photi was a strong swimmer and knew the lake, knew its dangers. She searched for him in the deep angry waters. "Photi! Photi!" she shouted above the noise of the increasing gale. Then the rain came, a solid sheet of water approaching with frightening speed. The wind whipped the lake into a fury. Within minutes, the waves had risen to six feet. The rain hit Tula with such force that it was like being swatted by an oar. She struggled to keep her footing on the slick, slippery boulder. She shivered as much out of fear as from the cold rain. She had to get off the boulder, she thought, before she was knocked off by the wind. Inching closer to the edge, she cautiously slid down onto the beach side. Her hair was dripping and her clothing clung to her. The drops were icy. On the beach, on the far side of the boulder, she scrambled around the huge rock and raced to the water's edge, searching the churning water for Photi.

Where is he? Then her eyes found him. He was struggling against the giant waves. She heard him cry out, saw his arms up above his head, still clutching the ring box. Even as she screamed, she knew Photi could not hear her.

The two men on the beach were now standing shoulder deep in the churning water, too frightened to go further, chewing on their cigars.

Tula cried out over and over, "Photi! Photi! Photi!"

After several minutes, two Coast Guard Officers carried a rowboat onto the beach.

"I'm going with you," Tula said.

"Sorry, Miss, no civilians allowed in the boat."

"I'm going," Tula said. "You're not leaving without me."

They took off and rowed in ever-increasing circles outward from the beach, fighting the storm, searching. One of the men told her that drowned men sank to the bottom and didn't come up for days.

"He's not dead!" Tula cried. "He's out there. We're going to find him!"

While the men rowed, Tula berated herself. She knew this lake, as well as

Photi why had she allowed him to go into the water? She blinked, trying to see in the rain. She no longer knew if the water she blinked from her eyes was rain or tears.

After an hour, the worst of the storm had passed, but the water still churned. There were angry whitecaps. Then, a few miles out, they sighted Photi floating peacefully, arms outstretched, face turned up to the sky.

"See? There he is. He's okay!" Tula said.

But as they rowed closer, it was plain that he was dead. They lifted the body into the boat and draped a blanket over it. Tula touched the blanket. "Photi! Not! You're not dead!" In this waking nightmare, Tula screamed.

When the boat landed on the beach, the rowers sprang out onto the sand and then turned back to lift the blanket-draped form. They walked a few feet on the beach and put their burden down. The blanket fell apart, exposing the long still form, his right hand clenched into a fist. One of the men pried open his hand, and in it was the ring box. He turned and handed it to Tula.

There was a rustling whisper from the onlookers. The little boy said, "Mommy, he found the box."

In the distance, Tula heard the ambulance's siren. She covered her face with her hands and sobbed. The boy's mother embraced Tula. "I'm so sorry," she said.

A trembling had started at Tula's forehead. Her temple throbbed. She put her hand up, to still it. The woman shook her head. The boy was crying now. Like and old woman, Tula turned to the boy and put her arms around him. She kissed his cheeks.

"Photi's dead—" Her voice broke. She couldn't go on. They were going to Indiana. He was going to be a big shot in the steel mills. He was going to save her from Andreas. And now he was dead.

After Photi's funeral, Tula kept her sorrow to herself. Week followed week, and during the day she walked to the Canal Street Bridge and looked out onto the water. In the evenings, sitting by the stove, she wrote in her Friendship Book: "There is this girl in the rain. And leaves are falling in the rain, as they die in the water, in the rain."

"I dream of you, Photi. There is something moving, slowly filling with water. We are swimming, side by side. I turn, and you are filling with water, sinking, sinking into the water. There's nothing left, is there, Photi?"

* * *

The first week in February, more than three months after Photi's death, Zoe and Andreas sat at the kitchen table, busy sorting through overdue tax notices for Baba's building.

Vasso and Angel were reading to Reni and Goldie. Tula sat by the stove. "Tula?"

She turned. "Yes, Mana."

"Pour Andreas some coffee, please."

She got up, poured the coffee, and set it on the table.

"Thank you," he said. Before she walked away, he reached for her hand. "Where is your ring?"

"In my drawer. I don't want to wear it."

Andreas said nothing but continued holding her hand.

Remote, she remained beside him, his hand on hers.

Finally, she said, "Let go of me."

"Tula, listen to me. You can't go on like this," he said. "You have to stop. You'll make yourself sick. Photi was a fine young man. But he's gone now, dead. Why are you so angry?"

Tula answered without looking at Andreas. "I keep telling myself, act normal. Act normal! But everything that is happening to me is making my life worse, and I hate it. Hate it, can you understand that?"

"Hush, Tula," Zoe said.

"No, let her talk," Andreas said. "You hate what, Tula?"

Tula stopped and looked at Andreas, her eyes shimmering with tears. "Things are just getting worse. This stinking building and all the taxes we owe, and the wedding and Photi dying for that ring."

"I know," Andreas said. "But this mourning is hurting you. You look tired all the time, circles under your eyes, my Black-eyed Susan."

Tula was silent. It didn't matter if she looked bad. She couldn't stop thinking about Photi. She'd remember him forever.

The next day, Andreas showed Zoe and Tula the check he had received from Mr. Pappas, his employer at the candy store. Money they needed to pay the back taxes. Andreas explained that Mr. Pappas, who owned several stores and tenements, also had his own private loan business. He said, "Mr. Pappas is an educated man from Athens. He is eager to loan money, with interest, of course. And I'm an employee, good for the loan." He glanced at Tula. "Well, let's go and get the taxes paid."

At the courthouse, an attorney met them.

"We'll get this tax matter cleared up in no time," he said to Andreas.

"Have you got the check?"

"I've got the check here." Andreas patted his breast pocket.

"I hope you didn't have to give up too much for that loan," the attorney said.

"Only my future." Andreas laughed.

Zoe, her face serious now, her eyes bright, said in Greek. "Andreas, you gave up your future for the money?"

"No, I'm only joking. Mr. Pappas will get his money back, with interest. He'll be taking money out of my pay every week until the loan is paid in full. In the meantime, he holds your flats as—" He turned toward the attorney. "What is the word?"

"Collateral, my boy, collateral."

"Yes, thank you, collateral. But don't worry. The property is safe in his hands, Zoe."

Chapter 13

Collateral. Tula couldn't get that word out of her mind. Did it mean that *Baba*'s building was not theirs anymore? Things got even worse when Andreas began talking about the letters he received from his brother Tasso in Nebraska. He was having trouble making ends meet and putting food on the table for his family.

Tasso's letters saddened Andreas and often left him in a rage. Soon Tula could not bear to sit and listen to him read about Tasso's plight, so she escaped into her bedroom, where Goldie and Reni would be sprawled on the floor doing their schoolwork.

That's how Tula began tutoring Goldie, who was almost five, and Reni, who was seven. For the first time since Tula had raced out of Socrates that rainy day, she picked up her schoolbooks and tasted the heady wine of teaching. And Goldie and Reni were thirsty for knowledge.

Vasso who was now almost thirteen, was finding school more unbearable every day. One evening after supper, Vasso confronted Zoe. "I want to quit school. You made Tula quit when she was thirteen. I hate school!" She shook her head, too furious to continue.

"What?"

"She wants to quite because she's d-u-m-b," Angel said.

"Shut up," Vasso said. "You teacher's pet, you!"

"Why do you want to leave school?" Zoe asked.

"I just want to!" Vasso was so angry that she couldn't sit still. She paced around the kitchen.

"So, do you want Andreas to find a husband for you?"

"No! I'll work."

Zoe was agreeable under one condition: that Vasso wait until she was thirteen. And at that time, Andreas found a job for her in the Dixie ice cream factory. She worked on the production line, slipping ice cream bars into their wrappers. Coming home at night she'd complain to her mother about how her fingers ached from the cold.

"Your decision," Zoe would say. "Besides, your wages will help with Tula's wedding."

It was the second week in April, when Zoe and Tula began preparing for Easter. Zoe was flouring her hands, getting ready to knead dough for the Easter bread. At the other end of the table, Tula twisted sweet lumps of dough to make *koulouraka*, the butter cookies. Some of the dough she formed into small circles, some into tiny braids, and lined them on the cookie sheet before popping them into the oven to bake until golden brown.

When the cookies cooled, she carefully put them in clean pillowcases and stored them in the buffet. After the Easter bread had cooled on the counter, Tula wrapped it in butcher paper.

"Ah, smells good," Zoe said, wiping her powdery hands on her apron. Tula watched while Zoe wrapped the last loaf in brown paper and tied it with butcher string.

"I'll check the mail," Tula said. Minutes later, she returned with a business-type envelope. She ripped it open. "This is a receipt saying all our taxes have been paid."

"See? I told you Andreas would fix everything."

"Yes, you did. But what did he give up for it?"

"Give up? Nothing. You heard him," Zoe said. "He just signed a paper. He will pay the loan back. Mr. Pappas is a good man, a man to trust."

"He did give up something, didn't he?"

"Tula, you ask too many questions. Andreas will take care of us, and we have *Baba*'s building, thank God."

* * *

The Saturday morning before Easter, Tula sat crossed-legged on her bed, chewing on her pencil. She wrote in her Friendship Book: "Another Easter without Baba, and I have such strange feelings. He would take me with him to pick out a lamb at the butcher. I remember the first time I went with him, I cried when he told me that baby lamb would be slaughtered for us. Slaughtered? Isn't that what *Nouno* Ondoni said about me when he fought with Mana? Off to the slaughterhouse. Am I being sacrificed?"

Tula walked into the kitchen, not too happy with what the day would bring. She wore her turquoise shawl around her shoulders.

Zoe, sipping coffee, said, "Take that shawl off. It belongs in the chest. I don't want Andreas seeing you wearing it. He's going to take you to the *caffeneio*, the coffeehouse, to watch the lambs roasting, yes?"

Tula nodded. "I don't want to go. Only men go to the *caffeneio*. All they do is sit and play cards, drink wine or Turkish coffee, and sing those songs about the old country. It looks like a barn. Smells like one, too."

"Don't say that, Tula. It's Easter time, and women are welcome at Easter. You'll see the lambs roasting on the spits in the backyard." Zoe looked at her daughter. "Well, are you going to take that shawl off?"

"I want to wear it. It's mine. Why can't I do one thing that I want to do? Why?"

"Don't sulk. I don't want you to wear anything *he* gave you. Understand? Now put it away, this minute. Andreas will be here soon. Do you hear me, Tula?"

"I hear you." She raced out of the room. When she returned, she was not wearing the shawl.

When Andreas arrived to pick her up, he gave her an Easter basket filled with red eggs. "For you, Tula. I dyed the eggs myself."

"Thank you."

"Here, let me look at those eggs," Zoe said. "You'll have to tell me how you did it. They are a perfect red, no discoloration. Did you use white or wine vinegar?"

"It's a secret I learned hanging around the *caffeneio*. A secret the owner's wife taught me." He laughed.

"Oh, *her*." Zoe made a face.

* * *

Ten minutes later, they walked into the *caffeneio*, filled with men sitting on wire-backed chairs. Tables held small coffee cups, some filled with coffee, others with wine. Two men played sad Greek songs on their mandolins. Sweat ran down their ruddy faces, and their black hair was pasted on their foreheads. Smoke from the outdoor pits filtered into the coffeehouse.

Some of the men were in the backyard basting lambs on spits, roasting over charcoal flame. An old man passed out a platter filled with pieces of cooked lamb's liver nestled in chunks of hard-crusted bread.

Tula's nose twitched to the delicious aroma. Was it the lambs? Was it the freshly baked bread or the fruity aroma of the homemade wine? For the rest of her life, whenever Tula smelled lamb roasting, she was back in this yard. Even the sound of the mandolin could do it for her.

Now a melancholy wail ripped from the fingers of the musicians, telling the tale of a long-ago shepherd watching his flock on the rocky mountains of

Greece. Most of the men sang, their arms linked.

The sea is ever sapphire blue,
The sky forever bright,
In beautiful Ellas, my homeland,
Far away, far away but ever
close in my heart.

Every time a verse was repeated, the men stomped their feet, sending echoes among the rafters. Every time a musician strummed a sad beat, someone would throw back his head and sing a stanza.

Caught up in the music and the spirit, Tula sang along with the men: "Far away, far away but ever—"

Andreas pulled her aside and whispered, "Tula, you know better. Women don't sing here." He groaned.

"Too bad," Tula said.

Before he could answer her, a stout woman came out of the kitchen, wiping her hands on a white apron. She greeted Andreas like an old friend. She was the proprietor's wife. "So you've brought your bride-to-be, good. Why she's no more than a child. Cradle robber!" She laughed, embraced Tula, and kissed her on both cheeks. "You've got yourself a good man in Andreas." She hugged him and then rushed back into the kitchen.

Andreas laughed. "I didn't tell her to say that, honest. I mean about me being a good man."

When the old clock on the wall struck two, the musicians packed up their instruments. Out in the backyard, the sun hid behind a cloud, and the proprietor and his wife were busy pulling the lambs off the spits and wrapping them in layers of brown butcher paper.

"Andreas, with such a big lamb, are you expecting a crowd on Easter?" the proprietor's wife asked.

"Only family."

"Did you enjoy yourself?" Andreas asked Tula as he lifted the wrapped lamb over his shoulder.

"No. You wouldn't let me sing."

"Women have to save their songs for their babies."

"Babies?" Tula's cheeks burned.

"Yes, babies."

"I don't want babies."

"Shhhh, we're not alone," he said. Two men walked by, grinning at them. "*Kalo paska*, happy Easter, Andreas," one of them said.

Andreas nodded.

"I don't care if they heard me," Tula said.

"Oh, my Black-eyed Susan."

They were both silent as they walked to the streetcar stop. Tula saw *Nouno* Ondoni watching them from the other side of the street. On his face was a look of bewilderment and pity. He motioned for them to come over.

"Andreas, old friend. Tula, my godchild. How are you? And what a fine lamb for Easter. You were at the coffeehouse?" Ondoni shook Andreas's hand and kissed Tula on both cheeks in greeting. "I'm waiting for my driver." He looked at his gold watch. "Should be here shortly."

Andreas laughed and said, "Yes, we were at the coffeehouse, and Tula wanted to sing along with the men."

Ondoni looked at Tula gravely. "She has a fine voice. Why shouldn't she sing?"

Tula stood silently between the two men. She frowned at both of them and said roughly, "Andreas didn't like it."

Andreas turned to Tula. "I'm sorry," he said. "I'm sorry if I hurt your feelings."

The sun was hot, the pavement warm beneath Tula's feet. The graceful skirt of her cotton dress fluttered in the breeze, while her thin cotton underslip stuck to her body. She felt the tension in the air between the two men.

Ondoni was charming in his best American style. He showed perfect manners to his old boyhood friend, Andreas, while speaking a refined English he had learned from the many books he devoured. The tension relaxed as they talked about themselves, told each other what had happened to them since their last meeting, reminisced about the old country.

Ondoni tilted his head and looked at Tula wisely. "My godchild, your wedding day is rapidly approaching, yes?"

Why did he mention the wedding? The conversation was going well without it. She nodded. She had been struck dumb. She stared at her godfather in his gray, tailor-made American suit and his newly-polished black leather shoes. He was younger than Andreas, although they had been childhood friends in Greece. They were the same height, standing head to head.

Closing her eyes, she thought about the day Ondoni had given her the Friendship Book. And how he had told her to write her dreams in it. Tula wanted to scream at him, "My dreams, remember? This wedding is *not* in my dreams!"

"Tula?"

She sprang back from her thoughts. It was Andreas.

"Say good-bye to your godfather."

"What?"

"See? His car and driver are here."

"Can I drop you two off?" Ondoni asked.

"No, thanks," Andreas said.

* * *

Soon the wedding plans began to take up most of Tula's time. Vasso became withdrawn as the wedding grew nearer. Angel and Reni were excited and raced around the flat humming the wedding march. They marked off the days until the wedding on the calendar.

Zoe and Tula scrubbed the floors, polished the furniture with rose oil, washed the windows, and hung clean lace curtains in the parlor. Andreas visited daily, often with gifts for the girls and violets for Tula. Friends and visitors filled the flat. The coffeepot was always perking, cookies always on the table for unexpected visitors.

But, for Tula there were too many things she didn't understand, too many things she didn't know about life. Doubts crept into her mind. She poured these doubts into her Friendship Book. "Things I believe would happen now seem only a dream. Would my godfather save me? I'm not stupid. And I don't believe in miracles. Not anymore. I must do things myself. Maybe it will be bad for a little while, the marriage, I mean. Maybe in a few years, I will be able to do what I want. I must believe that. I must make it happen. If I don't believe I can control my own life somehow, some way, I will die."

A week before the wedding, one late afternoon, Tula walked to the Hull House library, not for a book, but to get away from the visitors at the flat. They were driving her crazy with their silly questions, their laughter, their sly remarks. And it was by chance that she saw Ondoni when she left the library. He had stopped his car for a light on the corner. "Get in, I'll give you a ride home."

Ondoni drove easily, carefully, as he always did. Stopped by a red light at the intersection, he glanced at Tula beside him. He pulled a cigarette out of a pack, lit it and inhaled. The late sun filtered trough the windshield.

"How are the wedding plans going?" he asked.

"Okay."

"That's good."

"I don't want to get married. Mana can't understand. *She* should marry Andreas, not me. She doesn't care for me, never did."

"What?" Ondoni squinted at her in the sunlight.

"She doesn't care about me," Tula said.

"She care, maybe too much. There are other things to consider."

"So, now you're taking her side, too. I thought you didn't want me to marry Andreas. I thought you cared for me." She looked at him. His blue eyes stared ahead at the traffic. "I want to stay with you." She didn't mean to blurt that out. It was in her mind, in her thoughts. Why did she say it? "I mean, I want to go to school. Can't I stay with you? I won't tell. No one will know. Please?"

"No. That's impossible. At one time, I thought it was a good idea, too. Not now. It would only lead to trouble. You have to marry Andreas. I can see now that it is the only way. Your *Mana* is right. Things will work out. Later, maybe, you might even go back to school. Who knows? Didn't your Baba call you his scholar?" He stopped talking and looked at her.

She turned away from him and looked back out the window.

"We're almost there," he said, and he noticed her tears. "Don't cry, Tula. I know you mourn your friend Photi. He was too young to die. He had a bastard for a father."

"Yes," she said. "Too young."

She felt his touch on her shoulder. "You will always have me. Remember that, Tula." He seized her hand, lifting it to his lips, giving it a gentle kiss.

It was dusk when they got to the flat. He put his foot on the brakes, stopped the car, and reached over to open the door. "Please don't be sad. I want the best for you. I love you, Tula."

"I love you, too," Tula murmured.

Chapter 14

Plumes of incense rose heavenward toward the kaleidoscope dome of Holy Trinity Greek Church. A children's choir sang a wedding hymn. The sun streaming through the stained-glass windows put Tula's somber face into warm relief.

Just a month ago, this same sun had shone through the kitchen window while she cleaned dandelions. Her mother sat beside her with an envelope from Andreas. She had taken out the short note written in Greek which was wrapped around a sizable batch of bills. She spread the bills out on the kitchen table, then read aloud; "Dear Zoe, Please use this small gift to buy Tula anything she needs for the wedding. It is not a *preka*, a dowry, just a gesture on my part to see that my bride gets what is necessary for our marriage."

Zoe said, "How thoughtful of him."

Tula knew Andreas was trying to do the right thing. He didn't want to hurt her. Why did she hate him?

"Yes," Zoe said, sighing, "This money will help us."

Tula couldn't stop thinking of Andreas and his money. Money to purchase some delicate white lace and silk at Maxwell Street to make her wedding gown. Money to buy a lace veil falling from an orange blossom crown made of waxed blossoms.

Now, waiting to walk down the aisle, Tula wore the dress she and her mother had fashioned of lace with a silk underslip. It had short sleeve and an oval neckline and dropped gracefully from a fitted waist to Tula's ankles. Because of her height, it was longer in the waist than what the usual teen-age Greek girl of Chicago would wear. With tiny stitches, Tula had fastened pearl beads onto the fitted bodice. A dress fit for a princess, Zoe had said when they finished. And it was bought with Andreas' money.

Money. Always money. Andreas was the source of money, and Tula was the vehicle to extract the money from him. The morning of the wedding, Zoe had told Tula, "Ask Andreas for money." Zoe had no money with which to pay the priest or the church. Tula was disturbed.

"You don't have any money?"

Zoe shook her head. "We have spent the last of Andreas' money."

Tula knew what was expected of her. She had become resigned to her fate. Her duty was to save the family. Her duty was to get money. Someday, God willing, she would have money of her own. But for now—"How much do you need?" Tula asked her mother.

"About eighty dollars. It's not a large sum. Some bridegrooms offer it. I hesitated to ask. Andreas has spent much money—on your dress, on food for the wedding feast."

That morning, when Andreas stopped by and Tula was alone with him, she asked him once again for money, determined to keep her pride. Andreas did not seem surprised. He took out his wallet and handed her the bills. She thanked him with a smile but did not trust herself to speak.

Now, minutes before the wedding ceremony, Tula carried a bouquet of white roses and purple violets, with satin ribbons cascading down the front of her dress. Inside the beaded bodice hung the gold cross that had been placed around her neck at her baptism by her *Nouno* Ondoni. Goldie and Reni scattered rose petals in her path. Vasso and Angel, dressed in pink lace dresses, walked ahead of Tula. The bride had no father to walk down the aisle with her, and the groom only a brother to stand up for him.

Andreas was waiting. He had on a black frock coat with formal black trousers, a starched white shirt and a white tie and vest. Tula noticed that he appeared pale.

Tula inhaled the first faint scent of incense as she reached the altar and gazed up at the dome. Her eyes swept the altar, the marble bishop's chair to her right, the black curtain closing in the sanctuary, the life-size panels of the Virgin Mary and the infant Jesus on her left and Jesus on the other side, their hands and faces painted in warm flesh tones, their robes brilliant red and blue, and their crowns in highly embossed heavy silver.

Vasso and Angel had brought to the church many flowers to surround the altar and the great icons—wreaths of dahlias, chrysanthemums, daisies, and violets. There were vases of lilies on the steps that led to the sanctuary.

A square table had been set before the altar covered with an embroidered cloth holding the Gospel, a golden goblet of wine, two crowns of waxed orange blossoms held together with a wide satin ribbon, and the two gold wedding rings the bridegroom had provided. One side of Tula stood Vasso holding a tall white candle, with cascading white satin ribbons. On the other side was Angel holding another candle.

The church had now filled. The guests stood.

The old priest blessed the rings by making the sign of the cross over them and over the heads of Tula and Andreas. "The servant of God, Dimitra, is betrothed to the servant of God, Andreas, in the name of the Father, the Son, and the Holy Spirit." After repeating this three times, the priest placed the rings on them. The rings were then exchanged three times, by Tasso, who was the *koumbaro*, or best man, as a further expression and witness that the lives of Tula and Andreas were being entwined.

Then the priest placed on Tula's head and on Andreas' the stephanion, wreaths of waxed orange blossoms. Tasso held the satin ribbon joining the crowns as the priest, holding Tula's hand while she held Andreas's, led them around the table in the ceremonial walk while the cantor chanted.

Tula felt Zoe's eyes on her back and self-consciously touched the satin ribbons of her bouquet. She heard her mother sigh and that's when she felt loneliness and real panic. Then she turned just enough to see Andreas. His eyes, perfect hazel ovals, blinked in momentary confusion. Then he smiled, the kind of smile that carried a promise.

Tula had steeled herself for the more than one hour of chanting and reading of Scripture, for in the Greek Orthodox Church, the most important occasions in one's life were the baptism and the wedding. Tula remembered Ondoni's remark about the long service: "The ceremony is so long that it's no wonder they offer wine to the couple to sustain them on their long journey."

Finally, the old priest chanted, "O Lord, Our God, send your grace from heaven on these your servants, Andreas and Dimitra. Bless them, protect them, and make them fruitful."

There was weepy embracing of Tula by Zoe, Theo Sophie, and the other women, and kissing on the cheek by the men. All the while, Vasso, Angel, Reni and Goldie were handing each of the guests *koufeta*, shiny sugar-coated almonds wrapped in white tulle and tied with white satin ribbons.

Tula turned and looked over the crowd of well-wishers to search for Ondoni. Yes, yes, he did come after all. There he was standing in the back. But he was with someone—that woman Maggie.

Andreas took Tula's arm and guided her down the aisle as Goldie and Reni threw *koufeta* at them. The priest held the silver tray to accept the gold and silver coins offered by the guests. It seemed a long time before they reached the back of the church where Ondoni stood with that woman.

"Oh, *Nouno*, you did come," Tula said.

Ondoni smiled. "Yes, my little one." Her arms slid around his neck. Ondoni kissed her on both cheeks. Andreas stood watching, waiting.

"You look lovely," Maggie said.

Tula did not respond. Instead, she held Ondoni's hand, looked up at his face. "I'm happy you're here."

"I can't stay," he said. "We have to go." It was over in a moment. First Ondoni walked out of the church, then that woman. And they were gone.

"Andreas, Tula," the priest said, coming down the aisle. "For you." He gave them a red velvet bag filled with the gold and silver coins from the tray. Andreas respectfully kissed the priest's hand.

When Tula turned from the crowd to leave, her arm linked with Andreas', serenity was in every line of her face. It shone from her calm eyes, her composed smile. Only the faint color in her cheeks, and the pulse that beat in the hollow of her neck betrayed the emotional strain through which she had just come. She had composed her face, hiding her inner fears.

* * *

The wedding reception at Forest Park went on until midnight. In the center of the picnic grounds, young men danced in a circle to the beat of the *bouzouki* and the mandolin, whirling around with such skill and abandon, jumping so high that the other guests applauded loudly. When the dancers finally collapsed on the grass, Vasso and Angel brought them *retsina* wine and *ouzo*.

Although Zoe had the reputation of being the best pastry maker on Halsted Street, she had been relieved of this task by Thea Sophie and friends, each family bringing a large tray filled with *baklava*, yogurt cake, honey-dripped cookies, powdered sugar cookies, butter cookies and crisp fried, honey-drenched sweets called *theples*.

A long wooden table had been set out in the park with food to be relished with the wine—roast lamb, potatoes, green beans cooked in tomato sauce, *salatas*, seasoned with lemon, olive oil, dill and oregano. Another table strained under its load of shish-kebab, zucchini, okra, baked lemon chicken, fish *plaki*, artichokes with butter sauce. And from the bakery, loaves of hard-crusted bread.

At one end of the park, chickens and lambs roasted on spits, long casings of *kokoretzi*, sausages were turned on other spits.

Tula was surprised to see that there were even more people at the reception than at the church. She knew that Andreas had spared no expense to make this occasion a joyful one. *He did this for me*, she thought. *And Mana is a proud woman*. She could not refuse any of her friends, or even a casual acquaintance. She had asked everyone in the Greek community to the wedding.

When the time came for them to leave, Tula was surprised that Zoe would not go with them. Andreas and Tasso laughed.

"You don't need your *Mana*," Andreas said. "I'll take care of you from now on."

Tula looked away so they wouldn't see her tears. She clutched the violets and roses. She still held the violets when they walked into the lobby of the Sherman Hotel, in the Loop. Andreas carried a new suitcase. Tasso followed with Tula's suitcase. He put it down, shook Andreas's hand, kissed Tula's cheeks, and said, "I'll see you in the morning. What time?"

"Don't make it too early," Andreas said.

When the bellhop opened the door to the hotel room and Tula saw the bed in one corner of the room, she touched a handkerchief to her moist forehead. "I—feel sick," she said, and ran to the bathroom.

She came out a few minutes later to a concerned Andreas. "What's the matter?" he asked.

Her mouth was dry, and she felt a quivering in the pit of her stomach. "It's been a long day and I haven't eaten—"

"My poor Black-eyed Susan. Of course, you're hungry. I'll get something from the restaurant downstairs. It stays open all night."

"I'm so tired," she said, walking to the dresser. She took off her bridal crown and veil. Andreas was at the bed, pulling down the bedspread, fluffing the pillows. "Lie down, rest. I won't be long."

Tula sat on the bed while Andreas unfastened the straps on her satin shoes, caressing her feet.

"Don't," she said.

"You're my wife," he said. "Get some rest."

She turned her head into the pillow and slept even before the door clicked after Andreas.

Someone had taken off her stockings and covered her with a sheet. She stirred, stretched, and sat up. He sat on the only chair in the room, eating a sandwich. Her movement made him turn. He smiled. "Rested? Are you still hungry?"

She yawned. "Yes, I'm starved. How long have I been sleeping?"

He walked to the bed and sat on the edge. "Let's see." He looked at his watch. "About an hour. Do you like chicken sandwiches?"

"Yes, yes."

"Good." He handed her a sandwich.

She bit into it and said, "Mmmmmmm." She was hungry anything would have tasted good, but the sandwich was delicious.

He watched her, a smile on his face. After a while, when she had finished eating, he said, "If you like, I'll wait outside—until you get ready for bed."

"Ready for bed?" She felt her face grow hot. "Yes, maybe you should."

When Andreas returned, Tula was laying in bed in the dark with the sheet pulled up to her chin. She heard him walking about, saw his shadow shedding his clothes. When he came to bed she moved away from him under the sheets. Nervously, she fingered the pearl buttons on the front of her white gown.

He laid his hand softly on the back of her head. Slowly, he put the other hand on her shoulders and pulled her body gently so that she would turn to him.

"No, no," she said.

"Don't be frightened. Didn't your *Mana* tell you anything?"

"About what?"

Then he laughed. "My poor little innocent."

"No, I'm not!"

"I never thought that you, of all girls—with all your reading, all your book learning—would not know." Again he laughed and pulled her close, covering her face with kisses.

"Andreas, stop!" She pushed him away.

"I love you," he whispered. This time, he looked directly in her eyes. His hazel eyes filled with light. "I don't want to hurt you." He took her hands in his and pressed them to his face to make Tula believe his sincerity.

Still uncertain of her feelings, Tula wondered how she could manage the strength to refuse him.

He whispered, he coaxed, caressing her face, her neck. Each time she attempted to protest, his kisses stopped her. Now she was more curious than afraid. He touched her hair again, which cascaded down her back, and then, without the slightest protest, Tula allowed him to unfasten each of the ten pearl buttons of her nightgown. She wanted to see what would happen, to experience this feeling that was growing inside her. Later she could think about it. Later she could sort it out.

Why did she feel no shame when Andreas pulled her gown down to her waist? Why did she feel no shame when he touched the nipples of her exposed breasts? Why did she feel no shame when she saw Andreas naked, for one brief instant before he covered himself?

One moment Tula was wild with anticipation, the next she was filled with fear.

"I won't hurt you."

"No, please, I don't want to," she protested, moving from him.

"My precious, I need you, I want you," he begged.

Tula prayed, *Let it be over soon.* She closed her eyes, then cried out in pain when he entered her. Her body seemed to belong to another as he pressed upon her, rose and fell, in a slow rhythm, and he seemed unaware that nothing was happening between them, that he was doing something *to* her, not *with* her.

Let it be over soon, let me get through this. After the initial sharp thrust, it was not as painful as she had feared. It was not as agonizing. Her position under him was awkward. How could she move her legs to prevent this aching? She wrapped her arms around him. Opening her eyes, she stared into his face. Andreas' eyes closed, his mouth open. Did she regret this act she was observing because she wasn't participating in it?

Andreas emitted a final groan, a shudder, and then a sigh. He rolled off Tula's body. He kissed her cheeks and lips. "I didn't hurt you, did I?"

"Yes, yes—no, no." She was unwilling to admit the ache she felt inside. Turning away from his outstretched arms, Tula wondered how quickly she could leave, get out of the bed, away from him.

"It will be better the next time. A woman doesn't enjoy it the first time," he said. "Come here, let me hold you."

"No." Everything he said made her feel worse, farther apart from him. Was this love? Was this what Mana and Baba had done behind closed doors at night?

Andreas lay quietly beside her, and in minutes she heard his steady breathing, and he was asleep.

Morning came, and it seemed strange not to hear Mana in the kitchen and the sisters getting ready for school. Beside her, Andreas woke, reached out to touch her. She drew away. "Don't touch me." Tula choked back the tears.

"If you'll only let me love you, everything will be all right, believe me," Andreas said. Then he tried to comfort her by burying his face in her neck. The sheet fell from him, and she shrank away. There he was naked.

"I've got to get dressed," Tula said, sitting up in bed. She clutched her nightgown to her and ran to the bathroom. She could not understand what was happening. Why was she feeling this way? Yes, Andreas was her husband, but she wanted to go home. She wanted to go to school. She didn't want to be Andreas' wife. She sobbed as she dressed in a plain black skirt and a white middy blouse.

"Don't cry," Andreas pleaded outside the bathroom door. "Come out, please. I promise I won't touch you."

Should she believe him? Should she trust him? Finally, she came out and walked to the window, as far away from Andreas as she could get. There was a knock on the door, and Andreas said, "Who is it?"

It must be Tasso, Tula thought. *He's come for the proof.* She had heard her mother and Theo Sophie whispering and giggling about the wedding night proof. The proof needed to show that the bride was a virgin.

"It's me, Tasso."

"He's too early," muttered Andreas as he went to the door. "Why are you so early?" he asked.

Ignoring his remark, Tasso said. "How did it go, brother?" There was a strained smile on his face. Then he saw Tula and blushed. "I'm sorry."

"How did it go? Not even a good morning or how are you?" asked Andreas. "You're so anxious to hear about the wedding night that you've forgotten your manners. Shame!"

Tasso fumbled in his pocket. "Don't forget this is my first time as *koumbaro*. It's tradition. But I don't give a damn about the proof. We can forget the whole thing."

"No!" Andreas said. "Tula was a virgin. And it went well." He turned his back to Tula and motioned with his hands. "Just like this—in and out."

Her face grew hot. *It did not go well. He lied*, she thought.

Now Andreas walked to the bed and pulled down the bedspread, and there on the sheet a mass of scarlet dots had soaked through as if from a small wound. "See? There is your proof. Do you want to take the sheet with you?"

"Yes…I mean no, certainly not. It isn't necessary. You know I didn't want to do this—tradition be damned," Tasso said. "I'm ready when you are. Let's make it an early start. Don't forget Nebraska is a long way. You're the one who wanted to take this trip with me, remember?"

Tula wanted to scream, to curse. She didn't want to go to Nebraska.

"Yes, I think the trip will do Tula good. She's never been out of Chicago, never seen country. Right, my little bride? And then we'll take the train back, another new experience for her."

Finally, Tula spoke. "Yes, I want to see Nebraska," she lied.

"I'm glad, Tula," Tasso said. "I'll wait for you both in the lobby. Oh, almost forgot. Here's some more gold coins." He gave Andreas a red velvet bag.

Andreas turned and put the bag in Tula's hand. "This is for your *Mana* and your sisters. We will take care of them."

A short time later, Tula sat in the backseat of Tasso's old Model T, while Andreas sat next to Tasso in the front. A blanket of fog was breaking up into a golden mist as the wind blew across Lake Michigan. "A perfect day for a trip, with a perfect bride," Andreas said, glancing back at Tula, who sat between the suitcases. "I'm a lucky man," he added.

During the days it took Tasso to drive through the flatlands of Illinois into the wheatfields of Iowa, Tula was miserable. It seemed to her that they passed the same old wagons on the same old dirt roads, the same farmers waving to them from the same cornfields, the same roadside stands selling the same lukewarm lemonade. She was tired and hot. Three days into the trip Tula had her first frightening experience with nature. Tasso and Andreas had suggested a picnic in a farmer's meadow. They had bought some fresh fruit, cheese and some lemonade and settled down to eat, when a cow came out of the pasture and appeared as if by magic in front of Tula. She screamed. The men laughed, and the frightened cow ran back to her companions.

"What a city girl you are, afraid of a gentle cow," Andreas said. The two men wouldn't stop talking about the cow, not until Tasso pulled his car in for the night in front of some cabins. Then another experience made her forget about the intruder at the picnic.

When a stout cabin keeper showed them a cabin furnished with two maple beds, an old chest of drawers and a rocking chair, Tula cringed. This was worse then the other places they had stayed in. At least the others were hotels.

The cabin keeper eyed the two men and Tula. "For privacy, you can pull this drape and separate the beds. See?" she said. Then she pulled a worn brown bedspread fastened to a track on the ceiling.

"Good," Andreas said.

Tula glanced around the room. "But where is the bathroom?" Andreas laughed. "My bride is a city girl," he said.

The cabin keeper smiled. "I understand." She walked to one of the beds, reached under the patchwork quilt, and pulled out a chamber pot. "This is for emergencies at night. We also have an outhouse in the back."

Andreas took Tula's hand and led her to one of the windows. "See that little house out there? That's the toilet."

One night followed another, and Andreas had only touched her once. He had somehow talked Tasso into staying in a separate hotel room, even though it cost an extra two dollars and Tasso had grumbled about the expense. When Andreas held her, kissed her, made love to her, Tula thought about her bed in Mana's flat. Andreas was right, it didn't hurt as much the second time. But she did not like it. She hated it.

And then one morning, as Tasso was driving down a country road, Andreas shouted, "Stop, right now." He took Tula's hand and pulled her to a meadow filled with Black-eyed Susans. "Here are your flowers, my love. Here are the Black-eyed Susans," he said, gathering fistfuls of the golden flowers with the black centers. He pressed a bouquet into her arms.

Chapter 15

Married almost a year, Tula still had periods of resentment against her mother. She spilled out that resentment in her Friendship Book writing swiftly and easily. Now she scribbled onto a page while she sat in the back bedroom of her mother's flat, the bedroom she now shared with Andreas. Her mother had said it had more privacy and was next to the bathroom. Tula writes: "This summer of 1926 is my first as a married lady. Next month, July, I'll be married a whole year, and I still dread the nights with Andreas, dread going to bed, dread him asking me about the monthly flow, and why it hasn't stopped.

"I don't dare ask Mana. How strange. I'm living in Mana's flat, still Mana's daughter, but a married lady, and still afraid to ask her certain things."

She chewed on her pencil for a moment, then wrote: "I've spent most of the year helping Reni and Goldie with their schoolwork. I've been giving them extra assignments, just like a regular teacher. And they love it! Not like Vasso, who hated school, and now hates work, hates men, hates the world! Gentle Angel is becoming quite a beauty with her golden hair and gray eyes, Baba's eyes."

She searched under the bed for her box of movie star photos. She lifted the lid and sorted through the pile. She found the one of Rudolph Valentino in his sheik costume. She stared at the glossy photo and thought about Photi, her own sheik. Tears welled up in her eyes. "Mustn't cry," she whispered to herself.

Tula spent the mornings in her bedroom reading Angel's schoolbooks. If she couldn't go to school, at least she was going to study, to prepare herself for when she *would* be back in school. Reading in the mornings. And having one day in the week to do as she pleased was a bargain she had struck with her mother.

Yes, she had married Andreas. Yes, she had saved the family. Yes, he paid the bills. Yes, they lived in the flat with her mother. Now *she* wanted something. That's the way she put it to her mother when Andreas and she had returned from their honeymoon.

These thoughts filled her mind one afternoon as she walked to the streetcar stop. The afternoon was hers to do as she pleased. Would she spend the day at the Hull House library, searching for new books on geography, history, astronomy? Or would she ride to the Loop and see a movie? There was a new Charlie Chaplin film at the State and Lake Theater. Tula loved Chaplin; he always made her laugh.

The day stretched out for her, and no one would stop her. Not even Andreas. He was gone all day working at the candy store. She only saw him at night, and all he wanted to do was–. But she wouldn't think about that now.

She'd rather think about movies. Life on the movie screen was the real world to her. Not the life she was living. Now she walked down Halsted Street, she held her head down. She knew the old men sitting in front of the coffeehouse were watching her. The bentwood chairs on the sidewalk were filled with old men. They had nothing to do all day but sit and gossip and watch the passersby.

One old man, his mustache yellow with tobacco stains, sat apart from the others, smoking a water pipe, the gold liquid bubbling through the globe and into the hose, the mouthpiece clenched between his brown teeth. He tipped his frayed felt hat down over his eyes when Tula walked by. Tula didn't return the greeting, but she felt his eyes on her as she boarded the streetcar.

Was he the one who had spread the rumor about her, the rumor that she had a miscarriage? The whole neighborhood was talking about it. She suspected that Andreas had started it. He had denied it. But in their bedroom this morning she had said, "You might as well put a sign up over our bed: 'Tula isn't pregnant this month. She had another miscarriage'!"

"It's been a year since our wedding," Andreas said. "I can't stand them telling me I'm not a man. Yes, damn it, I started the rumor. There must be something wrong with you. If you're not pregnant soon, I'm taking you to the doctor."

She wanted to tell him that a baby would just add an extra burden in their life, but he stormed out of the bedroom.

Now Tula made her way down the streetcar aisle, found a window seat, and soon was gazing out the mesh-screened window. The street had not changed since her marriage a year ago. The same stores, the same people working in them, the same people shopping in them. Only she had changed. She was a stranger sitting there. She smoothed her dress down over her flat belly.

She turned from the window and looked up to see Ondoni, standing motionless in front of her, hanging on to a strap. "Hello, Tula," he said, as if he had seen her only yesterday and he sat in the seat next to her.

"*Nouno*! It's you?" That was all she could say. It had been almost a year since she last saw him. Where should she start?

Ondoni said, "My car's in the garage, so I thought I'd ride the streetcar. It's been years since I've been on one of these things. But they haven't changed. Still a bumpy ride. Where are you going?" His face was tan, browned by the sun. His damp blond hair curled over his forehead and his blue eyes crinkled in a smile.

"I'm going to the movies, can't decide whether to see Charlie Chaplin at the State and Lake or the new Rudolph Valentino picture at the Chicago Theater."

"Wish I could go with you," he said. "But I've got business. How are things going for you?"

"Great, couldn't be better."

"You're lying."

She turned from him, looked at her hands in her lap. "Yes, I am. I feel as if everything in the world is dead. I'm all alone, the only one left in this desert. And there is no one coming to rescue me—not even my sheik."

"I have the same feeling, too, sometimes," he said. "Being alone. Godfathers and goddaughters think alike, sometimes."

"Even if they're not allowed to see each other?" Tula asked. Then she mimicked her mother's voice: "When you see Ondoni, cross the street!"

They both laughed. He took her hand in his. "You're so thin. Hasn't Andreas been feeding you?"

"It isn't that. We have plenty of food. And Andreas took care of the flats, paying the taxes. They're ours now. He signed a promissory note. Mr. Pappas has it. I don't understand what it means, but—"

Ondoni nodded. "I know about that Pappas. I would keep my eyes on him. But something else is bothering you."

"Yes," she said. She felt herself flush, but she had to tell him. He would understand. "It's about Andreas and me. It's about—"

What could she tell her godfather? Could she tell him that sometime when Andreas kissed her, she fought him? And that sometime Andreas's touch gave her goose bumps? How could she explain to Ondoni that sometimes she hated Andreas and his lovemaking? And how could she tell him what Andreas wanted she could not give him?

Then Tula blurted it out. "Something is wrong. It's about babies."

"You're going to have a baby? That's it, isn't it? And you're afraid, poor child."

"No, it's not that at all. Andreas thinks I can't have any. He keeps asking me every month about—" Then she stopped. She could feel her face getting hot. "I don't know what to do."

"Canal Street, next stop," the conductor said. He pounded the lever at his feet with his heavy boot to sound the bell.

Ondoni looked up. "Andreas needs a good talking to. You're just a child yourself."

"No, I'm a married lady."

"Canal Street," the conductor said.

"That's my stop," Ondoni said. "I want to help you. Don't be afraid to come see me, please."

She watched him her heart acing. If only her mother would talk to him. But Mana wouldn't have anything to do with her brother. Meeting always by chance would that be the only way she could talk with her godfather? She had heard that Ondoni was doing well in his business and had become a wealthy man. He could help them if—

She yearned for the days when she and Ondoni would walk to the Hull House library. How they'd spend hours exploring the books on the shelves, finally selecting a few, always a variety, geography, world history, science, humor. And how they'd sit side-by-side reading, often sharing a page, reading to one another, having fun, giggling over a funny passage. And how the librarian would "shush" them, her finger to her thin lips.

* * *

That night, after midnight, Tula woke from a sound sleep.

Andreas at her side, whispered, "She's coming." Tula heard the doorknob turn in their bedroom door. She shut her eyes when she heard Vasso's cough before she walked into their bedroom. It was an unconscious signal Vasso had to alert them.

Vasso tiptoed across their room, not glancing at their bed. She was making her nightly trip to the bathroom, through their bedroom. The only way to get to the bathroom was to walk through to the last bedroom, which was where Andreas and Tula slept.

Zoe always reminded the sisters not to drink water before bedtime, so that they would not disturb Tula and Andreas by walking into their bedroom. Only Vasso made a practice of tiptoeing through at night.

Every time Vasso came into their bedroom, Tula felt she was watching them. She lay huddled in her corner of the bed, the warm sheets nice against her cold skin. She could not sleep. Instead, she looked at the holy lamp, the *kanteelee*, glowing in the dark. *Help me*, she prayed. Finally, Vasso made the return trip, back to her bedroom. Andreas heaved a sigh of relief. "Come here."

"No, I don't want to." She felt him lift her nightgown and touch her breasts. "No!"

He pulled her into his arms, kissed her. At first, she lay in his arms, not thinking, not feeling. She felt his tongue in her mouth, his arms round her, close, kissing, caressing, touching. In minutes, he had pulled her nightgown off and was on top of her. "We must hurry. Vasso might come back," he whispered.

"No, no."

His lovemaking was frantic, beads of perspiration on his body, his hair damp on his face. He lifted her hips with his hands and entered her—in and out, in and out, his breathing rapids. Then a shudder and he was on his back, moaning. "Damn that Vasso." Tula was numb, still, like a stone statue.

"I love you, my Black-eyed Susan," he said. "Or should I call you Ice Princess?"

She shook her head, because if she said anything, she would cry.

"All right, don't answer me. You're not an Ice Princess, you're a baby. When will you grow up?"

She lay on her side, away from him, her face turned to the pillow. Maybe she *was* a baby. She had been robbed of her childhood.

She soon heard Andreas snoring. She sat up in bed and searched for her nightgown, which was in a heap at the foot of the bed. She slipped it over her head and fastened every button. Only then, decently covered, did she lay back down. What was that? Did she hear something? Was Vasso coming back? No. She closed her eyes. *Please, let me sleep.*

Part III

Now if you love me, leave
me, that I may not swerve
but follow my own footsteps.
The Odyssey

Chapter 16

Tula was a prisoner during the winter of 1926. Day after day, the Chicago wind piled snow in high drifts and made it impossible for her to leave the flat. Isolated from the outside world, she lost herself in books.

She had discovered an old copy of Homer's *Odyssey* in a pile of Baba's books. White Angel and Reni did their homework, she sat by the stove and read. Her favorite passage in the Odyssey was about freedom. She ever copied it into her Friendship Book: "Freedom is neither wine nor a sweet maid—it's but a scornful, lonely song the wind has taken." She wondered, had Baba tried to find freedom in a wine bottle?

As for Andreas, on the rare occasions when he was home for supper, hearing him joke and tease her sisters and tell stories, you wouldn't know he had a care in the world, unless you studied his eyes. He didn't spend much time in the flat. He'd leave in the early hours and return late in the evening. He said it was his work that kept him away.

The weeks before Christmas were the busiest for him at the candy store. Hand-dipped chocolates had to be made, walnuts, cherries, and raisins marked with their special swirl. Boxes had to be packed and shipped. Mr. Pappas demanded perfection in this time-consuming work. Thousands of miniature works of art were created by Andreas.

After the holidays, there was a lull at the candy store, but Andreas did not come home. After work, he went to the coffeehouse or the back room of the grocery where men gathered to play cards. One Sunday in late January, when the weather had turned colder, he managed to come home early.

"Too cold to snow," Andreas said. He sat with Zoe and the sisters around the stove in the kitchen. Tula read to them from *Alice in Wonderland*. It was the last one from the pile of books she had borrowed from the library. The worn, thumbed volumes traveled from one sister to another. It was Tula who ventured out every two weeks, trudging through the snow to return the books and get more.

Now, as Tula finished the last page of *Alice*, Reni said, "Read *Little Women*, please, Tula?"

"I'll read it," Andreas said. He took the book from Tula. He was not a reader of books, but to ensure his welcome in the reading circle, he brought the sisters candy.

He leafed through the book. "Say, this story reminds me of you girls." Though a smile was playing around his mouth, his eyes were hard.

Tula wondered what he was up to. Since their argument, he had become distant. If she couldn't give him babies, maybe he'd leave her. She didn't care.

These days, Tula would notice her mother and Thea Sophie in deep conversation while they crocheted. She sensed they were talking about her. The two women would laugh like schoolgirls sharing a secret, but when Tula came in sight, they'd stop and exchange knowing glances. While the chicken soup simmered on the back of the stove, or the coffeepot perked, they whispered secrets.

Thea Sophie had all the answers. Didn't she teach her mother how to bake Easter bread, and how to crochet lace runner for the altar? Didn't she introduce Mana into the world of the gypsies and fortune telling? Even though Mana knew it was wrong to consult the gypsy and have her palm read, wrong in the eyes of the church, she could not help herself. The best Mana could do was to make sure the old priest did not find out.

"We have something to tell you," Sophie said one day when Tula had come home from the library. She could not contain herself, she was so excited. "Yes, we have good news, child!"

"She's not a child, Sophie," Zoe said. "She's a married woman. Someday, God willing, she'll be a mother. Tula, we're taking you to the gypsy. She'll cure you, and you'll have plenty of babies."

The next day, a reluctant Tula plodded behind Zoe and Thea Sophie as they walked into the gypsy store and faced an old gypsy woman. A scarlet scarf was wrapped around her gray hair. Smiling red lips revealed yellow teeth. A long black velvet robe covered her ample body and a gold cord circled her thick waist. As she drew closer to her, Tula's nostrils began to sting from the odor coming from the gypsy.

The gypsy spoke, "So, this is the childless woman. Why, she is no more than a child herself. How old are you, dearie?"

"Sixteen."

"So, young? There must be a strong curse on you, and it might take more than one visit to lift it. I will need a gold coin to start?" Her palm went up as she spoke.

Zoe reached into her coat pocket for a black-bordered handkerchief knotted at one end. She undid the knot and gave the gypsy the coin. The old woman bit into it and smiled. With a forward motion of her hand, she drew Tula near.

"Sit down, my dear." Three wooden chairs and a green velvet armchair surrounded a table. The maroon walls seemed to have been painted years ago. The storefront windows were draped in purple velvet.

The gypsy took a crystal ball and a deck of cards from a shelf. She looked at Zoe and Thea Sophie. "Did you collect the remains of the male fluid from their sheets? Did you snip hair from the husband's head, a fingernail from the wife? And dust from beneath their bed?"

Zoe nodded and produced another black-bordered handkerchief. She unfolded it.

"Good," the gypsy said. She reached over and took the handkerchief from Zoe, spit three times into it, refolded it, and slipped it under the crystal ball. She shuffled the cards and revealed an ace of spades. She frowned at Tula. As if in a dream, Tula watched the old gypsy take two candles and light them. The candle smoke and the gypsy's odor made Tula close her eyes for an instant.

"Open your eyes!" the gypsy screamed. "I can't remove the curse if I can't see into your soul."

She touched Tula's arm. Tula shuddered. The gypsy took her hand away. She smiled, her thin red lips slanted at an angle across her lined face. She whispered, "The curse must be lifted." She chanted while the rain beat against the store windows.

"Yes, it will be lifted!" Thea Sophie said, caught up in the ritual.

The gypsy cried, "Hush, hush!" She slumped over the table, her fingers circling the globe. Suddenly, a wrenching moan came from her. She closed her eyes and pressed her red lips on the crystal ball. She said, "I see a baby. Yes, a baby." The gypsy opened her eyes. "Put your hands on the crystal," she commanded Tula.

Powerless to call a halt to this madness, Tula's hands came up to clasp the crystal ball. It was as if she were in a trance and the stench of the gypsy overwhelmed her. Perhaps if she were still, very still, the old woman would back away, and this feeling would pass. The gypsy put her veined hands over Tula's for a moment. Suddenly, she reached over and unfastened a button on Tula's dress. She worked fast, her fingers flying across the row of buttons. She touched Tula's firm breasts, Tula, started, shivered. She looked down at her exposed breasts.

The gypsy said, "These breasts are too small for a baby to suck."

Tula's head came up, and she screamed, "No! No!" She flew at the gypsy like a savage, clawing at the old woman's face. "Don't you put your filthy hands on me!"

"Bitch!" the gypsy cried, and she slapped Tula hard across her face.

Tula pushed her roughly. "You're crazy, old woman!"

Zoe and Thea Sophie watched in horror. "No, Tula, don't!" Zoe said in Greek. "She means well. She will help you."

"I don't want that old bat touching me, ever!"

And with a sweep of her hand, Tula sent the crystal ball crashing to the floor. She ran out the door. She ran back to the flat, all the while wanting to curse, wanting to scream, knowing what had frightened her so, what had made her run from the gypsy. She didn't *want* a baby!

Cautiously, Tula opened the door to the flat, and when she saw the kitchen empty she ran straight to her bedroom and locked the door after her. She picked up her Friendship Book from the dresser and wrote: "That witch of a gypsy. How dare she touch me with her filthy hands! She can't read the future. Mana just threw her money away. A baby? What about what I want? Doesn't that matter?"

She clapped the book shut and shoved it under the bed. Then she took off her shoes, sighed, and sank back on her pillow.

The knocking on the door woke her. "Open up, it's me, Andreas."

She stood up and stretched her legs, surprised at how stiff she was from sleeping.

Another knock. "Open up."

She opened the door a crack and could smell the onions Mana was frying in the kitchen. Andreas walked in.

"What do you want?" she asked, her eyes down cast.

"Something happened at the gypsy's, didn't it?"

She walked to the bed and sat down. She looked out the window. *Andreas should have been the one to see the gypsy*, she thought.

Andreas said, "Tell me what happened."

Tula looked at him and spit out the words. "That gypsy is a devil!"

"My Black-eyed Susan." He stared into her eyes and smiled his hesitant, charming smile. There was something in his eyes she didn't understand. Somehow she felt trapped. *Run, run*, she thought. *Get out of this room, get out of this marriage.* The instant she thought it, she acted on it. She ran toward the door. She wanted to get out of the bedroom, away from him.

Before she could reach the door, he caught her in his arms. "Please, don't," he said. He held her tightly, as if he couldn't bear to let her go. He kissed her, gently, again and again.

"No!" she cried. She freed herself from him, wiped her mouth with the back of her hand. "Don't kiss me."

"Please, my Black-eyed Susan. We are married. I love you. Let's not quarrel. The hell with the gypsy. Come here and sit down." He patted the edge of the bed. He talked softly the way people do when they're in no hurry. "I'm tired of arguing with you, Tula. As for babies, they can wait. I want you to be happy. God answered my prayers. He sent me you."

"God didn't listen to my prayer," Tula said.

"He will."

"When? When I'm old?"

"Don't say that. It will happen." Andreas touched her face, ran his fingers through her long hair. "We will talk about your dream later. Now relax, sit here beside me, and forget about the gypsy."

"I hate her. I feel trapped—in this room, in this flat with Mana and my sisters," Tula said.

"I know. But for now, this is what we have to do. Here let me hold you." Tula trembled.

"I promise not to kiss you. Just hold you. Why, you're shaking. Let me hold you, please. I love you, my Black-eyed Susan."

Much later, the room was cool and dim and the flat quiet. She was in his strong arms. But there was a softness underneath suddenly such softness that she trembled. He kissed her.

Did she kiss him back? Did he carry her to the bed? Did she walk? Did he remove her dress? She couldn't be sure. She only knew that she lay beside him and she was in his arms, lost in thought. She didn't try to talk, didn't try to move. Why was her heart racing, pounding in her ear. "*Ola kala*," she whispered. She opened her eyes and looked at him. His eyes started back at her, full of wonder.

"*Ola kala*," Andreas repeated.

They made love wrapped in a satisfying peace. She was conscious of his lips on hers, on her neck, on her breasts, on her nipples. They had fallen into a rhythm of breathing as one—slow, easy, his mouth on her breast. She put her hand on him to feel the texture of his skin, slide it across warm muscle. This was a sensation new to her. He slipped his arms across her back and held her close. He looked at her with eyes so bright she couldn't bear it.

Thoughts and senses merged, became one. Why had she suddenly changed toward him, toward his lovemaking? She could not understand her feelings? What was happening?

He wrapped his arms around her. His touch sent shivers through her. She clung to him. Soon she was rising with the wave of love, again and again. She cried out, a moan from deep within her. Her arms held him so tightly she could feel his every bone. Then it was over. He sighed, release her.

"I love you," he said.

Tiny shivers passed through her. In all her life, she had never felt this way. This strange, brilliant feeling. Andreas snuggled next to her. Tula's eyes were wide open, fixed on the ceiling. He put his hand on her check and said. "I love you, and I think you are beginning to love me." He kissed her, a kiss full of affection, a kiss that to her surprise, she returned.

"Sleep now," he said.

"Yes." She stared at the ceiling. When she turned, he was asleep, his face as still as a child's. She wanted to watch him. *Is this happiness?* she thought. Happiness was not the silent film stars flickering like phantoms across the screen.

She was tired, but she couldn't sleep. Quietly, she left Andreas' side and went to the dresser where her Friendship Book lay, and by the light of the holy lamp she began to write: "I will try to make things different from now on. I fought with Andreas because I was afraid. I said angry things to him because I was afraid. I don't know if I'm happy now. I don't even know what happiness is, I've had so little of it in my life, but I do know that I am not afraid anymore."

Chapter 17

Andreas stopped leaving the flat after supper. Before, he always said he had to go to the coffeehouse to catch up on the news from Greece. But now it seemed to Tula that he was catching up on *her*. Sometimes they'd ride the streetcar to the Loop and go to a movie. On cold evenings they'd sit by the stove, Andreas in a rocking chair and Tula beside him reading aloud.

One Sunday afternoon after dinner, Andreas lay on the leather sofa in the parlor with Tula beside him rubbing his forehead. When Tula saw Angel come into the room, she jumped up as if someone had caught her stealing and ran into the kitchen. Andreas sat up, muttering something about a headache. It was plain to everyone that Andreas was courting Tula. Why else would he be home with her so much? He'd give her violets, like the ones in her wedding bouquet, the ones Ondoni had given her for her thirteenth birthday, and the ones she had placed on Baba's casket.

When she was sad, he had a joke to amuse her. He was always laughing and teasing her, and whenever he came into the room, her face lit up. They enjoyed even the cold snowy nights. Andreas and Tula would bundle up in warm coats, mittens, and wool stocking hats and take long walks. On Sunday morning, they'd walk to church and part at the door, where Andreas would stand on the men's side. Sometimes, when he didn't know he was being watched, Tula would look at him from across the aisle and try to imprint his face upon her mind. There were the hazel eyes, the nose, the mouth, the thick brown hair. And he would turn to find her watching him.

One cold night in March, Tula gazed at her sleeping husband beside her. She was lying on the bed in a pink flannel nightgown, his head cradled in the crook of her left elbow. He lay on his side, a nightshirt over his body, the sheets pulled up to his waist. His right arm rested on her stomach. His eyes were closed. "Are you sleeping?" she asked softly.

"No, I'm just resting my eyes."

"What?"

"Resting my eyes. Haven't you ever done that? You're not asleep, but halfway there. Still, you can hear what's going on around you. It's an in-between stage. Nice and peaceful, but not sleeping. Sometime you can see colors and bright silver stars racing in a velvet blue sky."

"What are you talking about?" Tula asked. Now that she wasn't afraid, she could talk to Andreas, really talk.

His eyes still closed, he said. "Close your eyes."

"Yes, you're right. I can see the colors, and the bright stars. Maybe this is what it feels like to be at peace with yourself."

He kissed her gently on the lips. "I've never been so at peace with myself. I have only one problem."

"Problem?" she asked.

"I want to bolt the doors to our bedroom to keep Vasso out. We need our privacy. Vasso's going to stay out of our room."

"And who's going to tell her?"

"I am," he said. "And I'm also going to get her a chamber pot or build her an outhouse."

Tula laughed. "Just like in Nebraska?"

Gazing at her, his face softened. He ran his fingers through her long hair. "You're so beautiful," he said.

She leaned over the bed to get her face close to his. She wondered if she should tell Andreas her secret—the secret that the flow had stopped. She hadn't even told Mana.

"Andreas, there is something I must tell you."

"Tell me." He closed his eyes.

"Don't go to sleep on me now. I've got to tell you. I think I'm going to have a baby."

He opened his eyes wide. "Baby? When? Oh, thank God!" he touched her face. "Thank you."

"And it will be a boy, I just know it."

"Yes, it will be a boy. My son, and he will have sons, and they'll have sons—on and on. Oh, my Black-eyed Susan, we'll call him Costa for my *Baba*. We must write my *Mana* in Greece."

"Before you write any letters, we have to get one thing straight. I'm sorry, Andreas, but I want to name our baby Leones, after *my Baba*. Your *Baba* had many sons, mine had none." She looked directly into Andreas' hazel eyes, which reflected understanding even during Tula's heated outburst.

"All right, the baby will be called Leones."

Tula struggled to control her voice, but it cracked slightly as she said, "Thank you." She was surprised he had given in so easily. She knew how much it meant for a Greek man to name his eldest son after his father.

Tradition!

The next morning, Tula told her *Mana* and with tear-filled eyes, Zoe said, "The gypsy did it, she worked a miracle. You must go to Dr. Voles at once."

After Dr. Voles confirmed that Tula was pregnant, Zoe went to Maxwell Street to buy flannel to make baby clothes. "Make sure you get blue flannel. It will be a boy," Tula said. And that's what she wrote in her Friendship Book: "I'm going to have a baby, and I know it will be a boy. It has to be a boy for my *Baba*. I will do what Mana could not do for him."

That evening was the first of many devoted to sewing for the baby. Sometime Thea Sophie joined them. They crocheted tiny sweaters and booties, lace-edged bonnets, all in blue, always blue.

The months of her pregnancy went swiftly. One evening, Tula and Angel sat hemming diapers behind the pot-bellied stove and acting out scenes with their favorite movie stars.

"I vant to be alone," beautiful twelve-year-old Angel said, and put her arms up to the ceiling. "Leave me alone!"

Tula giggled. "Just like Garbo, even to your blond hair." She applauded. "Oops," she said. "I felt something." She placed both hands on her stomach. "Here, Angel, put your hand here. Feel it?"

"Golly, yes, sure. Was that the baby?"

"Yes."

"Tula, remember what Vasso said when Mana had Goldie? I mean about where babies come from?"

"I remember. But Vasso didn't know what she was talking about. Where we pee, how stupid. I think Dr. Voles will cut me, and the baby will pop out."

"Why don't you ask Mana?"

Tula stood up and looked into Angel's eyes. "I can't."

Tula grew so big she began wearing the old dresses her *Mana* had worn when she was expecting Goldie. At night, she put on Andreas' roomy nightshirts. Her breasts were swollen and sore, and the baby inside her kicked constantly.

All the diapers, flannel sheets, robes, sweaters, booties, bonnets, and shirts had been put away in the bottom dresser drawer. Since they had no cradle, another drawer was taken out of the dresser. Tula had lined the drawer with a blue blanket and placed a feather pillow in it. A nice, comfortable first bed for the baby.

It was the last week of September, a Saturday morning, and a gentle autumn breeze blew through the open kitchen window. Tula, sitting at the table, stretched and yawned, and that's when she felt the first pain, low in her back.

She glanced up at her *Mana*, who was by the stove. Tula winced as the pain grew more intense and swept down her back.

"What's the matter?" Zoe asked.

Tula pushed her hair back from her forehead. She breathed deeply. *Maybe this pain will go away*, she thought. "I don't know. My back aches. I feel sick to my stomach."

Zoe's face grew as white as the apron she wore. "Tula, I think it's time for the baby. Go to bed, try to rest. I'll send Reni for Dr. Voles."

Later, when Dr. Voles finished examining Tula, he said, "It's false labor."

"What does that mean? Aren't I going to have the baby now? Aren't you going to cut me open with a knife?" She stumbled over the words and felt her face grow hot.

"What?" Dr. Voles asked. "Who told you I'd cut you open?"

"No one."

"Tula, do you know how babies are born? Your Mana didn't tell you?"

"Vasso told me something about the baby coming out—from down there." Tula blushed. "But I didn't believe her."

Dr. Voles put his glasses in his vest pocket. He took Tula's hand. "There is no cutting, if it's a normal birth. I don't foresee any complications with you. You see, Tula, there is a passageway inside, which has to do with birth. It's called the cervix. It enlarges to allow the baby to come out. This is what causes the pain, the contractions or labor pains. Your uterus, or womb, is like a sack holding the baby. It stretches, and the baby comes out through the passageway. Understand?"

"Yes, I think so. Does it hurt?"

"Yes, it does. We sometimes give something for the pain, but you're young and strong, and I don't see any reason to put you to sleep. What you had today was called false labor. Your baby is not ready to come into this nasty world." He laughed.

"No cutting?"

"No cutting. I promise."

"How will I know when—?"

"Usually, the first sign is pain in the lower back. The contractions are far apart at first, maybe thirty minutes. But in the last stages of labor, they are closer together. And the water bag breaks."

"Water bag?"

"Yes, your baby is protected in a bag of fluid."

"Really?" Tula liked him. He explained things.

* * *

A month later, at two a.m. on a Sunday morning, October 30, Tula felt a pain in her back. From the first twinges, she was sure that this was it. She had been worried that when the time came she wouldn't be able to distinguish between the contractions and the general discomfort she felt when the baby kicked. Sitting up in bed, she rubbed her back.

The grinding pains were different from anything she had ever felt. She looked at the Big Ben clock on the dresser and began to time them.

Beside her, Andreas slept. She sat tense, waiting, waiting. Twenty minutes later, she felt another steady stab of pain in her lower back. In the intervals between, the pain vanished. She looked at the sleeping Andreas, and in spite of the increasing agony she couldn't repress a smile. She knew little Leones was eager to get out into this world of theirs.

Trying to remain calm, she reached over and gently shook Andreas. He looked up and rubbed his eyes. "What's the matter?"

"I think it's time."

"Time?" he asked, now fully awake. In a matter of minutes, he was dressed. "Wait here, I'll get Dr. Voles."

* * *

Tula had been in labor for eight hours, her eyes squeezed shut, fighting back tears as another pain overtook her. At her side, Dr. Voles' high-spirited voice momentarily quelled her fears. But the next pain reached a crescendo, the confidence that he had given her disappeared. In the middle of the contraction, Zoe wiped the beads of sweat dotting Tula's brow. Her eyes were shut tightly, and she was gripping her mother's other hand. "Eeeeee," Tula screamed as another pain overtook her.

"You're doing fine," said Dr. Voles.

Tula bit her lips. *He's lying to me*, she thought. *I'm going to die from the pain. He lied.* And then another pain. "Eeeeeeeeeeeeeeeee."

"Help her, dear God," Zoe said.

"We're almost there," Dr. Voles said. He worked quickly and deliberately. "You're doing fine. The baby is coming, almost—almost there."

Tula felt a sensation of fullness. She cried, not a scream, but a series of unrelated sounds, huffing, choking. *Come on, baby, be a good little boy and come out.*

She felt Dr. Voles reaching in, pressing. Gasping, she began to tremble. "Ah," the doctor said. "The head is in a perfect position. Everything is all right. Tula your baby is coming into this world now."

"Yes, I can feel it," Tula said, no longer exhausted.

Finally, with one final thrust, the baby emerged. "You have a fine baby, Tula," Dr. Voles said, wiping the mucus from its nose. Before it was fully out, the newborn uttered a clear cry.

"Oh, Mother of God," Zoe cried, her face wet with tears. She knelt by the bed and made the sign of the cross.

My baby? He didn't say it was a boy. Why is Mana crying? Tula thought.

"Here is your son, your Leones," the doctor said simply as he lifted the perfect infant in the air before placing him on his mother's belly.

"A grandson for my Leones." Zoe sobbed, still kneeling on the floor.

Dr. Voles raised the baby's head and shoulders so Tula could see the baby crying, red with anger, unhappy to have left his mother's warm womb, blinded by the light of the lamp, and welcomed into the world by a clap of thunder.

"He's beautiful. Look at all that hair," Zoe said, now standing. "He looks like Baba, just like Baba."

Tula looked into his eyes, the newborn eyes, as gray as her Baba's "You have Baba's eyes." Her fingertip lightly touched her baby's hair and instantly she felt goosebumps on her arms and a shiver shoot up her spine.

"He's got a fine set of lungs," Dr. Voles said. He smiled. "I'll get Andreas. He'll want to see his new son."

"Please, may I hold him, touch him?" Zoe said.

And that is how Andreas saw his son, in the arms of Zoe. Turning her head toward the door, Tula saw it had been opened, and there looking at them was Andreas. He walked to her side and kissed her. "Thank you, my Black-eyed Susan."

Zoe placed the baby in Andreas's arms and quietly left the room. He stared directly into his son's eyes, and the baby returned the look. "My God, his eyes are gray!"

"Yes, the color of Baba's eyes. He's the most perfect baby," whispered Tula in awe. "Our son! Look at all the hair he's got. Look at the way he makes a fist, listen to him cry."

Dr. Voles returned. "Ah, so you two are getting acquainted with Leones. A fine boy." He searched in his case for a piece of paper, a certificate. "Let's see, what day is it, the time? Must get this down. It's October 31, Halloween, right?"

Tula smiled. "I counted his fingers and his toes. He's a perfect baby, and his eyes are the color of my Baba's—gray."

"All babies have light eyes, either blue or gray. They will change in a few weeks," Dr. Voles said.

"My son's eyes won't change," she said.

Chapter 18

Tula had a hard time at first during the weeks following Leones' birth. She loved her son but she didn't feel like a mother. She thought of Leones as her doll—as something to play with, something to amuse her. When he was hungry, she'd watch in wonder as he sucked on her breast, her milk bubbling up in his tiny mouth.

By the time Leones was six weeks old, Tula could tell that Andreas wanted to make love. She had shyly put off his advances, but Andreas hinted that it was time. One night, he seized the opportunity. He picked up his son and laid him in his drawer bed for the night. The baby curled up, tucked his hands between his knees, and promptly went to sleep. Andreas slid into bed beside Tula. "He'll sleep," he said fingering the buttons on the front of her nightgown.

"Oh, no, he'll be up in an hour wanting to nurse."

"If he's hungry, he has to eat."

"Someday I'll be able to sleep the whole night through."

Andreas placed his arms around her. "You've had quite a time with our son, haven't you?" he said kissing her lips. "I've missed you. I've wanted you for so long—so long."

"I want you, too, but I'm afraid it will hurt," she said.

Andreas lay beside her on the bed and drew her into his arms, kissing her lips, her cheeks, her neck. He slipped the nightgown over Tula's head and reached over to kiss her breasts.

Pushing him away, she said, "No, that's for Leones now."

Andreas looked up to see a smile on her face. "Leones, eh?" He circled a nipple with his tongue.

A sensation in her breast warned her that the milk was flowing, and Andreas was surprised with a spray on his face.

He laughed, wiping his face with the sheet from the bed. "Guess you're right, they're for Leones, for a while anyway. Here, let me hold you. I promise I won't do anything to cause you pain. Relax, lie down. You're my sweet Black-eyed Susan, my darling wife." He kissed her lips. "Is this all right?" he asked, touching her belly and below.

"Yes." Tula relaxed, confident that she could trust Andreas and enjoyed having him touch her and excite her.

Andreas was gentle in his lovemaking, and as soon as they were apart Leones began to cry. Andreas got the baby and placed him beside Tula. "Now, my son, you can have your midnight meal."

As the days had become progressively colder, Tula passed her time sitting by the stove, rocking Leones, while listening to the wireless Andreas had bought for her. One day, she wrote in her Friendship Book: "I feel like a mother should feel. When Leones nurses at my breast, he turns his head so he can watch me, reaching with his tiny hand to pat my cheek and coo. His body is filling out. After his bath, I stretch him out on a towel by the kitchen stove and rub him across his chest while he giggles. I take his little arms and form them into a x across his chest. He loves it."

Zoe, who had now become a grandmother, a *yiayia*, used the new telephone often to tell everyone about Leones' progress. At six weeks, the baby's eyes had settled on a permanent color. It was a miracle, Zoe had said when she saw that Leones' eyes had stayed gray.

Since Tasso, Andreas' brother, had stood as *koumbaro*, best man at their wedding, it was tradition that he stand as *Nouno*, godfather, at the baby's christening. Tasso was summoned from Nebraska. Zoe called on Thea Sophie to help prepare an elaborate dinner to follow the baptism. Andreas bought bottles of *retsina* and *ouzo*. Vasso and Angel wrapped the sugar-coated almonds, the *koufeta*, in blue tulle and tied them with blue ribbons to distribute to the guests.

The church ceremony was beautiful and Andreas beamed as he carried the baby into the flat for the party afterwards. Zoe, smiling with joy, said, "This is Leones' day, and Baba is looking down on us now and saying, 'Finally we have a son in the family.'"

Tula felt happy. Once the guests had left, she carried the wiggling Leones to the bedroom to nurse him. The she placed him in his drawer to sleep and took her Friendship Book off the dresser. She began to write: "Tomorrow I will be free. Free. Mana said it was tradition that a new mother could not leave the house until after the baby was forty days old. Tomorrow will be my day."

The next day, when Tula tried on her dresses, she discovered they were too tight. Her figure was a bit more mature in the bust and the hips. Finally, she found a fuller-cut dress she could wear. Where should she go—to the Loop to see a movie or a vaudeville show? To the library for some new books? She had read all of Angel's books and had taken detailed notes for she was still holding in her heart her dream to be a teacher, someday. For today, though, it would be a movie, because that's what she had missed most during her confinement.

Alone in the theater before the phantoms came across the screen, she had some time to think. She thought about Ondoni. He had not been at the baptism. He was never there when she needed him. She hadn't seen him for more than a year. She also thought about Baba, whom she still missed dearly. And memories of Photi had never left her. Now she had Andreas and the baby. They had taken over. But what did she, Tula, really want? What was she going to do for herself? Her dream to teach, had that died?

* * *

On Leones' first birthday, he was walking and making his demands known. He was a boy and could do no wrong in Yiayia Zoe's eyes. Even the sisters did his bidding, all he had to do was point to an object, and it was his. All he had to do was cry for an instant, and Angel would pick him up. All he had to do was scream, and Reni would play with him. He had these females wrapped around his chubby little finger, and he knew it.

A week after his birthday, Zoe and her daughters were in the kitchen listening to the wireless. Zoe sat holding a wiggly Leones, entranced with the joy that this boy was her grandson. She responded to his chatter with unconcealed delight. She kissed his cheeks impulsively. "You're my good boy."

"And a big boy, too," Angel said. "Time he got out of that drawer. Andreas should get him a bed."

Angel was helping Reni and Goldie with their homework. An eighth-grader, Angel would soon graduate from Socrates. Vasso already inquired at the ice cream factory about a job for Angel. Eight years is enough schooling, Zoe had said. It was time for Angel to work to help the family as Vasso was doing.

Vasso, now almost sixteen, had been at the factory for two years. She was a loner and still had that hot temper. No wonder men didn't find her attractive. Andreas had tried many times to introduce Vasso to an eligible Greek bachelor, but she rejected all of them. Vasso always found something wrong with them—they were too tall—they were too short—they were too fat or too thin. They had too much hair, or too little hair, or they smelled of garlic, or of too much cologne. She rejected all of them. Andreas finally gave up. "She doesn't want a man, she wants a Greek god!"

Tula suspected that even a Greek god was not right for Vasso. It seemed to here that Vasso was afraid of men. Vasso's only love was money and her lover was the Atlas Bank of Halsted Street.

Suddenly, Tula's thoughts were interrupted by Reni and Goldie. "We're finished!" Reni shouted "Come on, Goldie, let's practice our songs."

"Good," Zoe said. "So sweet."

Vasso closed her book, "Sweet, my foot. They sound like some screeching cats in the alley. Who told you kids you could sing, anyway?"

Reni made a face before she dashed out of the kitchen. Goldie thumbed her nose at Vasso.

Angel looked at Vasso. "She speaks, she's alive! I thought she was a-s-l-e-e-p." Angel grinned.

"Oh, shut up, Angel. You and your spelling."

"I think I've got Washington," Tula said, fiddling with the wireless. "Sounds like President Hoover."

"The President is a good man," Zoe said. "But he's not as good as Andreas. Look how Andreas fixed the downstairs flat, so Sophie could move in. Her rent helps us. Her late husband," Zoe said, pausing to do the sign of the cross," left her a little money."

Good man? Tula thought. *Was Ondoni a good man, too? Or was he evil. That's what Mana called him. How terrible to think of him as evil.*

President Hoover's voice on the wireless snapped Tula out of her reverie.

"What does President say?" Zoe asked.

"He says that 1929 will be a good year—plenty of jobs for everyone."

Chapter 19

It was September 1929, and Tula was wrapped in a dreamy, delightful sense of well-being, encased in the warmth of her family—and in the warmth of the turquoise shawl on this brisk autumn day. Never had she experienced this sense of contentment. Never had she experienced this, approval of Andreas, and the excitement that he brought to her life. Time and time again, she tried not to compare him to Ondoni, telling herself that it was unfair, yet the comparison inevitably entered her mind. Why did her thoughts dwell on Ondoni now on this autumn afternoon in the courtyard at Hull House? She touched the shawl, felt its softness.

She had taken Leones to Hull House to show him the monkey tree—her monkey tree. He was far too young to climb the structure, but she did want him to see it, and she did want to tell him that at one time she was "king of the hill." She held his chubby hand as they strolled through the courtyard. Leones would be two next month. He had plenty of time to learn about the monkey tree. Social workers in their familiar brown smocks watched as the children swung on the swings, and raced around. She didn't recognize a single face.

A fancy black car, a car that looked garish for the west side of Chicago, pulled up to the curb near the swings. Tula glanced at the driver who stepped out. He wore a hat, low over his eyes.

"My God!" she cried as she ran to him.

Leones's short legs tried to keep up with this mother but failed. He hung back and cried. "Mommy, stop!" Tula kneeled down and scooped up her son. She kept running toward the black car and its driver, her shawl falling from her shoulders.

"*Nouno!*" she cried.

Casually, Ondoni walked to her side and picked up the shawl, a broad smile on his face. "Here, let me help you with this shawl. It's held up well after all these years. So that's your son. He's a big boy, isn't he?"

"Big boy," Leones said, and went into Ondoni's arms.

"See? He's not afraid of me," Ondoni said.

"You're family. Why should he be afraid of you?"

"Let me look at you," Ondoni said to the boy. "Who do you look like? Lord, he's got your Baba's gray eyes."

Tula smiled. "Why haven't you come over?" she asked.

"You know your *Mana* doesn't want me to see you or your son."

Ondoni reached into his vest pocket and took out a gold coin. "Leones, this is for you, *kerasii*, my goddaughter's son." He put the gold coin in the boy's shirt pocket. "He looks like a happy boy. How about you? Are you happy?"

"Yes, I can truthfully say I'm happy. Andreas is very good to me. He has a good job. And how is *your* business?" She pulled the shawl closer to her.

"I've branched out—to New York. But I didn't drive all over Chicago's west side looking for you to talk about me. I want to talk about you—about your dream?"

"My dream? That's all it was, a dream. I'm a mother now, I have a son to take care of. Mana said it was foolishness. I—I—" Tula hesitated.

"Say it, Tula. It's still in your heart. Foolishness? No."

"Wh-what do you mean?" Tula asked almost in a whisper.

"I mean don't give up. It can come true."

"It can?" she asked.

"Yes. God willing, it can."

"Now who's talking foolishness? I'm a mother. I don't have time for school."

"Ah, but when I see Andreas, and I don't see him often, he tells me you study Angel's books. You devour them. And you tutor Reni and Goldie, he said. Isn't that true?"

Tula's cheeks burned. Why would Andreas tell Ondoni?

Ondoni said, "So the girl who wanted her dream is still alive and well."

"That girl is dead."

"That girl is dead?"

"Swing, swing," Leones said, pulling on Ondoni's shirt.

"All right," Ondoni said, putting the boy down. "I'll take you."

"No, you're busy. You'd better go. You'd better go back to your business. Vasso said she saw you a while back."

"Yes, but she crossed the street, never spoke to me. She is your *Mana*'s daughter, all right. Obeys her."

"You were with that-that woman, the one with the red hair."

"Maggie? Vasso doesn't miss a trick, does she? Yes, Maggie was with me."

"Well, don't let me keep you from your business."

Ondoni grabbed Tula's shoulders. "What are you talking about? I've been circling Hull House for months hoping to see you. I don't dare step in your *Mana*'s flat. I'm your godfather. I care for you, in spite of what your mother says. We have to talk, like old times. Talk to me, Tula."

Tula freed herself from his grasp and took Leones' hand. "There's nothing to talk about. These are not old times. It's 1929, and I'm not the frightened little girl who didn't want to get married and came to you for help. I'm a mother."

"I see." He glanced at this watch. "You're right, I do have to tend to business. Good-bye, Tula." He walked to his car and started the engine.

Tula watched as he left. Saying good-bye to him this time had been easy, in fact enjoyable in a cruel way. *Why should I be the only one hurting?* she thought. She took off the shawl, draped it on her arm. She didn't feel like wearing it now.

That evening at the flat before Andreas came home, Tula was alone with Leones. She sat down heavily on a chair near the stove, chewing her lip. On the table lay her Friendship Book and a pencil. She might as well write in it while the coffee finishes perking. "Why didn't I talk to Ondoni more about my dream? He knows what I want. Why was I so abrupt with him? I was afraid. I, too, had gone to Hull House hoping, praying, I'd see him. We missed each other so often, and the one time when we did meet, today, I was cruel to him. I hurt him, and I was hurting myself."

She slammed the book shut. *See if I care, you—you evil man sharing your days with that Maggie woman. Why do I hate her so? It's because she has you, Ondoni. She sees you, she talks with you, every day, every night. I should be the one seeing you, talking with you, sharing my thoughts with you. You always listen. You're my godfather. But I didn't have time for you.*

At the sound of footsteps at the door, she snapped out of her reverie. Andreas walked into the kitchen. "Coffee smells good. What are we having for supper?" he asked. He concealed a package behind his back. "I have a present for you, Black-eyed Susan."

"Violets?" She was being coy. "I love violets." He put a white box on the table tied with a wide scarlet ribbon. "No violets. Open this."

"It's not my name day. What's the occasion?"

"Open it."

She untied the ribbon, fumbled through folds of white tissue paper, and pulled out a black lace chemise, edged in delicate pink satin ribbon. "It's beautiful! Oh, Andreas." She wrapped her arms around him and hugged him. "You spoil me."

"I know. I'm glad you're smiling. You looked so sad when I came in. What's happened?"

She told him about meeting Ondoni.

"He's not part of our lives anymore. You have to forget him. I heard he's into some business that will get him in trouble with the law."

"The law?"

"Yes, but let's not talk about Ondoni. I have some good news. Mr. Pappas is talking about a partnership—with me. He's giving me this opportunity because I'm a good worker. I'm paying the money we borrowed from him for the flats, and he says that in time I can be a partner. These are good times for us, and I must take advantage of them."

* * *

But two months later, in October, the stock market crashed and things changed abruptly for Tula. Although she didn't understand it, she was worried when she read in the *Chicago Tribune* that bankers were committing suicide by jumping from skyscrapers in New York. Even in Chicago, men who had lost all their money in the stock market were killing themselves.

One evening after supper, Tula and Zoe had cleared the dishes away. Andreas sat by the stove, sipping coffee. "I'm lucky," he began. "I didn't invest in the stock market, didn't have any money to invest. Paid my bills and managed to feed and clothe us. But my poor brother, Tasso, lost everything. He thought the stock market was safe, and he put all his savings in it. He used bad judgement. Now my brother has lost everything, lost his store, lost his savings."

"Poor man," Zoe said. "Yes, we are lucky, thanks to Mr. Pappas."

Tula sat and listened, her head throbbing. She touched her forehead. Perhaps her headache would go away if she got some air. "I'm going outside," she said.

She stood on the back porch and breathed the cool evening air. But, her headache persisted. Her thoughts turned to Andreas. She realized that although he was a good provider, although he was a good man, they had never actually had a conversation with each other. That is, they had never carried a conversation with each other. That is, they had never carried a conversation to a point where each discovered something about the other. Did she know what he wanted? His goal? Was it to have a partnership in the candy store?

And what about her dream? She had told *Nouno* Ondoni that she had forgotten about it. It was in the past. Andreas was her life now. Her face grew hot when she thought about the black lace chemise and the lovemaking that had followed after he slipped it off her body. A shiver ran up her spine as she thought about it.

Now Tula leaned over the railing and looked down at the alley. She saw an old man urinating on a pile of garbage, the stream steaming in the cold air. She looked at him at the same time as the man looked up at her.

Feeling her face flush, Tula turned away. She stood and shivered. No, she didn't want to live like this, where bums peed in the alley and drunks lurked in dark hallways.

If only this headache would stop. If only my stomach would stop churning, she thought. She ran to the rail, leaned over, and vomited.

Zoe found her there. She saw at once that Tula had been sick. "What happened?"

Tula saw the concern on her face. "Don't worry, Mana. I'll be all right."

"Maybe it was something you ate," Zoe said in a gentle tone, she added, "It's really nothing."

Tula looked at her. "I'm going to have another baby, aren't I?"

Chapter 20

On July 18, 1930, the baby came into the world. She was born at home with Dr. Voles present. It was an easy birth for Tula, and it was swift—only four hours of labor. When little Leones toddled into the room with Andreas to see his baby sister, he took one look at the baby in bed with Tula and said, "Cissy has a red face and black eyes." The baby was christened Zoemu, but forever after Cissy was her name.

This time, Tula was happy to follow the custom and name the second child for her mother, Zoe. When the baby was born with black eyes that gave no hint of changing, Andreas couldn't be happier. His firstborn daughter was named for Zoe, and she had Black-eyed Susan's eyes.

Only Zoe was sad. She had prayed for another boy.

Angel was happy. She cried tears of joy when Tula asked her to be godmother. The two sisters had become close and shared many secrets and hopes. Tula had someone to confide in other than her godfather. Tula told Angel about her plans for the future. When her children were old enough to go to school, she was going back to school, too. In the meantime, she was studying books from the library. Angel in turn told her of her dreams. She wasn't always going to work in an ice cream factory. She planned to get married, although Andreas hadn't found a suitor for her. She was going to find her own suitor, someone who was educated. Angel and Tula spent time talking about their dreams while they crocheted collars and cuffs to sell to the factory employees. Angel was becoming more important to the family now, because of her job at the ice cream factory. She brought home much-needed money. She worked side-by-side with Vasso on the line dipping frozen ice cream on sticks into melted chocolate. The sisters would come home at night with their hands numb and blue from the cold. Still, Angel kept her sunny disposition. Only Vasso complained.

Fifteen-year-old Angel had grown into a beautiful girl. Tula would tease her about her blond hair and gray eyes. Not Greek at all, she'd say. And that's when Angel would remind her that Helen of Troy was a blonde.

Angel lived for the family. It was Angel who bought sheet music for Reni and Goldie, listened to them practice new songs, and took them to Hull House to audition for amateur hours. It was Angel who bought a ukulele for Reni, who at twelve was becoming quite a musician. Now there was Cissy for Angel to spoil. She was treated like a doll. Angel combed her hair, played with her, bought her new dresses. Sometimes it seemed to Tula as if she had no children. Leones was Yiayia Zoe's and Cissy was Angel's.

* * *

Only after Cissy was two months old would Tula allow Andreas to make love to her. She was afraid of getting pregnant again. Andreas tried to assure her that the rhythm method they had used in the past was safe. "You must be sure to mark the calendar. We must not be overwhelmed by our love," he had said. "Now that Vasso doesn't dare come into our room at night, we can be alone together," he added.

When Cissy was eight months old, the flow stopped again. Tula, angry, frantic, confused, poured out her frustration into the Friendship Book: "I don't want another baby. Andreas doesn't understand. We can't support another baby. We barely have enough money now." She put the book back in her drawer and rushed to the bathroom. By some miracle the flow had begun. That's when Tula took her pillow and a blanket from their bed.

"What are you doing?" Andreas asked.

"I-I can't sleep in the same bed with you."

"What are you talking about?" His face clouded over.

She waited for a moment before she spoke again. "I'm scared. I thought I was pregnant—again. I don't want any more babies. Where will we put the other baby—in another drawer? We can't even afford a crib for our babies. I'm staying away from you. Leones is sleeping with you, and I'm sleeping on his cot."

"Like hell you are. You're sleeping with me."

"I don't want to get pregnant. Don't you understand? I don't want to have baby after baby. How can we feed them? We can't keep bringing babies into this world. It's not fair."

"Fair? Listen, you sleep in my bed, or else I won't sleep in this house."

"I won't."

"All right." He slipped into his pants, put on his shirt, and stormed out of the flat.

Moments after Andreas slammed the door, Zoe came into the bedroom. After Tula tearfully told Zoe what had happened, Zoe tried to convince her that what she wanted to do was wrong, wrong in the eyes of God.

The next evening, Andreas came home from work late and said he had stopped off at the neighborhood grocery store to chat with the men in the back room who were playing gin.

"They asked me to join them. Maybe next time, I told them," he said.

"Go ahead. I don't care," Tula said.

Although Andreas acted toward his children as if nothing had happened, his manner had changed toward Tula. He was polite but distant. That night, he slept in the double bed with Leones. If he was angry, he did not show it. On the surface, life continued as usual. Zoe went to church and lit candles. She visited the gypsy and told her of the problem. Certainly the church and the gypsy should be able to help.

Tula settled into the household routine. She reread Angel's old schoolbooks until she had memorized them. She continued making lace collars and cuffs for Angel to sell at the factory. She hid half of the money she earned in her underwear drawer.

Thea Sophie came to the flat often to gossip with Zoe, who relished her visits. The smell of coffee would fill the kitchen while the two women chattered.

Sophie was a good friend and now she was their tenant. She always paid her rent on time. Sophie also helped Zoe with her pail garden on the back porch, where tomatoes, green peppers, basil, and oregano grew in heavily fertilized soil. She had done this for years. It brought back Greece to her, Zoe would say. Whenever Tula saw the porch garden, she laughed to herself. She knew why the plants grew so well. It was the horse manure. And this year it was Reni's turn to scoop up the freshly deposited manure with a shovel, after following the house-drawn wagons. Even Tula had scooped up horse's *kaka* for Mana's plants when she was younger. The porch reeked of manure.

One hot day in August, while Zoe and Sophie were watering the plants on the back porch and Tula had finished scrubbing the kitchen linoleum, there was a knock on the door.

It was the dry goods man. "Come in," Tula said.

He tipped his straw hat to reveal a baldhead. "I won't mess up your floor, Missy," he said to Tula "Is your mama home? Hot enough for you?"

"Yes, it is."

At that moment Zoe and Thea Sophie came in from the back porch. When he opened his old suitcase, the show began, as Tula called it.

The suitcase, throwing off a scent of old leather, was filled with silks from China, linens from Ireland, fine silk thread from India. Everything he showed was better and cheaper, by far, than what they could get at the Twelfth Street Department Store or Maxwell Street.

Tula felt the smooth texture of the soft flannel melting like butter between her fingertips. "Good material, will make fine blankets for your baby," the man said.

Zoe carried a yard of blue silk to the window to examine it in the light. Tula followed her mother and took some of the shiny, slippery silk in her hands. She lowered her voice. "It feels like, like starlight."

In less than an hour, the dry goods man had buckled the straps of his suitcase and was off to his next customer. Zoe bought the silk, Thea Sophie bought a cotton print, and Tula took the flannel.

The dry goods man wasn't the only visitor to the flat. On the first Tuesday of every month, the insurance man came to collect twenty-five cents for Zoe's insurance policy.

The Oriental man was also a visitor but not as frequently as the others. He was a small man of Chinese origin who came twice a year, his arms loaded with rugs, beautiful in design, vivid in color. Incense, that's what he smelled like, thought Tula. But not the same kind of incense as their priest, this was the mysterious incense of the Orient.

And the last of the men in Zoe's life was the brush man. He visited the flat monthly to show his supply of brooms, brushes and mops.

What kind of life is this? Tula wondered. Although she helped Zoe clean and cook, the days seemed empty for her. Is this what saving the family meant? The saddest time of year for Tula was the week school started. She'd watch Reni and Goldie take off with their satchels and their lunches of fried potato sandwiches. And then September drew into October and she'd hear the cold Chicago wind rattle the windows.

Outwardly there was no change in Tula, but inwardly she had become empty. There was no joy in her life. Even Cissy did not bring her pleasure. Although the baby crawled all over the house, she could not crawl into Tula's heart. Tula left her with Angel, and Angel filled the gap, disciplining her, teaching her, loving her. She had become a mother to her, as Zoe had become a mother to Leones.

One evening after Tula tucked Leones into bed, he said, "Where's Daddy?"

"He's out, honey. You'd better get some sleep, young man. I have to check on Cissy." She kissed him and left the room. Cissy was asleep in her drawer, and there was Tula's cot beside her, waiting for her. It was too early for her to sleep, and besides she was restless. She knew where Andreas was, and maybe this was the night she should confront him, in what had become his home away from home.

She walked down the dark stairs, pushed opened the door, and stepped out onto Blue Island Avenue, her street, full of grit from the factories, with streetcar tracks running down the middle. At the corner under a lamp post stood two young men fresh off the boat, squinting down at their polished leather shoes, talking rapidly in Greek.

Farther up the street, the swinging doors and windows of an old tavern were boarded up. She remembered another day, another time, when she was eight years old and had peeked through the swinging doors to watch her father, drinking wine and playing cards.

It started to rain. *How appropriate*, Tula thought. *I'm out looking for Andreas, and now it's raining. Even the elements are against me.* She raced for cover under the Plaka Grocery canopy. Rain pelted the windows of the grocery store as she peered through them.

She knew Andreas was in the backroom, drinking and playing cards. Making a fist, she rapped hard on the window. A young man came from the back room. "We're closed."

"I know that. I'm looking for Andreas. He's in the back room, isn't he? Let me in, I'm getting soaked."

He shrugged. "Well—yes, he is." He opened the door. She walked in and sat on an old barrel. She was shivering.

From the dim light in the hallway she surveyed the store.

Ripe oranges and apples filled the fruit bin, and carrots, broccoli and endives overflowed in the vegetable bins. On the counter were two huge jars filled with olives and peppers, and in the meat case, Tula saw a crock with feta cheese and a large head of *kasere* cheese, their pungent odors escaping the glass case.

In the back room, she could hear men talking and laughing. She smelled spicy Greek sausage frying. She waited. When she heard the back door open, she raised her head. In the dim light, she saw Andreas, his mouth set in an angry line. "What are you doing here?"

She jumped off the barrel. She wanted to scream at him. Instead, she said. "So you are here. What are you doing? Gambling? Drinking?"

He reached out and grabbed her arms.

"Let go of me!"

Andreas sighed and release her. "Is it so bad to spend time here with my friends? Drinking and playing cards, what harm is there in that?"

She was so angry that her hands shook, her lips trembled. "Are you coming home with me?"

"No."

"I'm not leaving this place until you do."

He did not answer her for a few minutes. Finally, he said. "I'll go home when I damn well please. No woman is going to give me orders."

Suddenly, Tula heard footsteps in the hallway. Ondoni appeared a bottle of wine in one hand, a coffee cup in the other. She was surprised to see him, but she did not show it. So he was responsible for Andreas being here. Damn him.

Ondoni said, "Tula, what are you doing here?"

"I came for Andreas. I should have known you were behind all this, Mana is right. You're evil."

"Andreas is his own man," Ondoni said. "He does what he pleases. He has a right to relax with friends after a hard day's work."

"I don't need anyone speaking for me, Ondoni," Andreas' voice had changed, and he spoke in a thick Greek accent.

Tula said, "Own man, are you? You're also my husband, and you have children who need you."

"What about my needs? I have needs, too." He looked at her. "It's time you went home to your children. Your *Mana* shouldn't have to do all the work. You should at least be a mother to them—since you're no wife to me."

She started to walk away. When she reached the door, Ondoni grabbed her arm. "Don't leave." He spoke in that beguiling voice of old. He had that smile she remembered. He put his arms around her, to console her, but she would not be consoled.

"You heard what Andreas said. I have to go home to my babies."

Andreas walked toward her. "I'm sorry," he began. "I didn't mean it."

"You meant it, all right."

She didn't want to accept his apology. But after a moment, she said, "Okay, let's not fight."

Ondoni filled his coffee cup with wine. He smiled. "That's better. Make up—kiss and make up." He winked at Andreas. "Is the fighting over? Good! Tula can now go home to her babies, and we can finish our card game. I think I was winning. Now kiss your wife."

Andreas put his arms around her. "My Black-eyed Susan," he began, but whatever he was going to say was lost, for at the moment Maggie walked in from the back room.

She ran her hands through her masses of curled red hair and said, "What's keeping you guys? The cards are getting cold." Then she saw Tula and smiled a sly smile. "Well, what have we here? Did someone say something about kissing?" Maggie did a sudden turn, kissed Ondoni on the mouth, and wiped her red lipstick off him with her hands, which she then shook saucily before Tula's face. "My, how prim you look."

Ondoni frowned.

"How vulgar *you* look!" Tula returned, with a glance at the red taffeta swatches and yellow silk roses adorning Maggie's tight black satin dress.

"Vulgar? Really? From the mouth of Mrs. Fashion Plate. How hoity-toity," Maggie said.

Ondoni moved toward her. "Shut up, Maggie."

"You bitch!" Tula cried.

"Tula, stop that," Andreas said.

Tears welled up in Tula's eyes. "And you're a bastard!"

"Listen, it's not what you think," Andreas said.

"Liar!" Tula sobbed.

Ondoni looked at Tula. "No. He's not lying. We're just playing cards, Tula. That's all it is."

Strange, she thought. Once she had wanted to model herself after him, drawn by his love of books, his determination to succeed. Now she realized that it was only the superficial aspects of her godfather's lifestyle that she wanted to emulate.

She almost laughed through her tears when she turned and heard Ondoni say, "Go back to your babies, Tula."

Maggie shouted, "Shit! She can stay here and talk all night. I'm going back to the card game." She threw open the door to the back room.

"Watch your mouth, Maggie," Ondoni said.

Although his words were calm enough, Tula saw a dangerous, golden spark burn in his deep blue eyes. He was troubled.

"I'm going home with Tula," Andreas said.

"You go to hell!" Tula cried in Greek, her black eyes flashing like hot embers. "Bastard! I wish you were dead!"

Andreas sighed and said, "Please, listen—"

"I'm tired of listening." She clenched her hands. Unable to find any more words, Tula ran out into the night and let the pouring rain wash away her tears.

Chapter 21

The arguments between Tula and Andreas stopped. Tula couldn't argue anymore. A lump would form in her throat, in her mind, in her heart. She couldn't answer the many questions she asked herself, much less what Andreas asked her.

She went back to her books—Alcott, Dickens, Bronte. She continued writing to the phantoms on the screen and was overjoyed when photos came in the mail from Clark Gable, Jean Harlow, Greta Garbo. They were still true to her. She poured her thoughts into her Friendship Book: "I'm trying to be a good mother to my children. They are my first concern now, to see that they grow up and succeed. And someday I will tell them, as well as my students, about the fantasy world of books and the theater."

The love she denied Andreas she gave to her children, to the books, to the films, to the letters.

Leones was not a baby anymore. In a month, he would be five. Tula took him for his first day at Dorr School. It was the second Monday in September 1932, and Tula had overruled her *Mana*. Leones was not going to Socrates School. It was a day of mixed emotions for Tula. She was disappointed that Miss MacMann was not at Dorr, for she had taken a teaching job in Indiana. But she was proud that her son would be attending the school she loved.

Where had the years gone? It was only yesterday that she had shared Photi's lunch. Now her son would be sharing his fried potato sandwich with someone. Tula asked herself, *Am I the only one?* But there was someone else locked in time. Vasso, at nineteen, only spoke when spoken to. She was still obsessed with money, still fearful of men.

On the other hand, Angel, at seventeen, was all that Vasso was not. Angel was happy and a joy to be with. In spite of the attention the young Greek men showered upon Angel, she had fallen in love with an American, Officer Robert O'Brien of the Chicago Police Department. Only Tula knew of their love. Zoe would put a curse on Angel if she found out that Angel's lover was not Greek. Zoe had said, "If any of my daughters marries an Americano, I vow that for every strand of hair on my head, that's how much sorrow and pain I wish on them."

Angel looked to Tula for advice. But the best Tula could do was to listen to Angel and to go with her when she met Robert so that Zoe would not suspect. It was an arrangement the sisters had made when Angel had started seeing him.

Now as the sisters walked into the Hull House courtyard, which had become a favorite meeting place for the lovers, Tula put her hand on Angel's arm. "Don't worry, things will work out. I can't stay too long, got to watch Reni and Goldie sing."

"Yes, it's their rehearsal. I hope things will work out for us," Angel said. And then when she saw Robert, she whispered to Tula in Greek, "Don't tell him about Mana's curse."

Robert walked up to them. "What are you two talking about in Greek? I'm going to crack that code one of these days." Tall, muscular in his uniform, he leaned over to hug Angel. "How are you, honey?"

"Okay," she said. "We were just talking about my mother."

"And when am I going to meet your mother?"

Angel blushed. She turned to her sister. "Tula, tell him about Mana, and why he can't meet her. Not now that is."

Tula glanced from Angel to Robert. "Tell him? Well, let me see. Our mother has this strange idea that her daughters should marry Greeks. Is that what you want me to tell him, Angel?"

Angel nodded.

"You're kidding," Robert said. "You don't think I can charm your mother, change her mind?"

Tula smiled. "I don't know. You've charmed Angel. But right now I've got to watch some talented kids, my sisters I mean, do their song and dance. Can I trust you two, alone?"

Angel giggled.

Robert said, "Trust me."

In a few minutes Tula found a secluded spot in the Hull House Theater and watched as Reni and Goldie performed.

* * *

One morning, Tula decided to visit Andreas at the candy store. She had an idea, and although their relationship was strained, he wouldn't refuse to help Angel, who was his favorite among the sisters. Tula would ask Andreas to talk to her mother about Angel and Robert. He could explain to her that

147

the two young people were in love and that it wasn't a sin for Angel to love an *Americano*. She hurried down to the candy store.

Mr. Pappas was busy at the register when she walked in. He either did not see her or chose to ignore her as he made change for a customer.

Andreas must be in the kitchen making chocolates, she thought. She walked to the rear of the store and pushed open the swinging doors. For a moment she stood in the hallway leading to the kitchen, breathing in the aroma of chocolate and caramel. Then she heard voices, Andreas and someone else, a woman, and she felt a cold shiver go through her. She heard Andreas say, "Maggie, how you make me laugh!"

It's her. Tula threw open the door, rushed up to Andreas, and slapped him hard across the face. "Why are you doing this to me? Why?"

Maggie cowered in a corner and Andreas said, "I want you to know, despite what you think you see here, I am not some monster."

She paused a long time before she spoke. "You make me crazy."

"Make you crazy? Well, Maggie makes me laugh. She's fun to be with. What you see here, you've driven me to."

Was that the truth? Tula thought.

Maggie's eyes avoided Tula's. She stood in her red high heels, her hands on her hips, her red hair hanging loose down her back.

A warm autumn breeze came through the open window. The sun touched the rows of chocolates on the marble table. Stacks of miniature white paper cups and empty candy boxes filled another table. Andreas stood with his arms folded across his chest, a clean white apron wrapped around his waist, an angry red welt beginning to form on his cheek. He rubbed his bruised cheek. "I'm only human. I can just take so much."

"You're my husband," Tula said.

"Maybe—once." His eyes were sad. "We don't have a marriage. Let's face it. We haven't had one for a long time. You wanted me out of your life, out of your bedroom, out of your bed. You had your books, your films. There's not enough love in you for me."

Maggie moved to put her hand on Andreas' shoulder.

"Whore!" Tula screamed. "Keep your hands off my husband!" She lunged at her, making a broad sweep with her hands for that mass of red hair and pulled with vengeance and hate.

Andreas jumped in between them. He pulled Tula away. She fought back, kicking, scratching, punching. And with a force that started them both, Andreas struck Tula across the face. She fell backward, lying on the floor. From somewhere far away she heard herself screaming, and then there was darkness.

They were buzzing around her, their eyes worried. Someone was holding her hand. Someone had a damp cloth on her forehead. From somewhere in the past, she heard Tasso's old Model T forging along past fields of Nebraska wheat. She heard the hooting of an owl. She was running through a field of Black-eyed Susans, arm-in-arm with Andreas, laughing, hugging, kissing. "Black-eyed Susan, here is your flower. Black-eyed Susan, I love you."

At home in the bathroom, Tula wiped her face with a damp cloth, then looked into the mirror. There was a red welt on her cheek where Andreas had struck her, but her eye was not bruised or swollen. Zoe stood silently beside her. When Andreas had brought Tula home an hour ago, Zoe was shocked. He'd left abruptly, saying he had to get back to work.

Now Tula changed her dress, brushed her hair, and said, "I'm going out for a while."

Soon she was at Ondoni's boarding house. Although she had many reasons for not wanting to see Ondoni, she had one good reason to see him: Maggie. She frowned as she walked up the steps to the boarding house. *Is that time in bed so important to Andreas? Is that why he turned to Maggie?* Ondoni would have the answer.

She walked down the hallway. She had the eerie feeling that there were unseen eyes on her. Certainly her reaction was based on nothing more than her own imagination. She should not have come. Her head down, her eyes fastened on the floor, she soon was in front of Ondoni's door. She heard footsteps behind her in the hallway and turned to see Ondoni's highly polished shoes. She wanted to rush into his arms, sobbing, tell him everything. He was her godfather, and he would help her. He would understand. He would solve her problems.

"Tula, what the hell are you doing here?"

"I have to talk to you, privately, not here in the hallway."

"You shouldn't be here. I've business, important business waiting for me in my office." He motioned to the closed door.

"This is important, too. Please, give me a few minutes."

"Come," he said.

She sat in the comfortable leather chair while Ondoni took his place behind the massive desk. Tula saw that the room had changed almost as much as he had. Instead of the metal bed in the corner, there was a blue velvet couch. An oak desk and chair were in the center of the room, and an Oriental rug covered the polished oak floor. The room smelled of fresh paint and new furniture.

How should she begin? "*Nouno*, there is something—I need your help."

"Let me guess, it's about Andreas, right?"

"Yes."

"Tula, are you all right? What happened to your face? Did Andreas do this to you?"

"Yes, that bastard hit me. And that Maggie, she's taking Andreas away from me."

"There is more to it than that, isn't there?"

"What do you mean?"

"I've had talks with Andreas. We don't just play cards at the grocery." Then as if Ondoni could sense her confusion, he spoke, his voice thick with emotion. "Maybe Maggie's gone too far this time. She was a beggar when I found her living on the streets. I took her in, cleaned her up, made her a lady—well, maybe not a lady, but a person." His voice was cold, controlled. "Listen, go home. Don't tell Andreas you were here, understand? Maggie has to be taught a lesson."

"A lesson?" Tula was gripped by fear.

"Maggie is becoming a threat to my family. Here," he said. She felt the glass of *ouzo* her godfather pushed into her hands. She drank most of it in a single swallow. They did not speak. The silence between godfather and goddaughter moved slowly from fear to the awkwardness of unspoken words. Finally, Ondoni broke the silence. "Tula, now I want you to do a favor."

"A favor?"

"That cop, that Robert O'Brien who's been hanging around Angel. That's got to stop. She mustn't see him anymore. Understand?"

"How did you find out about that? Mana doesn't even know."

"I make it my business to know. That cop's got to get out of Angel's life, and right away, do you hear? In my business, it's risky to have a cop that close."

"Your business?"

"Yes, my business. You're a big girl now, Tula. I'm not going to beat around the bush. Your mother was wrong. I'm not an evil man, but I do deal in evil. I make money satisfying other people's vices. I've come up in the world. But enough! I have to protect my territory, and that cop must go. Tell Angel to stay away from him. And don't worry. I'll take care of Maggie."

Chapter 22

Now Tula had another worry besides Andreas and Maggie. Angel and Robert were in love. How could she tell Angel not to see him again?

She knew that Ondoni would keep his word about Maggie. She knew his temper.

She stood in the dark bedroom, not moving, thankful that there wasn't anyone at home, thankful that she did not have to explain to Mana. She looked into the mirror and a drawn, frightened face looked back at her. She had to calm down, control herself. Mana and the children would be back soon. Andreas. Her thoughts would always return to Andreas. *He is seeing another woman because I won't share my bed with him. But sleeping with him means more children. I am not a baby machine.*

An hour later she awoke with a start. When had she fallen asleep? She had been dreaming of Cissy, her little girl. Now calmer, she reached for some paper. When she though of her baby Cissy, she thought of whom she had been named for—her mother, Zoe, not, the mother-in-law she had never seen. She began writing letters to Andreas' mother in Greece when she married Andreas. If nothing else writing letters was therapy for Tula. Her letters were deliberate falsehoods—never hinting of any difficulties or hard times. In her dutiful letters to Andreas' mother, Tula always said she and Andreas were doing well. In one letter, she also wrote about the new President, Franklin D. Roosevelt, inaugurated on March 4, 1932. She wrote of his promise to bring the country back after the crash of 1929, the New Deal he had introduced, and the promise to repeal prohibition which had made him popular. Things looked brighter for them and the country.

On rare occasions when the street photographer came to the neighborhood and Tula had a few extra dimes, the children's picture was taken, and Tula would include these photographs with the letters. Leones was growing, and every day that passed he looked more and more like Andreas. Whenever she mentioned Cissy in the letters, she called her Zoemu, her baptismal name.

One day after mailing a letter at the post office, Tula found Vasso sitting in front of the flat, her purse in her lap, her bank book open. To Tula's astonishment, Vasso was crying; but under those tears her face was set in anger.

"What's wrong, Vasso?" Tula asked.

"I've got no money," Vasso said. "I lost all the money I had in the Atlas Bank when that President Roosevelt closed all the banks today. The President stole my money!"

Tula asked, "How much did you lose?"

"Three hundred and eighty-seven dollars and fifty-two cents."

Tula had never dreamed it would be so much. "I'm so sorry, Vasso," she said. "I wish I could help you."

"The hell with it. The hell with the Atlas Bank!" She ran down the street and disappeared past the crowd of old men coming out of the coffeehouse.

Two weeks later, Tula received a letter from Andreas' mother, and it was all about Ondoni: "What's happening in Chicago? Why is Ondoni coming back to Greece? He said it has something to do with his citizenship—what does he mean? What did he do? My dear Tula, please tell us. Ondoni wrote and wants us to find a place for him in the village."

The kitchen door opened behind her, and Zoe came in. Zoe saw the letter on the table. "Is this a letter from Andreas' *Mana*?"

"Yes. It's about *Nouno* Ondoni. She says he is going back to Greece?"

"Going back to Greece? Good. I pity the people in the village when he goes back. He's evil!" Zoe made a fist and hit the table.

"Mana, don't say that."

Zoe frowned. "Foolish girl, you wouldn't listen to me when I told you not to see him. I didn't want him near us, not his filth. Count your blessings that he is leaving. Think about Andreas. Think about your children."

Tula stood, facing her mother. "Count my blessings? Well, I can count them on two fingers, Leones and Cissy. As for Andreas, he's not a husband to me anymore." She took her coat off the hall tree and raced out of the flat, slamming the door after her. She would get some answers.

* * *

At the police station, she hurried down a corridor and found herself in front of a desk, talking to the day sergeant, asking for Officer Robert O'Brien. The burly red haired sergeant said, "He's just coming off duty. He should be out here in a minute. Well, speak of the devil, here he is now. Hey, O'Brien someone wants to see you."

Tula turned and saw Robert in front of the double doors.

"Tula, what are you doing here?"

She drew her first easy breath. "I have to talk to you. Let's go outside."

"All right." He led her down the steps of the old police station. They walked to a bench a block away and sat down. Tula told him about the letter from Andreas' mother. He listened, eyebrows lifted, attentive.

After Tula had finished telling her story, Robert sighed. "Damn it, Tula, it was Maggie who blew the whistle on Ondoni." He took out a pack of cigarettes and drew out the last one. He crushed the pack , turned, and tossed it into a big barrel beside the bench. He lit the cigarette with a match, pushed the lid of the matchbox shut and held it in his hand.

"Maggie? Why?"

"He had her beaten up."

Tula felt the blood rush to her face.

"I don't know all the details," he began. "She was found in an alley, with a broken jaw and three cracked ribs. They took her to Cook County Hospital. Two days later, her broken jaw wired together, she wrote a note asking to see the district attorney."

"Oh, my God."

"She was hurting, bad," he said. "She wrote everything she knew about Ondoni and the rackets and signed the statement. Maggie named names, gave details."

"She named Ondoni?"

"It took a lot of guts on Maggie's part. Now the DA has promised her protection," Robert said.

"Protection?"

"The DA found out that Ondoni never applied for citizenship, and that's what they got on him—he's an undersirable alien."

Tula's memories of Ondoni flooded her starting with the turquoise shawl. Her *Nouno* had given her courage to go to the casket at her *Baba*'s funeral. Her *Nouno* had given her silver dollars. Her *Nouno* had given her strength to outrun the boys who wanted to jazz her. Her *Nouno* had given her the Friendship Book.

And he had Maggie beaten. Because of her. Did Andreas know?

"Would you like me to take you home?" Robert asked gently.

"I'm okay, honest. I'll just sit here for a while." He left her sitting on the bench, confused, her body trembling.

* * *

That evening, Tula waited for Andreas to come home. She had a lot to say to him. She paced the kitchen. Where was he? She heard a soft knocking on the kitchen door. "Who is it?"

"Andreas. I forgot my key."

Tula waited for a few minutes, then opened the door. "We must talk," she said quietly.

"Yes, we have to talk. I can't go on like this any longer," he said. He poured himself a cup of coffee and sat across from her at the kitchen table.

Tula sat down. "I got a letter from your *Mana*. She wrote that Ondoni is going back to Greece. Did you know?"

Andreas nodded. "Yes, I know."

"And?"

"I want to talk about *us*. Do you understand? Ondoni, too, but about us first. Please, listen," he said.

"I'm listening."

"After you found Maggie and me in the candy store kitchen, I told her we were through. I made the decision not to see her again—ever. I realized you and the kids are my life. Then I went to Ondoni, told him, and he laughed at me. He said I didn't have to worry about Maggie, he had her taken care of. I soon found out what he meant. He took care of her, all right, sent her to the hospital. I went to the hospital to see her. She lay like a wounded animal in bed, her jaw wired, her ribs cracked. She didn't want me to see her like that, she didn't want me to know. Then I got mad, real mad, and went back to Ondoni's to teach that bastard a lesson. I couldn't get in, his men were all around. But I have a score to settle with him."

Tula muttered, "I didn't want this to happen. I didn't wish this on Maggie."

Andreas flinched. "I know." He put his hand on her shoulder, bowed his head, and murmured in a low voice. "Black-eyed Susan, please forgive me. I was a fool to put you through this. I know what I did was wrong. I love you and our children. Please take me back."

"You hurt me, Andreas. I was like a madwoman when I went to Ondoni. I regret going to him. I didn't know he could be so cruel." She looked into Andreas' eyes and saw pain. Should she forgive him?

"Let's go to our room," Andreas said.

Tula felt lightheaded. He took her hand to guide her. So much time had passed since she'd allowed him to touch her, to possess her.

Andreas gently lifted Leones from their bed where the child was sleeping and put him in the other room with Cissy. When he returned, he locked the door and turned to Tula. He kissed her. Had she been waiting for his kisses? Why all of a sudden did she have no fear. She was safe. He would protect her.

"Do you know what this means to me?" He lifted her and put her on the bed. As he removed her clothing and it fell to the floor, her body felt warm, tingling. Andreas caressed her with surprising tenderness. His motions were slow and hesitant. *He is afraid*, thought Tula.

"Come, Andreas, make love to me." She saw how her words stunned him, and then he smiled, a broad smile.

Chapter 23

Tula paced back and forth across Chicago's Canal Street Bridge. The weather had grown cold as it sometimes does in October, and the mist that enveloped the city showed no sign of dissipating. She shivered, pulled her worn turquoise shawl tightly against her black dress, and glanced over her shoulder. The day before, she had received an urgent call from Ondoni to meet him on the bridge. Where was he?

When a car slowed before crossing the bridge, its wheels rattling the old wooden timbers, her steps quickened toward it. She peered into the semidarkness, her black eyes reflecting the late afternoon light. *No, that's not him.*

Ondoni had said, "There'll be stories about me in tomorrow's newspapers. I'll explain. Meet me on the bridge at six-thirty. That's the last place reporters will look for me." Now on the dock, laborers in overalls and longshoremen in bulky clothes and rubber boots joked and laughed as their shift ended. A low whistle from one of them caught Tula by surprise. With back erect and shoulders squarely set, she was determined to defend herself, if only with her rolled-up newspaper. She wasn't a child. She was twenty-two, a woman. As she caught the laborer's eye, he gave her a broad smile and a tip of his cap that unmistakably said, *I mean no harm.* She walked toward the center of the bridge, intensely aware of the smells that filtered up through the old boards— fish, crude oil, engine fumes. She glanced down at the water, tried to see the rock, the boulder she and Photi had claimed, the boulder Photi flew from, like a soaring bird that day he drowned.

She unrolled the newspaper. "West Side Gangster to be Deported." The front page showed an old passport photo of Ondoni Kolvas when he was a teenager, twenty-two years ago. He appeared thin, frightened, his unruly blond hair falling across his forehead. She wasn't certain that the newspaper stories about Ondoni were true. She wanted to hear it from him. In her mind she could hear her mother saying in Greek, "*kakos anthropos,*" evil man.

Pacing back and forth with a copy of the Chicago Herald rolled up as a weapon, she waited for him. She glanced at her watch, the gold one he had given her as a gift for her name day last year. Where was he? She tried to see beyond the bridge, but the city was now hidden by a shroud. Mist had surrounded the docks and the warehouses.

A huge dark car pulled to a stop in the narrow street. What she saw, then, was, first a pair of fine leather boots extending from the vehicle's open rear door, next gray trousers with a sharp crease, and finally a velvet-collared gray flannel coat. Ondoni emerged from the backseat and the driver jumped out and stood guard in front of the car. Ondoni paused for a moment to light a cigarette and glance around.

Then he came to her, smiling, with a nosegay of violets in his hands. "For you."

She had waited too long and was angry now. She tossed the flowers. She glared up, waving the newspaper in his face. "What's this? Explain?"

"Oh, my Tula," he said, embracing her, kissing her on both cheeks. "My godchild. I *can* explain." He took her hand and walked to the railing. For several moments she stared at the water. She didn't know what to do. So she turned her attention back to the newspaper. The story said that Ondoni was the boss of Chicago's biggest mob, the notorious West Side gang.

"It is true," Tula said, handing him the newspaper, her anger spent.

"Yes. They made me an offer, either deportation or Joliet Prison."

His frank remark shocked her. "Prison?"

He nodded. "I made my first mistake a long time ago by not becoming an American citizen. I wasn't going to stay here, so why bother? I was going to make my fortune and get out—go back to the old country and live like a king. Instead, I got involved, got greedy."

"Mana was right?"

"Yes, your *Mana* was right. She denied me as a brother a long time ago— when your father died." He leaned on the rail and looked out onto the water. Suddenly, forcefully, he said, "I tried to make amends, to help with money. But she refused to take it. I knew I did wrong taking money from your *Baba* when I was working for him. But things happen. We can't go back and right the wrong. Maybe I'll be better off in Greece, climbing the mountains, working in the vineyards. There are old friends in the village. My friends in Chicago have run out on me. Maybe for the good, they're too powerful, and I don't want to be at the bottom of this lake tied to a cement block. You're the only friend I've got Tula. I want to hear from you. Write to me, promise."

"Yes, I will."

He began to speak rapidly in Greek. "I was at one time honest, decent, of good character, and now I'm a criminal—"

Tula heard only a little of what he said. Her Greek was more than adequate but she had difficulty following when it was spoken so rapidly.

"Maybe with me gone, things will be better," he was saying now. "Maybe you will be able to reach your dream."

He took Tula by the arm and led her toward the man who stood beside the car waiting for him. "I wanted to see you one more time," he said. "I'm glad we talked. You are my family." He embraced her. "I must go."

She nodded. He got into the car, and it pulled away.

Part IV

The whole earth sobbed.
The Odyssey

Chapter 24

Tula sat in the kitchen and carefully brushed Leones' cowboy hat. She unpinned the sheriff's badge from his plaid shirt and set it on the table to be polished. The toy gun and holster were draped over a chair. A carved pumpkin was on the table.

This routine of getting Leones and Cissy ready for the Halloween party at Hull House made her feel happy.

"It's my birthday!" Leones said. He turned and hit Cissy in the chest. "Take that, you dumb clown." Cissy began to cry and rubbed her eyes, smearing her clown makeup.

"Don't hit your sister," Tula said, taking Cissy in her arms. "Don't cry honey. Here, let me fix your makeup. I'll never get you two ready for the party. Are the balloons in your bedroom? Cissy, did you wrap your present for Leones?"

"Yes-s-s."

"I'm six! I'm six! I'm getting presents!"

"Hush, Leones." Tula turned as the kitchen door opened and there they were, two Keystone Kops. Angel's blond hair was tucked into the bowl-shaped hat, and her face glowed as brightly at the brass buttons on her uniform. Robert's freshly cut hair smelled of barber tonic. He carried his helmet under his arm, striking a pose.

"How do we look?" he asked.

Tula leaned back and eyed them fondly. "You both look great. You're sure to win for best costumes at the Policemen's Ball."

Angel smiled at her sister. "Your kids look pretty good, too. Are they going to Hull House?"

Tula nodded while she fixed Cissy's makeup.

"Yes, and I'm going to have a birthday party there, too, I'm six, you know," Leones said. "How do you like my gun? Bang, bang!"

Robert shook his head. "Don't shoot a cop, Leones, that's bad news." And then he laughed and picked up the boy. "So you want to be a sheriff."

"Yes, and I wanna see your gun, a real gun."

"Nope, that's not a plaything, and I don't show it. Sorry, buddy."

Angel said, "I must be hungry or something because I can smell that spicy sausage from the Italian carnival. Let's go on the porch and watch. We've got time before the ball, and you said Mana won't be back for an hour or so, didn't you?"

"Yes, the coast is clear." Angel was still keeping Robert a secret from Zoe. After Tula measured coffee into the pot, she busied herself arranging biscuits on a plate. "I got a letter from Ondoni."

"What's he say?" Robert asked.

"He's working in the vineyards, just what he's wanted to do. And he's even climbed a mountain. He said he's turning into a real villager. He sounds happy."

"Then he doesn't blame me for getting deported?" Robert asked.

"I think he blames himself more than anyone." She reached into the cupboard and took out some cups. Leones crept up beside Tula and untied her apron. She flinched. "Don't do that! I almost dropped the coffee cups!"

"My, you're jumpy," Angel said. "What's the matter?"

"I don't know, must be all this Halloween stuff," she said. "The goblins are getting to me."

"Come out to the porch with us, get some fresh air," Angel said.

Leones ran up. "Want to see our b-a-l-l-o-o-n-s?" He spelled out the word. "See, I can spell, good, too. Want to see them? They're in the bedroom."

Angel laughed. She spelled, "S-u-r-e. I'm glad we're getting another champion speller in the family." Then to Robert, she said, "You go on outside. I have to see the kids' balloons. I'll meet you on the porch."

"Fine," he said. "Tula will keep me company."

"Right," Tula said. She carried a tray with coffee cups and a plate of biscuits. The hallway was dimly lit by a bare bulb in the ceiling. Ahead of them, taking up one wall, was a curtain stretcher with lace curtains stretched taut on it. Robert eased around the stretcher and opened the door to the porch. A beam of light spilled into the hallway.

At that moment, Tula noticed a shadowy figure in the vacant building across the alley. And then, in the fraction of a second before anything happened, Tula knew that Robert was a dead man. She watched, numb, as the shadow took aim and opened fire. The shots caught Robert in the face and neck, and his body spilled onto the porch. The music from the merry-go-round below drowned out the gun's explosions. The shadowy figure across the alley disappeared.

Tula dropped the tray, the coffee spilling on Robert. She screamed. Angel

161

ran to his side, crying, "No! No!" She knelt down beside him. She clutched his hand, her nails deep in his skin, and then she glanced down and saw the white marks, the little arcs in his skin where her nails had dug.

"You're all I've ever wanted," she said looking into the bloodied face. "Oh, God, please bring him back," she gasped, wiping tears from her eyes with a trembling hand. "Mana! Mana, your curse worked!"

"Don't," Tula said. "Don't say that!" Tula began to shiver. How cold it had become. "We've got to call the police," she said. "We've got to get some help."

Dazed Angel cradled Robert's bloodied head in her arms. She was muttering. "We mustn't tell Mana about us. You're not Greek. And Mana will put a curse on us. She will. She will."

Chapter 25

On Blue Island Avenue, every event was noticed by the women peering from windows and the old men lounging behind the doors in the coffeehouse and grocery store. And so the day after Officer Robert O'Brien's death when an unmarked police car stopped in front of Tula's flat, everyone knew about it in a matter of minutes.

Tula was also peering between the lace curtains in the parlor. She had been reading the Chicago Tribune: "Policeman Gunned Down in Gang Slaying." She read the front-page story several times, not wanting to believe it. She was not surprised when the police car came to a stop in front of the flat. Two men got out, big, burly men who looked like movie gangsters themselves. She was sure they had come to question her about Robert's death, and she didn't want them talking to her mother. She wouldn't understand. Tula got to the kitchen door just as she heard their knock and she called to Zoe, who was in her bedroom. "I'll get it." She opened the door.

"I'm Detective William Doyce from Precinct 22," one of the men said. He motioned to the other. "This is my partner, Detective Swanson. Are you Tula Korinthes?"

Tula nodded. Doyce said, "May we come in and talk to you for a few minutes? It's about Officer Robert O'Brien."

Zoe appeared in the kitchen. "What do these men want?" she said in Greek.

Tula said in Greek, "They're policemen and want to ask me about Robert."

Detective Doyce glanced at Zoe and said to Tula, "We'd like to talk to you alone, will that be a problem?"

Tula shook her head, then spoke to Zoe in Greek.

Zoe said, "All right. Call me if you need me."

Tula nodded and said to the men. "Please sit down."

They sat uncomfortably on the kitchen chairs. Tula sat facing them, her hands on the table. Detective Doyce opened the conversation by saying, "We knew Officer O'Brien and your sister were seeing each other for some time. When they were here yesterday did you notice anything suspicious? Did you see anything, anyone?"

"Across the alley, in that vacant building, all I saw was a man in the shadows," Tula said. "I didn't see his face—"

"No description? Not even how tall he was?"

Tula sat up very straight in the chair. "No."

The other detective said in a harsh voice. "We know all about your uncle, Ondoni Kolvas. We know about his contacts, before he left the States. If you help these contacts in any way, you may be getting in very serious trouble. Understand?"

"Why would I help them? They killed Robert, and my sister is sick—she can't get over his death, she won't believe it. What are you saying?"

Detective Doyce asked gently, "Is she here? We'd like to ask her a few questions."

"No. She won't talk to anyone!"

"Maybe she can come down to the station later, when she's feeling better. The sooner we talk to her, the sooner we'll be able to clear this up. Someone killed a police officer, and that someone has to pay." He chewed on his lower lip. "Let us know if anyone contacts you. Anyone, and that means your uncle, too."

"But he's in Greece. He doesn't know about this—"

"Don't' be too sure about that," Doyce said.

Tula looked at him, astonished. Then she got up and went to the door. "You'll have to go now," she said.

Tula closed the door on their backs firmly. Zoe came into the kitchen. At the stove, she heated the coffee and took no notice of Tula's weeping. She poured Tula a cup, poured one for herself, and guided Tula to a chair.

"Too bad. That man of Angel's was good. Too bad he was killed," Zoe said. She made the sign of the cross.

Tula looked up in surprise. "How did you know about Robert?"

Her mother said complacently, "Angel thought she was so clever. I've known about him all along. Sophie told me, the neighbors told me, the men at the coffeehouse told me. But of course, I couldn't bring it up, not until Angel did. And now it is too late." She pulled a black-bordered handkerchief from her pocket and wiped the tears from her eyes.

* * *

Robert's funeral made the front page of the *Chicago Tribune*.

The mayor and other dignitaries attended, but Angel could not. The next day, she quit her job at the ice cream factory. She shut herself in her room. "Leave me alone!" she said. She wouldn't eat, wouldn't talk. Even Leones and Cissy could not bring a smile to Angel's face.

Day after day Tula tried with no success. Finally after a month had gone by she walked into Angel's room and said, "Angel, this has got to stop. We're worried sick about you."

"Don't worry," Angel said. "I'm okay."

"Please, can we talk?"

"Sure. What do you want to talk about? Mana's curse? What did she say? For every hair on her head, that's how much pain and sorrow she wished me."

"No. You're wrong. She didn't mean that. She would have loved Robert, if she had known him. Angel, don't do this to yourself."

"Did I ever tell you how much we loved each other? Did I ever tell you he didn't want me to be afraid? But we mustn't tell Mana about him. Never!"

Tula turned away from Angel's ravaged face. "Angel, please, don't do this to yourself."

"Get out of here!"

Sighing, Tula walked out of the room.

* * *

In April 1935, six months after Robert's death, the killer had not been caught, and the *Tribune* featured the story as 'the unsolved murder of the year." Tula flipped through the newspaper. On the front page was a story about the new Civilian Conservation Corps: "When he was elected, President Roosevelt promised, 'Nobody is going to starve.' Now, two years later, the whole country is involved in an effort that promises to restore confidence and economic well being to the country. Economic well being. No one will starve."

And in the bedroom, her sister Angel was starving herself, Tula thought.

One morning after Angel had refused the breakfast Tula brought to her room, Tula called for Dr. Voles to come.

"She won't eat," Tula said. "We can't force her to eat. She just takes a bit and says she's not hungry."

"Here, let me take your pulse," Dr. Voles said to Angel. Gently he reached for her wrist. He lifted one eyebrow in alarm. "Hmmm," he said. "Let's take a look at you." He raised her blouse and saw how thin she had become. He placed his stethoscope to her back and said, "How did this happen? She's just skin and bones."

"She just won't eat," Tula said.

Dr. Voles said, "She needs food. She's starving herself. We'll have to get her into a hospital."

"I don't want her in hospital," Zoe said.

Angel stood up. "No, I don't want to eat. I can't eat. There is this noise in my head. It won't stop. Make it stop. Please."

"I'll try," Dr. Voles said. "But you must help me, Angel. You've got to eat something. Tell me, when did this noise start?"

"A long time ago—when Robert was on the porch watching the carnival—there was this terrible explosion." She sobbed and flung herself across the bed.

Dr. Voles wrote a prescription and gave it to Tula. "Here, get this filled. It's a sedative—it will calm her down. And see that she eats. If she hasn't eaten well in a week, I'll have to put her in the hospital."

The day before Dr. Voles' second visit, Angel walked into the kitchen where Tula sat along at the table.

"Tula, why hasn't Robert called me? Why?"

"Angel, sit down, let me pour you some coffee."

Angel began to cry. "It's because of Mana, isn't it? Because of Mana's curse." She looked around the kitchen. "He's not going to call, is he?"

"No, he's not. Robert's dead, Angel."

Following that conversation, Angel came out of her room during the day. She began to eat. There were no more outbursts of crying or screaming in the night. Vasso, who shared a bedroom with her, said she slept well. Angel did not mention Robert, and the others followed her lead and did not bring up his name. When Reni and Goldie sang their songs, Angel listened and smiled her approval. When Leones and Cissy brought out their storybooks, she read to them. Tula wanted Angel back, the Angel she had always known, the Angel she loved. A month passed, and Angel was getting better.

One night, Tula slept soundly next to Andreas. A light touch brushed her cheeks, enough to startle her awake. Her hand went up to her face and came in contact with someone's cold fingers. A voice whispered in her ear, "Be quiet. I'm leaving. I'm going to him."

Tula gasped. "Angel? Wait!" She sat up in bed and turned on the lamp. Angel, a knife in her hand, darted out of the room. Tula jumped out of bed, raced across the room and flung open the door. There was no one there. Was it a dream? She shook Andreas.

"What's the matter?" he asked, rubbing his eyes.

She told him what had happened. "Are you sure it was Angel? Are you sure she had a knife?"

"Yes, she's going to hurt herself. We've got to help her."

Zoe burst into the room, her black eyes wide with fright. "It's Angel. She's got a knife. God help us. She ran downstairs."

A sleepy Vasso followed close behind Zoe. "I'm calling the police. Angel's crazy."

"Listen," Andreas began. "She's not crazy. She's been through hell. All of you stay here. I'll get her. Make sure the kids are okay and stay in the flat, Tula."

"No, I'm coming with you." She raced down the stairs and outside after her sister. Tula saw her under a lamppost. In the light of the full moon, her hair appeared so blonde, almost white. Her unblinking eyes sparkled. The soft white cotton gown clung to her thin body. She sliced the air with the knife. She shouted wild nonsense.

Windows flew open, filled with curious faces. "Shut up. We want to sleep!" shouted the fat man, leaning over his windowsill.

"Call the police!" shouted another.

"She needs a padded cell," said still another.

"Bitches, bastards!" Angel cried, pointing her knife at the faces in the windows.

Tula walked slowly, her heart pounding. Angel spun around and faced Tula. Her gray eyes started at her. "Stay away from me, bitch!"

"Get away from her, Tula, she'll hurt you," Andreas said.

In an instant, Tula was beside her, and she raised her hand to grab the knife. *I've got it!* Tula thought, but before she could wrestle it from Angel's hand, the knife ripped into her own hand. Tula froze. She'd never expected Angel to stab her. Dazed, shocked she saw the gash in her hand. She fought with Angel under the lamppost and again felt the flashing blade of the knife on her hand.

Andreas grabbed Angel by the arm and twisted the knife out of her grip. It skidded across the street and bumped to a stop at the curb. Angel's legs went limp, and Andreas caught her.

A siren ripped the quiet, and a police car pulled up. Two officers jumped from the car and rushed to Andreas and Angel. One of them spotted Tula and her bleeding hand and reached into the backseat of the squad car for a first aid kit. "Here, let me help you."

"Angeleke!" Zoe screamed, rushing to her side. "My baby, my baby!"

"Get away from me, old witch. Get away from me!"

"Please don't call your *Mana* such names," Zoe said.

Angel spit in her face. "You're not my *Mana*. You're a witch. Your curses work! You're a witch!" Then she grabbed a handful of Zoe's hair and pulled.

The policeman got between Zoe and Angel, grabbed Angel, braced her against the side of the squad car, and handcuffed her. "Take it easy, girlie," the officer said.

An ambulance turned the corner and came to a stop. The white-coated driver jumped out. "What's the problem?"

"This young lady's been cutting up people with a knife. Help that other one over there. She's got a mean cut. We've got the one who knifed her shackled. She ain't going no place."

While one attendant bandaged Tula's wounds, another approached Angel. The men led her to the ambulance. Angel screamed. She spit at them.

"The little lady's getting' rough, eh?" the officer said. Tula and Andreas watched helplessly as the men lifted Angel, kicking and screaming into the ambulance. As the ambulance drove away, Zoe wailed.

* * *

Tula willed herself to remain calm as they walked up to the mental patients' floor of the sprawling redbrick, hospital building. Andreas walked ahead and motioned for Tula and Zoe to hurry. They entered an office and the doctor left his desk and came over to them. He held a folder in his hand. Tula concentrated on his eyes. Behind the glasses, they were bright blue. Tula and Andreas began asking questions. "What's wrong with Angeleke? When can she come home? Is she all right? Why did she act that way?"

For a long time the doctor was silent.

Tula looked at the doctor. "When can we take her home?"

"We know for certain, she can't leave today," began the doctor. "Angeleke is a very sick young lady. She's had a breakdown. She must remain here for the time being. We can help her. We can't tell at this stage how long she will be here. But her mother must sign these release papers before we can treat her. And she must get treatment, right away."

Zoe said, "I will never sign, never." She spoke in Greek, and Andreas told the doctor what she had said.

"I'm sorry," the doctor said. "But if she doesn't sign, we have to resort to other measures."

Zoe dabbed at her eyes. "No, never."

"Maybe if you see Angeleke," the doctor began. "Then your mother can see she needs care."

Tula nodded, "Yes, we want to see Angel."

Tula, Andreas, and Zoe followed the doctor down the corridor to a room with bars on the doors. He used a key to get in. On the bed lay Angel, in a straitjacket. She stared blankly at the ceiling, damp tendrils of blond hair on her forehead, her eyes glazed.

Tula gasped at the sight, but it was the smell that got to her—vomit, disinfectant and urine.

"Angel!" Zoe cried. "What have they done to you, my baby?"

Angel turned her face, her skin as white as the sheets, her breath coming out in short gasps, her body rigid, legs caught in a tangle of sheets.

Tula ran to her sister's side, but the doctors barred the way with his arm. "No. Don't touch her," he said.

Tula wept for the Angel who would not know the love of a man. She wept for Mana who must forever carry the guilt of the curse. She wept for herself, who would have to do without the only sister who cared. And she cried because for the first time she had seen madness. It could take over someone as gentle and kind as Angel.

Chapter 26

There was no Angel to welcome home from work, no Angel to read to Leones and Cissy, no Angel to encourage Reni and Goldie in their singing. The house contained three forlorn women, bored with their routine, involved in their own thoughts as they sipped their coffee on this Saturday morning. Vasso, ever restless, put her coffee cup on the table and paced around the kitchen. Zoe studied the coffee grounds in the bottom of her cup. Tula looked out the window to see Leones and Cissy playing on the sidewalk while Reni and Goldie watched them.

"Can't we *do* something?" Vasso whined, rushing to the window as though she expected to see the blazing sun hide behind a dark cloud. "This must be the hottest July of the century."

"Go for a walk, or go watch the kids with Reni. It's too hot to move," Tula said, fanning herself with a newspaper.

"Girls, girls, please—" Zoe implored.

Tula watched Vasso rush out the door. She finished her coffee and glanced at her mother sitting alone at the table, her mouth moving silently. At first Tula thought she was praying, and then she realized her mother was not talking to God but discussing her problems with Baba. Tula strained to hear. "Why is Vasso so angry? Why is Angel sick? What can I do for Tula? Please tell me."

Tears stung Tula's eyes.

"Tula, a letter for you from Greece!" Thea Sophie burst through the door and shouted, startling Zoe and Tula.

Tula jumped and went to the door. "From Ondoni?" She looked at Mana.

"Go. Go read your letter," Zoe said. "Thea Sophie and I have much to talk about."

Tula raced out of the room, ripped open the envelope and read:

"I've been working for Andreas' younger brother, Petro. He's mayor of the town, and I must tend his vineyards while he governs. I spend my time in the field. The grapes are plump and ripe. They shine with the morning sun. It is backbreaking work.

"I think my coming back to Greece was not by chance. I belong here. I've

170

got a dog, or rather the dog has me. It found me at the village square and followed me home. I call him Phelo, which you know means 'friend.' I've also adopted a donkey. Don't laugh. You know how much I loved cars, but now my donkey, Homer, is my transportation. I call him Homer because I think he's blind. We are a mangy group, a scared dog, a blind donkey and me.

"Only once did I leave the village for a trip to Athens to see the Acropolis. I walked the slippery rough stones to the Parthenon and strolled to the Porch of Maidens and stared at the marble maidens and thought of you. Later I walked through the crowded streets of Athens. I spent time in the marketplace. A vendor forced a garlic clove on me, the smell making my eyes water. He said one clove would protect me from the evil eye. I didn't tell him that I needed more than one clove.

"As for evil deeds, I cried when I heard what evil spirits had done to Angel's mind. I can't write your mother, although I tried. But as God is my witness, I had nothing to do with that policeman's death. Please believe me, my goddaughter.

"I want to ask your forgiveness for not being a proper godfather to you. For not seeing that you got an education and could attain your goal to become a teacher. Hold on to your dream! And forgive me for getting Andreas involved with Maggie. I never meant that to happen. Do you remember Homer's *Odyssey*? Do you remember how Penelope, the wife of Odysseus, waited years for his return? I think of you as Penelope waiting for Andreas. I know it's too late for me, but it's not too late for you, my godchild.

"I've found some sort of peace here in the village, in the vineyard, in the mountains. I didn't find it in Athens, where I had the feeling something terrible was about to happen, as it has done in Germany with that man Hitler running the country. He is the true gangster. And it is happening in Italy, too. But in the village I find peace.

"I will close now my dear godchild.

"My love always, Ondoni."

Sighing, Tula put the letter back in the envelope. She believed him when he wrote he was not responsible for Robert's death. He would not lie to her.

Chapter 27

Tula had assumed that Angel would be cured in a short time. But it had been six months. It was only when she received a letter from the hospital stating that Angel was scheduled to receive a series of electrical shock treatments that Tula realized that it would be a long time before their Angel would return.

She wrote in the Friendship Book: "I saw Angel for the first time after her treatments. She no longer needs the restraint of a straitjacket. She no longer screams. She no longer whines. She just sits quietly in her room and stares out the window. Our Angel is gone."

Tula's own life was at loose ends. She took things as they came and trusted that for every disappointment there was an equal balance of good fortune. But the good fortune was long in coming, and with two children to feed she could stand some security. She asked only for some good years for her children. Leones was a loveable child, with strong enthusiasms and a passion for his Yiayia Zoe. He learned every word of Greek Zoe would teach him. He took the instruction seriously, and he started memorizing some of Homer's poems in the original Greek. As for Cissy, more and more she resembled her mother. Only five, Cissy sat and read the picture books Tula got from the library.

"She's another Tula," Zoe would often say.

Now only Andreas and Vasso were bringing in money, and Vasso resented turning most of her paycheck to Zoe. Tula could still hear Vasso's voice. "I'm tired of supporting you and your brats. Angel took the easy way out. And you and Mana crocheting those stupid lace collars and making me sell them to my friends in the factory, I'm sick of it!"

From the moment Tula got up in the mornings, she thought of nothing else but their lack of money. Bills, bills, and now they had another burden, another bill, Angel's hospital bill. Tula thought that if she didn't stop thinking about the bills, she too would go insane.

And lately Sophie was not as prompt with her rent. Sometimes she neglected paying rent for two, three months. But Zoe wouldn't say anything to her dear friend.

Movies were luxuries now, but on some days, Tula walked to the Hull House library. It was the most soothing remedy available for her problems and worries. Books soothed her, thick and thin, bound in everything from mellow golden leather to cheap cardboard. She chose *Moby Dick*, a rich purple tome with heavy gold-stamped lettering and thick pages that smelled of mellow paper. Next she discovered a collection of Robert Browning's poetry. To be thorough, she snagged a couple of biographies and historical novels. Before long, there would be too many selections to fit in her sack.

In the library's semi-gloom, Tula thought about Andreas and their flat. The neighborhood was already a land of ghosts its men out of work, many of them gone to another part of the city or to another city where they could earn money and escape the poverty of Blue Island Avenue.

On her long walks to the library, Tula saw the apple vendors on each corner and men begging on the streets. Sometimes she walked as far as the Canal Street Bridge, and spent hours looking down into the water.

* * *

One morning, Vasso was rushing around getting ready for work. Andreas stood in front of the kitchen window sipping his coffee. The scent of freshly baked bread filled the kitchen. Leones and Cissy giggled at the table, happy as the bright new day. They munched on thick slices of bread. Tula smiled. And then she saw Vasso reach across the table, snatch a slice of bread, and tuck it into a napkin.

"Think my kids will eat all the bread?" Tula asked. "Is that why you're hiding it?"

"No!"

"Here, take some more, take two, three slices!" She threw the bread at Vasso.

"Stop it!" Zoe said.

"I've had enough of this bickering," Andreas said. He picked up his hat and left the flat, slamming the door after.

"See what you've done?" Zoe frowned. "You two must stop fighting. Be thankful we *have* bread. We are a family."

"We're not a family." Vasso spit the words out. "And as for Andreas, he's always leaving. You never know where he's at, do you?" She glared at Tula.

"Keep your nose out of my business," Tula hissed.

Cissy began to cry. Leones shook his head, a bite of bread caught between his teeth. "Don't cry, Cissy."

A knock at the door halted the argument.

"It's me Sophie, open up."

Sophie blushed as she entered the room. "I didn't mean to interrupt your breakfast. I'll come back later."

"No, no," Zoe said. "Please sit down. Tula, get a cup of coffee for Sophie."

Maybe she's come to pay the rent, thought Tula, getting up.

"Thank you, yes, that sounds good. I've come to tell you about Mr. Pappas."

"What about him?" Tula asked.

"Mr. Pappas came to see me last night. His talk confused me. Mixed up my head." She made a gesture toward her head. Then she asked, "Is Andreas here?"

Tula shook her head and was surprised at the look of relief on the old woman's face. "Good."

Sophie said that when Mr. Pappas came to her door, he was with another man, an *Americano*. They asked her about her income, about the insurance her departed husband had left her. They asked about Andreas and if he collected rent from her every month. Sophie blushed. "I know that sometimes I'm late with the rent, and sometime you overlook it altogether," she said.

"We are friends," Zoe said.

Sophie made the sign of the cross on her chest. "Yes, dear God, we are good friends."

It was after Zoe offered Sophie another cup of coffee that she continued. Mr. Pappas had informed her that from now on he would collect the rent. He said that Andreas had not been paying on the promissory note, and that he, Mr. Pappas, was the owner of the flats. She was made to understand that if she told anyone that he had been to her flat, she would meet with some misfortune. Sophie's hands shook as she told Zoe she could not keep her word. She had to tell her good friend, Zoe.

"Don't worry, Sophie, he won't harm you."

After Sophie left, Tula asked Zoe. "What can we do?"

Zoe said, "Nothing. Too many things are happening. What next? God help us."

The next week, on September 15, the Holy Day of the Cross, Zoe and Sophie took the children to church. Tula sat alone in the kitchen, listlessly crocheting. Her cup of coffee, untouched had grown cold on the table. The telephone rang and rang. *Maybe it's Andreas*, thought Tula as she rose to

174

answer it.

"Hello?" There was static, and above the static a voice, faint, distant, asked, "Is this Tula Korinthes?"

"Yes," she said.

"This is the overseas operator. We have a call for you from Greece." Above the static, the heavy-accented voice spoke rapidly while Tula was still assimilating the fact that it wasn't Andreas calling. "You can go ahead," said the operator.

"Tula? This is Andreas' *Mana*. Is that you, Tula?"

The voice was choppy, faint, breathless with urgency.

Tula's eyes open wide. "Andreas' Mana?"

"Yes, I'm calling about Ondoni."

Tula clutched the phone and leaned against the solid support the wall offered. "What about Ondoni?" She bit her lip. Her hands trembled.

"Oh, Tula, my Tula." There was a moan, a gasp. "O-ndoni is dead!"

"What happened?"

The crackling static muffled her words. "Some shepherds found his body at dawn at the foot of the mountain. His neck was broken, he fall from a great height."

"But he was a good climber."

"I know," the voice said. "Poor Ondoni! He had some visitors from America last week. They kept to themselves, only talked to Ondoni. They left yesterday afternoon."

"From America? From Chicago?" asked Tula.

"Yes." And then the old woman sobbed.

"The priest will pray for his soul, my Tula. Good-bye, child."

"Good-bye." Tears welled in her eyes. Now she had lost Ondoni, too. She ran out the flat down the stairs without looking back. She turned onto Halsted Street, and the sun blasted her full in the face. As she ran her throat felt full of dust, and sweat ran down into her eyes. She stopped to wipe her face with the back of her hand, and suddenly was too weary to run anymore. Taking a deep breath, she started moving slowly down Halsted Street to Ondoni's boarding house. Lies! All Lies! Ondoni is not dead! She looked up and saw that the white sky had filled with wind clouds, and behind, looming high and dark and threatening, were black ones rushing toward the sun. When she approached the door of the boarding house there was an eerie silence all around her. It was going to storm. She must get into Ondoni's house. The first raindrop his her face, cool, soothing.

She could see the storm coming, sweeping across the street like a great silver sheet. She pounded on the door. "Let me in!" The thunder clapped so loudly that she felt she had been slammed against a brick wall. Tula fell to her knees and hugged herself. The noise that followed was like nothing she had ever heard, a clap of thunder so loud that she toppled over. There was no one to catch her as she slid to unconsciousness.

Chapter 28

She looked up into a pair of concerned eyes. Someone had put a cold cloth on her forehead, and she was sitting on a chair in the kitchen of Mana's flat. Zoe held her hand, while Sophie hovered.

"I'm all right," Tula said. In halting sentences, Tula told them about Ondoni and the call from Greece.

Zoe held her fist up to her mouth, her eyes wide with grief. Sophie let out a long, raspy moan and made the sign of the cross. She sighed, "My poor friend. You have lost your only brother." She offered Zoe some water.

* * *

Later, although it was only nine o'clock, Tula had gone to bed hoping that sleep would dull the pain. Instead, she lay wide-eyed, staring at the ceiling. From the kitchen, she could hear her mother's sobs.

Then she heard footsteps outside the bedroom door. Andreas came in, sad-faced. "My Tula," he said. He kissed her wet cheeks and held her until she stopped crying. They sat on the edge of the bed.

"Ondoni is dead! Say it's just a nightmare."

He looked at her. "You loved Ondoni very much, didn't you!"

"No! I hated him, hated him." She moved away from him, across the room to the window seat and sat down.

"You're lying."

"Y-Yes." She buried her face in her hands, rocked back and forth. "Yes, yes."

"Black-eyed Susan, I know what's in your heart. Be still. You must rest."

She stretched out on the bed, feeling lightheaded, as he removed her slippers and then his shoes and lay beside her. He held her. Andreas' concern seemed to restore her sanity. Yes, Andreas cared for her. The strong rhythm of his heartbeat in her ear lulled her, calmed her, soothed her. She was tired, very tired. He held her face and kissed her mouth, brushing it tenderly, and she responded, forgetting her pain, her sorrow.

Her body ached for him. In the dark room, he undressed her. She surrendered all her qualms and fears to him. He possessed her, and she clung to him, willing that in some way this act could rid her of the pain in her heart, the sorrow of Ondoni dying.

The next morning he held her and kissed her gently before he left for the candy store. There seemed to be a new clarity in her thinking as though for the first time in her life she knew what she was doing. Was this the first step toward healing her grief? She looked out the window at the bright September sun. This was going to be a good day. She turned and stared at her reflection in the dresser mirror, and her eyes caught a small yellow rubber ring on the dresser. She began to shake inside, and it was all she could do to stand up. What had happened last night went round and round in her head. *He forgot to use the rubber*, she thought. *He forgot!*

For one month, Tula lived with uncertainty. Outwardly she appeared calm. Never once did she show that she was worried. She made sure that Leones and Cissy were dressed for school, fixed Cissy's curls, smoothed down Leones' cowlick. She made sure Leones' high-top boots were polished and Cissy's patent T-strap shoes were shined.

Soon it was October, and still no sign of the flow. Tula began taking hot baths, trying to bring on the flow. She wrote frantically in her Friendship Book: "I must not be pregnant!"

One morning, after Andreas had left for the candy store and the children were in school, Tula ran to the bathroom and vomited into the sink.

Although Tula suffered with morning sickness throughout the month of November, she told no one. She poured her thoughts onto paper: "How foolish I was to succumb to Andreas' wishes. Another baby. Another mouth to feed. How can we do it?" She laid her hands on her flat belly and glanced at her reflection in the dresser mirror. She did not look pregnant, but she knew the inevitable effects of her condition had begun to mark her body.

One night a frigid rain pummeled the bedroom windows and Tula tossed in a fitful sleep. In her dream she heard Leones crying, "You're not my mommy," and ran into his Yiayia Zoe's arms. Tula tried to run after him but her legs were paralyzed. Suddenly with a start she opened her eyes and sat up in bed and heard Leones' cry from the other room.

Tula grabbed her wool robe and rushed to him. He was coughing, a hacking cough, in between sobs and screams. In spite of her precautions Leones had gotten sick. She heated a flannel cloth on top of the stove and placed it on his chest. With a sigh Leones finally slept.

The next morning both Leones and Cissy were delirious with fevers. From that day on Tula and Zoe took turns standing vigil at their bedside. After the third day, seeing that Leones and Cissy were worse, Zoe came into their room with two glass tumblers and two candles.

"No, you're not going to put *vendouses* on them. That's witchcraft. I don't want you lighting candles on their backs, and covering them with glasses. No! I don't want to see my babies' skin swell and pucker up under those glasses."

"But it will pull out the bad blood. It is good. I did it for you when you were little and sick."

"I know, I couldn't stop you then. I can now. I'm calling Dr. Voles."

That afternoon after Dr. Voles examined the children, he said. "Plenty of liquids for them. They're young, and will get over this. But it's you I'm worried about. Tula, how are you? Let me look at you."

"I'm fine," Tula said. "Just need a good night's sleep."

"If that doesn't help, I want you to stop by the office," he said.

"I think I know what's wrong with me," she said.

"What?"

Her eyes blinked and then she said. "I'm going to have another baby."

"I suspected as much."

"I don't want another baby."

"I'll pretend I didn't hear that."

Tula felt her face grow hot. "It's true. I don't want it. We can't afford it. We don't have any money. I don't—" Tula choked back the tears.

"You can't sweep it under the rug like dust. What are you saying?" He picked up his medicine bag and walked out of the room and into the hall without another word.

At first, Tula blamed herself for the pregnancy, but eventually vented all her rage on Andreas. If it hadn't been for his demands, if he had kept his promise and used the rubbers. If, if, if.

The long hours at her sick children's bedside gave her time to ask herself just what she was going to do about this baby? She only knew she had to find an answer and she knew Andreas wouldn't help her. She knew something was bothering Andreas. Was it their lack of money? Even though Andreas and Vasso pooled their salaries to pay the bills, it wasn't enough.

Although Vasso gave most of her salary to Zoe, she still insisted on saving a little for herself. And instead of putting it in the bank, she kept her savings in a metal box under her bed. The key to the box she hung on a chain around her neck. She never talked about the money, but somehow everyone in the family knew about it. Reni and Goldie joked about Vasso's fortune behind her back. Even Tula dreamed about the money and imagined what she would do with it—buy Leones a new jacket, or a toy train—buy Cissy a doll with real hair and herself a new coat, like the one Claudette Colbert wore in the movie magazine she saw in the drug store.

At night when Andreas and Tula were alone, it was getting more difficult for her to hold her tongue. Even when she did, she knew that Andreas felt the silent bitterness and was quick to start a quarrel. And Tula, realized that Andreas felt guilty about the unwanted pregnancy and the bills, would point out that Leones' shoes needed soles or that Cissy had grown out of her coat. Andreas would remain away from the flat for longer periods of time. One night, an argument began when Andreas saw Tula gathering up her nightgown and robe, preparing to sleep with Cissy on the cot.

"Starting that again?" he asked.

"I'm not sleeping in the same bed with you."

"Good! Why don't you move out of the flat, altogether. Get the hell out of here."

"Maybe I will." Tula shrugged her shoulders though she could not help feeling wounded when Andreas verbally attacked her. "If I had the money, I'd leave—you're to blame for everything."

"Why is it always me?"

"Because it is. I wish I'd never met you—never married you. I don't want this baby!"

"What?" asked Andreas, unwilling to let the remark go unchallenged.

"You heard me. Do you think I can raise another one in this flat? Do you think I want to spend the rest of my life living with Mana, hiding in bed with the covers over my head, worried that my sisters will come into our bedroom? I love Leones and Cissy. I want something better for them. I can't do that by have more babies."

He turned to her. "I don't know how to make you happy. I don't know what you want. You're not a child. You're twenty-five years old. Forget about the books, forget about the movie stars. Think about your family, think about me. You've hurt me, Tula."

"I've hurt *you*? That's a laugh," she said. "What about that Maggie? Go to her. And as for this—" She pounded her belly with her fist. "I'll get rid of it, watch me!"

"You're not serious, are you? It's a sin."

"I don't know, I don't know." She shook her head, her eyes filled with tears.

"I've waited years for you. I waited and saved to marry off my sisters, send them dowries. Your Mana helps you with our babies. We will manage."

"Manage, how?" Her hand trembled as she shook a forefinger at him.

He pushed her hand away. His face flushed, his eyes blazing. "Get rid of it then. Get rid of it! But don't you ever mention that baby to me. Ever!"

"Damn you!" she said.

The next day, when her anger had abated, she looked for something to occupy herself. She tore the blankets and sheets from the bed and shook them out on the porch until her arms ached. Then she remade the bed with painstaking care. After she fluffed the pillows and put them on the bed, she sat on the edge of the bed. What was she doing? She ran into the kitchen. Frantically, she began scouring the sink.

Then she removed the dishes from the cupboards, lined the cupboards with fresh newspapers, and replaced the dishes. Zoe calmly watched Tula's frantic activity as she sat at the table crocheting a lace collar. "What's the matter with you, Tula?"

"Nothing. Can't I do some cleaning without you asking me what's the matter?"

"I only asked," Zoe said, and then excused herself and went downstairs to talk to Sophie.

Alone in the kitchen and exhausted, Tula sat at the kitchen table, her head in her hands. When she closed her eyes, her head pounded. When she opened them, her eyes ached. She must do something about the baby. Now! Today! She shouldn't cry about it. She must do something! She knew she couldn't go to Dr. Voles. She had to get help from someone else. And then she thought of Vasso. She knew people at the factory. Someone there could help her. She grabbed her coat and rushed out of the flat.

The chimneys of the factory stood up from among the old buildings. Red brick that dated back to the last century had softened to a muted color with the passing of the years, so that the factory no longer lived up to its imposing name...Deluxe Ice Cream. An iron fence guarded the building, and Tula walked around to its gate.

Now that she was there, waiting for Vasso, she didn't know what to do. This hardly seemed the place for the sort of talk she had in mind. She heard the factory whistle and out poured the workers from the main door, chatting, joking, laughing, bundled against the wind. Only Vasso walked alone. Tula stood by the gate. When Vasso saw her, there was concern in her dark eyes.

"Tula, what're you doing here? Something happen at home? Mana all right?"

"Yes, everyone's all right. I just had to talk to you, alone." The wind lashed about her legs like a whip.

"About what?"

"About this baby. I've got to get rid of it. Please help me."

The familiar twitch was evident at the corner of Vasso's mouth. She shrugged her shoulders. "Are you crazy? How can I help you?"

"You know people in the factory, someone who can help me."

"You'll get hurt, Tula. It's a sin."

"It's a sin to bring another baby into this world."

At last Vasso said, "I do know someone. Once she told me she had a tumor in her belly. She was swollen a little." She demonstrated with her hands outstretched over her waist. "Then she came back to work a week later, thin as a rail. She told me she had the tumor removed. She winked at me when she said that. A few days later she told me in confidence she had been pregnant, knocked up—is what she really said. I'll talk to her tomorrow." She looked at Tula. "But she's not a very nice girl."

Chapter 29

The following night, Tula went to the girl's flat. After introducing herself she got right to the point. "I want to get rid of this baby."

"Don't mince words, do you? Well, come on in."

Tula followed the girl into the small space that was crowded with furniture—a table in one corner with four chairs around it, a hot plate on a counter, a small icebox.

At the other end was an unmade bed, a dresser and a vanity, with a large mirror. Jammed against the only wall that boasted a window was a threadbare couch and a maroon velvet armchair. An end table pushed against the couch held an ornate lamp with a torn lamp shade. A muted rag rug covered the wood floor.

"In some kind of trouble?" the girl asked. "I thought Vasso told me you were married."

"Yes, I am, but I don't want this baby."

The girl turned away from Tula, reached for a cigarette. "Got any money?"

"Yes."

"This is going to cost you. How far are you?"

"Three months."

The girl shook her mass of black hair, hugged her red kimono to her. "I ain't taking any responsibility, if something goes wrong. Understand?"

"Yes, I know." Tula squeezed and unsqueezed a handkerchief in her fist.

"I need ten bucks up front. Do you have it? It you don't we can stop talking right now. This ain't no relief station."

Tula undid the knot in the handkerchief and took out two five dollar bills, part of her savings from crocheting.

"Good," said the girl, snatching the money from Tula.

The girl gave Tula a small bottle. "These are quinine pills. Should do the job. If not, there's another way." She smiled and produced a knitting needle. "But this is the crude way. You can have the needle, no extra charge." She laughed.

Tula felt faint and leaned against the table.

"You okay?"

"Y-yes."

"Just before you go to bed, take the pills. Soon you should start bleeding. It won't take long. The bleeding should stop in a while. If not, that's your problem. That's it. If you don't mind, I've got a hot date, got to get dressed." She made an impatient gesture.

Tula got up to go.

As the door closed behind her, she burst into tears.

It was midnight, and Tula, still awake, stared at the ceiling. She held the bottle of pills. Sleeping beside her was Cissy. *Do it! Do it!* Tula thought. Where was Andreas? But he didn't care. Didn't he tell her to get rid of it? Didn't he? Do it! She eased herself out of the bed. Her hand tightened around the bottle. She kissed the sleeping Cissy and walked to the bathroom. When she saw her reflection in the bathroom mirror, she covered her face with her hands in shame. She turned on the water and filled a glass. One by one, she put the pills in her mouth and swallowed them, gagging on their bitter taste, washing them down with the water.

What now? She couldn't stop shivering, not so much from the cold but from terror. She sat on the rim of the tub, hugging herself, shivering. Did an hour pass? Two? She looked out the small window onto the desolate street, the snow piled in dirty mounds. Nothing moved. Then she threw up, violently, holding her head down over the toilet. She could feel the blood flowing from within her, staining the bathroom floor, coming out in a gush. Then the pain started. She moaned at the first contraction. When a cramp overtook her, she doubled up on the floor, soaked in perspiration. Soaked in her own blood, the pains shooting through her.

Now her greatest fear was that she would not abort, that somehow the pills had hurt her baby. As if in a dream, she saw three black-cloaked women, the Furies, slashing at the unborn baby. "No! No" Stop!" she cried. The Furies did not stop. They worked faster, snipping, slashing. And then from somewhere far away, she heard a scream and lost consciousness.

* * *

In bed, she drifted in and out of the nightmare—those three Furies in black—the baby—the shears. She fought with them, clawed spit. What had she done? God please let me sleep. And she slept.

When she awakened, her stomach was sore, her whole body covered with sweat. She lay in bed, trying to ignore the dampness of the sheet under her body. She was afraid to close her eyes and drift back to sleep—to dream of those black-cloaked women. Then she saw him.

"You're all right now, my Black-eyed Susan."

Dr. Voles, at Andreas' side, nodded. "Rest now. I'll see you tomorrow."

After the doctor left Tula looked up at Andreas. "The baby?" she asked.

Part V

Ah, what great joy to free
the mind.
The Odyssey

Chapter 30

"Why did you do this, why?"

Tula couldn't answer Andreas. She settled deeper into the soft wool blankets and murmured, "I don't know."

And that's how the nightmare began for her. The baby still grew inside her. One excruciating day followed another, and the women in black haunted her. They stood before her, shears in hand. They were not pleased with her. After consulting with each other, they began snipping, directing the future of her baby.

Every Sunday, Tula lit a candle in church for her unborn child. She'd carry the candle to the altar and place it in a scarlet glass under the icon of the Virgin. One Sunday, when she put the candle in front of the icon, the flame died. That's when Tula made a bargain, for what she had attempted to do—abort her baby. The bargain was to see that her children would survive and would succeed.

"Very nice," one of the Furies said. Her hand clasping the golden shears hovered over the infant's head, "but we still need something more from you."

"Something more?"

"Yes," the second Fury agreed. "Let us take these silver and gold threads and wrap them around the infant, perhaps a bit of blue, and some pink."

"Don't harm my baby," Tula cried.

But the Furies weren't listening.

Now she even shared the bed with Andreas. But he didn't seem to care and spent less time in the flat. For the sake of the unborn baby, she did not quarrel with him. Night after night, while Andreas was out, she sat with her mother and crocheted bonnets and sweaters for the baby.

And they talked about the unborn baby, about Angel and about Ondoni.

"Ondoni was a troubled child," Zoe said. "Even in the village, he had been a handful. But the real trouble started with his sickness. The sickness he contacted on ship, in steerage. The sickness that ruined his life. I called him evil. Was he evil?"

"No, he wasn't evil. I think you know deep down in your heart that he wasn't evil. He tried to outsmart others. He was clever, sometimes brilliant, but evil no."

In these talks in the kitchen, over coffee, everything changed for mother and daughter, their bond became stronger.

"How do you feel?" Zoe asked.

Tula didn't answer, continued crocheting.

"How are you?" Zoe insisted as if she had the right to know.

Tula looked at her mother. The planes of her face fit together with clever precision. The coffee pot ticked and perked as it passed through another cycle. A sparrow hopped on the open window, pecked at the bread crumbs left by Cissy.

"I'm fine."

That evening, the family gathered around the kitchen table and listened while Reni and Goldie rehearsed new songs. Leones and Cissy added to the festivities by clapping after each song.

When Reni and Goldie began singing, "I'm in heaven, when we're out together dancing cheek to cheek," Tula joined in giving them a rousing round of applause and a "Bravo."

"I love the way you sing that, almost as good as Fred Astaire and Ginger Rogers," Tula said.

"Sure," Goldie grinned.

"I can't stand that cat screeching they call singing," Vasso complained.

"Stop that!" It wasn't the first time Tula criticized Vasso's behavior, causing a round of harsh words. But it was Vasso's preoccupation with money that angered Tula the most. If she dared question Vasso about anything, she would say, "I pay most of the bills. You just keep having babies. Without me, those babies would starve!"

To that Tula had no response. Yes, Tula's babies needed Vasso. The new baby was due in May. As the time drew closer, she began taking care of Leones' and Cissy's every need. And that left Zoe with time to invite Sophie to their flat to share the evening. The two women would begin hours of conversation and crocheting that would end only when one of them, usually the older Sophie could no longer stay awake and would leave for her flat.

Tula listened as the two women laughed and cried recalling their childhoods in Greece. As they talked, they ate thick slices of crusty bread dipped in yogurt, savoring every mouthful.

Cups of steaming hot Greek coffee were never far away. Zoe would sip her coffee and in the same breath hurl insults at Mr. Pappas. And then she'd cry for Angel doomed behind bars in the mental ward, and for Ondoni, buried in Greece.

Sophie talked about her horse. As a girl she rode the horse to the vineyards and fields on her father's land. She laughed when she told of stomping the grapes with her bare feet until her toes turned red.

Tula listened and crocheted for her baby, never contributing to the conversation. As her body grew, her face seemed to shrink, and she became all eyes. When the older women asked her if she could feel the baby, she would change the subject. She must not tempt the Furies.

The rains came in April carrying the grime-filled snow into the gutters, flushing the streets clean. Windows flew open. Spring cleaning began.

"Easter is early this year, there's no time to waste," Zoe said.

"Mmmmm," Tula said. "I can already smell the delicious lamb roasting on the spit. I must be hungry, and it's only 10 o'clock in the morning."

"It's the baby that's hungry," Zoe said, pointing to Tula's belly.

That evening when Andreas came home he told them that this year they could not afford a whole lamb, but he had made arrangements with a friend to share one.

"What? Share? It will be our luck to wind up with the tail," Zoe said in Greek.

"Don't be foolish, we are going to share, fair and square. I can't afford a whole lamb. I'm not made of money, old woman."

"Don't talk to *Mana* like that," Tula said.

"We'll soon have another mouth to feed, we must save," Andreas said.

"That's not my fault!" Zoe said. "Don't blame me for the unborn child!"

Tula shut her eyes tight, squeezing them and then opened them wide, but they refused to focus. She sat down in a chair, her palms on her swollen belly, closed her eyes and waited for the dizziness to pass.

"Are you all right?" Andreas asked.

Tula held her breath, let it out slowly, all the while telling herself she had to relax. She nodded "Yes."

Across from them, Zoe rung her hands and shifted her weight from one foot to the other. She made the sign of the cross on her chest. "What has this man done to my family?" She fell to her knees on the floor, moaning, rocking back and forth.

"Get up old woman," Andreas said.

"Don't," Tula cried. "Can't you see she's upset."

Zoe raised her face, looked at Tula. "I can do without you both. He's trying to send me to the asylum to join Angel."

"No! No!" Tula cried.

Zoe wept. "It wasn't me who sent Angel to the mad house. I swear I did not curse her. Angel!" Zoe tore at her long hair, pulled out strands from their roots, hair pins fell to the floor.

"*Mana*, please." Tula held out her hands to comfort her mother.

Zoe in a rage now screamed. "It wasn't my curses! Please God, tell them I didn't do it! Tell them, please."

The next day, Sunday, Tula looked in the dresser mirror as she tied a black scarf around her head. She turned away in disgust at the gaunt face and dark-circled eyes that looked back at her. She went to church and lit two candles. Would God have mercy on her?

That night, she slept peacefully, not disturbed by her usual nightmare. The Furies were being kind she thought the next morning, as she was awakened by the rain beating on the window pane. She crawled to Andreas' side of the bed. Where was he? Had she overslept? Why had he left so early?

She got up and looked in the closet. Anything missing? Only Andreas' blue suit. Why did he wear his Sunday suit to work? Her eyes went to his shirts. Were there fewer hanging there? The closet somehow seemed emptier, larger.

"Oh, no!" The leather suitcase was gone. *He's gone!*

"The hell with you, Andreas!" she screamed. "Go to your whore!" She looked up and saw her mother at the door.

"What's the matter?"

"Andreas left me, he's gone. What am I going to do?"

The next day Tula was sitting in a back booth of the candy store with Mr. Pappas. Outside, the rain continued.

"He's gone?" he asked. "Well, he left the store a day ago. Didn't appreciate what I tried to do for him and his family." He eyed Tula. "He didn't give a damn."

"But—" Tula began.

Mr. Pappas quieted her with a hand on her arm. "No, he didn't give a damn. See this store? It's losing money. He could have helped me make it successful. But, no, he had other interests. Why, we did better in 1931 when men were selling apples on corners. Roosevelt said he'd fix everything. Now it's 1936, and I'm ruined."

"I'm sorry," she said, "But did Andreas say anything before he left?"

"No, nothing out of the ordinary. I've been pressing him for full payment of the note, but you know that. He could afford to pay off the note. Don't you

190

have two sisters working at the ice cream factory, earning good wages?"

"Only one works. My other sister is sick," Tula said.

He nodded. "Yes, I forgot. Well, anyway, I dissolved the partnership, had to, no business. See, the store is empty."

In this moment, Tula learned of the power Mr. Pappas had over her life. She knew that he was the enemy and would exercise his authority even more now that Andreas was gone.

"Where have you looked?" he asked.

"I—I don't know where to look. I came here first."

"Try looking for Maggie. Then you'll find him," Mr. Pappas said.

Days later Tula accepted that Andreas was not coming back. She packed his things in two cardboard boxes and hid them in the closet. She filled her days with the children. Leones was moody and fought Cissy. She took them to Hull House and watched as they climbed the monkey tree. She clapped when Leones reached the top and shouted, "I'm king of the hill!"

After supper, she read to them, the same books she had read to Reni and Goldie—*Alice in Wonderland*, *Little Women* and *Tom Sawyer*.

Now only Vasso supported the family. And she would not let Tula forget it for a moment. She sulked at the supper table and spent many nights in her room. "Probably counting her money," Reni would say with a giggle.

Reni and Goldie concentrated more and more on their singing, appearing in local amateur hours and at weddings.

One Saturday in mid-May Reni burst into the kitchen, Goldie following close behind. "Tula, we've decided what we're going to do this summer," she said.

"I thought it was decided," Tula said. "You're going to work with Vasso at the ice cream factory." Tula's hand came up from kneading dough in a low wooden trough.

"No, we're not," Goldie said.

Tula looked at her younger sister. What could she do with them? They were dreamers. If they said that they were off to Broadway or Hollywood, she doubted she could stop them. So much energy, so much vision in those young eyes, she thought. "Tell me," Tula said. "I'm all ears."

"We're going to sing! We're going to enter all the amateur contests there are and with the prize money we'll help pay some of the bills. Sometimes the prize is $100! And besides someone will discover us and give us a contract to Hollywood or Broadway!" Reni said.

"We're not getting any younger," Goldie added.

"Good grief!" Tula said. "Goldie, you're only fourteen, and Reni's sixteen. Old? Anyway there are hundreds, thousands of singers in Chicago waiting for that big break."

"Don't be a wet blanket," Reni said. "We can do it, like that." She snapped her fingers. "So it won't be easy. But we have to try, at least try. We don't want to live on Blue Island Avenue forever, not in this dump," Reni said.

Goldie glanced at Tula. "We're got to think of our futures. Look at you, Andreas left you. He didn't care about your future or the baby."

"Shut up!" Reni said. "Goldie didn't mean that, Tula."

"I'm sorry," Goldie said.

Tula did not look at Goldie. And with more energy than she believed she had, she pounded the dough, kneading it, pulling it, forming it into loaves. No, she must *not* think of Andreas!

Attempting to change the subject Reni said, "I want to make oodles of money, get a fur coat like Carol Lombard, dye my hair blonde like her."

"Not if *Mana* has anything to do with it," Goldie said.

Calmer now, Tula said, "Carol Lombard? Isn't she the one whose picture is on your dresser, Reni?"

"Yes. At least I have taste. I don't have a photo of a dog, Rin Tin, Tin, on the wall like Goldie does."

"So what? I like dogs."

When Tula thought of them with their dreams of Hollywood and Broadway, she remembered her photos of the silent film stars. Now they were in a box in the closet. She hadn't written to a movie star in years.

"That's what it's all about, dreams that come to reality," Reni said. "You gave up on your dream to become a teacher, didn't you Tula?"

Tula shaped the mound of dough into two loaves fitting them into greased pans. "My dream. It's too late for that, now." She looked down at her swollen belly. Then she said to Reni, "You should think of finding some nice Greek boy, and get married, not go chasing a dream."

Reni imitated Zoe's "tsk, tsk, tsk." Then in her own voice said, "You mean like Vasso? And sorrowful Nicko coming over with any excuse to talk to Vasso, who ignores him? Or like Angel in the nut house? Or like you?"

Tula shot back. "Don't be rude and cruel! Dreams are just that, dreams, not reality."

Reni said, "Isn't it strange, the minute I speak the truth, I'm being rude and cruel. I'm not saying your marriage was a complete failure. You've got Leones and Cissy, and now—" She looked at Tula's swollen belly.

Reni's words hurt Tula, but she did not want to show how much, so she changed the subject. "When do you plan this big push for fame and fortune, Reni?"

That's when Zoe stepped into the kitchen and Tula welcomed her. "Do you know what Reni and Goldie plan for this summer?"

Since Andreas left, Zoe no longer was up to anything beyond the simple tasks of cooking. She even neglected Leones and Cissy.

"How should I know?" she asked, looking at the loaves of bread rising. "Mmmmm, even unbaked bread smells good," she said, pinching the dough.

"We're going to sing this summer," Reni said rapidly in Greek. "We're not going to work at the ice cream factory."

"Really? Is this one of your jokes, Reni?"

"No, *Mana*."

Goldie added, "We're going to try out and maybe win the amateur hours."

"Do you object?" Reni asked.

"Object? No. That's a good idea," Zoe said in Greek.

"It is?" Tula gasped.

"Of course. I've given up telling my daughters what to do. It didn't work with Vasso. It didn't work with Angel." Zoe sat down.

"*Mana*, do you really think they have a chance?" Tula asked.

"Certainly."

"You're amazing."

"I've learned my lesson." Zoe smoothed the finished collar she had been crocheting and set it on the table. "Finish your coffee, Tula."

Tula lifted her cup.

Chapter 31

One morning, after Tula finished putting the dishes away, there was nothing to do. She had made the bed, washed the breakfast dishes, and made sure Leones and Cissy were not quarreling when she sent them off to school. Oddly, she felt relaxed. Her mind, for once, wasn't running in circles, looking for a way to escape. She didn't even think of Andreas. Finally, her thoughts came to rest on the baby inside her. She was content to let them dwell there. And she opened her Friendship Book to write: "I must abandon all pride and continue my pact with the Furies. It's almost time. The baby will be born soon. And nothing else seems important when I'm waiting for labor to begin. Certainly not Andreas. Had he known from the beginning that our marriage would not last? And that stupid impulse that led me to sleep with him, allowed him to make love to me that night when the baby was started, that day I heard of Ondoni's death. A life for a life."

She was startled when she heard a knock on the door. "Tula, it's me, Thea Sophie." Inside, the old woman hugged Tula. "Where's your *Mana?*"

"She's at Maxwell Street. She thought I needed some quiet time, time to be alone."

"All is well with you?"

At that moment, Tula felt a sharp pain, and she must have made a sound because Sophie jumped up and said, "What's the matter, Tula?"

"Nothing, nothing, please sit down. It's just an ache, a backache."

Suddenly, Tula felt water trickling down her legs as she sat there with Sophie.

"Your water!" Sophie said. "What can I do?" She rushed to the bedroom and returned with some underclothing in her hands. She asked Tula to lean over while she removed her cotton dress, damp slip, and wet underclothing and deftly put the dry clothing on Tula.

"Better?"

"Yes, thank you."

"When I was young," Sophie began, talking rapidly in Greek, "I thought the midwife had to break the mother's bones to let the newborn baby pass through."

A groan was Tula's only response. Her hands clutched the seat of the chair and her mouth twisted as she felt a wrenching pain.

"You're really going to have this baby today. I wasn't as fortunate as you are. I couldn't have babies." Sophie wiped a tear from her eyes with the back of her hand. "I'll call Dr. Voles. Look, it's stopped raining."

The sun fell through the kitchen window in a magic arc, alive. The sky was a misty blue and a slow wind blew pads of clouds through the air. Tula cautiously lifted herself out of the chair and went to the window.

"Yes, it's going to be a beautiful spring day." She was thankful that Sophie had come when she did. She closed her eyes and put her hands on her belly. With each pain, her heart hurt. She sat in a chair with tears drying on her cheeks.

When Dr. Voles came, he guided Tula into the bedroom. "Let's see what we have here." He smiled and turned to Sophie. "We'll need some clean cloths, perhaps you can find a sheet or two, and some towels and some hot water. Everything will be fine."

Dr. Voles began his examination. Then he said, "I have to take you to the hospital. I can't deliver this baby here."

"What's the matter?" Tula asked between pains.

"The baby's not in the right position."

Minutes later, Dr. Voles and Sophie helped Tula out of the doctor's car and into the hospital lobby. A nurse quickly appraised the situation and came toward them with a wheelchair.

Tula felt weak and frightened. It seemed the baby was pressing up against her lungs. Beads of sweat dotted her forehead. She began to feel dizzy. She tried to control the anxious feeling that almost compelled her to scream that she was going to have this baby, here, now, right in the wheelchair. But she didn't want to have it. Please, give me some more time, Furies.

Tula was whisked into the delivery room.

"It'll be all right," Dr. Voles said kindly. "We'll have that baby out into this world in no time. Don't worry." He smiled.

There was no way she could tell him how she felt at this moment, how grateful she was to him. Then another pain gripped her, and the pains kept coming. She breathed in quick shallow pants.

"The head is coming!" Dr. Voles said. He eased the head out and in one final push the baby was born in the midst of a rush of fluid. The doctor slapped the tiny buttock to shock the baby into taking a breath. There wasn't a sound. Wiping the mucus from the infant's mouth and nose didn't help.

The baby remained limp and blue.

The baby was dead! The Furies had won! Tula screamed, "My baby is dead! I killed my baby!"

Dr. Voles said to the baby, "Cry, damn it, cry!" There were tears in his eyes. Then, holding the baby's feet, he slapped the infant again. "Breathe, breathe!" he commanded. Back and forth, back and forth, he swung the baby.

Tula's fear turned to rage at the Furies who had haunted her all these month. The Furies had won. All the candles, all the bargains were for nothing. She looked at Dr. Voles in a fog. She saw the nurse crying. She closed her eyes and took great gulps of air, breathing for the baby.

Then there was a sound. The baby spit up some mucus and gasped for breath. The cry was weak but Tula laughed through her tears. Color rose in the infant's face. The wrinkled tiny mouth, wide, wailed, the tiny eyes shut tight.

Dr. Voles said, "You've got a tough little baby here, Tula. You've got a tough little girl. She's a fighter, if there ever was one."

Tula's hands trembled, desperate to touch her baby girl. She looked at her daughter and saw wisps of blonde hair on her head, and when she opened her tiny eyes, they were gray, like Angel's. She would be her Angel, her Angeleke. It didn't matter that Andreas was not there with her. She had her baby, her Angeleke.

The following day when Zoe came to see her new grandchild, the baby was sucking at her mother's breast.

"I'm calling her Angeleke, after Angel," Tula said.

"She has her hair and her eyes too," Zoe said. "A beautiful Angeleke, our Kiki." And the name of Kiki remained with her.

And on that day, because they lacked money for Tula to stay in the hospital longer, she and the baby were going home. It was a rainy day and the nurse had bundled Kiki in a flannel blanket. Zoe brought Tula and the baby home on the streetcar. Tula stared glumly out the window. Somehow the street had changed character in the rain. Was it an evil street as Ondoni had forecasted? Tula hugged her daughter close to her. Zoe put her hand on Tula's shoulder. "We're almost home. Don't let the baby get wet. Wrap her in my shawl, too. Here's our stop."

Carefully, Tula stepped down. She looked at the flat—home at last. She was struck by the feeling that something was wrong. What were Leones and Cissy doing out in the rain?

The children ran to their mother. "Mommy, we're locked out," Leones said. "Someone put a big lock on our door. We can't get in."

Tula turned and saw Vasso stumbling, sobbing, running toward them, carrying a metal box. She fell into Zoe's arms, sobbing. Finally, they all walked up to Sophie's flat.

The old woman let them in and poured them coffee, while the children took off their wet clothes and spread them to dry in front of the stove. Sophie wrapped the children in blankets and they sat on the floor in front of the stove. That's when Vasso began her story.

Two men came to the flat in the morning while Leones and Cissy were getting ready for school. They told Vasso they were acting for Mr. Pappas and that the flat had to be padlocked for non-payment of the promissory note.

"Andreas took care of everything didn't he?" Vasso asked.

Later that afternoon, Tula sat in the candy store waiting for Mr. Pappas to finish with a customer. But when he talked to her, no amount of reasoning on her part would change his mind. "I warned Andreas. I told him he was behind in payments. I'll open up the flat for you to take your furniture and clothing, but that's it," he said.

The next day, Nicko helped them move their belongings to Sophie's flat. Nicko, a short stocky man, who was one of Vasso's cast off suitors and also a friend of Andreas, was more than willing to help them.

It took a week before Vasso found a flat to rent on the southwest side of Chicago near Sixty-third Street and Kedzie, a great distance from the old neighborhood. On the last day before they were to leave, Tula could not bear to pack her few belongings. She held baby Kiki in her arms and listened to the strange sounds in the rooms, as if the phantoms of fifteen years had been set free.

That night lying with her children in bed, she couldn't sleep. She held Kiki against her, Leones and Cissy slept at the foot of the bed. Poor Leones was so sad, so easy to anger now, why? And when Tula cried, the tears fell on her sleeping baby.

A cold breeze came from the open window. She got up, put the baby back in bed, and dressed in the dark. She sat at the window and waited for dawn. For the first time in years she heard the clippity clop of a horse-drawn carriage. It reminded her of *Baba*. Sparks flew from the hoofs as they struck the streetcar tracks. She watched and waited till the sun came up from behind the buildings.

Nicko arrived to help them move. While he loaded the truck, Tula talked to some of the neighbors who came to say good-bye. None of her friends came. Miss MacMann was teaching in a New York school. Esther married and moved to the north side of the city. Miss Kaloda was living in Evanston. George had stopped talking to them, blaming Tula for Photi's death.

After a time the only things in the flat were Sophie's. Then Tula chased the children out of Sophie's flat. Leones, his eyes tearing, rebelled.

"No, I won't leave!"

"What's the matter with you, Leones? Why are you acting this way? Why are you always mad?" Tula reached for her son, held him.

"It's because of Daddy. He hates us, doesn't he? He left us because he hates us, and I hate him, and you, and Yiayia—"

"Oh, my poor little boy. All the time you've been crying inside." When she had calmed him down, Tula took his hand. "Let's go find Yiayia." In the kitchen, they found Zoe, with a strange, dazed look on her face.

"I can't believe we're leaving the old neighborhood." Zoe covered her face with her hands and cried.

"*Mana*, don't cry. Everything will be all right. *Ola kala.*"

Zoe could not stop crying.

Then Vasso came in and said, "Leave her alone. Let her cry. She has a right."

Suddenly, strength rose in Tula. She looked at Vasso, then at her mother. Finally she put her arms around Zoe. "Let's go, *Mana*. We have a nice flat waiting for us. Let's go."

Chapter 32

The front page of the *Chicago Tribune* was spread out on the kitchen table. "Jessie Owens Breaks Olympic Record with Four Gold Medals."

She scanned the story:

"Berlin: Aug. 3, 1936—Jesse Owens, Ohio State's Negro son, stepped into his designated role as Olympic 100-meter sprint champion today amid the thunderous acclaim of another magnificent crowd of 100,000 at the Reich Sports Field Stadium.

"The United States stole what to date had been distinctly a German Show. The invincible Jesse Owens also won the broad jump at the Olympic record distance of 8.06 meters. The broad jump was one of the most dramatic events of the entire day. He hit the take-off board cleanly and sailed through the air—"

Tula felt pride while turning the pages of the newspaper. "Good," she said as she read. She was glad that Jesse Owens had won. And Adolph Hitler was not man enough to witness the medals presentation. She sipped her coffee and her thoughts went to Ondoni and his last letter. Strange how perceptive Ondoni had been about Hitler's hold on the German people. Now, Jesse Owens, a Negro, was "man of the hour."

Dreams do come true, thought Tula. Turning to the book page of the *Tribune*, Tula read that *Gone with the Wind* was on the best-seller list. The film rights had been quickly snapped up, and the search was on to find an actress to play Scarlett O'Hara. She had read earlier that Clark Gable was to play Rhett Butler. Tula had a picture of Clark Gable tucked away in her box filled with photos of movie stars. She remembered that she had written to him after seeing him in the film *Red Dust* when he played opposite Jean Harlow.

Now she turned to her mother, who sat at the window of their second-floor rear apartment, her elbows resting on a folded towel, staring out into the alley. Zoe's depression, which had increased since the move, and then been alleviated briefly by Thea Sophie's visits, now returned. Sophie no longer dropped by to gossip with her, as she had done in the past. There were no neighborhood women to join her sipping coffee, and discussing the issues of the day in Greece and on Halsted Street. Tula knew that she was her mother's only confidante in this new neighborhood, in this apartment, which was in the back of an office building, facing an alley. No longer could Zoe hang out the parlor window and greet passersby. The only passerby she saw from the back windows were garbage men, delivery men, and children racing through the alley.

They no longer had a potbellied stove in the kitchen. Now heat was provided by radiator steam. But Tula knew that Zoe missed the old coal stove and the glow the isinglass windows gave to the large kitchen. This kitchen was tiny, barely enough room for the table and chairs they brought from the old flat.

The other rooms in the apartment also were cramped. Vasso, Reni, and Goldie had to share a bedroom. Zoe slept in another room with Cissy. The third bedroom was Tula's and baby Kiki's. Leones was forced to sleep on the sofa in the living room.

Stepping into the small living room, Zoe would complain, "No windows in here, too dark. Not like Halsted Street. Not like the old place, not like home."

"*Mana*, the old neighborhood is not home anymore. Forget about it."

Then Zoe would wipe her eyes with her black-bordered handkerchief and say, "*Baba*, where are you?"

Tula listened as Zoe wept new tears for him in this strange apartment and cursed the evil destiny that had brought her here. "I came to America, land of dreams, but no, Tula—better for me if I stay in village."

Tula could not console her. Zoe would sit in the kitchen weeping. Her face haggard, eyes swollen, she would say, "I curse the day George Kukkones wrote to my *Baba*. George is evil man. And his son, Photi, and angel, may his soul rest in peace."

One day word came to Tula that George Kukkones' heart stopped while he was brushing down one of his horses in the barn. And when Tula went to the old neighborhood alone and saw him lying yellow and gaunt in his casket, she did not weep. It was only when she boarded the street car for home and saw a glimpse of a man, tall, slim, with dark curly hair, a broad smile revealing a chipped front tooth, that she surrendered to the despair that had been threatening to drown her. And she wept new tears for Photi. The women sitting next to her gave her a sympathetic look, offered her a handkerchief. But Tula couldn't tell her why she was crying. At that moment sitting in the street car, Photi's presence seemed so real to Tula that she thought she was losing her mind.

What am I doing? she thought. And then she remembered her promise to her children. She was a mother suddenly thrust into the role of single parent. She must see to her children's future. Wasn't that the promise she had made? She had to get a job. She started looking for work in the want ads of the *Tribune.* One read: "Wanted: People who have good penmanship to address envelopes, $1 for 100." She stuffed it into her purse and went to the address posted on the ad. An hour later, she returned, lugging a large box of envelopes.

That evening and other evenings that followed, Tula devoted her time to addressing envelopes in her precise Palmer penmanship. She had begun to understand something of life when Kiki was born. Her children needed a mother who made plans for their future.

One night she sat at the kitchen table, envelopes pilled around her and wrote in her Friendship Book: "This job is my first step, my first act of freedom. How dare Andreas leave us! He did not even bother to wait for the birth of his baby. He did not even bother to find out if it was a boy or girl."

She rested her head in her hands and closed her eyes for a moment. Then she had a vision of him—chest bare, naked, his manliness erect—with Maggie! *Damn him!*

At the small gas stove, Zoe was simmering some strong coffee in the long-handled brass pot. "What's the matter, Tula?"

"Nothing."

"You—think of Andreas?"

Tula nodded.

Zoe said, "He did wrong to leave. It's too much for Vasso, too many to feed."

"I'm helping, a little."

"There are too many bills for Vasso. Reni must leave school, get job."

"What? She only has a year to go before she graduates. You can't do this to her, *Mana.*"

"How will we eat?" Zoe clasped the gold cross hung by a chain around her neck. "Vasso do everything."

"If only that son of a bitch Andreas hadn't left. If only he hadn't run away with that—whore. Shit!"

"You have a foul mouth now. You speak dirty words. Shame."

"I've learned. I've had a good teacher—Andreas."

Zoe took out from her apron pocket a handkerchief and blotted her eyes. "Tula, you've changed, grown so bitter."

That evening after supper Zoe called her daughters together. She said, "Reni, leave the dishes. Come, all sit down."

"What's the matter?" Reni asked.

"We must talk, Reni—about school," Zoe said. The words hung between them. "Since Andreas left us, we only have Vasso' paycheck to live on and—not enough. You have one more year of school—but a year is a long time and we need money, now. You are a clever girl. You have enough school, more than sisters."

Reni's face grew pale, her eyes defiant. "I don't want to quit school. This is 1936. You can't make me, like you made Tula. I'm not Tula. I'm going to graduate. I'm going to be a singer."

"Me too," Goldie sobbed.

Reni shouted, "I won't quit!"

"You must," Zoe said.

Tula had lost again. How many things she had wanted to do for Reni. Tula tried to discover the wrong—but there were too many wrongs.

"It's unfair!" The hatred in Reni's voice slashed across Tula's nerves that had gone raw with pain.

Vasso said. "Unfair? Like hell it is."

The next morning, Tula heard someone running through the apartment. Then she heard a door open, and another, and finally her bedroom door flew open and Vasso stood there, trembling, crying. "They stole my money, they're gone! They took my money!"

It was several minutes before Tula got the complete story out of Vasso. "Reni and Goldie stole my money and ran away. Reni didn't want to work for her money, so she took mine."

Almost hysterical to discover that her savings were gone, Vasso began accusing Tula of plotting with Reni.

"No, I didn't," Tula said. "We've got to find them before something happens to them."

"I'm calling the police," Vasso said.

Twenty-four hours later, Tula went down to the police station and filed a missing persons report. Bus and train stations were given the girls' descriptions. Tula spent all day and half the night in the police station waiting for word.

At two o'clock in the morning, a detective tapped the shoulder of a sleeping Tula. "Miss, I think we've got a lead on your sisters," he began. "Two girls fitting your sisters' descriptions were seen getting tickets for California yesterday. They're in Omaha now. We've told the police there to put them on a train for Chicago. A matron will be with them, just in case. It's not safe in these times for young girls to travel alone. They'll be at Union Station in four hours."

In four hours Tula returned to the police station with Zoe. As soon as they walked into the station Tula spotted Reni and Goldie sitting on a bench. At their side was a silver-haired matron in a navy blue uniform with brass buttons. She walked up to Zoe. "Are you their mother?" Zoe nodded and reached out to embrace Reni.

"Don't touch me," Reni cried. "Don't you ever touch me!"

Goldie said, "We're going to run away again."

Back at the apartment, to Tula's surprise she saw Nicko in their kitchen sipping coffee, while Vasso busied herself placing a few of Zoe's *biscota* on a plate. It wasn't often that Vasso had male visitors. In the old neighborhood, on Halsted Street, there was a time when Vasso had many suitors, friends of Andreas, men who saw her at church, sought her hand. But they weren't aware of the true Vasso, they only saw a young woman, hard working, slender, aloof with symmetrical features.

So for a long time, Vasso, like Penelope in Ithaca, managed to stall all the suitors. All the suitors disappeared, except for Nicko.

Tula wondered at the turn of events. Was Vasso interested in Nicko? For she knew that Nicko was infatuated with Vasso. And he certainly seemed to be enjoying the domestic scene in the small kitchen, Tula surmised. Baby Kiki sleeping soundly in a wicker basket. Leones and Cissy, on the floor with their coloring books. Reni and Goldie burst in on this scene and ran to their room.

"Please forgive my daughters' manners," Zoe said.

Nicko dismissed the remark with a wave of his hand. "I understand. I'm glad they are all right. Yesterday when Tula asked me to look for them, I went to every flat in the old neighborhood."

"Thank you," Tula said. "Did you come to see about Reni and Goldie? As you can see, they're home. Not happy, I might add."

"I'm glad they're home, but I've come on another matter."

"Oh?" Tula looked at Vasso.

Vasso just smiled.

"I have some information," Nicko said. "I know where Andreas is staying."

Chapter 33

"Why don't you take Nicko into the living room, Tula?" Vasso suggested. "I'll bring some coffee in a little while."

When they reached the living room, Nicko settled into the comfortable horsehair chair, and Tula sat on the leather sofa opposite him. Should she get to the point, ask him right away about Andreas? Nicko pulled out a box of Turkish cigarettes and offered her one. "They're Turkish."

"No thanks. I don't smoke." She moved a brass ashtray on a stand by the chair. "How is your vegetable business, Nicko?"

"I'm doing okay, considering the times, with many out of work. At least I'm not selling apples on the corner, like some men. But I'd better tell you about Andreas—and Maggie."

A shiver shot through Tula. She looked at Nicko. "Was she with him, that *putana*?" Her voice cracked.

"No. She wasn't. Not when I saw him working at the Apollo Café in Indiana Harbor. He's a cook, and Maggie's a waitress there. But they don't work the same shifts. Andreas told me that when I started delivering vegetables to the café."

"Why doesn't he come home?"

Nicko shook his head. "I don't know. He told me he had planned to come home—once. But now he is convinced you don't want him. He said you're better off without him."

She got up and paced. "Better off without him?"

"He's ashamed."

"He should be. He doesn't want his family. He didn't even bother to ask about his baby, the baby he's never seen. He doesn't care."

"You're wrong. He does care. He is suffering."

"Let him suffer. I've suffered." Tula turned her head and saw Vasso with a tray.

"Ready for some coffee?" Vasso asked.

That night Zoe asked Tula, "When are you going to Andreas?"

"I don't know. I have to think about it. Maybe I'm better off without him. Do I really want him to come back?"

"I only ask because Vasso is curious. There are too many bills. I made a promise to you that if Reni and Goldie got home safe that they could finish school. We will manage," Zoe said.

One day the following week Tula took the bus to Indiana Harbor. She had brought along a lunch in a paper sack—and her Friendship Book and while the bus rumbled along she opened the book to a blank page and wrote: "I have to change my life and the direction I'm going in because it seems unlikely now that I will ever achieve my dream if I stay on this path. I have to go in another direction. I have to decide if I really want him to come back to us. *Ola kala*."

She closed her book and through the bus window she watched the autumn wheat being harvested. Soon the wheat and cornfields of Illinois slowly changed into the smoke-belching steel mills of Indiana.

Tula knew that she had made the right decision for her family, her children. She felt confident as the bus pulled into the depot. She searched in her pocket for the scrap of paper Nicko had given her with the address of the Apollo Café. He said it was on Main Street and had drawn a map for her. She wrapped her shawl around her shoulders, now re-crocheted in several places, with yarn almost matching the faded turquoise.

The Apollo Café might have been on Halsted Street, thought Tula when she went inside. The same smell of chicken soup simmering in the kitchen, the same dark-haired men sipping coffee at the counter. She was surrounded by the warmth, laughter, the familiar babble of Greek. Tula wound her way around the room and found Andreas sitting at a booth in the rear, a white apron around his waist sipping coffee, smoking a cigar. A glance around the café assured Tula that Maggie was not there.

Although she could not see his face clearly, she knew his pain by the way his shoulders drooped.

She stepped up behind him and touched his shoulder. He turned, startled, his eyes wide, his mouth open.

"What? What're *you* doing here?"

"Nicko told me you were here. I had to come looking for you, Andreas. Why didn't you come home?"

"I was afraid. Too many bills, not enough money. Mr. Pappas, that bastard, said he was going to kick us out of the flat. I couldn't face you, couldn't face your *Mana*."

"He did kick us out."

"I'm sorry. I'm not as strong as you think I am. I'm only human. I hurt, I worry, I get scared."

"But you didn't think about us, about the baby you've never bothered to see." How strange, thought Tula, that she would be calmly talking about the new baby. She surprised herself, she was so calm, so much in control. So this was Andreas, this scared, worried man?

"I missed you," he said. His voice broke.

"Like hell you did." Now Tula was feeling her anger. "I don't know why I came here. I don't know if I want you back."

"No, my Black-eyed Susan, come sit next to me."

She sat across from him in the booth and looked at him. He looked afraid.

"I'm so ashamed," he began. "I ran away. But I love you, believe me."

He was saying all the right things all the things she wanted to hear. Yet she hesitated. Finally she asked. "What about *her*?"

There was shame in his eyes. "Yes, I thought I loved her once. But not anymore. Maggie no longer matters." He changes the subject. "And how is our baby? God, how I prayed she would be born well. After what you tried to do—" He could not go on.

"Do you truly care about our baby?" She tapped the table with her fingers. "I don't want you to come back to us until we settle some things, here and now. I need promises from you. Promise never to see Maggie again. Promise to be a good husband, a good father to our children. And the last is really not a promise, because it is set in my mind to do it. I'm going back to school, night school, maybe correspondence school. But I'm going to get my diploma, my certificate to teach."

"I see—" Andreas began.

"Don't interrupt. I haven't finished. We're moving out. I'm tired of living with my mother and my sisters. I want my own place, maybe not a house, not yet. But I do want a house before I die, my very own house, with a backyard and an apple tree."

Andreas smiled then. "Houses cost money."

"You'll work. I'll work, too. And we will save."

At that moment, Tula was convinced that her life was changing, that this was the turning point. At last she could see a future. Then she said, "The last bus leaves at ten o'clock. I'll be on it. If you really mean what you say, come back with me."

"I'll be there."

Hours later as she waited in the depot, she thought about their conversation. Strange, but she didn't remember Andreas agreeing to all her promises. She was so busy talking, so determined in mapping out their lives that she hadn't given him a change to promise. That was it. But she knew by the look on his face, that he had agreed to the promises.

Suddenly she could see Ondoni clearly in her memory. Ondoni, Andreas and Photi. She ran their images through her mind, remembering everything.

Finally she got up and walked the length of the depot, past an old man who mumbled to himself as he worked a crossword puzzle in a newspaper. She walked past the lunch counter where three customers sat on stools munching sandwiches and drinking coffee. Her stomach was knotted in hunger and that's when she blessed Zoe's foresight for packing her a lunch. Tula found a bench and open the brown bag which contained a fried potato sandwich, olives, feta cheese, dried figs and an orange. *A feast*, thought Tula as she devoured the food, even the fried potato sandwich.

As Tula waited in the depot, she wrote in her Friendship Book. "*Ola Kala*. My future is clear. I will work side by side with Andreas."

Then she heard the bus pull into the terminal. Startled by a hand on her shoulder, she looked up and saw Andreas. Worry clouded his face.

"You did come," she said. "Hurry, we've only got a few minutes."

"Tula, wait." He sat down beside her. "We have time, we must talk."

She saw the look in his eyes, saw his jaw tighten. *Let him speak first*, she thought. *He has something to say.*

"I can't go with you...not now." He closed his eyes. "But that doesn't mean I'm not coming back to you and the children." He rushed on. "I am. But there is something I must do first."

She flung her arms out. "Go, get away from me! I was a fool to come here. You don't want to come home. Go!"

"All aboard for Chicago," the driver called.

"Get out of my sight!" she said. She was angry. There was a tightness in her chest, she couldn't breathe. "I don't need you!" Tula pulled her shawl close to her—but her hands were trembling. So she put her hands in her lap.

There were tears in his eyes. "Don't hate me."

She got up. She started to speak to him, but when she glimpsed his sad eyes, she caught herself. Instead of the harsh words she had meant to say, she found herself saying, "I have my own plans. I will take care of my children. We don't need you."

"Tula, don't say that. I will come back, I promise."

"I know about your promises." A thought dark and threatening crossed her mind, but she chased it away. She boarded the bus and sat at a window seat. Her trip had been a fool's journey. And when the bus turned the corner, and stopped for a red light, she saw Andreas crossing the street. She shouldn't leave him with those angry words of hers. He would come back to her and their children. She must talk to him one more time, tell him—

She tapped the window to get his attention. Then she saw the woman walking beside him, chatting, holding his hand. Maggie plodded along awkwardly, her body heavy with child.

Tula arrived home after midnight, her head spinning with unanswered questions and she was relieved to find only Zoe rocking a fretful Kiki. Still dizzy with the effect of the confrontation and the final happenings, she ached down to her toes. She greeted Zoe with a kiss and sat in the kitchen slipping off her shoes to reveal pink and bruised toes. As soon as this was done, she sighed. "Ah, that feels better," she said, rubbing her sore feet. "Here, let me take Kiki, you look tired."

"I am," Zoe said. She put the baby in Tula's arms. "Tell me, is Andreas well? Is he coming home?"

Tula looked at her baby, not sure she wanted to tell Zoe the day's happenings. Then she said. "Yes, he's coming home—As soon as he takes care of some unfinished business."

"Then why do you look so sad?"

"It's about her—" she began. Then she told Zoe about seeing Andreas and Maggie from the bus. Finally she told her that Maggie was pregnant. She could have made something up but she had always tried to be honest with her mother.

"With child?" Zoe asked.

Tula nodded. Kiki was asleep in her arms, now.

"I'll make some coffee," Zoe said.

And then the two women talked. They spoke about Vasso and her work, and about Reni and Goldie. They talked about how tall Leones had grown, and how Cissy's hair curled like Reni's. And about how Kiki resembled Angel in every way…her blond hair…her gray eyes. And then they talked about Angel in the mental hospital. And then Tula took the sleeping baby in the bedroom.

A month later, when the special delivery letter came from Cook County Hospital, Tula was addressing envelopes and Zoe drinking coffee in the kitchen. It was a brief note stating that Angeleke could be release to her family on weekends. The letter said she would require constant care and that she still was taking medication.

"Is she all well now?" Zoe asked.

"No. But she's getting better. She can come home, for a day or two. Do you want Angel to come home?"

The color drained from Zoe's face. She drank the last of her coffee and set the cup on the table. "Do I want Angel to come home? What are you saying? Don't I love her? Don't I miss her? She is my flesh and blood, my daughter."

"Yes."

"But we must keep the knives in a secret place," Zoe said.

Tula said nothing.

"We don't want her to cut someone, like she cut you."

"She's better now. They wouldn't let her come home if she was dangerous."

"I don't know. What if she hurts the baby?"

Tula was surprised at Zoe's answer. In her mind she saw the image of Angel in the hospital bed, bound and tied, her face a horrible mask. She could not live with herself if she did not bring Angel home. "Angel *must* come home."

"You're not her *Mana*. What do you know? Who will care for her? Watch her?"

"Mana, it's Angel we're talking about," Tula said.

"But she is not the same Angel. She must stay in the hospital."

When Vasso came home that evening, Tula showed her the letter. "She'll kill someone the next time. She's better off in the nut house."

And so Tula wrote a letter that evening when everyone was in bed. She said that it was decided by the family that Angel should remain in Cook County Hospital.

Chapter 34

It was January 1937, more than four months since Tula went to Indiana Harbor to see Andreas, and still no word from him. She started out the window. The snowstorm that began at midnight had turned to no more than snow flurries now, and had almost stopped when Tula went to the mailbox to find a package from Greece. Andreas' mother had been writing to Tula informing her that Andreas' oldest brother, Petro, was still mayor of the town. Hitler was mentioned in every letter. War was at Greece's doorstep. There was no indication that Andreas' mother had remembered a word about what Tula had written her…about Andreas' running away from his family.

Sometimes Petro wrote to Tula. He knew about Andreas' departure and had expressed concern for Tula and the children. Reading Petro's letters brought comfort to Tula. Now Tula tore through the package and found another letter from Petro and a leather bound notebook.

"My dear Tula," began Petro.

"I'm enclosing a notebook that belonged to Ondoni. Since Ondoni was your godfather, it is only right you should have it. I found it while packing to move to the mountains. We are leaving because the Germans are on our doorstep. Europe is on fire! Spain has its civil war, in Italy it's Mussolini, and Hitler wants all of Europe. I hear the Japanese have joined him and they plan to divide up Asia and the United States. But I'm bitter, and writing nonsense. As mayor of the town, I'm concerned about my people. Your President Roosevelt can't help us. Even God can't help us, now. All the young men are in the Army. The old people are hiding in the mountains, living in caves.

"The women, not only the *Yiayias* are dressed in black, mourning for Greece. The British have tried, but can't help…they can't even help themselves. Even their king has abdicated, but he gave up his throne for an *Americaneetha*, so all is not lost. He is lucky, he is marrying the woman he loves."

Tula read the letter to Zoe. Later she went to her room to look at Ondoni's leather journal. She opened it to a page where there was a pressed dried violet and an unfinished letter dropped out.

She read: "My dear Tula,

"I'm writing hoping you'll never read this, Tula, and then hoping you will. It's my confession, to you and to God. But I think God has given up on me. At the time I discovered my great sin, I thought, thank God, Tula doesn't know. You may find this hard to believe, but as God is my witness, I did not know. So that is why I'm asking for your forgiveness. Now I will tell you who killed Robert. I did! I was not there when the bullet struck his body, nor did I give the order. But I killed Robert. In my heart, in my soul, I killed him. I'm responsible for his death. I'm responsible for Angel's madness.

"My so-called Chicago friends killed him and then they sent their messengers to Greece to tell me. They thought I'd be happy. To tell you that I cried when I heard, will not lessen my grief, will not make Angel sane. To tell you that I plotted to kill the messengers as the ancient Greeks had done when they brought them bad news will not bring back Robert. But I will settle my score with the messengers. I am meeting them tomorrow—"

The unfinished letter was written the day before Ondoni's death. Tula sat on the bed and held the letter. Suddenly the room seemed to be filled with the fragrance of violets. And she seemed to see Ondoni's face, hear his voice. "Forgive me, my godchild."

* * *

The next day, Tula dressed carefully, putting on her navy skirt, white cotton blouse, silk hose, leather pumps, her best. She searched in the old trunk for the turquoise shawl and threw it over her shoulders. She had slept badly and looked haggard. She picked up the porcelain ring box, with the Black-eyed Susan on its lid. She slipped off her wedding and engagement rings and put them in the box.

She had things to prove, if only to herself. She walked into the kitchen. Just as she was about to take a cup from the cupboard, Vasso came up to her. "Good morning, you're up early. And all dressed up in your good clothes— going somewhere?"

Tula poured some coffee into her cup. With her eyes closed she held the cup close to her face, breathing its aroma. "No, just decided to start the day different, maybe it will change my luck."

"I doubt it."

The sisters looked at each other and then Vasso's glance went to Tula's ring finger. "Last night, after you'd gone to bed, Nicko came. He left this letter for you. It's from Andreas."

Tula's hands shook as she opened the envelope. Andreas wrote: "Soon I'll be coming home. Just a few more weeks, and I will have enough money saved. I quit my job at the café and am working at the steel mills. Since the threat of war, the steel mills here are going full blast. I'm making more money. I'm anxious to see you, Tula, and the children, especially the little one. I'm sending you twenty dollars. My love always, Andreas."

Tula put the bill in the envelope, folded the letter, and put it in her skirt pocket.

Vasso asked, "What does he say? Is he coming home? Did he mention her?"

"No. That damn bitch!"

Vasso sipped her coffee and waited. Tula walked to the stove and poured herself another cup of coffee.

"What are you going to do? I see you've taken your wedding ring off," Vasso said.

"I'm going to straighten out my life, that's what."

"Sure you are. Talk, that's all it is."

"No, it isn't. I'm not staying in this hell hole forever! Andreas is coming back. He is!"

"Hell hole, you're right on that count. And as for Andreas, he's never coming back to you. Never! And I'm sick of supporting you and your brats."

"I help. I'm working."

"Making pennies, just peanuts. I'm sick of working in that damn factory, coming home, hands frozen. I'm sick of running through the alleys, scared out of my mind, bumping into bums peeing and sticking their cocks out at me."

"Don't Vasso." Tula tried to touch Vasso's arm, but Vasso drew away. "Andreas is coming back. He said so in his letter."

"Like hell he is! Wake up!"

"Vasso," Tula began, but she couldn't say the terrible things in her mind. She stopped speaking, her coffee cup shaking against the saucer as she held it. The coffee spilled on the tablecloth.

Vasso sat there staring at the stain.

Tula said, "Even if he doesn't come back, I'm leaving. I'm taking the kids and leaving."

"Good."

They looked at each other.

"Is there anything else?" Tula asked.

Vasso did not answer.

"I hate what you've done to this family, Vasso."

"What I've done?"

"And here, take this twenty dollars." She tossed it on the table. "You're looking at it like it's the last crumb of bread in the house."

"Tula—"

"What?"

"Nothing." She looked at the bill on the table.

"Damn it, take the money."

"Yes, I can pay some bills with this—" She stuffed the bill in her pocket.

"Yes, pay some bills," Tula said.

"I mean—"

"I know what you mean. You don't want me here, or my kids. You didn't want Angel back. You never wanted to get married. What do you want?"

"I certainly don't want to go through what you're going through. Men! The hell with them. You're a perfect example. A pack of kids and your man runs out on you." She walked out of the kitchen without saying another word, leaving the money on the table.

Tula's first impulse was to go after Vasso. She could see how much pain Vasso felt at being the sole provider in the family. But the agony of the confrontation was too much for Tula. She could not answer Vasso. She had learned about pain. She walked out of the flat into the street.

It was time to end this dependence and look for help at the relief station. On the next block, Tula paused at a dress shop window, a mannequin wore a stylish dress of blue silk with a wide lace collar. It seemed to Tula just the thing she would wear when she became a teacher. She was dreaming again, she thought as she entered the dimly lit relief station.

Rows of desks, their tops loaded with file folders, lined one side of the large dull gray room. Several social workers were seated behind the desks. A counter with two clerks behind it was at the other end. Tula took her place in line, joining dozens of men and women. All she could think of while she waited was that in a few hours her life would change. The rest of her life would be of her own making. A humiliating beginning in this relief station, perhaps but it was only the first step.

That evening, after the supper dishes were cleared, Tula said to Zoe, "I'm leaving, taking my kids and moving out."

"Nonsense. Where will you go? You have no money."

"I went to the relief station today. It seems there was a purpose to my dressing in my best clothes. They said they can help me. A clerk, a very nice young woman, looked in the files and found a place for me, a basement flat, just a few miles from here. I told them my husband left me. I filled out some forms. The kids and I are leaving next week. I can't wait any longer for Andreas. He has been gone more than a year. He'll never come back. Vasso was right."

Tula packed her few belongings and left within the week. A social worker made arrangements for Tula to move to the basement flat. Around the corner were stores, a bakery, a grocery, and a butcher shop. On the next block was Marquette Park.

Tula was given some used furniture from the Salvation Army and was supplied with food vouchers. On their first night in the basement flat, Tula gathered her children around the kitchen table and said, "Listen, your father will be coming home soon. But until he does, we have to do our best, understand? Leones, you're getting big, and you're strong. You will help the most." She looked at her eldest daughter. "Cissy, my bookworm, you'll help with the baby and the cooking—that is, if I can get your nose out of those books." She hugged her.

Tula looked at Leones, his face red and cheerful above his faded plaid shirt, and then at Cissy, staring silently down at her hands, and at Kiki, rocking back and forth in her high chair. Her children.

Later, when the children were in bed, she pulled out her Friendship Book and wrote: "My children are no longer babies. I'm away from *Mana* and Vasso, and I know my life is just beginning. I'm not going to depend on relief forever! Addressing envelopes is just a start. It's ridiculous to think that Andreas will come home. Better give up on him. I've got to think through my plans for the future. Living on relief is not what I want out of life. I can make it, and make a future for my kids. As for Andreas and his letter, the hell with him. Is there some price I must pay before I'm allowed to be happy?"

She had resolved now that she wouldn't let anything get her down. She could live without Andreas. It wasn't the first time she'd been alone, and it wouldn't be the last time.

Tula moved around the parlor. Suddenly she heard shrill voices coming from the bedroom. She heard Cissy crying. *Something must be wrong*, she thought. Before she got to their room, she heard Leones say, "Be quiet, you want Mom to hear you?"

"I don't care," Cissy sobbed. "The kids in school said we don't have a daddy, that I lied when I said we did."

"What do you care what the kids say?"

"And he's coming home, isn't he, Leones?"

"Sure he is. Don't pay attention to those stupid kids."

Tula stood outside their door and listened. When she looked down at her hands, Andreas' letter was crumpled into a ball.

As the days passed, Tula went to the relief station, waited in long lines for surplus food, mostly cheese, flour, cornmeal, powdered milk, and occasionally oranges and apples. At the corner bakery she bought day-old bread. While Leones and Cissy were in school, Tula addressed more envelopes and walked with Kiki in her arms to the office to return them and collect more.

Every night while the children slept, Tula addressed envelopes. She worked around the clock addressing envelopes, taking care of the children, and dreaming about her goal.

On Sundays, Tula and her children took the streetcar to the Greek church in the old neighborhood. She was comforted by the church rituals, the old priest with his censer, the sound of the children's choir, and the voice of the cantor.

Despite her money worries, Tula pampered and praised her children. Leones was becoming more and more like Andreas every day. He was a good student, and excelled in spelling, taking after Angel. As for Cissy, she was Tula's clone. Always reading, always questioning the text.

In the summer of 1937, while Tula waited in line to turn in her envelopes, Mrs. O'Hare, the woman who ran the office, called to her. She was a robust, friendly person who reminded Tula of her teacher, Miss MacMann, even to her Irish brogue.

"Tula, come into my office. Yes, and bring your darlin' little girl. I want to talk to you."

Tula entered the small, windowless cubicle.

"You do good work, Tula. Your handwriting is excellent, and we haven't caught one error. And you're always on time. Would you consider working for us here in the office?"

"I have Kiki and two other children in school."

"I know. I'd like to train you to be my assistant office manager, at a good salary. We could make the hours coincide with your children's school schedule. As for Kiki, there is a day nursery for working mothers down the block."

"I—I don't know what to say."

"Think about it. It will get you off relief. Let me know your answer by tomorrow. Is that enough time?"

"Yes. Thank you!"

Getting praise from Mrs. O'Hare and a job offer was heady stuff for Tula. *A job, a real job*, she thought as she walked out of the office building. *I can do it!* She knew that before she became a teacher, she'd have to get her diploma and a teacher's certificate. And the only way she could do that was to earn some real money. With a real job, she could save enough to pay for her schooling. She raced right back into the office. Spotting Mrs. O'Hare near a corner file cabinet, she walked up to her. "I don't need time to decide. I'll take the job."

"Good."

"I'll get my mother to watch Kiki."

Tula's job meant spending about five hours a day in the office sorting through envelopes, placing them in specific piles for various companies. She also was required to assign boxes of envelopes to the 'home workers' and keep records of their output and the sums of money they received. She learned fast. As for Kiki, she thrived with Zoe, who began teaching her Greek, as she had taught Leones and Cissy.

As assistant office manager, Tula learned a lesson from Mrs. O'Hare that would ultimately be more useful to her than anything she had ever learned. Mrs. O'Hare was an original and she insisted that all those on her staff look for a fresh perspective on every job and never take anything for granted. One week, Mrs. O'Hare assigned one of the office girls, who knew how to type, to type the addresses on the envelopes, instead of writing them by hand. That gave Tula a wonderful idea. Why not send *all* the office workers to night school to learn typing so all the envelopes could be typed?

"Excellent!" Mrs. O'Hare said. "Do you want to go too, Tula?"

Suddenly, all her carefully laid plans were materializing. She had a job. She no longer depended on relief. She clipped a want ad for a correspondence school.

"High school course in two years! Lack of high school training bars you from a successful career? This complete course is specifically designed for home study by leading professors. It meets all requirements for college entrance. Be a teacher, architect, and engineer, a writer! Send for free bulletin. American School, 28 Drexel Avenue, Chicago, Illinois."

That's how she'd earn her high school diploma.

Tula soon became accustomed to doing her home-study work at night, sitting with Cissy and Leones at the kitchen table while they finished their homework.

One day, Tula was in the outer office waiting for Mrs. O'Hare to complete some paper work and join her for lunch, when a man entered and paused at the counter, looking about him uncertainly. He stared at the women typing with a respectful expression which Tula noticed frequently on the faces of those who entered the office and immediately saw ten women typing at rapids speeds. He then walked over to her and asked whether Mrs. O'Hare was in.

"Yes, she is. She's in her office. She'll be out in a few minutes, if you care to wait."

"Do you work here?" He wanted to know.

"Yes, I'm the assistant office manager."

"He was an odd-looking young man. He had a thatch of the lightest blond hair she had ever seen, and under it was a freckled face. And his blue eyes were alert and alive. He was tall and skinny, with large hands, the backs of which were covered with the same freckles that were splashed on his face. And he was staring at Tula with such apparent pleasure that she felt herself blushing like a schoolgirl. He reminded her a little bit of Ondoni.

"May I help you?"

"I'll wait for Mrs. O'Hare, if you don't mind."

"I' don't."

"I guess you have work to do."

"Yes, I do."

"Well, that's obvious," he said. "I don't usually say silly things. What I mean is—"

"Yes?"

"Men can type too."

"Oh?"

"That's a really dumb thing to say, I mean about typing."

"No, it isn't."

The young man nodded and at that moment Mrs. O'Hare appeared and walked over to join them.

"This is Mrs. O'Hare," Tula said. "I don't know your name."

"No, of course. I never told you. I'm sorry."

"I didn't ask you," Tula said.

"No, you didn't, did you? My name is John Ryan."

"Mine is Tula."

"Tula?"

"Yes, just Tula."

"John Ryan?" Mrs. O'Hare asked. "Of course, you're Mary Ryan's son. I'm glad to see you. How's your mother?"

He took the hand she held out and nodded. "She's fine and sends her best to you."

"Lord be praised. Here you are a fine young man. Time flies. Your mother and I went to school together, back in New York. What are you doing in Chicago?"

"I'm looking for a job. I'm a bookkeeper, an accountant I mean." He reached into his pocket and pulled out several sheets of paper. "Here's my resume and letters from previous employers."

Mrs. O'Hare took the papers and nodded. "Let me see what I can do. We're expanding, John. You don't mind if I call you John?"

"No, not at all."

"We're going out to lunch. Would you like to join us?" Mrs. O'Hare asked.

At the restaurant, Tula watched him with interest. It was not that he was charming; she had known many charming men not to be over impressed with charm. But he had a naivete, a kind of boyish simplicity, that was delightful. No, he didn't remind her of Ondoni, she thought. He reminded her of Photi.

Tula had never been so relaxed, chatting away, actually talking. *How old is he?* Tula wondered. Twenty-five, twenty-six, at the most. Her age.

"But we haven't talked about the job," Mrs. O'Hare said.

"No, we haven't."

"John, let's get to it."

"All right."

"We do need an accountant. The business is growing, thanks to Tula's suggestion to have our envelopes typed. I need a good accountant."

"I understand."

"When we get back to the office, we'll talk salary and all that stuff," Mrs. O'Hare said.

Tula had not said a word while Mrs. O'Hare and John Ryan spoke. Now all she said was, "Good."

Both Mrs. O'Hare and John Ryan looked at her.

He asked Tula, "Do you work at the office every day?"

Mrs. O'Hare said, "There are days when Tula is visiting our various clients, but most of the time, she's at our office."

"Great!" John said.

*   *   *

The Sunday before Christmas Tula and the children stopped by Zoe's flat. Strange it seemed that Vasso was always out when Tula paid a visit. However Reni and Goldie greeted her and the children with open arms.

"How's your spelling?" Reni would ask Leones.

"I can spell elephant, listen, e-l-e-p-h-a-n-t."

"Wonderful! And how about you Cissy? Read any good books lately?"

"I'm rereading *Little Women*, my mother's favorite," Cissy said shyly.

While the children chattered with Reni and Goldie sitting in the small windowless living room, Tula and Zoe talked, and sipped their coffee.

The day before Christmas, 1937, the streets on the south side of Chicago were full of people shopping for presents. The bookstore on the corner held a good supply of books. This was Tula's destination. She bought *The Little Mermaid* by Hans Christian Anderson, which she planned to read to Kiki. For Cissy, she selected a copy of *Little Men*, another one of Tula's favorites, and for Leones *Treasure Island*. Yes, books were what her children were getting for Christmas, and books were what they wanted. *Thank God*, thought Tula.

For the celebration of Epiphany, on January 6, which Zoe always referred as Little Christmas, Tula and her children took a bus to Zoe's flat, and then they all rode on the streetcar to the old neighborhood, to Holy Trinity Church, for the service which would commemorate Christ's baptism in the river Jordan.

The old priest prayed over the water in the front, then sang the baptismal hymn before immersing the cross in the holy water. After blessing the congregation he gave to each member, a vial of the holy water to take home. When Tula returned to the basement flat, she sprinkled a little of the water in each room, after first her children sipped from the vial.

In the afternoon on the day of Epiphany, Tula, the children and her sisters sat down to Zoe's traditional roast chicken dinner. Later all of them took the streetcar to the Canal Street Bridge. A crowd of Greeks had gathered around the priest on the bridge. In the midst of the service, the priest threw a cross into the waters to sanctify it. Young men were lined up at the bridge, ready to jump into the cold water. The young man who recovered the cross would be blessed by the priest. Seven young men threw themselves fully clothed into the cold water. In a short time, one emerged, chilled by the cold water, triumphantly waving the cross in his right hand. Tula was started to see that the young man, with curly hair and a wide grin, bore a remarkable resemblance to young Photi.

"I see Photi in that boy's face," Zoe said.

"Yes, *Mana.*"

Chapter 35

Tula felt truly blessed that holiday season. Mrs. O'Hare had given her a raise and more responsibility in the office, and Cissy and Leones were doing very well in school. Kiki was thriving under Zoe's care.

The Friendship Book told the story: "Good fortune has enveloped us. Thank you, God, thank you Virgin Mary. My children are well, I have a good job, and I'm going to school. My dreams are coming true. I have no worries. I don't even have bad dreams. Andreas is in the past. I have a new friend, John Ryan. He can never to more than a friend, but he has brought laughter into my life.

"As for Vasso, she was avoiding me, but now we are more comfortable with each other. She had been promoted to supervisor at the factory, and she no longer complains about frozen hands. *Mana* says that Nicko has been coming over, courting her, but Vasso rejects him. Good fortune also has smiled upon Reni and Goldie. They have part-time jobs after school at the radio station, singing commercials. *Mana* is becoming the matriarch of a female dynasty. She also is becoming accustomed to their new flat, either accustomed or resigned to it. Only last month she bought some large clay pots and planted tomatoes, basil and geraniums in them. She's set them out on the back porch overlooking the alley. We don't need Andreas in this family." With a sigh Tula closed the book and put it away.

Often on Saturdays, Zoe would take the bus to Tula's basement flat, and the two women and the children would walk to Marquette Park, to pick dandelions, *horta*. Later at home, they'd wash the greens, boil them, and season them with lemon and olive oil, and serve them for supper.

Beyond the park on a hill was the city college. That usually was their destination after they had filled their shopping bags with *horta*. When they got to the college, Tula and Kiki would press their faces against the entrance door. In her mind Tula could hear the sounds of students rushing to class, bells ringing and lockers slamming shut.

When winter came, the snow, sleet and bitter cold prevented Tula and Kiki from meeting Zoe for their Saturday walks. For the most part, on Saturdays while Cissy and Leones were occupied with their books or toys

Tula spent the day cleaning the basement flat. Polishing the old, scared furniture from the Salvation Army with rose oil, scrubbing the worn kitchen linoleum, cleaning the antique gas stove, would that make the flat a home? Tula wondered. Sometime when her home-study work was finished, she'd sit by the window and watch the passersby. She was grateful for her children being in good health, even though they were clothed in second-hand garments from the Salvation Army, they were warm and they were loved. She seldom thought about Andreas. He was her past, this was a new life for her. And she thought about John Ryan. He filled her days with smiles and laughter. He was a good friend.

It was during one of those cold March Saturday mornings while Tula was reading from *Little Mermaid* to Kiki. Cissy and Leones were at Zoe's for the day. Tula shut the book and said, "Let's go, honey, I'm getting cabin fever."

Kiki smiled. "Going out?"

"Yes. We're going out. I'm tired of this flat. We're going to the park." In a matter of minutes the two were in the park, tossing snowballs at each other, making a snowman. Finally exhausted, they found a bench, wiped the snow off it and sat and watched the few brave crocuses bursting from the snow, their saffron yellow faces turned to the sun.

So it was on that cold March day that Tula and Kiki resumed their Saturday walks to the park. And when April came, Tula with renewed vigor took a paper sack to the park and searched for dandelions. With a paring knife she'd cut deep into the soft earth to the roots of the tender plant.

She felt now that feeling that had comforted her as a child, when she went with her mother to search for the first spring dandelions to make a meal. Now she was doing the same thing with her daughter. After an hour of picking tender dandelions the sack was full. Zoe had taught her how to strip the plant of its outer leaves, only saving the most tender. Was it her imagination or could she now taste the delicious dandelions?

An old man stopped in their path and said, "That's it girlie, pick those ugly dandelions, those ugly weeds."

"Ugly weeds? They're not weeds. They're good food. They're *horta*," she said.

"Whatever you say, girlie, just keep picking them, save us taxpayers a few bucks." He strolled down the path.

Tula turned to respond to him, when to her surprise she saw Vasso sitting on a secluded bench, partly hidden by bushes. She, too, was sorting dandelions from an old leather shopping bag. Tula remembered the bag. She had carried

222

it many times in the past, when her mother and she went dandelion picking. Now the sun shone on the warn leather bag and on Vasso's high forehead, her dark hair was covered by a black kerchief. Immediately Kiki cried out *"Thea Vasso!"* and ran into her arms. When they hugged, Vasso burst into tears. She wiped her eyes with a black bordered handkerchief and said, "Come, sit, Tula. Spring is almost here. The winter was too long and too cold. I missed you."

"I did too," Tula said.

Vasso's eyes were dry now, and although her face was pale, much more than Tula remembered, it seemed younger.

"Sit here." Vasso offered her hand to Tula. When she took it, Tula felt drawn to her sister. *Vasso, too is getting older*, she thought. Only a few years ago Tula had fantasized about Vasso dying and leaving Tula free of her bitterness, but since then Tula had remembered aspects of Vasso's character— aspects that had changed Tula's mind. She remembered the way Vasso supported the family. In a way, she was the one who had saved the family during the hard years—Tula knew that in her own way, Vasso was fiercely loyal to the family.

All those thoughts crowded through Tula's mind in a few seconds.

"Tula, all is well with you and the children?"

"Ola kala." Tula smiled.

"Ah, yes, *ola kala*." And then she said, "Do you think of Andreas?"

"No."

"Maybe that is just as well. You are working, you are studying for your diploma." Vasso sighed. "Then why do I see that look in your eyes?"

"You don't see anything in my eyes. I'm free of him, understand? That's my business, not yours."

Vasso's face changed, grew red as if she'd been slapped. "Tula, why? I care for you—for your children."

"Is that why you're never home when we visit *Mana*?"

"I-I-I—"

"Can't find the words, can you, Vasso? My kids haven't eaten any of your bread lately, have they?"

"Stop! Can't you forget? Can't you forgive? I was wrong."

"Yes, I forgive." The two sisters embraced.

In Vasso's voice, Tula read her agony and understood. Then the sisters began to talk. That was how Tula found out about Andreas, Maggie and their baby.

"Tula, it seems no one knew where you had moved. So Nicko contacted me about Andreas." Vasso's information was startling. But Tula was not truly surprised. She had told herself many times that Andreas would never come back to her.

Vasso sat on the bench, quietly cleaning the dandelions.

Tula watched her sister and then blurted out. "What about the baby, the one Maggie had?"

"The baby, a boy, was born dead," Vasso said. She grabbed Tula's hand, held it in hers. Then she said, "Andreas stayed with Maggie for a while. I'm not sure how long. You know how Nicko is, his facts are never right." She spoke softly, calmly. "That woman left for New York. Andreas didn't go with her, but he did give Nicko a letter for you. Vasso searched in her black purse and found the envelope. "Here."

Tula opened the envelope. The letter was dated April 23, 1938, a few weeks ago, and it said:

"My dear Black-eyed Susan,

"I'm sending you a sum of money, two hundred dollars, and Nicko has promised to deliver this letter and the money to you. I've told my story to him, no use repeating it now. I'm not coming home, Tula. I know I've hurt you enough. Forget that there ever was an Andreas. Go on with your life."

Enclosed were several bills and a small gold frame with a watercolor of a Black-eyed Susan. Tula felt cold. She drew a breath. Finally, she folded the bills and put them and the picture in her pocket. "He's not coming back."

"Yes, I know. Nicko told me. Divorce him! Forget him."

"My God, Vasso, I don't believe you said that. Divorce?"

"I mean it. He's no good for you. You're still young. You have your whole life ahead of you." She smiled. "You are working, studying. Someday you will marry again."

"Me? No, never!"

Vasso smiled. "Somehow I remember those words—coming out of *Mana*'s mouth. You are attractive. You will find a good man."

Tula hesitated. "I know a good man. His name is John Ryan. He is a friend, a good friend. I've had enough of marriage."

"Well you do have your beautiful children. And someday I know you'll be a teacher. You've changed, Tula. You've grown into a very strong woman."

"You've changed, too, Vasso. Will you ever marry?"

"I doubt it. But thank God, Reni graduated from high school. But she will work in the factory, and when Goldie graduates, she too, will be on the line."

"The factory is your life, Vasso?"

"It's not bad, now that I'm supervisor. As for Reni and Goldie, they have something else to fall back on, their singing at the radio station. Who knows? Their dream is still alive, just like yours, Tula."

A laugh, very much like Tula's came from the bushes. It was Kiki. Tula leaned over the bench. "Kiki, get out of those bushes, this instant."

Kiki crawled out from under the bush, her hair full of black dirt, green and yellow smears on her face. She passed her hand over her mouth and said, "Dandelions, icky." She ran to her mother. Almost two years old, she had a delicate face framed with blonde curls. Her huge gray eyes started at her mother.

"Kiki, I told you not to put things in your mouth."

"Pretty flowers," Kiki said, handing her a fistful of dandelions. Tula hugged her.

"Thank you, you little smarty."

"Just like you," Vasso said. "You'll make a fine teacher. Isn't that what Baba used to say?"

"Yes, those were *Baba*'s words. Vasso, will it happen? Will my dream happen?"

Chapter 36

Tula worked side by side with Mrs. O'Hare and John Ryan. She was a working woman, dealing with people and, strangely enough, enjoying herself.

After work, she would pick up Kiki at her mother's flat and wait for Leones and Cissy to return from school. The day Tula was able to buy new clothes for her children, clothes that no one else had worn before, she rejoiced. She knew now that she was on her way to achieving what people called the American dream.

But the American dream had some drawbacks for Tula. She wanted to be her own person not the typical American working woman. That's what John Ryan called her. He teased her about wearing blinders, having a one-track mind, all work.

One day at the office when he said that, Tula exploded. "Don't *ever* say that again!"

"All right, forgive me. I certainly shouldn't have said that. But I care for you. I don't want you to work, work, work. Have some fun, Tula."

"Fun? Listen, I'm lucky to have this job. Lucky to have my kids well and happy. For the first time in a long time, I'm able to buy them new clothes. Do you know what that means?"

"No, not really. I'm glad for you, though. I care for you, Tula. I know you haven't encouraged me. I understand. The relations between men and women are never very simple. It takes time. We can be happy together."

Tula continued sorting envelopes.

"I know how the past can live on in people," he said. "But for you the past was a long time ago. Let go, Tula."

"I can't discard the habits of a lifetime."

"Tula, listen, try to understand. You and your husband never seemed to be happy, from what you told me. Divorce him. When we're together, we laugh, we have fun."

"What did you say?" Tula asked.

"I'm saying it's good between us. We've known each other for a year, and yet we make no demands on each other."

"We're friends," Tula said.

John was leaning on her desk. "I want it to be more."

"When we're together, yes, we do laugh and have fun. There are men and women for whom marriage is a good thing. But I don't think I'm one of them," Tula said.

"That's what you have forced yourself to think," John said. "What's wrong with you? You fuss over your children. You fuss over your job, your home-study program. What about *you*, Tula?"

"Me? I'm doing what I want to do, finally. I've got a dream, John."

"A dream? It seems to me you've crawled into a cave. When are you going to crawl out? I care for you. I want to marry you."

"No, don't say that. I care for you, as a friend, nothing more. I have another plan for my future. Please find a good woman and get married."

The next day, John Ryan turned in his resignation to Mrs. O'Hare. In two weeks, he was on his way to New York City.

Several weeks after John Ryan left, Tula sat in the kitchen listening to the radio that Andreas had given her so long ago. A warm September breeze filtered through the open window. Leones was sprawled on the floor reading the Sunday comics.

"Mom, turn on the 'Sunday Comics on the Air.' You know the one. I want to hear comics read."

"Okay, but after that, I'm turning on the news."

A half-hour later the children had gone out to play, and Tula settled with another cup of coffee, to listen to the news.

The news on the radio was bad. "Great Britain and France have declared war on Germany, following the invasion of Poland by the Germans."

"Oh, my God!" Tula said, spilling her coffee, and staining the tablecloth.

The next day, Zoe came to visit Tula carrying a letter.

"Let me see the letter," Tula said. She read Petro's letter aloud.

"Greece is not prepared for this...this hell war! The German and Italian troops are at our back door, our borders. The British are trying to help us, but God they don't have enough manpower. Already Poland has fallen and the Russians are in Finland. The world is on fire...except for you in America. Thank God you are safe.

"Why doesn't your President help us? We are desperate. The village has been evacuated...all women, children and old men have moved to the mountains...live in caves. I have set up headquarters in the village, taking directions from the Army. Tula, it doesn't look good. My brothers are in the Army, my mother is in the mountains, with my wife and children...resisting in their own way." Tula put the letter down.

Over the next three months the news would get worse. One day while Leones and Cissy slept soundly in the back bedroom of the basement flat; Kiki wandered into the dark kitchen crying. "Mommy, where are you?"

"Right here, honey," Tula said. Her home-study book was open in her lap, her Friendship Book on the table. Kiki found her in the rocking chair and crawled into her lap. Tula's arms went around her. "Now my baby's safe."

She hummed softly to quiet her. The only light was the faint beam coming from the radio on the kitchen counter. Tula listened to the static voice of the radio commentator.

" Latest bulletin from Europe. Hitler is pinning his hopes on U-boats, allied merchant ships are sailing in convoys with armed escorts...bringing to the British much needed food, raw materials for their factories, and fuel to keep aircraft and ships in action.

"Bulgaria has allowed German troops to pass through their country to invade Greece. In spite of help from a small British Army, many Greek soldiers have been killed and captured."

Tula's hand trembled as she reached over to switch off the radio. She pulled Kiki close to her. She craved comfort as much as her baby did. Minutes later she put the sleeping Kiki in the rocking chair and for a moment she was sympathetic to Kiki's nightly wanderings.

Then she reached for her old friend, her Friendship Book, and began to write: "In this house, this basement flat, there are needs. The needs of running, laughing children as they struggle to grow up. Leones with his pitching arm, his swift legs, his athletic chest, his cheerful disposition as he protects us. He's the man of the family. Yesterday I was in the kitchen when I heard him talking to a friend who wanted him to come over and play catch. Leones said he wanted to, but he couldn't leave his mother. She needed him. That frightened me. I realized I was becoming a burden for a ten-year-old boy. And Cissy, with her serious dark eyes to offset Leones' mischievous gray ones. Cissy with her books, a vital part of her. So much like me, yet so much her own person. I'm my own person, too. I'm not living in a cave, in spite of what John said. I'm living for my children, for my dream. And sweet Kiki, with her golden locks pressed against my cheek as she falls asleep, her hugs as she wiggles into my arms. It would be so easy to give up, to let go. But no, I can't allow that. I will never give up! I have three children to think of, and myself. I've survived hardships before. I'll do it again! And the Holy Mother is watching over us and that has made an enormous difference in our lives."

Tula closed her book. "I must be strong," she said. This is her family, her home, she thought. She needed its deep, quiet comfort. It was an old place, the heart of it the kitchen, with its wooden floor poking through the worn linoleum and the yellow daisies in the weathered wallpaper. On the gas stove, the coffeepot stood, a silent reminder of Zoe.

Tula still was thinking about her fears of the war when she heard footsteps in the hallway. Probably someone in the next flat. But the footsteps stopped in front of her door, and there was a light tap. She caught her breath and gasped, fearing terrible news. *It must be Mana*, Tula thought. *She has bad news, that's why she's out so late.* It was after eleven at night. The light tapped continued. She was thankful she had latched the door from the inside with a chain, beside bolting it. She couldn't be too careful. She placed the sleeping Kiki in the rocking chair and walked to the door. "Who is it?"

"It's me."

Opening the door a crack, with the chain secure, in the dimness she saw his familiar face, his hazel eyes.

"Oh!" she cried. For a moment, she couldn't breathe. She slammed the door shut. She couldn't let him in. No!

He tapped on the door, "Please let me in, Black-eyed Susan."

Although her fingers felt clumsy, she finally unlatched the chain and let Andreas in. He placed his suitcase on the floor.

"Hello, my Black-eyed Susan." Shyly he offered her a bunch of violets.

She didn't take them. "After all this time, all you say is hello? What do you want, Andreas?"

The man who stood before her did not look like Andreas. He was too gaunt, too pale, too beaten. He wore ill-fitting old clothes. Where was the Andreas who took pride in his clothing?

Where was the Andreas with the starched white shirts, the creased trousers, the tailored jackets straining over broad shoulders? Finally he put the violets on the table and removed his old felt hat. He twisted his hat between his hands, awkwardly smiled at her. "So, am I welcome?"

"I never thought I'd see you again," she said. She turned to switch on the kitchen light, flooding the small room with light from a bare bulb in the ceiling. She looked at him. Did she want him back? For a long time, in the silent room, all she could hear was her own breathing.

She could feel half hate, half love, resentment, anger. Was desire still there? Or was there just bitterness. Was there love?

"I-I want to make it up to you—" He stammered. "I'm not the same man I was."

She wanted him to feel guilty, more guilty than he felt now, standing there with his hat in his hand. She felt bold, brave. Oh, how she had looked forward to this meeting. Oh, how she had imagined in her mind what she would say to him—or how she would punish him!

"Why did you come back?" she asked, her eyes searching his.

"Because I still love you." He spoke softly. "Is that so wrong?"

"Wrong? *You* have to answer that question, Andreas."

She couldn't tell him that it was wrong. She knew of the emptiness of his life. She knew that the baby—the one he had with Maggie—had died. She couldn't hate Maggie, not anymore. She knew of the woman's sorrow.

He said, "No it's *not* wrong."

Tula looked at this drawn face. "I'm not sure I'm ready for more pain. I may never be. I've got a new life. I've got a job. I'm studying to get my diploma."

"I know."

"I don't know if I can trust you," she said.

"I can accept that. I know I have to start again, work to get you to trust me again, prove myself."

"I'm sick of you trying to prove yourself."

"You never used to be so hard on me."

"I never had a chance to. You were always gone, staying late at work, or seeing that whore. I don't feel sorry for you."

"I know." He stared at her. "You're the most wonderful woman I've ever known."

"How do you know that?" she demanded. "You don't even know me. We never talked. You don't know the first thing about me."

"I do know the first thing, damn it!" He was angry now. "I know you're my children's mother. I know you're a hard worker. I know you want to succeed at all costs. I know you have guts."

"I have guts?"

There was silence as they sat side by side at the kitchen table, the bare light bulb above illuminating them. He reached for her hands. She drew away.

"Yes, you're independent, arrogant, and pigheaded at times, but above all you're sentimental—and the funny part is, I don't like people like that, pigheaded, sentimental, because that's what I am." He smiled a shy smile. "But I not only like you, I love you."

"It's too late for this, Andreas."

"I just want to stay, until you tell me to go away," he said.

"And if I tell you to go away now?"

He fumbled with his hat in his hand. Tula watched his hands, strong, long-fingered, broad hands.

He reached out and touched her arm very gently with one of his fingers, tracing a line down to the back of her hand. She turned to him, and his eyes filled with tears. He closed his eyes and shook his head. And then a small voice cried, "Mommy!"

Tula turned to Kiki, who lay in the rocking chair, rubbing her eyes. "Mommy."

"Yes, darling, I'm here." She picked her up in her arms, hugged her. Then she turned to Andreas. "This is your daughter, the daughter you've never seen. You never stayed up with her when she had colic, was delirious with a fever, or scared by a nightmare. You never heard her say her first word."

"I know. I can't tell you how sorry I am. Please, please, forgive me." Then he said. "May I?" He took her from Tula, brushed the child's forehead with kisses, caressed her blond hair. "My baby."

"Mommy, Mommy!" Kiki cried, frightened, arms reaching out to her mother.

"Here, let me take her. She doesn't know you. You're a stranger. Have you come back to mess up my life?"

At that moment, Leones chose to stumble into the room, sleepy-eyed, a tall, gagling boy who with every passing year looked more and more like Andreas. "What's happening?" Leones asked. Then he saw his father. "Is that really you, Daddy?"

Andreas hesitated only a moment before he moved forward to hug his son. "Yes, son, it's me. It seems you've grown a foot since I last saw you."

"Are you still mad at me?"

"Mad at you? I never was," Andreas said. "I never was."

Coming up behind Leones was skinny Cissy, with Tula's black eyes and Tula's long brown hair. "Daddy?" she asked, her hands lost in the folds of her flannel gown.

He embraced her. "Hello, my precious," Andreas said, hugging her, kissing her. "I have missed all of you so very much."

"Are you home for good?" Cissy asked.

Andreas rocked both children in his arms, there in the kitchen, kneeling on the floor. "I'm home," he said, and softer still with his eyes on Tula. "I love you."

Why is he doing this to me? Tula thought. She had finally come to the conclusion that he would never return. She had her life together. Why was he giving her so much pain? Then she looked at him for a long time and slowly nodded her head. "Yes, your daddy's home."

Andreas got up. "Tula, I don't want to pressure you. I can go find a room someplace."

Tula shook her head. "No, stay," she said. "You can sleep with Leones." She felt her face flush.

"Yes, that will be fine." He couldn't take his eyes off her.

That after a time Andreas managed to fit into their life at all was because of Leones, who acted as if his father had been gone only a short time and had not brought unhappiness to the family, or hurt his mother.

Quietly, Andreas slipped into the niche of their life that he had occupied before, and he tried to make them happy. He found a job in a restaurant. He took Leones out to the park, played catch with him. He brought Cissy books and listened as she read from them. As for baby Kiki, Andreas had captured her heart. A few days after his return, they'd become friends, and she'd run to him. When he'd lift her and toss her in the air, she'd scream with delight.

They fell into a routine. Andreas worked, Tula worked. They came home all gathered around the table for dinner. Then Tula did her home-study lessons, and if she had a minute she wrote in her Friendship Book, always the questions about her future with Andreas. "Will it be right?" she wrote. "Will Andreas stay, be a good father? I don't know, and I wonder if he knows. He *is* trying.

Daily Tula returned to the office. It had become second nature to her. All of the girls were now typing their envelopes. Because of Tula's suggestion, the output of envelopes was greater. Tula had hired two high school students to do the filing, another to sort and count the envelopes. Mrs. O'Hare was so pleased she gave Tula a raise. More and more Tula threw herself into her work, thrived on it, and Mrs. O'Hare and the staff became Tula's second family. In the office, amid the clatter of old Remington typewriters, Tula and Mrs. O'Hare became a team.

It was a bittersweet moment when Andreas handed over his paycheck to Tula, and she realized it was less than the wages she earned working for Mrs. O'Hare. She was almost finished with her correspondence school studies and soon would receive her high school diploma.

One night when the children were in bed, and Tula had finished her home-study work, Andreas and she talked about their future. Tula poured another cup of coffee for Andreas.

"We've got to move out of this basement flat," Tula began.

"Soon. With both our paychecks, we have saved, but not enough to move," Andreas said.

"I want a real place to live in," Tula said.

"Soon, soon," Andreas promised. "We'll have a home of our own. You don't belong in this basement flat."

"Yes, a real house, with a backyard, and—"

"And an apple tree, my Tula, my sweet." He leaned over and kissed her cheek.

It did not matter that he had left them. Seeing Andreas every day was a different kind of pain from not being able to see him at all. She looked at him, and her eyes filled with tears.

After his return, he had slept in Leones' room. They had not made love, although their lives were joined, joined by their children, by their work. But their bodies were separate. It had been a long time since she'd been his wife in the real sense.

"Do you want some more coffee?" she asked, reaching for the coffeepot.

"No." And without another word he took her hand and led her into her bedroom, the coffee forgotten.

Chapter 37

One hot Saturday in late August, Andreas came into the kitchen with the morning mail and found Tula sitting at the table looking at the small porcelain ring box, the one he had given her so long ago with the Black-eyed Susan etched on the lid.

She had been looking at it for a long time. It was a relic of a forgotten past, several lifetimes ago. And yet it had survived all these years. It was battered, but it had survived. Tula sat staring at it. Finally she looked up to see Andreas' troubled face.

"Black-eyed Susan, I—I," he began.

He wasn't calling her Tula anymore. She found herself looking at his open face, at his hazel eyes. She marveled at the notion that this man had nothing to hide, that his face was as unveiled as the look in his clear hazel eyes. He sat down heavily on a chair beside her, chewing at his lip, his eyes resting for a second on her, fumbling with the letter in his hands. His face was more relaxed now, but still wary.

"Uncomfortable" did not begin to define Tula's state of mind as she now looked at Andreas. *Something is wrong*, she thought. Andreas' handsome face was within inches of hers, his mouth ready to smile, his hands reached across to touch hers. Their eyes locked. Then Tula caught her breath. Suddenly, she couldn't breathe. It couldn't be the August heat. It was the look in Andreas' eyes. She wiped her brow with a handkerchief. It was hot and she needed a glass of water, that's what she needed. She walked to the sink, turned on the tap and filled a glass. "Ah, that tastes good," she said taking a sip. But still she could not look at Andreas.

Instead she stood at the sink and glanced around the kitchen as if she had never seen the room before. She looked at the worn spots in the linoleum, the rips in the flowered wallpaper, at the red clock over the icebox—at time so frivolously wasted. In one corner there was a pile of boxes, filled with old clothing and blankets, ready to be shipped to Greece as part of the Greek War Relief program they were involved with at the church. Only last Sunday they had spent part of a summer afternoon in the basement of the church sorting and packing blankets and clothing to send to Greece. Andreas and

Tula were among a dozen volunteers knee deep in piles of clothing.

"God willing, some will go to my village," Andreas had said. Even the children helped, after they had gained a promise from Tula to visit the park later. Time was fluid, instead of solid that Sunday afternoon. They enjoyed a picnic, watched the children swing, helped them on the slides. After a full day, they had remained in the park to gaze at the summer sky, a canopy of brilliant stars above them in the night.

Now on the table lay the porcelain box and the letter. Andreas patted the seat next to his. She sat down, sipped the cold water and reached for the letter. Quickly Andreas covered the letter with his hand. "You can read it later," he said. "First, I must tell you what I must do."

"Must do?" she repeated. Tula leaned back in the chair and stared at the letter on the table, and other questions exploded like fireworks in her mind. Why had Andreas felt it necessary to cover the letter? Was the news so terrible? Was he going to leave them, again? Tula shuddered.

Andreas picked up the letter and folded it, put it in his shirt pocket.

"You're leaving us," she said.

"Yes." He sighed.

For the first time, she realized how *gloomy* the room was—worn, old furniture, windows eye-level to people's feet. Suddenly, the place seemed far more isolated than she had ever imagined. She wanted a house, but they were never going to live in a real house.

Why is she so calm? she thought. In a level voice she said, "Don't do this to me. Don't do this to our children."

"It's not the same. Not like last time."

"It doesn't matter. See? I don't care." Her voice was in control, her hands steady.

He leaned over, took her hands and kissed her brows, her cheeks, her eyelids.

She pushed him away. She was angry now. "I can't trust you. Because when I start trusting you, then bang—you do something like this. A slap in the face, that's what it is."

"Wait. You haven't given me a chance to explain. It's the letter. I must tell you about the letter."

"The letter?" She put her hands to her face. "I knew it was terrible news when you hid it from me."

"I'm sorry." He pulled the letter out of his pocket. "In this letter, my *Mana* writes that my brother, Petro—" He had to stop, his eyes tearing. "Petro was hanged in the village square by the Germans. They had to set an example since Petro was mayor of the village."

Tula caught her breath and gasped. "Oh, God, no!" Her hands shook as she picked up the letter. Petro killed! Petro who had written her all those letters. Petro who had become her friend, her confidant when Andreas left her. Petro, Petro.

"And Petro's wife and daughter," Andreas continued. "They took them to a camp in Poland, Germany, who knows?" Now he sobbed openly.

The rest was a blur to Tula.

Andreas said, "Somehow *Mana* got this letter out of Greece. I don't know how. She's living in a cave in a mountain, outside the village, hiding by day. God knows how they did it. I don't know where she is, but I've got to find her. I must help!"

The early September rains began the day after Andreas left. It rained steadily for two days. That afternoon, Zoe and Tula sat in the kitchen.

"It's strange, the way things happen," Zoe said. "Andreas is in Greece fighting with his countrymen for freedom. And you are here, working on your own freedom. You've completed your home-study program, eh?"

Lost in a world of her own, Tula missed Zoe's comment. "What?"

"Never mind. I'm wandering too much. I want to give you something that I took from you a long time ago, if that make sense. Would you believe that I walked all the way to your flat, walked and thought about what I was going to say to you? Not that I couldn't have taken the streetcar, but I had a lot on my mind. I had half a mind to turn back, because I could see what I wanted to suggest was—well a dream, a fantasy."

Tula shook her head. "I don't understand."

"You will, listen." She took a sip of steaming coffee. "Remember what I told you once? Don't give up on your dream?"

"I've never given up," Tula said. "Not even in the worst times. I'm twenty-eight years old. I have three kids. I've got a good job. I've got my high school diploma. Andreas will return to a different *me*."

"That's my Tula. We've been through a lot together. I have made many mistakes with my girls. Forbidding Angel to marry her *Americano*. Now she's locked in a room with bars on the door and windows, her mind gone, her spirit broken. Tula, I can't help her, but I can help you. I'm sorry for forcing you to marry so young. God has given me the strength to mend that wrong, to encourage you."

"What do you mean?"

Zoe pushed herself away from the table. She stood up, took Tula by the shoulders, and shook her gently. "Take your dream in your hands. Follow it!" She was crying now.

"*Mana*, I will!"

"I will help with the children and in any other way." She made the sign of the cross. "I am so sorry."

"Sorry for what?"

"For living in the past. For being unwilling to face a future not to my liking. I've always had things my way with my daughters. It's hard to change."

Tula regarded her mother with tears in her eyes. Her hand covered her mother's. "Andreas loves you, Tula. Don't ever doubt that. He was a man haunted by many devils. He will come to peace with himself in Greece. Sometimes love isn't always what we hope it will be."

"But wasn't it for you and *Baba*?"

"Yes. He left me too soon."

The next morning, Tula woke up with an idea forming in her head. This was the day. She stood at the window and watched the scarlet leaves fall from the tall maple tree across the street. The children were waiting for their breakfast. So much had changed. Time was important, she must not waste it. She couldn't stop smiling.

She telephoned Mrs. O'Hare and informed her she would be late for work. She had an important errand to go on.

When she hung up, she reached for her Friendship Book, now worn, only a few blank pages remaining. And she began to write: "This is my decision day. Andreas made his decision to fight in Greece, and I have made my decision. No more waiting." Then she heard a voice.

"Mom." Tula turned to see her eldest, Leones. Twelve years old, older than Tula had been when Baba died. She looked at her son, so much like her Baba, with those gray eyes, that unruly dark hair, the serious look on his young face. So much like Andreas, tall, lean, quick to smile.

Then she said, "I'll be there in a minute. Help Cissy—put corn flakes in the bowls, get the milk out of the ice box."

"Okay." He turned at the door and said, "I'm giving a book report today on H-o-m-e-r-'s O-d-y-s-s-e-y," He spelled out the title. "It's your *Baba*'s book." He looked at the kitchen clock. "Aren't you going to work today?"

"I called, I'm going in a little late. Kiki and I have something to do," Tula said. And she thought, her son the champion speller, just like Angel.

And as Leones closed the bedroom door silently, Tula looked around the room. Today was different, nothing would ever be the same again. She cast a last look over her shoulder at herself in the mirror and closed the door, her back straight in a navy blue skirt and white blouse, her hair combed back. As she left the room, she almost collided with Kiki. "Mommy, Mommy, *ola kala?*"

"Yes, honey." She swept Kiki up in her arms. *Ola kala!*"

Later, after Leones and Cissy left for school, Tula bundled Kiki in a warm sweater and wrapped her turquoise shawl around her shoulders. In fifteen minutes, they were climbing the hill behind Marquette Park. When they reached the top, the city college was there.

With Kiki in tow, Tula pushed through the double doors. Inside they stood for a moment in the hall lined with lockers and filled with noisy students. She whispered conspiratorially to Kiki. "Look at those kids. See the books they're carrying? We'll be doing the same thing, soon."

Kiki's gray eyes met hers in wonder. "Really?"

"Yes, yes, honey." She had to make it happen—now! Tula thought of Dorr School and of Miss MacMann. She thought of Socrates School and Miss Kaloda.

She found her way to the main office, her mind racing. She reached the clerk's desk.

I must make it happen, Tula promised herself. She thought of studying for her teacher's certificate, and then more college year.

"I want to enroll in night classes," Tula said to the clerk.

"Enroll?" the clerk asked, peering through her bifocals.

"I'm twenty-eight years old, and I want to start working toward a teacher's certificate. I've finished my home-study program for my high school diploma. Is twenty-eight too old for college?"

"No, certainly not. Just fill out this form. Classes begin next week."

"I know."

Hand in hand, Tula and Kiki walked out of the building. She listened as Kiki rattled on excitedly about school. "I can go to school, too. I'm big...big for school." Her eyes danced, just as Tula's did as she listened.

"Yes, Kiki."

They walked down the street to the park, the wind catching Kiki's blonde hair as she talked about school. The morning mist and overcast had cleared, and now when Tula looked up at the sky, it was the deepest blue she had ever seen, almost turquoise in color. Unconsciously, Tula ran her fingers down her turquoise shawl—the shawl Ondoni had given her so many years ago.

"Ondoni, it's going to happen," she said aloud. She walked to the park's entrance and sat on a bench with Kiki beside her.

The trees were alive with color, and she was alive with hope. Now at the park's entrance an old man pushed a flower cart filled with daisies, roses, and violets.

"Flowers? Might be the last time before it gets cold."

"See how pretty?" Kiki said pointing to a bunch of violets.

"Yes, pretty," Tula said. She knelt and picked up Kiki, filled her arms with her daughter. "I'll have that bunch of violets, the deep purple ones. She gave the old man some coins."

"Excellent choice," he said, handing her the violets.

She held them to her nose, caught the faint fragrance, and traveled back to another time, a time when as a ten-year-old she carried violets in a long procession.

So now on this autumn day in 1939, a windy day, the kind of a day that *Baba*, who loved Chicago, said occurred only in Chicago and only in the autumn, when the wind blew across Lake Michigan and when white clouds crowned the city, Tula buried her head in the nosegay of violets. But she didn't feel sad at all.

Epilogue
How it Ended

Chicago, November, 1986

For the rest of the night I sat in Tula's house reading the worn cloth-bound book, the one she was planning to give me. "It's a surprise," she had said when we spoke earlier in the day.

I leafed through the book and thought about the stories she had told me about the family—her mother, Zoe, the sisters, Vasso, Angeleke, Reni and Goldie; the day at the bridge before Ondoni was deported to the old country, and the struggles and hard times with Andreas. Sometimes when she spoke, she would be traveling back in her memories, and I would listen while she relieved conversations, sometimes arguing to settle old scores, sometime bursting into laughter. She had lived more than seventy-five years surrounded by family, and now she had died alone. There had been no one to hold her, no one to kiss her.

I should have insisted she live with me. But she had not wanted to leave her house. "I want to die in this house," she would say. I should have insisted! Her life might have been saved. But Tula was strong-willed. I could not control her. No one could. Although her mother, Zoe, even Ondoni and Andreas tried.

Andreas—page after page she wrote about their problems. But she knew deep in her heart he would not stop her from obtaining her dream, to become a teacher. He would not! It was her obsession.

Finally I came to the last page of the book. Glued to the back cover was an envelope. It had my name on it. Tucked inside was a letter. It was dated 1985. At the top of the page in her precise Palmer penmanship, Tula had written, "When I Die." My hands trembled and I dropped the letter. My eyes filled with tears when I read:

"I want to be buried beside Photi. He was my true love. We were two lost souls, he with his physical pain brought on by his bastard father, and me with my mental anguish, brought on by—I don't know. Did I bring on my own pain? Did my mother? Did Andreas? Ah, Andreas fought the good battle in Greece, trying to save his homeland. But he was not good at saving our marriage. May he rest in peace in his soldier's grave in Greece. As for Ondoni, dear godfather, he too had his demons, and they followed him to the village and caused his death. He meant well but his life was twisted. No, he was not an evil man. He was a troubled man, a lonely man, but not evil.

"After Andreas died, I never loved another man, never married. There was a time when I thought I had found a new love, but it was an illusion. Andreas was a good man, in his way. His only fault was that he tried to teach me how to become a woman, but I was afraid of becoming a woman, a wife, a mother, afraid that reality would crush my dream. I expected too much of him.

"I had my dreams and I didn't want anyone getting in my way. I was obsessed with my goal. My goal? Now I realized that my children were my ultimate dream, my real goal. When Andreas left us, I thought we would perish, but it strengthened our bonds, and they remain strong to this day."

* * *

Now Tula's last wish generated considerable discussion in the family. And I wondered why my sensible mother had not asked to be buried beside her parents. Her other requests were also strange, but we granted them. She wanted her casket to be placed in an ebony carriage, pulled by four white horses, following the path from her *Baba*'s bakery on Halsted Street to the old Holy Trinity Greek Church, passing Hull House, and the courtyard where she reigned as "king of the hill," passing Dorr School and the playground where she had sat on the swing while Photi pushed her high into the clouds, and Socrates School where she learned her beloved Greek language.

At her funeral while I walked in the procession beside the family and friends, the icy November air penetrated into my bones. Somehow her death seemed to have touched almost everyone in the old neighborhood with sorrow. Children, teenagers, and young adults solemnly followed us. They carried flowers—roses, carnations, daffodils, Black-eyed Susans and violets.

I glanced back at the crowd of children and young people. They were Tula's students, generations of students, whom she had taught to love books and to cherish learning.

Later back at Tula's house, when the last of the mourners drifted away, I washed the dishes, put away the remains of the baked fish, *Retsina* wine and bread, and looked out the kitchen at the calm sky. All the early morning wind and rain that seemed part of Chicago in November had evaporated. I was alone in Tula's house.

It was after midnight when I began the long process of sorting through Tula's possessions—the old turquoise shawl, the boxes filled with yellowed photos of movie stars, the gold cross Ondoni had fastened around Tula's neck at her baptism, her teacher's certificate and the old worn cloth bound book, her book of secrets.

I am Tula's daughter, Kiki.